CON S

The Pra

SPHERE BOOKS LIMITED

A SPHERE BOOK

First published in the United States of America as
BROTHERS IN BATTLE in 1989 by Pocket Books,
a division of Simon & Schuster Inc.
1230 Avenue of the Americas, New York, NY 10020
First published in Great Britain by Sphere Books Ltd 1989

Reproduced, printed and bound in Great Britain by
Cox & Wyman Ltd, Reading

ISBN 0 7474 0384 8

Sphere Books Ltd
A Division of
Macdonald & Co (Publishers) Ltd
27 Wrights Lane, London W8 5TZ

A member of Maxwell Pergamon Publishing Corporation plc

Korea, 1950.
Tanks of the communist North Korean People's
Army crash over the 38th parallel, and the Land of
the Morning Calm erupts in bloody chaos . . .

The broiler of September sun had bloated the
corpses quickly, and their gases made them swell
even as the skin began to darken. They stank; the
island smell, Jap smell was strong, thickening the
air of this abattoir. Air trapped inside the prison
walls had a peculiar texture, like almost visible fish
scales; like the belly of an ancient feathered
serpent, slithery and disgusting.

The fucking flies, black and green and greasy, they
carpeted the crushed heads, crawling and buzzing
and eating. The animals, the fucking Japs who did
this to their own kind. You killed the fathers, but
the sons grew up to carry long bayonets and
sharpened entrenching tools. Who would kill the
grandsons?

To the men of the Second Infantry Division, who fought from the Naktong to Kunu-ri, and whose successors still man the DMZ.

To the people of the Republic of Korea, whose pride outweighed the agony.

And lastly, this is dedicated to my mother, May LeCroy, who threatened me if I didn't.

Many thanks to Raymond Kell, Honorary Consul, and Dr. James and Alice Sours, experts on Korea, who got the ball rolling.

Kamsa-hamnida to these good people for research guidance:

Kim Hyun Uk
Kim Ki Hwan
Yoon-Hi Byung
Lee Jong Ryool
Pasik Naksuh
Cha Myong Hee
Cho Yong-Soue
Lee Chan Yong
Yoon-Sun Kim
J. Woonghill Kyhm
Song Ji Yong
Yu Tae Wan
Song Ji Young
Kim Eun Woo
Chung Hee Ryu
Bong-Shik Kang
Kim Kwang-Ok
Seong Cheol Lee

CHAPTER 1

Seoul, Republic of Korea, June 25, 1950—This country was in-
vaded in force by communist troops and tanks of North Korea
early this morning. U.S. Ambassador John Muccio cabled Washington that "this constitutes an all-out attack upon the Republic of
Korea."

곧은   나무   먼저
찍힌다.

"The ax falls on the straight tree first." (Korean
proverb: The good die young.)

A glop of slime off a slaughterhouse floor might feel like
this—gummy brains, a hot freshet of blood, and sharp little splinters of bone. Sam hit the ground before the falling
body did and rolled to cover in a ditch. *The body;* see—
one goddamned microsecond and it flashed back, all that
horseshit thinking. That split head had suddenly ceased to
be Cpl. Lee Hyung Ki. Now it was a body, inoperative, a
blank file, a casualty. Write it off.

Listening hard, Sam heard a man shift weight up the hill
and disturb pebbles, and then he caught the sneaky, oiled
movement of a rifle bolt. Only one shot had killed Hyung
Ki before they could reach the KMAG radio jeep tucked

1

into the kitchen lean-to. But a burp gunner waited up there, too.

Sam whispered to the ineffective that used to be Hyung Ki in Korean soft as a leafstir, fine as the five thousand years the language had polished words one upon the other. "You always had that failing best left to foreigners, *chingu* mine. You were impatient. Now you must wait a moment longer so I may send bearers to ease your journey."

Although the Koreans had abandoned that tradition two or three dynasties back, it made more sense to Sam Connover than angels or double-headed dogs waiting on the other side. If there was another side.

Flies gathered many-legged at the smear on Sam's cheek, but he did not brush them away. He watched a seething blanket of blowflies fresh lifted from stinking rice paddies; they made a busy, green-black blanket upon Hyung Ki's half a head.

When the communist People's Army crossed the 38th Parallel at 0400, they knew exactly where they were. Sweeping by the outpost and its jeep, the *Inmun-gun* dropped off a pair of sharpshooters and hurried down to the Imjin tributary to tackle the main body of the 11th ROK regiment. Just after daylight, Lee Hyung Ki's touch of foreignness took him outside to meet his bullet. The fighting by the river was just rising to fever pitch, and if Sam still believed, ever had believed, he'd have rattled off some memorized plea, crossed himself, and spit over his shoulder—any magic to help—because he heard the tanks come rumbling up into line beyond the ridge, those squat T-34s with the 85mm cannon, thirty-five tons of steel that could go almost truck-fast on the flat. The entire army had nothing to stop them.

The Russian-built jobs started whacking away with their big guns, and Sam swallowed at each fusillade, clearing his ears. His father would have already been praying, but that god of the round-eye and pale skin probably wasn't out

2

of bed yet. If so, he'd still need heavy thunderbolts to stop those T-34s.

Pastor Connover's final exhortations hadn't brought him anything but a reasonably quick death, the way the story went. Did that mean *bushido* and samurai steel outbled the soft answer and turned cheek? Damned right.

One of the bastards up the hill finally moved. Sam thumbed open the chin strap of his steel pot and flung it rolling along the ditch that covered him. The guys on the rise were pretty good—a four-round burst kicked the helmet around, and the rifleman bounced dirt close by, making the blowflies lift from Hyung Ki's broken face.

Sam flowed up to one knee and shot both young true believers in the bellies, two 30-caliber rounds each. Only then did he wipe the leftovers of his friend from his cheek. "Your retinue, Hyung Ki. Not much, but travel in peace— *ahnyong-hi kashipshi-o.*"

Then he hurried to the jeep and tried to raise the Korean Military Advisory Group in Seoul on the radio. There was a lot of cross traffic and even more panic. Sam didn't figure anybody down there wanted to know more than what time the evac planes left. Evac planes? From what Sam had seen of Ambassador Muccio, embassy dependents would be lucky to hitchhike out on fishing boats. Gunning the motor, he flung the jeep from cover and raced west across open ground for the shallowest ford in the Imjin.

A tank shell blast whirled his jeep around like a beanie propellor but dropped it pointing the right way. Sam fanned a watery rooster tail across the river as the jeep gave all it had. Just as he swerved behind a rock, a handful of slugs from a burp gun chewed up his spare tire and a ricochet sharded out a chunk of windshield.

Straggling pine saplings wavered through the river dunes here, and once into some shadow Sam jerked the jeep to a stop and bounced out with his M-1. He was in the middle of Colonel Chong's command post, where men hunched low and busy as rice birds at long poles and satchel charges of explosives. Dug-in ROKs were firing back across the river, popping at every movement. They were between the old rock—the Yellow Sea on their left—and the hard place—at least a North Korean division on the right.

"Colonel?"

"Ah, sergeant. Anything clear on the radio?"

"Not much; everybody's falling back."

"Except this regiment," the colonel said.

"Yes, sir." Sam got the same feel this officer always projected. It was the rare aura of leadership that cut right through Sam's adrenaline hype and a heartbeat set on full automatic. Then Sam noticed that Chong was heavily hung with Compo C, igniters stuck in and some frag grenades hooked on. "What the hell—sir?"

"We used our 2.6 launchers; they did no harm. The 37mms we abandoned as useless, although we did manage to damage one tank with all the shells planted as a mine. There has to be a way to stop them—or a dramatic try."

Helplessly, Sam looked beyond the straight, slim man to his son, Lieutenant Chong. The lieutenant's face was waxen, set, his eyes glittering with unshed tears. He said, "The divisions on our right flank have been destroyed. This unit stands alone—but we *are* standing."

"Colonel," Sam said, wanting to snatch up the man, toss him in the jeep and take off for Seoul, "please, sir—it might not be a Dunkirk. American occupation outfits from Japan, one from Hawaii—*damn it*, colonel, the ROK army *needs* you."

The country needed Chong Jun Ka. If the baby Republic of Korea were to live beyond even this attempt at infanticide, if it would ever reach a place among modern nations of the Pacific, men like Colonel Chong would guide it. There were other brilliant Koreans, but damned few who would shed restrictive traditions and look forward. But

4

Sam couldn't kidnap him. If the man chose to die this way, it was his right.

WHAMM!!

Sam was thrown over into the boulder and reached to catch the colonel, but when the smoke cleared, Chong was still on his feet. His choice was to meet the first tank across the river because he was so damned much man, and his feet were planted in the core of the earth.

There'd been another man close to Sam before the whiskey got him. Uncle Kelly Connover made his twenty years to retirement with inches to spare; only a good company commander stood between Kelly and a boarding out for alcoholism.

Why think of Sgt. Kelly Connover now, with fucking tanks revving up to wade the Imjin and kill off practically the only ROK regiment that hadn't run? Because Kelly said, if a man started out lucky enough to soldier, and stayed lucky enough to find him a war, why then, he might get to pick when and how to die. Civilians didn't have that dignity. In the end, neither had Kelly.

Colonel Chong put his hand upon Sam's forearm. "You have been as my own blood to me. We learned much from each other, *tong-saeng*. I ask that you and my older son, the *chongi* here, continue to enlighten each other."

Sam glanced around the boulder, then down at the M-1 held across his knees. "I am flattered by being called younger brother, sir. It would be a great honor for me to address you as father."

Chong's easy smile stayed in place, although small arms fire picked up on both sides of the river, and Sam thought he heard the heavier thump of whatever the NKs called their 4.2 mortar. That meant their backup was in place, and within minutes the T-34s would come on.

"Strange," the colonel said, "if I do not look directly at you, Samuel, I hear only the accent of Cholla-do, when it was an older province whose scholars delighted in linguistic complications. I see only the foreign soldier when I look into your eyes. Some day I hope all Republic of Korea soldiers will have the same look of eagles."

Then he turned to his true son. "Take them south while it remains possible, lieutenant. My son."

"My father," the lieutenant said, and he didn't try to hide the unsoldierly tears.

And then the first tank clanked into the shallow water, its pair of 7.62 machine guns sweeping ahead, firing high with its cannon. NK infantry in their mustard-color uniforms lifted from the ground and followed.

Colonel Chong walked steadily to meet his tank, the river swirling around his knees, his slight body heavy with plastique explosives and with the heavier responsibility of showing his regiment how a brave man died. When he threw himself under the tank, and the blowup scattered river rocks and water through the haze, Sam propped the forestock of his M-1 against the tall rock and fired carefully, steadily, until the empty clip *pinged*. Colonel Chong would have servants to help his way, too. And he had stopped his T-34. One track gone, it slewed and braked while others crossed above and below its place.

Lieutenant Chong said quietly, "May I have the crew?"

Before the hatch opened, other desperate troops ran at the coming tanks with pole charges. Some went down in the river, bloodying the Imjin without setting off their explosives. Some made it to the churning monsters, only to be ground up and spit wide in the blasts.

The hatch of Colonel Chong's crippled tank swung up, and Lieutenant Chong killed the man who opened it. Firefights broke out all along the near side of the water, and the tanks just rolled on through, outdistancing support infantry.

Sam said, "Time to haul ass."

"I would stay," Chong said, "but my father ordered me to take out our survivors."

"Like I said—haul ass." Thumbing a fresh clip into his

rifle, Sam added: "Any kind of rear guard? They might get lucky, with the tanks just rolling ahead."

"Two platoons leapfrogging back. They will reach the sea or escape through the hills."

Slapping down the jeep's ruptured windshield, Sam jumped in and handed Chong a canister. "Willy Peter. If you feel lucky, heave it at the open hatch."

It was a long pitch, and Chong came close. The bright spray of white phosphorus lighted the turret for a moment, but no more. "Hang on," Sam said, and he raced the jeep through the scattering of pines and down the Suwon corridor directly behind a T-34. He swung off onto the first side track.

The *inmun-gun* crossing the Imjin, screaming their goddamn *mansei! mansei!* without even recalling it was the *banzai!* of the hated split-toed dwarfs who had occupied and stripped their country for thirty-five years, the hated Japs. Ten thousand years of *what?* Sharp-edged swords and long bayonets and now thirty-five-ton tanks; *mansei-banzai!* Ten thousand more years of hunger and suffering and death. There would always be bloody work for butchers of men. Why didn't Sam Connover throw up, instead of tasting wine in the smoky wind? Because he was expert with ax and cleaver; because *mansei* rolled as easily off his tongue as the rebel yell at Manassas, or the wordless roar at other chopping blocks. His holy father was born to the collar and cross, Sam Connover to olive drab and blood. If not, he would have chosen the job.

Stopping the jeep this side of a rise in the ground, Sam got out with Chong to walk up and look around. What was left of the 11th Regiment was making its way through the hills, scattered here and there in small but still-disciplined groups. No infantry without antitank weapons could have done better.

"They are to collect at the railroad station in Seoul," the lieutenant said.

"If some idiot son of a bitch doesn't panic and blow the Han River bridges and trap everybody on this side."

"*Morah-go?* What?"

Sam shifted into Korean: "You have seen Fat Chae, the illustrious chief of staff?"

"The darling of the *kho-jaengi,* yes."

"He is popular at embassy drinking parties, but I do not trust him now. I think he will run for Pusan. We must get our troops across the Han quickly as possible."

As the jeep sped down the ancient invasion valley of the Khans and Manchus, traffic thickened. Trucks filled by ROK soldiers with and without weapons, but grinning as if they all were part of some big joke; other military trucks with better-dressed civilians jammed into the back, complete with luggage, women, and children.

"Money." Lieutenant Chong spat. "My father warned of this. Those are the warlords who profit from misery, why honest men despise soldiers of any army, even their own; especially their own."

"Your father," Sam said, cutting around a civilian bus top-heavy with a mixed bag of civilians and military, "was the wisest of men. He foresaw the needy refugees that will fill these roads, the wounded and sick, the lost children."

"And ordered my *tong-saeng* to prepare. Younger brother has the most difficult job. I can fight; he must run and care for our own family as well."

Now ox carts thickened the traffic into the capital, and men stooped under A-frames with staggering loads; and the old people; and the children. Oh, yes, the children.

"The railroad station," Sam said. "I will get transportation at the embassy and come back for the regiment. If I am held up, do not allow the Han bridges to be blown, if you have to kill the engineers."

"If I can. But your officers at KMAG may not allow you—"

8

Sam pushed the jeep between swaying ox carts and frowned. "From here on, they do not allow or disallow. The games are over, my brother. The dead are real."

Lieutenant Chong swung his carbine over one shoulder and climbed down to head into the railroad station. He didn't smile, and Sam saw the memory of it run swiftly through the man's eyes—the bloody river, the explosion, the death of his father.

Faster now, up on sidewalks or along side streets with his horn blasting, Sam whipped the jeep onward to the embassy compound. KMAG officers might not allow, Chong said; word must have run across the front that Korean Military Advisory Group people had mostly taken off, or had no orders to go or stay.

And KMAG officers meant the well-meaning souse Captain Prescott on his weekend bash in Seoul instead of up at Kaesong when the communist shit hit the fan; that much was a blessing for Sam, and one less problem. The embassy meant Lt. Col. Julian Barron, a spit-shined son of a bitch if ever West Point graduated one. He would stir a hand in every TWX going out to the godhead in Tokyo, but no matter how hectic the embassy and KMAG evacuation got, Colonel Barron would always hope to catch up with M/Sgt. Sam Connover, RA 7009245—the too-well-protected *enlisted* man who had somehow, impossibly, seduced and carried on a stateside affair with the colonel's wife.

Colonel Barron would hope, of course, for Sam to get his guts blown out. He might even stay in Korea long enough to make certain of that.

Maggi Barron; Sam drove through the compound gates and angled for the motor pool. Maggi Barron; it was the first time he'd thought of her since—when? Certainly not since the shooting started, and for busy months getting settled in with his KMAG assignment.

Sure, he had said, *I love you, Maggi. I must; I never told that to another woman.*

That soft smile of hers, and: *I'm not sure that proves anything, sergeant.*

I'm here with you, he said; *that ought to prove I love you. You're also the only officer's wife I ever—oh, damn, Maggi!*

Yes, she whispered, *I imagine we are damned.*

CHAPTER 2

New York, NY, June 27, 1950—The United Nations today asked
its members to go to the aid of the Republic of Korea. Yesterday,
North Korean invaders ignored the Security Council's call for an
end to the aggression.

공복에 이경을 침도
안바르고 삼키려한다.

"As hungry as a man who tries to swallow a big
bell." (Korean proverb: A hunger for gold, fame,
and power, disregarding honor.)

Call me Rich because I ain't, and ain't likely to be. He
grinned and swallowed the grin because nobody else on the
road to Seoul was smiling. People carrying all they owned
and staggering off in hopes of living long enough to use the
stuff—well, they just didn't show a lot of teeth, not even
to bite back. Already the bite was gone from this stream of
Korean refugees, and the war barely had a running start.
They weren't boozed up, either.

He kept the jeep putting along, beforehand wisely lashing down all he and *Stars & Stripes* owned in the back-
seat, everything tucked and roped and strapped under a
shelter half. All except a firearm or two, the Speed

Graphic, and the bottles he used as propped guides for the steering wheel. He was pretty good at driving with that kind of help. One big greeny jug was about half full of *soju;* the smaller bottle of juice he used as a chaser was supposed to be made from apples. It did taste like ground-fall apples and seeds and maybe tree bark dusted with cowshit.

But the *soju* now—Rich kept the jeep cruising slowly on the shoulder of the road and had another go at it. Like Japanese *sake,* this started out as rice, but where the Jap crap was winy, this stuff was so strong it had to be healthy. He eyed the scum of bugs floating on the mostly clear liquid and figured they'd died at first touch. All the nasty microorganisms Korea had to offer, and God knows some of them hadn't even been named, well, they ought to flop over in his belly at first touch, too. Antiseptic value, laddie buck, as well as anesthetic.

A humped old man with a face like a pumpkin left in the field way past frost reached at the empty front cushion next to Rich and said something in gook. Rich knew enough to glance back over his other shoulder in time to catch a couple of kids prying at his shelter half.

He tried to prop the apple stuff between the seats and tipped over the bottle. That pissed him so much he jerked the carbine from the floor and fired a rolling burst into the air. The little shits trying to grab C-rations vanished; old pumpkin face jumped the ditch, and some woman squalled loud and long.

Oh, hell; they scurried along the road and got off it and some of them just kind of flopped down and waited to be run over. Or shot. If only they didn't look so much like fucking Japs. He gassed the jeep and weaved around them and finally got out ahead to a clear space. Oh, they didn't act like the first Imperial Nips the old America Division got introduced to in the hospitable jungles. Those were all hotshots, still full of that *banzai* horseshit and wearing uniforms that looked like uniforms.

It was after eight or ten more screaming, bloody islands that the Japs started looking like these gooks running from somewhere to nowhere. Scabby little turds with ribs showing from their rags, stinking in their cocoa-log bunkers or ratholes or caves—half-dead or maybe better than half, but you still had to go in and make goddamn sure.

Hell—Rich blew the horn and made them jump, two guys laboring under loaded A-frames—if these gooks didn't look so much like Japs, he might have tossed the hungry kids a can or two of rations.

A rattling ROK army truck with women and kids hanging all over it came edging out of a side road no wider than a rice-paddy dam. The driver tried to push ahead of the jeep, but Rich remembered spilling his rotten-apple chaser and fired the rest of the carbine's banana clip. He had a clear road again and choked down a big swallow of *soju*.

Coughing, he hung onto the wheel until the jeep zigged straight and his eyes cleared to see another old man make the sign of the cross. Hell; he'd missed the old gook by the width of a bar rag. Crossing himself? Rich shook his head and rebalanced the *soju* jug. He didn't change clips in the carbine. If there was any more shooting ahead, the *Stars & Stripes* jeep and all these sweaty gooks were going the wrong way. Besides, a grease gun barrel kept nudging the little double sticks of the four-wheel drive at his right boot. As far as he could remember, it was loaded.

He blared the horn again and yelled at a hot blue sky empty of a single glittering example from the greatest air fleet the world had ever known. "Hey, old gook! You ain't learned it yet, but Saint Mike's rear echelon don't wear a Purple Heart!"

Saint Michael, protector of soldiers and flyboys and everybody but Japs as crazy as stomped sand crabs who swore by that divine constipation in Tokyo—well, nobody ever saw him with his armor dented, and look what the hell his vision caused little Joan of Arc. Where was he when they lit the matches?

Maybe the church got him screwed up with some other Michaels—like Mike II, *The Stammerer;* now he sounded like the perfect platoon leader for combat GIs, better than Michael the Brave who messed with the Turks until they jerked him inside out and shot craps for his empire.

You only go on that way when you're drunk and hiding, Teresa said. *You know I don't appreciate you attacking the church.*

Now how the hell can I be drunk, hiding and attacking the church all at the same time? Hiding from who, anyhow? It's still Sunday, ain't it? Holy shit, if I miss another Monday—

Hiding from yourself, his wife said. Now there was a woman who should have been sainted. Saint Terry, for suffering through his shit for eight years. He thought it was eight years. Suffer the GI wives, any children caught in crossfire, and the gooks! The Japs had a payoff coming and didn't collect enough.

You don't come right home from camp, and when you do, you're payday-drunk and complaining about my church and your army. Terry had this trick of sitting up in her old towel-looking robe with rollers in her hair and wasn't about to let him sleep. *You had your chance, Richard. All that big talk about the GI Bill and going to medical school. I would have worked day and night, and you know that, but your army—your goddamned army!*

Blasphemy, Saint Teresa.

Oh, you're such a smartass! You had to get back in that lousy uniform, and you think I don't hear you crying in the night like a sick baby—but you're not a baby! You're a medic, and a damned good one—all those citations—

You don't understand—

No, I don't! At last, I'm admitting I don't understand

14

you at all, unless you can't wait to get into another war.
You suck on a bottle and then you're a baby, and talk about
not enough Japs dying by A-bombs and how we ought to
drop some on China and every other slant-eyed country in
the world—

They multiply so fast. One cave, two Japs; two caves, a
hundred goddamned Japs. We can't knock them in the head
fast enough. Terry, you can't say I didn't try. There was the
newspaper job and then the photo studio—

And me waiting tables when you were supposed to be in
school. You could take your citations to any hospital, if you
couldn't make it in school. You'd have gotten a good job
right off, and never reenlisted—

It was the only time he could remember screaming at
her: *They never stop bleeding! Don't you know they won't*
stop bleeding?

He sat on one side of the bed, his wife on the other. He
fought the vomit in his throat, seeing that kid with yellow
hair and acne. He always remembered the acne, but he
hadn't even known the kid's name, just another casualty
down and guys yelling *medic! medic!*

The boy might have stretched it to seventeen years old,
but a mortar shell broke his kneecaps, and then some passing Jap stuck the bayonet to him nine or ten times just for
fun.

Can I help you, sarge?

Jesus Christ—the little bastard lay there with the slime
and blood and liquid shit pumping out of his body cavity
and asked if he could help. Rich was in it to his elbows,
pushing stuff back and trying to force greasy things to hang
together. All the time, that fucking Nambu kept going
whack! whack! whack! and kicking mud over them.

Can I help you, sarge? I mean, can I hold onto something and we can crawl on out of here?

Yeah—stop bleeding or die quick.

Help? Not that day, you fuzzy-faced nameless bastard,

because Saint Michael was having a bowl of rice in Tokyo, and this poor helpful son of a bitch died before Rich could even get the ampule of morphine in him.

He yelled something else at his wife, and it must have been pretty bad. That time she didn't just go to sleep in the other room; she phoned her old man collect for money and caught the train back to Missouri. The divorce papers caught up with him about six month later, and he signed without looking except where to write his name.

He was at Schofield Barracks by then, and already the Old Man said your ass is a high noon popsicle if you start any more fights with civilians in Honolulu. Rich couldn't tell Jap from Chink from certified beach boy by just their eyes. He had to quit punching them anyhow; they were all kicking his ass.

He shuddered and killed the *soju* and tossed the dead soldier into the ditch. Where the hell would M/Sgt. Sam Connover be about now? At the embassy, if he had any sense, but Medal of Honor clowns weren't known for much sense. If Connover was half-assed smart, he'd be on some fat assignment stateside, where he could hang around the PX coffee shop and pretend the clipboard he carried was for something besides doodles. Nights, he could cruise the NCO club for wives whose husbands were shipped out, or go downtown and dazzle civilian women with money for the booze and bedding.

That's what Rich Shriver would do, if he had the big bong. But he would never let the president hang the Medal of Honor around *his* neck, even if he turned stupid/lucky enough to earn it. The ribbon would remind him of a string of guts and a blond kid with acne. He never did tell his ex-wife about that boy.

"What, you old bastard?" Damned if it wasn't the same old pumpkin face, but now limping badly, mumbling in gook and pointing at the empty seat. After checking over his shoulder, Rich said, "Oh, shit—climb in. No, goddamnit—don't throw that crap on top of my stuff back there. Keep it on your lap, you toothless son of a bitch. If I find Sam Connover, or just a goodly supply of *soju*, out you go on your hookworm-infested ass."

The old man nodded. *"Soju, soju."*

Maybe all gooks weren't dumb. They weren't? Everybody on this thin gravel excuse for a highway was pissant stupid, or they wouldn't be here at all. The men would be bolted down inside those NK tanks, getting even for Hiroshima, and the women—no, they weren't Japs. They were Koreans. He had to keep reminding himself.

Rich motored down the middle of the road and squinted. He couldn't see any right close by, but maybe there were a few good-looking women who could peddle enough ass in Pusan to buy a berth to Yokohama.

"Pusan," he said, and the old pumpkin cackled. *"Pusan, soju—yea, yea."*

Yea, yea? He was too old for a cheerleader. Everybody was too young or too old to be cheerleaders around a war. Everybody ought to have more sense, too.

If only these gooks didn't look so much like Japs.

CHAPTER 3

Seoul, Republic of Korea, June 28, 1950—Battered ROK troops, some in blind panic, streamed into this city today. Survivors of battles along the 38th Parallel, they claimed the North Korean armor was unstoppable.

엎친데 덮친다.

"Stamp on the back of a man on his belly." (Korean proverb: One misfortune follows another.)

Blood, sweat, and tears.

Chong Nam Ki squatted with his back against the cooling bricks of the Seoul railway station and thought the English leader had been right, although nothing had been said of the impotent rage and the scaly dragon of agony that later came to thresh in your belly. Then, of course, there was the potter's mix of road dust and rice field offal. No beautiful celadon would ever be made from such a lowly stirring. The great potters broke many vessels that came from the kiln, each carefully worked piece that the artist considered to be flawed. Only the perfect was entitled to remain.

It had become different. The strong and the beautiful

like his father lay broken, while the worthless trash from the north continued. Nam Ki looked up as a soldier wavered from the steady flow of refugees and made a tired salute. The man carried his M-1 rifle slung and still wore his web belt. Nam Ki discovered that he was not yet too weary in soul and body to feel pride. This survivor of the 11th Regiment made how many—perhaps forty? So few left of the regiment Colonel Chong had showed how to fight and taught how to die well.

"Jotah!" he said and motioned the man inside to the collecting point. "Good!" So many owed their lives to these few—if indeed many of these terrified refugees lived to see another dawn in their Land of the Morning Calm, this blooded land that saw too little peace and had belonged to the people for only two years. Five thousand years of suffering and struggle under tyrants and foreign dominance only to flee from their own blood, from their brothers to the north turned into wolves.

Many owed much to so few. The *yongkuk* leader had been a political poet, which may have influenced Father Chong to see that Churchill was first read among all the foreign military books he brought swiftly into the country. Mother Chong had murmured, as she always did, but with thought and firmness, as also was her habit, "But why must the family Chong, of all respected names in Korea, concern itself with things—military?"

Held almost rigid by weariness as the trucks on the road tried to jam themselves through the plodding throng, Nam Ki smiled, remembering that his mother had always pronounced "military" as if the word had a disgusting flavor. After all, she would whisper sometime later, warlords and their pitiful bandits in uniform are only one small step above that lowest and most menial of occupations, that of—butcher of animals.

Almost at Nam Ki's bent knees, an ROK army truck crowding the sidewalk blared its horn, and the driver shouted at Nam Ki, who stood up and cradled his carbine. The driver's eyes widened as he must have realized his error. The crowd and other vehicles were too dense around the truck for him to pull aside or back up. Nam Ki held those eyes with his own. Then he glanced up at the back of the open truck and saw it so packed with women and children, with grandmothers and grandfathers, with rolled bedding and sacks of food that the people could barely move about.

Nam Ki looked quickly back at the other man in the cab, a sergeant who seemed less inclined to look away. Nam Ki shifted the muzzle of his weapon.

An old man bracing thin elbows upon the cab pulled at his white beard. At least one of these *harabawgi* was not afraid, for he said: "Officer, these two took all our money in payment."

The sergeant swung casually out upon the running board; Nam Ki's gun muzzle followed him with deliberation. The *sangsa* said, "The old one is crazed with fear and his great age. We took no money, and we fought with our regiment until it was overrun by the communists. We are good soldiers of the 10th Regiment."

Father Chong had been firm upon the uses of discipline. Not like the Japanese, he said, for soldiers will more readily follow officers they respect than those they hate. But, Nam Ki, all military emotions must be spiced with a justifiable sprinkling of fear. When your orders must be enforced, do not hesitate.

Wearily, for he was becoming light-headed, Nam Ki said, "You are liars and deserters, as well as thieves. Climb down into the street. The 10th Regiment died south of the Imjin River. Your uniforms are not even stained, and the bumper markings of the Whitehorse Division still show upon this truck."

Nam Ki had been correct to watch the sergeant. The man's fatigue jacket bulged with money and the small

riches of the poor. His sudden wealth made him a trifle
slow bringing around his carbine. So as not to break a
prized pocket watch or fountain pen, so as not to rip the
wadding of *whan* or make the money unusable with blood,
Nam Ki shot the sergeant through the forehead. The bullet
snatched him from the running board and hurled him into
the wall of the railway station.

"Lieutenant!"

Nam Ki tried to drop to one knee and fire at the driver,
but he was so tired that he stumbled. The driver clapped
both hands atop his soft cap. The man who called out was a
corporal of the 11th Regiment who still owned his rifle and
carried a communist submachine gun. He aimed it at the
driver.

"Lieutenant, shall I kill this dog also?"

Nam Ki considered. The smoke from his carbine had not
yet cleared, and already the refugees were piling from the
truck, children crying and only the younger women crying
with them. The grandmothers expected sorrow and were
more experienced at coping with tragedy. That, Nam Ki
was certain, was both the basic weakness and a pillar of
strength for his people.

Again he considered. Genghis Khan sent living and terrified word ahead of great bloodlettings and burnings, so
that cities in his path surrendered rather than face the final
fury. "He lives for this day, if only to tell other deserters
the fate they may expect."

Of course, the Khan often slaughtered populations of
surrendered cities as well, but then, he was Chinese.

"Run, dog," the corporal shouted, "before this officer
allows me to shoot you in your coward's belly!"

The gunshot had cleared an opening through the flow of
refugees, an open sand bar that would soon again be
drowned. Across the clearing bounced a KMAG jeep, its
radio antenna waving. Nam Ki's brave corporal stepped up
beside him, the communist PPSH at the ready.

"*Aniyo!*" Nam Ki said. "No; these are friends."

Sam Connover, so close to their father Chong, almost brother to Nam Ki; the other man was a black sergeant.

Pulling the jeep onto the sidewalk, Sam Connover stopped it and looked at Nam Ki. "May our father rest forever in peace and honor."

The corporal blinked and stared; Nam Ki thought the man didn't believe his ears, couldn't accept the formal and fluent Korean phrasing coming from any foreigner.

"Thank you," Nam Ki answered.

Old men from the truck swarmed about the dead ROK sergeant like magpies upon an unguarded rice pile, pecking and jerking at his clothing until they recovered all taken from them and a bit more. Perhaps wiser, perhaps only more afraid, the women and children still huddled in the truck.

When the graybeard grandfather started to climb back Nam Ki said, "No; this is an army vehicle, and I have soldiers to transport. I keep the truck; you hurry across the Han River as quickly as you can, and keep going. I am certain we cannot hold Seoul, and possibly little else."

The old man clenched full hands inside his jacket. "We have no more money."

Nam Ki leaned back against the wall as Sam Connover got down to the walk. The black man only swung his combat boots over the side of the jeep; Nam Ki saw the American .45 submachine gun across the man's lap, the weapon the GIs called a grease gun.

The ROK corporal moved to the truck tailgate. "Old one!" His voice was furious. "You speak to a *yangban,* to one whose father just died so that old fools like you may live another day. This man is of the family of Chong—directly descended from that of King Sejong—if old fools even know that much history. Get out!" He waved the submachine gun. "Get down—all of you—now!"

Gratefully, Nam Ki accepted the cigarette Sam Connover

offered, and the *Me-in* said, "That one would make a good officer, I think. How many survivors, Nam Ki?"

Nam Ki coughed. His eyelids were gritty. "Forty. Not enough."

Sam Connover tilted his head at the jeep and said in English, "My friend Matt Jackson, called Stonewall in the boxing ring. Stonewall—Lt. Chong Nam Ki."

"Hello," Jackson said, and Sam Connover spoke again: "Best we get them quickly across the Han. The bridges are being mined and Fat Chae is in a panic, but forty good men can hold roads open."

Ah, the ROK army chief of staff—very short and heavy and the darling of the U.S. embassy cocktail parties—Fat Chae. Fat Chae having the two Han River bridges mined, with so many retreating ROK soldiers to be trapped in Seoul, entire columns of stragglers pouring in from both coasts and down the Suwon Valley; many thousands of refugees—the terrified people fleeing the mad dogs of the north. If those bridges were not held open until the last moment, all these Koreans would face would be death, conscription, or forced labor, especially the remaining soldiers.

Even if the weapons were lost, the soldiers should be saved and resupplied; use their training and use what would become their deep shame for deserting. Turn that shame outward into anger, hone it into the sword edge of duty, and the communists would face a different kind of ROK fighter.

Nam Ki became conscious of stench and swirling dust and thick, damp heat pressing down like a sleeping cover. It had rained last night, beginning the refreshment of rice land, beginning the rains that the farmers desperately needed to grow food, the rains that had held off too long this year. It wasn't needed now; there would be no farmers left in the valley, only the butchers of men.

"My family," he said, frowning into Sam Connover's eyes. "My mother—young Wae Ki—"

"Your brother obeys our father. He readies all for the trip south. He has sent your mother and sister to Pusan. Now he understands how important it was not to come into the army."

Pushing himself away from the railway station wall, Nam Ki said, "I will collect my men. If there is time to see my brother—"

"KMAG is scattered," Sam Connover said. "The embassy panics also. Jackson and I are with you until something happens."

"The United Nations—America?"

"There is so little time; perhaps help will come, perhaps not."

Nam Ki straightened. "Then we fight alone."

As he walked into the station he heard the black sergeant say, "Man—I don't know what shakes me more, you rattling off in gook, or that guy wasting his own soldier for hauling ass."

"The man's like his father, a real *soldier*."

When Nam Ki stood before the survivors of his regiment as they sprawled upon the tile floor, he could still hear—although barely—the black man reply: "Shee-it, I believe it. You notice the head shot he laid on this busted ROK?"

Nam Ki rubbed his eyes and fought to hold his body erect. He whispered to the corporal who had stood by him in the street. "Your name?"

"Lim, sir; corporal—"

"Second lieutenant," Nam Ki said. "Lim *Sowi*, lead the regiment into our truck. Choose a driver. We follow the *kho-jaengi* jeep to Yongdung-po or where they lead. When the bridges are blown, I do not think that the communist tanks can swim the Han."

Suddenly he wanted to throw up. The Imjin was shallow at the ford where Colonel Chong's blood turned the water scarlet, where bits of the great Chong family bone and flesh and so many explosives meant nothing to the T-34. Chong family bone, the unchanged "true bone" of the *chingols*, aristocrats for two thousand years.

If the *balgaengi* tanks could swim, if they somehow began to ford the last major barrier between them and the defeated ROK army, would it be wrong for Nam Ki to disobey his father? Should he not also attack a tank with his own body? He must wait for such a moment. Only then would he be sure.

CHAPTER 4

Seoul, Republic of Korea, June 27, 1950—Fears are rising here that the city must fall soon. There is some confusion about the evacuation of Americans. U.S. Ambassador John Muccio announced that he expects diplomatic immunity for all.

그물에 든 새

"A bird in the net." (Korean proverb: A life in danger, having lost freedom of movement.)

General Wright frowned a moment longer at the spread of red markings on the overlay, regiments and corps and probably armies, if the truth was known. Geometrics over here and indecisive blobs over there, somehow like tentacles on a Portuguese man-of-war, not only painful, but deadly. If this disintegration of ROK forces and the disappearance of KMAG didn't adjust, any of the good guys left had sure better know how to swim.

That wasn't funny; if help didn't get here damned soon, an evacuation would be gory, with none of the excuses and so-called glory of Dunkirk. It would be only a massacre on a nameless beach that nobody would want to remember, much less dignify by giving it a name.

"Ho damn," he said. "Barron, is this the latest? The map shows ROK II Corps in place outside Uijongbu, and I've seen their trucks shagging over the Han."

"Inadequate reporting, sir. You know these Koreans—"

"No, and neither does anybody else, it appears. Troops at Uijongbu and KMAG can't be found; ho damn! That's an American outfit; nominally, anyhow. It can't be as screwed up as the rest of this embassy rat's nest."

Colonel Barron's wordless sound was noncommittal. "Intelligence from the field, compounded by linguistic barriers and confused via improper channeling, can be—indeed, may be expected to be—"

"Do you always talk like a trade school manual?" Wright had inherited a book soldier. The man's voice sounded like a book, like fresh paper sharply folded and creased according to the latest army regulations.

If Barron had tried to come up through the ranks, he'd have wound up as a warrant officer in Personnel, real good at shuffling paper and quoting regulations. Wright felt for a cigar and found the butt he had let go out hours past. He bet himself that when he lighted it, Barron would make a face but quickly recover. He did, and Wright chalked up another in his win column and wished he could cut through all bullshit in this compound. Already it looked like a kicked ant nest; that would get worse, too, a heavy shitstorm.

There in the tender part of his memories, Wright winced; since Frances had died, even innocent profanity made him feel guilty. Make up something, she'd asked. So many of them are just looking for excuses to get you caught in a RIF. Manners and morals and attitudes count more than ability, between wars, and any opportunity to get rid of us by a reduction in force—

We, she said, this wondrous woman he couldn't believe had actually married him. *We*, when he was a mustang and she the daughter and granddaughter of generals. He gained and held his star because of Frances, through her guidance and wisdom. How he still missed her. Frances smiled at him the first time he broke off earthier expletives and tested his sanitized ho damn upon his wife. Thank you, darling, she said.

". . . since the general has just arrived and I have been on the scene for quite some time, and since Ambassador Muccio is technically still in command of this embassy and the Korean Military Advisory Group, may I suggest—"

"You may not! I don't give a country shit about technicalities, colonel, only that my orders are obeyed, and damned quickly. Now haul your West Point ass into a jeep and get me some eyeball G-2, some field intelligence, then double time back, if things are as bad as I think, and start evacuating these civilians. Two thousand damned civilians; how the hell could there be that many in this miserable, field-stripped country? Worse—how can we get them out? Never mind. Any other comments, colonel?"

"No, sir. Of course not."

"Of course not."

Julian Barron saluted, wheeled sharply, and left the briefing room. Christ, what a boor. How had the infamous Brig. Gen. Buckley "Butt" Wright gotten onto MacArthur's staff in Tokyo? A mustang like that, battlefield commission in World War I; marriage to Washington connections reaching far back. But to fly such an officer into an embassy situation, a clown with no more diplomacy than a payday private—

Outside, Julian didn't see a jeep or a three-quarter, either. Where was his driver? These damned Koreans; the smartest thing for the U.S. occupation and the U.N. to do would have been to leave the Japanese army in control here. The Nips knew how to instill discipline and get action.

"Need a ride, colonel?" Julian turned to stare at the jeep come silently up behind him, at the markings of *Stars & Stripes,* the military newspaper headquartered in Tokyo. Faintly, he recalled seeing this sergeant around KMAG and the compound. The man was slovenly, a uniform disgrace and a heavy drinker, but he was here from Tokyo before Butt Wright and before the invasion, and good publicity had never hurt an officer's career. A new war would call forth new heroes for the public, and new names for the Pentagon.

"Thank you, sergeant," he said. "I decided upon a quick loop around the city for some direct intelligence. Maybe you'll find something newsworthy, too."

The jeep jerked around in a tight circle, scattering a band of American civilians who had come out to pile embassy documents for burning, and to make more careful stacks of personal belongings. Dust rolled, and Julian waved his handkerchief under his nose in a futile effort to rid the air of rice-paddy stink. Out through the gate and heavy on the horn, the sergeant worked the jeep into the swirling tide of refugees, yelling obscenities when it was blocked to a halt. Julian saw ROK army trucks forcing refugees into ditches, bumping them with grill or fender, and once turning over an old man's cart. Some of the military vehicles carried only troops, but most were mixed with civilian passengers and often the soldiers were without weapons; some wore dirty bandages.

"They look like Japs," the sergeant said. "They'll always look like them *banzai* bastards to me."

"Watch that truck," Julian said, and he grabbed at the dash for support.

"No more refugee shots," the sergeant said. "Tokyo don't know what the hell to do with any more, and that fucking GI Speed Graphic has got a bellyache again. I mean to lose that bastard first chance and use this Rollie I bought on the Ginza. You see something worth my film, just holler."

"Holler—sir," Julian said, and he hung on as the jeep lurched, got two wheels in a shallow ditch, and fought out under four-wheel drive. The sergeant shot the vehicle through a gap in the mass, and Julian cracked his elbow. Slamming to a stop, rolling a great red-yellow cloud of dust, the jeep slewed and bumped the mud wall of a shack.

"One knee on the seat," the sergeant said. "Hold that elbow and kind of hook it over the windshield—look over your shoulder at them kids running. Yeah." The flash popped, and the man was back in the jeep and grinding it off before Julian settled back onto the seat. "Get your name and hometown when we get back. Name's Shriver, colonel, but everybody calls me Rich because I'll never have a dime."

"Get me back to the embassy," Julian ordered. "Sergeant Shriver, you certainly don't sound like a correspondent."

"Don't have to. I write like one."

Julian almost fell out as the sergeant twisted the jeep sharply around a curve and bounced it through a dip in the dirt road. "You're also a lousy driver and insubordinate." The man turned his head and actually smiled at Julian.

"You don't have to send me to the front, colonel. It's about to catch up with us. Watch them Japs—gooks—all heading for the river, all going south. Not one old mama-san is pointed for Inchon Harbor. They know there ain't but one freighter, and it's some kind of Norwegian shit boat. No evacuation that way—sir."

Julian snapped back before he realized that he was arguing with an enlisted man. You never did that; you commanded. But this one didn't seem to give a damn, and perhaps in his own way he was like General Butt Wright, with high friends in Far East headquarters. With correspondents and photographers, you never knew. In time, of course, you hung their hides out to dry, anyhow.

They moved through the gates of the embassy, and Julian lifted a hand to wipe road dust from his face, then thought better of it. The general would be more impressed. Turning to the sergeant, he said, "The ambassador does not intend to evacuate." Remembering the general, he added: "If it can be helped. If it must be, I'm certain enough planes will come in from Japan."

Shriver grunted, fumbled beneath his seat, and brought out a green glass bottle. He drank and said, "Ain't no planes, colonel. They're all rusting away in the New Mexico desert, and the pilots are out selling insurance."

Julian lost his composure. He stood beside the jeep and held a deep breath that didn't help. "You're only a goddamned sergeant! You don't even deserve the stripes you have, and I'll see about them. What do you think anybody in the lower ranks knows? Do generals take you into their confidence? Does the Pentagon ask you for advice? You goddamned old-line soldiers irritate me, pretending the army couldn't go on without you, perpetuating that fairy tale that noncoms actually run the army. In Korea the only difference in the chain of command is that the ambassador stands at the top. The ambassador will know when and how to get our people out, and *if* we must. There is diplomatic immunity and high-level decision making you will never understand."

Shriver had another drink. Julian was tempted to slap away the bottle and put the man under arrest, but the compound was in such an uproar, and now the ROK guards were holding back frightened Koreans seeking safety within.

"All I know is what happened at Kaesong. Every swinging dick the communists caught is dead. But we're so lucky—us lower ranks—to have people like you and Ambassador Muccio thinking for us. Does old Butt Wright know it?"

The jeep roared off, back through the gates, forcing the sentries to leap aside. A clutter of Korean refugees ran by, slant eyes fixed upon the embassy buildings as if they were Buddhist heaven or Confucian Eden, or whatever they believed in. As if any evacuation could possibly include natives; as if anyone wanted that. Julian dusted his hands upon his shirt and went in to face General Wright again.

CHAPTER 5

Seoul, Republic of Korea, June 28, 1950—Gunfire rocks the suburbs of this capital city. Civilian refugees hamper movement of ROK troops that seem leaderless.

소경이 개천 나무라기.

"The blind man blames the ditch." (Korean proverb: The fall is due to his lack of sight, not the world.)

Sam Connover watched Lt. Col. Julian Barron hurry across the seething compound and into the embassy. The son of a bitch strode as arrogantly as if he headed for the reviewing stand at Fort Lewis. The parade ground was the extent of Barron's soldiering, the tough part for City Hall officers who had to stand retirement parades and hang peacetime medals on other officers.

Filling his second extra gas can, Sam lifted it to the rear brackets of his jeep and wondered what Rich Shriver had been doing with the man. Rich would rather sit through a Troop Information and Education lecture than get near brass of almost any kind, much less a known chickenshit. Then Sam grinned and climbed behind his wheel. Barron had better keep an eye on his ass, or he might come up short. Rich had set up ambushes for better men.

Not a luckier man, though. Sam eased through the confusion and panic of the civilians, round-eye and Korean, who swept here and there in sweating clumps. Barron was the luckiest man Sam knew; Maggi had married him. She must have seen something not discernible to other eyes. A woman like that, so much deep, warm woman to be wasting herself on Colonel Barron.

The quick thunder of tank guns reached the compound like Gabriel blowing Recall that nobody was ready for and stilled the crowd for a moment in disbelief. Close, Sam thought, closer every time. The jeep angled around back near the kitchen door. Inside, Stonewall Jackson was loading up on canned food, on wines and bottled water. Even if they received orders to the contrary, they would still rejoin the 11th ROK and perhaps collect a few KMAG stragglers along the way. If they wouldn't stand and fight, they could hit and run.

Sam parked the jeep and checked over ammo and grenades, plentiful for now, no doubt soon more precious than Manchu diamonds. He should be concentrating upon survival and bleeding the invaders, not thinking of Maggi Barron. It was always so in the army—GIs talked of nothing but soldiering when they were in town, and of women and whiskey when they were back on post. But Maggi Barron was no town woman, and Sam always reached high as a soldier. Mrs. Barron would have wasted her comfort, her still depths and sudden storms of wild excitement, upon Sam as well. It would have been no one's fault.

One night of what might have been, should have been, thousands of nights, but would the fine edge dull and the soothing, the aching perfection change? Contented soldiers turned fat and careless; smiling soldiers had their combat boots set on a line of departure that promised them a short war. That was their choice, but keeping their heads up their asses usually took other guys with them. That made their suicides into mass murder.

The damned army, Maggi had said, a faint outline of shadowed rose and unbound hair, long sweet legs drawn up to her chin there on the side of the bed. It was the first time Sam knew the true meaning of hair unbound; the last time, too.

He coiled when the embassy's kitchen door crashed open, kicked from inside. Stonewall Jackson pushed a cart piled high with luxury foods and wines. He said, "You believe that asshole wanted a requisition?" Sam saw a stateside civilian, still in kitchen whites and chef's cap, sitting on the shiny tiled floor and holding his face in both hands.

"One more load," Sam said, going in and stepping over the guy's spread legs. "We'll pass it out to our ROKs and the younger Chong's refugees, if they need it." The man on the floor looked up but didn't say anything. Sam said, "You're learning. The North Koreans will be here within hours, and your only bet is get out for Inchon. There's one ship in the harbor; if you're lucky, you'll be in Japan tomorrow or next day."

The man lifted his head now, his hands sliding to his lap. The left side of his face was puffing. "But the ambassador said—and Colonel Barron—"

"The *balgaengis* do not listen; they come to kill, and they are proficient. But often they take the time to enjoy themselves before proceeding, the time to loot, rape, and torture."

"Huh?" the cook said, and Sam realized that he was really home again, home to his next war and the growing-up memories held in his inactive file. He had spoken Korean.

Changing gears, he said, "Outside of Kaesong, just a few hours ago, I saw a woman with bamboo poles stuffed up her vagina. When the bastards couldn't jam any more into her, they lifted her up on them. All her blood ran down and mixed with the dust. If they do that to their own kind, what do you think *you* can expect?"

Jackson came back, his cart rattling empty. "You telling jody war stories? Somebody convinced that ambassador, looks like. Convoy pulling out for Inchon. But fucking KMAG don't know whether to shit or go blind."

The cook leaped up and staggered out the door.

"Shit or go blind?" Sam pulled smoked hams off a shelf. "You sure you're not a country boy? All that jive about big cities—"

"Salt Lake City keeps growing, but nobody worries about a cow in the street. Picked up on a jeep trailer they leaving; we can take another load. You know the ROK's about to blow them bridges? I say we split right now. It ain't that water's cold; I just ain't swimming against no turd rafts."

Pivoting, Sam flipped up the carbine muzzle when something scraped to his right rear. Colonel Barron and a pair of civilian attachés stood in the hallway door. It would be so damned easy—an accidental shot, a ricochet; Maggi a widow. Then what? At the end of their night, they had both said love; neither mentioned the future, much less marriage. Maggi would know it was no accident, and being Maggi, could love no longer.

"Looting already, sergeant?"

Sam warned Stonewall with his eyes, then said, "Supply; better us than the gooks. Better we get it across the river before Fat Chae or some other cocktail-party general cuts off Seoul." He started out with the last hams and a sack that held jars of caviar.

One of the civilians whispered, but it carried: "Colonel, that's our Congressional Medal of—"

"I know who he is, and I *know* what he is," Barron said aloud. "Right now it seems our showpiece hero has deserted his command and is about to retreat without orders, to desert."

"Shee-it!" Jackson said. "How you live this long, man? Fuck this bunch, Sam; let them swim the Han. They fit right in with all that floating shit."

Sam watched Barron's face go purple under what seemed to be artfully applied streaks of dust. "S-sergeant! Goddamn you, sergeant! You—you—"

Jackson didn't actually smile; he just showed teeth. "Black bastard? You a turd, but you ain't no complete fool, because I still got time to fuck you up for life before us *soldiers* have to cut out. What orders you talking about? None of you motherfuckers back here even sent orders up to say fire or run or—"

"Shit or go blind?" Sam asked. He left the kitchen; Jackson could take care of himself. Sensing Barron hurrying behind him, Sam stepped to one side and half turned. "Like the man said, colonel—"

Barron's face was pale now, the dust streaks almost dark against his cheeks. "Oh, not here, Connover. Not now. But soon and somehow, somewhere. Did you actually think I would allow you to seduce my wife—*my* wife—and laugh about it to your lousy friends?"

"Lousy *enlisted* friends," Sam said, "but nobody's laughing; not then, not now. It's better for Maggi if you let it be, colonel. I intend to."

"How magnificent of you, how gallant. It won't save you. I will still have you killed."

Sam's face tightened, pulling across his cheekbones. "Up your candy ass, Barron. You're supposed to be doing your job, getting KMAG under some kind of control, and here you are playing a vengeance game. This isn't Hollywood, and it's not a classroom exercise. This is down and dirty, and fuckups like you can get good men killed. Go do your job and get the hell out of my way so I can do mine.

Because if some of the KIAs you cause are my men, you won't have to come looking for me. I'll find *you*."

Jackson brushed past with another armload of booty. "Shee-it, Sam—you sure you ain't no big-city boy? You starting to sound like a badass street cat."

Sam gunned the jeep and liberated trailer away, and as he passed through the gates he looked back and saw Colonel Barron motionless, staring after them.

CHAPTER 6

Seoul, Republic of Korea, June 28, 1950—Communist troops entered the capital this afternoon. American civilians and dependents have been evacuated from Inchon Harbor by a Norwegian fertilizer ship.

풀끝에 앉은세.

"A bird sitting on the tip of a blade of grass."
(Korean proverb: An unstable mind or position.)

He saw the tall buildings rising over the houses, stone buildings that were always shows of authority, towering above the common homes, the hovels of the workers that they would never own. From his kneeling position, Ho Chuk Gun saw the stillness in the outer rings of thatch-roofed houses and heard silence waiting in the empty alley below the roofs of tile, the temples where false gods had held power for thousands of years. The population of Seoul was attempting to flee its liberators, the masses deafened by lies and kept blinded to their destiny. That would change.

Had any man ever been so honored as Senior Lieutenant Ho Chuk Gun? Of all officers, he had been chosen to spearhead his company into Seoul. This corrupt city, this center of foreign imperialism was his to split open so the rotten heart could be cut out. Chuk Gun was the point of a great sword, the men behind him its cutting edge. All the military might of Pyongyang rolled behind them.

Chuk Gun clenched his teeth to avoid smiling; a leader must remain serious. A ruthless soldier does not smile and does not hesitate, does not flinch from his duty. Chuk Gun wanted to laugh and shout because this capital of the so-called Republic of Korea was about to fall, as all the south would fail. Of course, he did not. Hands strong upon the stock of his submachine gun, breathing the rainsweet air of victory over this land no longer divided and no more to be ruled by foreigners, he signaled his company to rise and follow him.

Nothing could stop them, these true soldiers, not the misguided peasants in foreign-made uniforms, and certainly not the cowardly long-noses who ran at first sight of the dedicated men of the *inmun-gun*. When Chuk Gun stood up, a rifle fired from one of the stone buildings and the bullet whined by his head. He did not flinch, for he was not afraid, and his heart sang. He hand-signaled forward and did not have to look to see if they followed. Children of the Democratic People's Republic of Korea, of course they obeyed. Now they knew their worth; now they had dignity and pride.

Moving forward, alert and keyed to all his senses, Chuk Gun wanted to shout at the people hidden in the houses, at those still easing unseen down the streets. He needed to tell them that he too was peasant stock, that he too had hungered and eaten tree bark because the landlords took the rice for taxes, that he had suffered under the Japanese and hated them all his life. Look at me now, you fools! I am an officer, a leader, even though I was only a poor farmer. Now I have education and pride. These great gifts I bring to you from our father, Kim Il Sung.

The hidden rifleman fired again. Behind Chuk Gun a man grunted and went down. Someone would look after that one later, and the range to the suspect building was too far for a burst from Chuk Gun's PPSH. One traitor was not enough to slow this advance while heavy weapons were called up. That was a weakness in foreign tactics, holding up an entire attack in order not to lose a man or so to a sniper. *Inmun-gun* soldiers knew how to die.

Breaking into a trot, Chuk Gun headed directly for the target. To his left, something moved, and he forced a quick burst at it. Kim Sangsa appeared at his side, so he motioned the sergeant to the right flank and smashed in through the front door. Too late, he saw that a woman tried to hide behind a counter, too late to stop his gun. The boy with her looked to have been about military age, anyhow; he left both bleeding in the wreckage of the marble counter. He leapt for the stairs but stopped partway up when the grenade exploded—the thump so heavy and a thin scream of metal ripped small; a stick grenade. Sergeant Kim had made his flanking movement well. Without a glance at the woman and boy, Chuk Gun trotted across the lobby and out into the street.

The blood smell stayed in his nostrils until the stench of the city pushed it out. He was tall and strong; he was quick and accurate; even better, he was a patriot doing his duty. This was good, this awareness that raced through his body, the powdersmoke taste in his mouth, and the sunshine of Seoul sliding over his face. That sun was weakening, its light stained with the smoke of burning houses, the hours left to it short. The Yin and the Yang, and this night Chuk Gun's unit should sleep well in the capitol building of the great traitor Ee Sung Man, he who called himself Syngman Rhee now, as if the foreign lettering and foreign sound made him better than ordinary Koreans. That was their objective, the capitol building. If they were given the chance to crush all resistance along the way, along the broad pathway of Taengyong-no, that tree-bordered street where the electric cars ran was a fine place to leave examples. Chuk Gun had never seen electric cars.

The exhausted soldiers of the 11th ROK Regiment slept in the back garden of the Chong home, filled with the last of the *kimchi* and cooked rice. Chong Nam Ki turned and almost stumbled through the house until he reached the front seating porch. He had slept but two hours and his eyes ached, but a clock inside him waked him to hurry.

His mother still wept, her pain even more evident because it was soundless and wordless. Never had she appeared so old, for her hands had ever been skilled with lip stains and powders of the court. Surely those were new lines drawn about her mouth and eyes, or channeled there by her bitter tears. Mother Chong could not even mourn in solitude, which was the manner of the highborn classes.

"I listened to your younger brother," she said, "and had a little *kimchi* put aboard the vehicle. We have dry rice and beans and peppers, a little *soju*. I did not forget dried octopus."

"The *kimchi* crocks are heavy, so my soldiers will have grateful stomachs."

Now she sleeved her cheeks and stood erect. "Do the communists celebrate *Chusok?* Will there ever be another thanking time for harvest and all wives putting down *kimchi* for the entire winter?"

"I do not think that the *balgaengi* celebrate, or know how to laugh, mother." But they knew how to kill. He sat crosslegged upon his own porch for probably the last time. "The servants—do they help Wei Ki bury valuables? If so, they—"

Again his mother patted her face with the wide sleeve of the simple dress she wore except for state occasions. "War does not change all things. Our servants are our second family and will never betray a trust. Not one has run off. It is time for tea."

Tea was one of the decadent foreign habits scorned by the *yangban* who would still change nothing, who yet accepted nothing not purely Korean. Father Chong had said: Take the good things, no matter where they were born. Discard things that do not work, no matter how long they have been revered.

His sister Soon Ki brought the low rice table, the ancient black table their father had eaten from. It was many layers deep with lacquer over an intricate mother-of-pearl design. She placed the brass teapot upon a small tray, protecting the finish of the *pahp-saeng* out of lifelong habit. Mother Chong brought drinking bowls at the moment Nam Ki's brother kicked off his rubber slippers and came onto the porch.

"All is ready," Wei Ki said. "Here is your map of the hiding places, older brother. I will try to leave food for your men."

Mother Chong poured. Nam Ki held his bowl in both hands; the dark, steamy aroma was far better than the standard Korean drink after eating, and that only in winter: unseasoned rice water. He said, "Soldiers can always find food. There will be more refugees than you can feed, so care for the children." The tea was hot; he closed his eyes.

"As our father wished," Wei Ki said, and Nam Ki wondered if there was a note of resentment in the boy's voice. Did the young fool imagine he had missed a moment of glory when their father blew himself to bloody ribbons?

"War makes staying alive difficult. Keeping others alive becomes more difficult. Out father was very wise to think this far ahead."

To save the young in a land that demanded devotion for the old; to foresee roads clogged with frightened people and lost children; to plan for secret hoards of food and coverings on the route to Pusan—all that was the clear vision of a seer. Father Chong also dreamed his own death and followed that plan of the gods. The family gods overlapped, from Taoism through the more civilized religions of Buddha and Confucius, but the shaman was never forgotten. War forced men to think upon religion and other lives to be hoped for.

"There is little time," he said, and he rose as his mother collected the tea bowls. What would she do with them? Who would next drink from them? She must realize that this house, home to the family Chong for at least ten generations, would be destroyed by northern jackals after they defiled it in every possible way. The Chongs were gathered for the last time upon this porch. He sat upon its entrance stone to pull on his boots and go wake his soldiers. His eye caught his sister's movement as she removed their father's rice table.

"Give it to me," he said.

Soon Ki stared, and he repeated his words. For a moment he held the *pahp-saeng* close, feeling his father's hands upon its smooth surface, hearing the echoes of his voice. Then he raised the little table and smashed it upon the entrance stone. Bits of pearl flashed in the lowering sun, shattered lacquer spun high, and a long splinter of teak thrust into the side of Nam Ki's hand. Dropping the twisted table leg, he watched a droplet of blood form upon a ragged frame of black wood.

Soon Ki cried out and fled into the house. Mother Chong said nothing, but her hands held tightly to her dress. Younger brother nodded once, as if he understood.

Then servant Old Kim rushed across the yard from the open central gates. "Soldiers come—foreign soldiers! Hide!"

"We hide from our own these days, grandfather. Those are friends. You do not recognize the man who guides the jeep?"

The old man shrugged. "Foreigners."

Sam Connover stopped the jeep, its trailer wagging like the tail of a fat dog, and Nam Ki appreciated the piled-high food and ammunition. The black sergeant still rode with Sam Connover, which approved him as a soldier to be trusted.

"Fat Chae is south of the river—alone," Sam said.

General Chae Byong Duk, little more than five feet tall, 245 pounds, and ROK army chief of staff; panicked now and fleeing for his pig's hide, abandoning Seoul and his scattered troops.

"The bridges," Nam Ki said. All his father's planning, all the blood sacrifice of the 1st Division before the tanks, would be gone for nothing, if his son failed to get family and soldiers across the Han.

CHAPTER 7

Suwon, Republic of Korea, June 28, 1950—General of the Army
Douglas MacArthur flew into this beleaguered airstrip this afternoon. After a meeting with ROK President Syngman Rhee and
U.S. Ambassador John Muccio, MacArthur took a short trip by
jeep. Retreating ROK troops cheered him.

비단옷 입고 밤길같는다.

"Dress in brocade and stroll in the dark." (Korean
proverb: Useless effort.)

Julian Barron was confused. He was more tired than he'd
been in his life, even during plebe year at the Academy,
but worse, he was confused. He had been close enough to
touch General Douglas MacArthur, and that great man
hadn't seemed to know exactly what was going on. He
rode about, corncob pipe and scrambled-eggs visor, drawing a retinue in crisp suntans. Even the president of Korea
trailed behind with the U.S. ambassador. But the general
acted as if Seoul would not fall tonight, and if that improb-
ability should occur, why, it could be brought back with a
snap of the kingly fingers. And heresy that it might be,
Julian knew better.

He rode his jeep behind Ambassador Muccio's long after MacArthur had flown back out of Suwon with his court jesters, thirteen staff officers, and a pair of EM, five hours on the ground, and only one direct observation. Choking on dust seething with God only knew how many varieties of germ and microbe, Julian shuddered. He had seen the evil little bastards, more deadly than disease, heard fire from the snipers already infiltrated into the city. If the general knew that U.S. troops were coming, he didn't say how long it would take them to arrive. If it wasn't this evening, and if they didn't come equipped with at least antitank weapons and tanks of their own, Seoul would fall, and shortly thereafter, everything north of—what, Pusan? There could be nothing after Pusan, no war and no army.

Good Christ, today a pair of prop planes had actually strafed the streets of Seoul. Yak fighters, somebody said; right after they made their pass and headed for Kimpo airport, Julian remembered what the *Stars & Stripes* reporter said, that the greatest air force the world had ever seen was rusting away in the New Mexico desert. The transports that brought General MacArthur from Tokyo were unarmed, and if there was a fighter escort, Julian didn't see it. Of course there were hundreds of operational aircraft in Japan —or scattered over the Far East. But there weren't in Korea, not in direct ground support. An entire air force parked in the desert halfway around the world.

Why should he recall what some lowly sergeant said, what any damned sergeant said? Because he felt the power and responsibilities of his rank lessen every hour, felt himself caught up in something too big and far too deadly. Julian had no place in it, and that was a thing he had always been certain of, his position in life as an officer, a leader of men, and—yes, damn it—husband and father. Before the first crack in the world's sanity appeared with his wife's betrayal.

Now he had no book of army regulations to check, no

school solutions to theoretical combat situations, and he was fast losing respect for his superiors, especially any civilians thrust into command. Good Christ, wasn't suffering under Butt Wright enough, without doubting the entire Far East Command and the focus of his own life?

Julian's driver, Lieutenant Smitts, Switts, or something like, flicked on the lights, and Julian coughed on the constant dust. Two jeeps bounced and swerved ahead, one carrying Muccio, and the other personally driven by General Wright, his horn blasting. Refugees still hurried along the roadsides, but the stream seemed to be thinning, or maybe it was because he couldn't see them all in the dark, only the whitish blobs of moving shadow. They were always moving, going anywhere in a desperate need. These Koreans knew something, and what they knew scared him, too.

"Shit," the lieutenant said, "we can't get back into the city. Look at the gooks all over those bridges. My Val-Pac and two cartons of Luckies are across that bastard river."

Up ahead, in the dust-swirled beams of the jeeps, General Wright climbed down and put his fists on his hips, staring at the tangled mass clogging every inch of the vehicle bridge and the railway bridge, too. Wiping his face, Julian got down and walked to the man, dreading another confrontation but somehow welcoming it. Wright fit into all this confusion, crude and tough. At the end of his career, he could do just about what he wanted without worry. Just now he kicked the front tire of the jeep and kicked pebbled dirt out at the river. The refugees kept coming, crawling along bridge girders, insect-crawling over each other, moving inches at a time, lapping like tired waves around carts and a few trucks. "Ho damn! Mr. Ambassador, did your people destroy all files?"

Muccio's suit was patterned with dust, and his face looked drawn. "I don't think so, general; the evacuation got off late, and—"

"Yes," Wright said, "the evacuation. So all the G-2 files are still there, naming every Korean who ever worked for us. Death warrants, sir—we've killed them all."

Hunching his shoulders, Muccio said, "Oh, I wouldn't go so far as to say—"

Wright's head snapped around, and his face was half shadow, half glare from the headlights when he looked around at Julian. "How many vehicles abandoned in the compound, colonel?"

Julian did a swift count: the three jeeps here, the six-bys that carried the dependents and other civilians to Inchon Harbor. "Fifteen, sir."

"And the monthly liquor supply—didn't it just arrive? Tax-free at forty thousand dollars is a lot of booze to leave behind. Colonel, what would you say is the value of all that gourmet food?"

Blinking, Julian wondered what this was all about. Around the jeeps boiled the refugees, and a few ROK soldiers stood by the near end of the bridges, uneasy with their weapons. For all the numbers, there was so little sound from the crowd. "A hundred thousand dollars won't miss it much, sir."

"Counting the short load liberated by Connover and Jackson?"

So weary that he didn't flinch at Connover's name or wonder how the general knew about their set-to in the kitchen, Julian answered yes and felt a pang of conscience about the ambassador, who turned away and got into his jeep. Butt Wright had erected a cross here on the bank of the Han River and driven the spikes with a sure hand.

The general chewed on a cigar, its lighted end bobbing as Wright watched the bridge and the teeming mass of fleeing Koreans. Seoul showed more lights this night than Julian could recall seeing before. The general's maps and communications center were across the bridge, impassable from this side and almost so from the other. There must be two thousand white-clad civilians swarming the span, not knowing where they were going, only that they must go. Again, Julian felt an echo of their panic in his belly.

"You're real sharp with figures, colonel; regular adding machine."

"For what good it does here." Good Christ, where did that come from?

Wright stepped closer, the stink of his cigar enveloping Julian's face, but it was no worse than the rice paddies, so Julian took it without blinking. Wright said, "There's a place for numbers and little details, but it ain't here. But you surprise me, a book soldier discovering that."

The smartmouth correspondent's don't-give-a-damn words came back. What the hell you going to do, colonel —send me to the front? Wait a few minutes and the front'll be here. The front and flanks and rear area were all here on the river, together. Where the hell could the general send him, back to Fort Lewis? The warning buzzer that had protected Julian Barron most of his life sounded but didn't ring clearly through the fog of his fatigue.

"I was surprised, too, general, embarrassing the ambassador with a kangaroo court. I don't care about the screwup —sir. He tried to get orders out of Tokyo and Washington, but nobody knew what to do about KMAG. And no matter how they had to ride, the civilians got out safely."

He had said too much. Wright didn't have to send him anywhere; the general could run through an order busting him to lieutenant and assign him an infantry platoon. If it weren't for the reduction in rank and pay, that might not be bad. Down at that level, you knew what you were doing, or thought so.

"Ho damn, boy—there might be hope for you yet. Did I upset our technical commander? Ho damn, I have to do something until this bridge situation clears, if it ever does. Embarrass the guy? He's State Department with political connections, and this is the most embarrassment he'll ever get."

An ox cart fought off the bridge, its motor power now a desperate family. Pulling the cart jammed with belongings, pushing at it and wrestling with it, the men and women struggled with it to the edge of the riverbank. Julian watched them pause for air, for a moment's rest, four men and as many women, three small children. As he watched the earth gave way under one cart wheel and the whole thing creaked and sighed over into the river. A bundle of white clothing floated back under the bridge before it sank.

Julian thought that the Han didn't exude its usual mud and crap smell this night; the smell was of sweat and terror and hopelessness.

The general leaned back upon his jeep fender. "Nobody will even know about the embassy screwup and how much money was lost. Did the North Koreans get a present of fifteen GI vehicles, not the ROKs? No headline will ever say anything about the embassy employees who will die because those clowns left all personnel records intact. That's what pisses me off—the poor bastards who die because of incompetents. Now another bunch of clowns has us stranded here, while most of the ROK army is trying to cross these bridges to the south. We need to get back and see what we can destroy. Especially those records that embarrass our civilian boss. In government service, there's only one rule: PYOA, protect your own ass. Any ambassador ought to think on his feet, but that's beyond them. They'd have to accept responsibility for wrong calls."

"Something like the army," Julian said. He might as well take the extra step. If Wright wanted him, he already had enough.

The Korean family lowered a boy into the water. He felt around with his feet, then shook his head. The grandmother gook began to wail.

Butt Wright flicked a battered Zippo at his dead cigar.

"Something like, but some of us believe the army picked the right ho damn men for wading shitstorms."

Gulping air, the Korean kid dived. Headlights from the little MacArthur welcome convoy, more bobbing lights from the bridge, spread ugly yellow puddles upon the turgid water. It was still hot, this far into the night, and reminded Julian of the weekend he'd spent in New York City, the air muggy and difficult to breathe. He had been scared then, too. The girl was the sister of an upperclassman, although Julian had suggested a professional for himself.

Nothing doing, Brocklin insisted. Little Suzie needs it, and you sure as hell need it, and I can vouch that baby sister can fuck better than any call girl, because she loves it. The night was hot and sticky and a mistake. It might have been all right, if she hadn't finally laughed. She tried to cover that, and then apologized, and helped him to some sort of climax. He woke just before dawn to hear her in the other bed with someone else. Julian didn't want to know who.

Gasping, the kid broke the surface, holding a dripping packet high. It was clothing, and when his elders urged him to try again, he dragged out onto the bank and shook his head, still gasping. He crawled into shadow, and Julian couldn't see his face. One of the middle-aged men climbed down into the river.

"The bridges are mined," Julian said. "That's why ROK soldiers are hanging around this end. We won't get back, general. There's a ferry; maybe KMAG survivors are getting out with it."

"Knew that," Butt Wright said, "but I appreciate you telling me. You just might find the true believer if you scratch deep, boy. What say to a field command, an infantry battalion? I saw the idiot sticks on your collar."

Julian shocked himself. "Thank you, general. If U.S.

troops come in, you mean?" He'd transferred to Korea for a field command, hadn't he?

Wright chewed his cigar. "Oh, they're on the way, what we've got. The great man sent for them, thinks the enemy will stop at first sight of American uniforms. I think our occupation troops aren't up to the task here. But American soldiers are on the way, and I know of a weak battalion CO in the bunch."

Julian felt better. He was worth something, his expertise called for, his sharp mind to seek a way out of this mess before too many troops were committed. "Until then, sir?"

The general pushed himself erect, and Julian saw that the old man was as tired as anybody else. "Keep your jeep and driver here. If any dumb bastard tries to blow this bridge, stop him." Wright's cigar was out again; he pitched the butt into the river. "If you don't get stopped yourself. I'm taking this ambassador south a bit, and see if I can find a unit that might fight." He paused, and the women beside the river screamed, but Julian refused to look that way.

Wright said, "You'll hate me more for giving you a command than you do now. If you screw it up, then ho damn—give your soul to God, because your West Point ass is mine. Welcome to the United States Army, colonel. This is why we get called 'sir.'"

CHAPTER 8

Seoul, Republic of Korea, June 28, 1950—This city was overrun by communist troops tonight. Many thousands of disorganized ROK soldiers were trapped north of the Han River when the bridges were blown.

돌다리도 두들겨 보고 건너가라 .

"Test even a stone bridge before crossing."
(Korean proverb: Safety first.)

Inch by sweating inch, fretting that the motor would overheat any minute, despite shutting it off while the bridge was packed so tightly that nothing moved, Sam Connover kept it together. Carbine cradled, Lieutenant Chong rode the trailer; behind him came the deuce-and-a-half with the family and a gathering of lost children.

"Surrounded by ROKs," Jackson said, one long leg stuck outside the jeep, boot resting upon the right fender. "Never been guarded by a whole regiment before, but I'd as soon be riding a bulldozer right now, cutting a way through this mess. We liable to get wet asses anyhow. You feel this bastard shake? Going to rain some more, too. Shee-it."

Sam eased up on the clutch and the jeep nosed forward, then stopped. "That's not thunder you hear, but artillery. Not ours, and a forty-man regiment isn't much, either." He smelled the fear around them, the desperation and death sweat. He bitched, to hold off thinking about explosives below them, about already spooked ROK troops hearing that enemy artillery with their shaky hands close to the plungers.

It's a soldier's privilege to bitch, his uncle always said; you got to watch the bastard when he ain't bitching. That's when he's dangerous. Kelly Connover taught Sam a lot more about the army than Sam's father taught him about being a man of God. That was because Kelly didn't force it, didn't keep a switch handy while a kid kneeled sore and miserable on a stone floor and learned too damned many of the scriptures by rote.

"You just trying to cheer me up," Jackson said. "Look how I'm smiling. Forty *good* men be plenty; if we split time we even see a tank. You catch all them mothering lights on the other side? GIs?"

"Some; I see a few jeeps and hell of a lot of running Koreans. What bothers me are the ROKs who aren't cutting out—those engineers."

Jackson grunted and pulled in his leg. "Shee-it, and I'm a man crimps pins on grenades so they can't no way fall out. Take a gorilla to pull that pin in one jerk. Compo C, you guess? How much, I wonder."

"Enough to kill everybody on this damned bridge; enough to cut off every ROK soldier and civilian trying to get out of Seoul before the north gooks turn it into a bloodbath." A military problem he had no hand in solving irritated him, and if trusting only to his own decisions got him into hot spots, it had also kept him alive.

My knowhow, reverend, *my* expertise, and a good share of Kelly Connover's luck passed along. Since God and I aren't exactly barracks buddies, I'd disagree with you,

55

Reverend Connover; no act of God got my tail out of a crack. Not without my help.

Why didn't He turn thy stiff and holy neck into steel, so the samurai sword of the infidel be turned? Why didn't He keep you from that common grave with all those parishioners who believed with you?

"Getting close," Jackson said. "Can't remember being so glad to see land—unless it was getting off the ship in Pusan. Seasick? Every time I felt a knot in my throat I swallowed. It was my asshole coming up. Tell me something: How come you call North Koreans gooks and get pissed when anybody says it about the people down here?"

"A fine distinction. I don't know what else to name the bastards; they're not Koreans anymore, but some kind of animal mutant. All Koreans suffered under Jap colonization, but the People's Democratic Republic crossed that *bushido* butchery with Russian paranoia and smeared the result atop the inferiority complex Koreans have had since they discovered they didn't live in the best of all possible worlds. Arm and motivate that, and you get vicious, bloodthirsty, and goddamned deadly *gooks*."

"Sounds like the psych course I took in a weak moment," Jackson said. "Flunked, and a good thing, too. Started trying to analyze how come fucking officers like Barron act that way, and there ain't no cause but some guys get born chickenshit and spend the rest of their lives getting better at it. Hey! Look at that bunch at the bank, holding hands and scuffling around underwater like they trying to find something."

"Or somebody," Sam answered, sucking a deep breath of thick night air and easing his grip on the wheel. It would be irony of ironies for this brave remnant of a fighting regiment to be destroyed by their own army. It was about to happen to other stragglers, to unlucky people who would be thrown away in Seoul this night. For the idiots were going to blow the bridges; Sam was certain of that.

"Speak of the chicken," Jackson said. "Be certain that prick been on the right side of the river ahead of everybody else. Shee-it; he get in the way, let me drive. I'll run over his ass."

Sam kept going. Out of the corner of his eyes, he saw Jackson's grease gun rise, its wire butt braced against Matt's knee. A young lieutenant stood beside Colonel Barron, staring and pointing at Sam and his people. Doggedly, heads down and bone-weary, the 11th ROKs held a tight column on each side of the vehicles, the point ahead carrying bayoneted weapons at the hip.

Lieutenant Chong kneeled upon the jeep trailer and shouted to his troops, telling them he was proud of them. The Chong family in the truck and their little covey of children applauded. Refugees turned dripping faces to look, wide-eyed and disbelieving.

The KMAG officer yelled, "Hey, you sergeants! Where the hell are you going? KMAG is pulling out."

Still, Barron said nothing, but Sam felt the sharp points of his eyes. Jackson turned to stare back as they passed. "That so? *We* ain't."

So many people clogging the road, its thin blacktop worn through and patched with gravel only. The Jap garrison in Korea during the war was made up of the lame and the halt invalided from China, and the standard police force to protect the bureaucrats who came to run the country thirty-six years back. But during that war, everything went out of Korea to support the emperor's war machine; nothing so minor as road surfacing came in, or rice or medicines.

"You think Butt Wright ordered everybody to split?" Jackson lowered his weapon.

"Not him; Tokyo, probably. That watch you liberated from the embassy stores still running?"

"Saved it from the enemy, like it says. You interested in time? I ain't since we put ass to that river, and it don't look like Lieutenant Chong means to call for a bivouac yet. You see how much stuff these poor ROKs are carrying?"

"Can you see that damned watch?" Grit was inside Sam's fatigues, crunchy against his teeth, and he breathed more dust that wouldn't settle until heavier rains turned the road to slop. "The gas gauge is broken, and I've been refueling by time spent in first gear."

Not that far behind them, a gigantic explosion shook the road and stopped the flight of the refugees. It was followed by three more heavy blasts. In the shock waves that rolled down the road and over them, Sam turned off the ignition and closed his eyes.

They had done it; the sons of bitches had dropped the Han River bridges and killed thousands of their own people, trapped thousands more helpless in the city being overrun by communist troops. Sam understood the confused, face-saving thinking behind the stupid, self-serving deed. He understood because he had been born not too far south of here, because he thought as a Korean when it was called for. Right now, he wasn't proud of that.

Before the women squatting beside the road moaned any louder, Jackson said, "It's oh-one-hundred; a new day, man."

Nam Ki posted sentries and drank a little of the foreign wine that Sam Connover and the black man brought to the small fire where the Chong family sat in bleak silence. The children had been fed something and tucked under blankets upon the earth. His mother still held one child close, a little girl no more than a baby who whimpered softly every few minutes. Flickering light marked faces around the fire— Mother Chong, his sister, his brother who did not appear so young now; Sam Connover and Jackson *Sangsa*. Encircling them all were the forty faithful of the regiment. How many friends had he?

The poet Yun—pillowing his head upon his crossed

arms, Nam Ki thought it was Yun who claimed no need for more friends than five:

> water and stone,
> pine and bamboo—
> the rising moon on east mountain.

A very long time ago Nam Ki had thought to be a poet, had dreamed of combining calligraphy with the older art of word painting. Perhaps some day Korea would again need its poets; perhaps he could try once more—if he could brush-stroke past the killing and the pain. If anything else was to be left in the world, beauty must be returned.

Lifting his head, he saw the blurred outlines of Sam Connover's face.

> . . . You look at me but with no words;
> That is why, O brother, you are my friend.

Yun would not mind the small change from moon to brother—if the poet was Yun. It was easier to think of poetry than an enemy tank and Father Chong's blood floating the Imjin; upon Buddha's peace rather than the morning to come. Should he send a squad with the truck or keep every sorely needed man to set up a roadblock? If the family were to be destroyed by deserters and looters, if Father Chong's plans were to come to nothing—but the other need was vital, also. Not all *balgaengi* would remain to rape Seoul; an armored spearhead was certain to be aimed for Suwon as soon as ferries were found to carry the iron monsters, as soon as a pontoon bridge could be laid across the Han.

The T-34s could be hurt, the road walled off by the explosives that Sam Connover carried, or slowed by hand-dug ditches and great stones rolled downhill into the first narrow pass. Nam Ki sighed into and out of sleep. He could recite poetry to the Red dogs, too. Where were the fresh troops, where was the time? But somehow, some way, they must be delayed until American help arrived. Father Chong had believed such help would come. They will not turn their backs upon Korea again, he had said; *Me-kuk* is a great country that has shame for giving us to the Japanese before. Even though Sam Connover wasn't sure American planes and soldiers would come quickly, Father Chong believed, and therefore so must Nam Ki.

When his eyes snapped open again he had been covered with a blanket, and the women were heating American C-rations in a pot of water. Stretching, Nam Ki smelled coffee from across the fire and nodded to Sam Connover. The man Jackson was at the jeep, passing out different kinds of food to a line of ROKs, their midday meal to come. Nam Ki had slept longer than he intended, but his body of troops was functioning smoothly, and the family was already repacking the truck and soothing stunned children who wanted to know where their own parents were.

When he returned from the bushes, Sam was on the jeep radio and looked up as Nam Ki approached. "Nothing much; garbled messages to KMAG—get out, come back. Much communist traffic from short-range radios, but nothing we did not expect."

The jet screamed overhead and was gone before Nam Ki could draw another breath. "American plane. They are coming, my brother. We are not alone."

Sam Connover nodded. "Which way do you expect the *balgaengi* tanks to attack?"

Hesitating, Nam Ki accepted a canteen cup of hot coffee. That this great soldier should ask his advice was flattering, but one more stone upon the load Nam Ki carried. "Suwon, Masan, then Taejon. The road is open, but we can block it in places and gather army stragglers along the way. I do not expect the *Me-in* to arrive for several days."

"At least," Sam Connover agreed. "After you have eaten, then?"

Handing back the empty canteen cup, Nam Ki said, "Rations as we travel. Even the Sorak mountains are more beautiful when viewed upon a full stomach."

The black man walked up, frowning. "You try any of this caviar stuff? Knew it wasn't nothing but fish eggs, but I thought they'd at least cook the damned things."

Nam Ki took the open jar. "Thank you." Would he ever be as calm and unconcerned as this man? He signaled to Lieutenant Lim to get the men moving and climbed back into position upon the jeep trailer, where he could see forward and to the rear. To fight one war prepared a soldier for the next one, it seemed, but Nam Ki would as soon be respected as an artist-poet—except that he had no choice. As his group left the field and moved south along the road he heard jet planes again and looked up to see the mark of high-flying bombers above the clouds.

Again the wisdom of his father had proven true; assistance was arriving, but by the time ground troops got to Korea, there might not be a place for them to land.

CHAPTER 9

South of the Han River, June 30, 1950—The North Korean army hurled tanks and infantry over this river today, striking south to bring all Korea under the red flag. Some units met fierce resistance.

내절 부처는 내가 위하여야 한다.

"The Buddha in my temple is best worshipped by me." (Korean proverb: One must serve his own master.)

They crossed on the ferry only minutes behind the tanks still easing one by one over the pontoon bridge, Ho Chuk Gun and his victorious company. Two days and nights in Seoul might have dulled his men's cutting edge, so Chuk Gun was happy to get them on the attack once more. Tasting the damp air, the rice-wine flavorings of the day, he hid a smile behind his hand. The English embassy still smoldered in the heart of the city, and the deaths of the foreign fools within its white man's walls were his gift to Seoul's peasants.

Not only the sun and his accomplishments warmed Chuk Gun, but the bright memory of the *yongkuk* cowering before the *inmun-gun*. Make them remember, Colonel Paik had ordered; see that every running dog of the capitalists pays his just debts to the people. Ah—and so they had, and the people would never forget.

Drifting only a little, the boat reached the riverbank, landing near five corpses that seemed to have been holding hands in a chain extending down into the river. The explosion that had demolished the bridge had killed them with one mighty blow. Chuk Gun strode off the flatboat as the ferrymen struggled to hold it firmly aground with their poles.

Such blind ignorance, for the common people to be so steeped in imperialist propaganda that they ran before their own liberators, fled and died without ever knowing the benefits of a classless society.

Turning as his men trotted past, Chuk Gun said to the boatmen, "Go back quickly for more soldiers."

Sullen and fearful, the men did not answer, did not send him southward with a cheer. He had no time to correct them now, but when the Han bridges were rebuilt they would also be in uniform. The new order would need many men to protect itself.

"To Suwon," he commanded his troops, and trotted ahead. Thinking on that particular group of bodies on the riverbank, he could only wonder at such animal stupidity. They were not young children; all had bowed to the despised Japanese and, after the Russians freed Korea, had continued to lose their dignity to the bandits and traitors who came after the war.

A tank rolled by, trailing only a bit of dust but spraying half-dried bits of mud from its tracks. Its sergeant commander saluted Chuk Gun. It was as it should be, a salute instead of a kick, pride instead of shame. The *sensae*—always the Japanese way of things—never the Korean *songsaeng*, slapping the boy trying so desperately to learn;

the Japanese teacher beating that boy with a bamboo rod because he had forgotten and spoken in his own language.

Farmer's son, the teacher spat; what good is learning to such as you? You will always stoop over a rice paddy, always stand to your knees in offal. Get out, you stupid Korean!

"Lieutenant?" Chuk Gun's next-in-command moved up beside him.

"Yes, *sowi?*" The boy was a proper second lieutenant, young and dedicated. When all land below the parallel came under the red flag, both of them might have the opportunity to train in Moscow.

"Sir, I respectfully suggest that scouts be sent ahead on this side of the road. A farmer has said that objects were hidden in the earth by foreign soldiers."

"Mines, but no more than one or two. The cowards were running too fast to delay for long. See how much equipment has been thrown away in their fear. Wherever they run, we will catch them. Wherever they hide, we will find them. Have the scouts watch for turned earth and mark the spots. Others will remove the mines."

Raising his right hand, Ho Chuk Gun gave the signal to trot. The faster the army moved now, the sooner victory would be complete.

More tanks clattered past, five, ten, their cannon muzzles sniffing south, their joyous crews eager for more combat. No traitor soldiers, no foreign advisors could stand to the *inmun-gun* intent upon recovering every *li* of its own land.

Sam Connover put his hand on Matt Jackson's arm. "No use; we can't help them from here, and even if we go down there with all we've got, we just add to the casualty count."

"The poor bastards," Jackson said. "Oh, man, the poor bastards. So goddamned many gooks, so goddamned many tanks." Gunfire rolled up the ridge to where they lay above the village of Osan. Only the first of July, Sam thought; the firecracker celebrations were early, and most of the American GIs below would never stand a hometown parade on any Fourth of July. They were dying fast.

Lieutenant Chong said, "We can attack the flank and relieve some of the pressure."

"And die with them? It will be more useful if we circle down and booby-trap that creek crossing, then kill some of their infantry before we run again. But you are the commander, Nam Ki."

Jackson said, "You're telling him we ain't going to do shit?"

"Sorry; I forget which language I'm in."

"How you say it don't count, man. *All* our asses in Korea along with them poor bastards getting wasted down there."

The tightness was upon Sam, the thinking that telescoped one quick idea upon another. It was a special knowing that came over him in combat, his own sense of rightness. Back in that other war just around the corner, an officer had called that a blessing for Sam. The *Moksa* Connover would not have agreed; secure in his fortress of God, the pastor of Chunju city usually agreed only with God, or the other way around.

"Task Force Smith, the radio said." Sam lifted field glasses. "So damned sure of themselves that they're using open channels. I make out a few bazookas, one battery of 105s; maybe a reinforced company. I'll bet they're short of ammo and food, short of water and everything but optimism—oh, Christ! There, a direct hit on that T-34! High explosive right on the nose, and the damned tank keeps coming."

Smoke and dust whirled high in the air. *Rapraprap!* went the light machine guns of this American sacrificial group run in from Japan. The flat *crack!* of tank 76s answered, and Red mortars pinpointed the American artillery positions. Sam held the glasses to his eyes and winced at the carnage.

Chong Nam Ki put his mouth close to Sam's ear. Blast after blast thundered from the valley floor to shake the earth under their bellies, and Sam caught his first taste of gunsmoke. He breathed it deep and nodded as Nam Ki shouted that he would start down the reverse slope and see to the tank trap.

Jackson pushed himself back from the ridge. "Can't watch that no longer. Leaving those guys in a shitstorm is cold, Sam. How you get so fucking cold?"

Crawfishing back, the spices of burned powder on his tongue, Sam ducked away from the skyline and looked down the slope. "I'm guessing three hundred guys down there. They'll have to retreat damned soon. Our forty-three men won't stop the gooks."

"Didn't say you were wrong, just that somewhere between V-E Day and here you got your balls froze. Come on, Frosty—let's go down and do *something.*"

The angle was steep; Sam stumbled, and Jackson held him up; Jackson sat down and cursed as he slid into a boulder. Behind them gun thunder reached up into the hot sky, and Sam hoped they could set the ambush before Task Force Smith pulled out and Red scouts turned into this side road, before at least one tank and support infantry made certain that no enemy troops lurked in this fingerling of a farm valley.

The budding emerald shoots of a small paddy showed the good last week's rains had done the crop. But the tiny community tucked into a flap of mountain stairstepped by dikes looked deserted. No dog barked; no children sat upon the dikes to pull strings and keep rice birds away with fluttering papers strung around each small field. Even before the sound of guns had reached their peaceful valley, these interlocked, intermarried families had joined the flight to Pusan, to anywhere that might offer a few more days of safety from their brothers striking down from the north. It had always been so in Korea, and perhaps through the Orient, where those about to bleed from warlords never needed a modern communications system. They *knew,* and they got out of the way.

As Sam knew, and did not try to escape.

Samuel, his father said, you grow more Korean each day that passes.

Is that bad, father?

It is not for us, boy. We come here to save their souls, not to emulate them. They are heathens, boy. They are yellow men, and we must ever be conscious to remain different.

Are all God's children different, father?

"They already got it about dug," Jackson said. "We better see to camouflage. Hey! Tell that bunch to leave enough support so foot troops can walk over ahead of the tank without getting suspicious. Here—grab a handful of that brush and help sweep off the top."

Sam climbed atop the wooden span. Two of its middle braces had been carried away and hidden. It was about twelve feet to the rocks below, their bottoms only dampened by the recent rains. The drop might not kill any of the crew but ought to cripple the tank.

The killing would come when the crew tried to get out, either through the turret or the escape hatch in the steel belly of the T-34. The killing would have already begun above the bridge, where heavy crossfire was set to cut down the infantry. Then the 11th ROK and its AWOL advisors from KMAG would hurry on south, hitting again and running again when they were given the chance.

Jackson straightened up, started to toss his brush broom into the dry stream, changed his mind, and tucked it into his web belt. "Slick as owl shit. They strut right over and here come the tank. I'll be around that bend to nail the crew. You coming?"

"How'd you get so cold?" Sam asked.

Jackson only glanced at Sam, his eyes saying it for him: shee-it.

One on each side of the creek bed, gone to cover, they waited. Sam watched the quick distribution of Nam Ki's troops, the placement of machine guns and 60mm mortars. The son of Colonel Chong was good. And the son of Connover *Moksa*, was it good when that one went "home" to the country he had never seen to become, not the divinity school student his father wanted, but the adventurer that Uncle Kelly had been, the soldier?

Like the warning hiss of a snake, Jackson's whisper reached Sam: "They're coming. I hear that tank. You see if Chong put rifles on the other side of the road? We don't want them mothers hiding behind all that iron."

"It's covered. The guy knows what he's doing."

"I sure hope so. If a whole battalion comes running up that road when we cut down on this bunch—"

"I'll beat you to the jeep."

And then it was the silent, watchful time, the stretched minutes when the adrenaline pumped hot through Sam's body and near his chin, every grain of sand grew big and faceted, every small sound was magnified until he could hear a weed grow, hear the hammering of a cricket's heart. Every sense sharpened, so that the smell of hot earth enveloped him and made him part of its sensual depths. Rifle snugged to his cheek, all-seeing eye fixed upon the lining up of the M-1's sights, Sam married this leached soil, this only proper bride for a soldier.

For a long moment, while the scouts of the Red Army eased across the bridge, Sam thought of Maggi Barron, of the harmonies of her so calming. But he was calm now, tensed to the ripple of a muscle, yet very still inside himself. The connecting file came close behind the pair of scouts who now were focused upon the deserted farm-houses. Then the rest of the platoon walked in, careless and smoking, talking softly.

And the tank, its turret swinging gently, the long gun searching right, searching left, motor rumbling, treads clanking. The tank commander stood in the open hatch. Sam drew a deep breath when the driver hesitated, while the 11th ROK held discipline and did not fire a shot.

It came slowly onto the bridge, and the commander shouted down the turret. The tank gathered speed and rolled onto the center span. The bridge collapsed, and the T-34 crashed to the rocks below.

Everyone opened fire. Ricochets *spranged* from the roadway, from the tank itself; two mortar shells fell, perfectly placed, one at the head of the column, the other at the rear. Sam squeezed off a round at a tanker and dropped him when the man thought he was safely out. That left room for another to try, but Jackson got that one. Nobody else crawled free, because then fuel spilled onto the hot engine and exploded. Inside, cannon shells and machine gun ammunition went off. It was over in minutes.

Stiffly, Sam walked up to the road, well away from the blazing tank. Stonewall Jackson walked beside him, and they met Nam Ki where the troops were assembling. Except for the occasional late round popping inside the tank, there was quiet. Nobody cheered; no man shouted *mansei!* to hail a victory Korean fashion.

They were better soldiers than Sam had realized. They knew this was but a small victory, and that they might never see another one. With Task Force Smith beaten and withdrawing toward Taejon, the port of Pusan was far away for everyone.

There, no doubt, they would have to stand and die. So nobody cheered.

CHAPTER 10

Washington, D.C.—President Harry Truman ordered U.S. ground forces into Korea.

제가 제 뺨친다.

"Slap your own cheeks." (Korean proverb: Bring harm to yourself.)

Rich Shriver sat on a broken table and held the little Royal on his lap, two-fingering its keys. *Taejon*, he wrote, *sits behind the first defendable river south of Seoul. They say 120,000 people lived here until a week ago. A lot of them don't believe the Kum River line can be held by the first American division to arrive in Korea. They left right after bedraggled survivors of Task Force Smith came to town.*

Some righteous officer in Tokyo would probably censor hell out of that paragraph, but the debacle couldn't be kept under wraps forever, and there was more to come. Rich didn't think the line could be held either, not by Japan garrison troopers so young, fat, and spooky. They had no better weapons than the sad bastards clobbered at Osan, and they had also been dragged from their shackmates and hurled into combat. They hadn't made their own beds or

70

shined their shoes since they came fresh-faced from basic training stateside to the best duty in the world, to cheap houseboys and lovely women trained to please. They hadn't expected to be asked to die and thought it didn't seem fair. They still believed in right and wrong.

Typing a few more background lines, Rich did some propaganda on the 24th "Taro Leaf" Division. The outfit had a tough CG, but General Dean couldn't hold the Kum River line by himself. After that fell, Taejon would go in the toilet.

There is a familiarity about it all, he typed, *Americans short of everything but blood, the bad guys better trained, armed and ready.*

For a week, whenever his liquor supply got low, he had found himself looking around for jungles. Damned right it was familiar, slant eyes and the rot smell, the shit smells and that unforgettable odor of the dead. Japs stank different than GIs; not more or less, just different. Diet, of course, and how quickly the jungle heat liquefied the guts inside the swollen bags that once were men. You could never mistake the smell of a dead GI once it had choked you. It was sweeter and thicker than a Jap. The closest thing to it was a dead rat.

"Holy shit," he said, balancing the typewriter upon his knees while he reached for the *soju* bottle. Just north of the Kum he'd gotten sidetracked and trapped in a battalion aid station. Jap—damn it, *gook!*—fire pinned him down with the medics and wounded. He couldn't hack that anymore and didn't give a damn if they all thought he had shit in his neck. When the fire lifted, he got the hell out as fast as he could. The guys on litters who stared up at the baking bowl of a sky they couldn't see—that didn't bother him. It was the kids who chewed their lips and wouldn't cry, the kids who would not stop bleeding and died trying to be helpful. Screw them all, the bastards who said be brave, be brave, and the stupid shits who believed them.

71

Coughing because this jug of *soju* was green and raw, he blinked down at his news feature and wondered where Sam Connover was. Any time a firefight got close, it was natural to think about Sam. He called in the enemy the way Rich zeroed in on booze, and their talents would someday turn them both into melting heaps of dead rat smell.

"Unholy shit, then," he said, then took another drink and lighted a C-ration cigarette; a Phillip Morris, what else? That hadn't changed between wars, either. Somehow the Luckies and Camels got lost and you got stale Phillip Morris to go with your jungle rot.

That was a break, no jungle rot here. (Hell, no, boy— ain't no sharks around this island; the crocs keep them away.) Korea offered Jap-B encephalitis, the cute bug that got into your brain and set it afire until it tried to break out of your skull and killed you. This ancient soil, enriched by centuries of human shit, lay in wait with hemorrhagic fever, an even cuter disease whose victims bled to death through the pores of their skin. Then there was typhus, malaria, and dengue, and a hundred other silent killers that western medicine hadn't yet named.

But the worst killer was a slant-eyed little son of a bitch with a red star on his cap, and the penicillin cure was anything that blew him open.

Rich ground out his cigarette on the floor of the shack, smearing it in with his boot toe and ruining the oiled paper covering. Probably the owners would never return, anyway. *But the GI will get tougher by each increment that arrives in the Far East. It isn't so far from the ETO and the South Pacific that some veterans won't show up. They are already the hard core of experience around which a new fighting force will be built.*

"Not all bullshit," he muttered. "They always kick our asses at first. Then we turn meaner and rougher and better at killing. We bust gold teeth out of dead Japs with rifle butts; we pickle their cocks in a jar of alcohol in case their *bushido* code is right and they wake up in paradise ten days later. But then they can't fuck any of the geisha the Shinto priests promised them."

Rich looked up as a man stamped into the shack with a roll of maps under one arm. He hadn't bothered to remove the stars from his collar: General Butt Wright. "Good roof here, sergeant?"

Frowning at the others who came crowding inside—the GIs come to install a sound power phone and SCR 300 radio, the lieutenant rattling a folded map stand, and Lt. Col. Julian Barron—Rich stood up with his typewriter. "Would G-3 and its Operations section have it any other way, sir?"

He rescued his tall *soju* bottle before Barron recovered enough to take a step toward him, saying, "Damn it, soldier—"

The general grinned. He didn't hold off pointing where he wanted things set up, but he grinned around the ragged cigar he chewed. "Name of the game, son. The lower ranks locate; the higher ranks appropriate."

Barron cleared his throat. "Drinking native whiskey is—"

"Adapting," Wright said. "Will you part with a snort, sergeant?"

Rich handed over his bottle, and the general took a long pull. "Ho damn! Where'd they get the kerosene to put in that? Kind of green, too."

"Ain't it?" Rich scooped up the rest of his equipment. "I'll go pull rank on some corporal, sir. Would anybody have any idea where Sergeant Connover is?"

The general dropped his cigar and didn't have to grind it out. "Probably not dead. Sam Connover is immortal, I think. There's an ROK unit on my left flank; try there."

Passing close to Colonel Barron, Rich saw the stony set of the man's jaw and felt the enmity sharp around him. Was all that from their little set-to at the embassy in Seoul?

Did it bother this desk soldier that the general played good old boy? Rich didn't think so. It must be something else, then. Sam Connover? Sam had a knack of pissing off officers who soon realized that they couldn't reach a man who wore the Medal of Honor. Barron would know that. Maybe he just enjoyed being a turd.

Before he got to thinking too much, Rich piled his gear in his jeep, opened the padlock that held its steering wheel cramped over, and climbed aboard. Butt Wright was setting up a sort of unauthorized command post south of the Kum. General Dean of the 24th ran his own CP, but this meant the river defenses were about to be broken.

Rich lifted his head. If he hadn't been so busy with rice whiskey and trying to do a color piece for *Stars & Stripes*, he'd have heard it before—that rumbling of artillery to the north and the closer sound of GI trucks coming into Taejon.

It wouldn't be long before dispirited infantry shuffled into town; the walking wounded were already here. He didn't want to see them, or hear them, but he knew damned well they were already here. Hotshot combat medic Rich Shriver couldn't do anything for them. The bastards never stopped bleeding.

CHAPTER 11

Miryang, Republic of Korea, August 31, 1950—Since U.N. forces established the Pusan Perimeter, fighting along the Naktong River has been the bloodiest of the war. Stretched thin, U.N. forces are holding.

한 일을 보면 열
일을 안다.

"If you see one deed, you can tell ten deeds of a man." (Korean proverb: A man is judged by what he does first.)

The mortars came in with the hissing of giants, one—two—three, and the third shell was too close. Julian's nails dug into the palms of his hands as the ground rocked, as dirt stung through the CP tent dug into the low hill.

"Medic—*medic!*"

"The replacements," Charley Heath said, "the poor damned kids that just came up."

Julian couldn't answer his executive officer right away. He fought to control his shakes while the S-3 sergeant brushed dirt off the map overlay. The three of them filled the scooped-out hole that had been Julian's world for miserable twisted pieces of eternity. Part of his mind insisted

75

that it was only a matter of weeks. The rest of him screamed *liar!* inside his head. This was the new part of Julian Barron, grown like a cancer since he took command of the battalion.

"They're yelling in Korean, too," Major Heath said. "That's about all we've been getting—handcuff volunteers with about a week in the ROK army. No English and can't field-strip their weapons."

Finding his voice, Julian said, "Sergeant—check on the medics and bring back a casualty report." He sounded okay, so he chanced lighting a cigarette. He'd been smoking a lot since he came to the Naktong River.

"I'm gone," the sergeant said, and slid out of the tent flap into the night. Julian couldn't remember the man's name right away.

. . . *whiisSSHH!* . . .

—WHAMM!!—

Another mortar shell, one of the bigger 82s, and this time the earth bucked. Pebbles ripped holes in canvas around Julian, and a hot steel fragment slapped over the situation map. Charley Heath snatched up the sputtering gas lantern and turned off the light. In the total blackness of a grave, Heath said, "That's the worst damned sound in the world, an incoming mortar. Artillery doesn't seem half as spooky. If I can find that phone and get counter battery across the river—"

Somebody crept up to the CP hole, too noisy to be a gook. "Hey, major, you know you got a dead man out here?"

"Good Christ," Julian said, "the sergeant. He was just here, and I sent him to see—"

"That you, Norred?" Heath called.

"Sir?"

"Drag him aside and let me know if the medics are doing any good across the road."

"Good Christ," Julian repeated. "We sit here and the

lousy gooks blow hell out of us. We just sit here, and sit here."

He heard Heath scratching around in the dark, pulling the holed canvas together. Julian had lost his cigarette and couldn't find its spark. He forced his hands out to feel for the situation board. By the time he found it, Heath had repaired things with a blanket and relighted the lantern. He had also contacted the 4.2 mortars for counter battery.

Fresh earth made the CP smell even more like a grave, and the light didn't help all that much. The nights belonged to the North Koreans, and the little bastards were probably infiltrating at this moment. Julian got another smoke going, cupping the spark in his palm to hide his attack of nerves as well as any glimmer of light that might draw a bullet. Under cover or out, combat men acquired the habit fast. For better or worse, Julian was a combat man now.

His exec said, "I'll handle the board the rest of the night. Tomorrow we'll levy the Personnel or Adjutant General sections for another man."

"I didn't even know his name," Julian said, cigarette smoke dry and bitter in his mouth.

"Scott, Melvin J.," Heath supplied. "Don't let it dig too deep, colonel. We learn that—after so many of the originals go, the men we had coffee with at Fort Lewis, the noncoms we reenlisted. And the old friends; this outfit has lost all ranks from light colonel down, since the first day we took up this damned position."

Holding smoke deep in his lungs, Julian thought of the PX coffee shop at Fort Lewis, the habitual morning break for City Hall troops and anybody else who could make it—line officers, civilian workers, wives and other dependents. He coughed and pawed for his canteen; the water tasted like a big hotel's rest room smelled.

That was where he had noticed them for the first time, his wife and Sergeant Connover. Oblivious to all about them, they shared that look of expectancy that only lovers wear. Never mind that Maggi was a field-grade wife and from a long line of West Point ancestors; never mind that the man was a scarred and tough enlisted man, or that the entire post could buzz with gossip. They stared into each other's eyes across one of the little tables near the record machine that played "Mister Sandman" and "Slow Boat to China." Even though Julian saw it for himself, it took a while for him to believe. Maggi simply wasn't that kind, and even before their son's death—the death she blamed on Julian—he hadn't considered her as overly sensuous, and surely not ready to stray.

The light MG ten yards from the CP's right front opened fire, a long, rolling burst; a string of quick, sharp pops that hammered into Julian's skull. He shook his head and widened his eyes to lean forward and stare at the situation map. So damned many blobs of enemy red, such a thin, stretched line of friendly blue. Julian damned General Butt Wright for talking him into a field command, and twice damned him for holding off until the Second Infantry Division hurried in from the States to plug a gap in the Pusan Perimeter. Maybe he would have made it just fine among the survivors of the 24th as promised.

At least, the 24th once had room to run; there was nowhere it could go now, but the Second had never had a retreat option. Behind its desperate lines lay the village of Miryang, and beyond that, the port of Pusan. The perimeter was a lumpy half circle where collapse meant disaster.

Brapbrapbrap! The MG fired again, and a Browning Automatic Rifle joined the echo with its flatter *bupbupbup! Bup bup!*

Major Heath said, "Better they fire at shadows than let one gook pass. At first it was tough to get fire at night. Nobody wanted to give away his position. After they got a lapful of gooks with bayonets, they figured that the NKs already knew where they were."

Christ; Julian knew all that, and it irritated him that

Heath should keep going over the same ground, as if Julian had only arrived this evening, as if Julian had made some major command mistake. He wasn't going to make a mistake, and started to say so to Heath. But living like a frightened animal had made some changes in Julian's thinking, and he considered the possibility that the major might be talking to help them both relax. But if their positions were exchanged, Julian wouldn't do it. From the first he would have resented an outsider coming in over him to grab the higher rank.

Julian jumped and had to catch the map board when the soldier slid into the CP. It could just as easily have been an infiltrator, for killing commanding officers and wiping out the nerve centers of battalions or even regiments was a specialty of the communists. He ground out, "What the hell?"

GIs here had a nasty habit of not looking at him, but of reporting to Charley Heath directly. This one said, "Major, we caught us a prisoner, a sure enough goddamned officer. He was fucking around that knocked-out village behind us. Want me to take him over to Rocky?"

Julian snapped, "Bring the prisoner and the interpreter to me, here."

"Ah—" Heath began.

"What, damn it?"

"Sorry, sir," Heath said, and Julian felt the soldier glance at him before shrugging and backing out into the night.

When the man was gone Heath said, "It's close quarters, colonel. And Sgt. Rocky Watanabe's methods aren't by the book. I wasn't sure if you'd—"

Both the machine gun and the BAR opened fire and held it for about twenty seconds. Julian became aware of a monster headache. Small arms picked up the shooting; the two-toned *ka-chung* of M-1s, the lighter, nervous cracks of carbines. Julian was fast becoming expert on the different voices of weapons.

"My battalion, major; my decisions."

"Of course, sir."

No sarcasm, Julian thought, military acceptance with a lack of accent. Julian had practiced that bland delivery for years. Even if he hadn't been sent out from Butt Wright's unofficial, roving CP, Heath probably would have run the battalion without a silver leaf. Promotions were all screwed up, but when they arrived, they were apt to come in bunches. A good job for a while longer here, and Julian might very well be running the regiment; a full colonelcy, eagles. He swallowed another sip of purification-pills water and spat.

Heath said, "After Rocky questions the PW, I'll make some coffee. Been saving some heating tabs." Again no hint of discontent, and no servility, either. Maybe Charley Heath just didn't give a damn beyond doing his own job well, and he had survived this far.

Julian heard them coming and shielded the light with his helmet liner when the gook was pushed into the tent. Crawling behind him was another Oriental, heavier and meaner looking, with scars in his eyebrows.

"Sergeant Watanabe," Heath said, "a Nisei from Hawaii; used to fight in the Honolulu Bowl."

"Paid better than this," Watanabe grunted. "Okay—I already talked to this son of a bitch. We got a tough guy, Mr. Senior Lieutenant. He was in that wrecked village for a reason, but he thinks he won't say why."

The North Korean was muddy and ragged; one eye was swollen shut, but the other glared at Julian. Miserable-looking little bastard, but then they all were. It didn't seem possible these troops had shattered the ROK army and bloodied three American divisions. Four, counting the casualty drain on this one.

"Can you sit on him, major?" The Nisei sergeant drew a carbine bayonet from his belt.

Damn it, every EM in this outfit seemed set on ignoring

Julian's position. He blinked when the man threw the Korean face down on the dirt for Heath to straddle.

"Grab that wrist, colonel."

Julian did it without thinking, then frowned. The man hadn't asked, hadn't even said "sir." Then Rocky had a knee pinning the gook's other wrist and, with a little help from Heath, inserted the tip of the bayonet under a fingernail. Two, three quick raps against the handle with the butt of a .45, and the bloody nail peeled off.

Julian flinched as Rocky said something choppy in Japanese, a language all Koreans understood. The Korean didn't cry out; he didn't answer, either. Rocky peeled the second nail with an expertise that showed this wasn't his first difficult interrogation.

Then the Korean pissed himself, and Julian almost let go the wrist he held with all his strength. He would have, but for the cool eyes of Charley Heath watching him. My battalion, Julian had said; my decisions. The urine odor was strong, and the gook's breath rasped in his throat. Rocky demanded some information, the Japanese words harsh and loud, threatening. He worked the bayonet point, bloody and slippery, under the third fingernail.

The Korean said something through clenched teeth, then opened his mouth sideways against the dirt.

Rocky said, "Stupid shit; could have saved both of us a lot of trouble. I can see him holding out against you round-eyes and not believing he wouldn't be able to scratch. But he sees me and hears Tojo talking to him, he ought to know I'd take his goddamned arms up to the shoulders. Stupid shit."

Julian sat up, snorting his nose clear. "What information does he have? I hope it's important, because if somebody from Corps, or even division—" Julian shut up. He had never seen torture before, much less taken part in it.

The Nisei stood up. The PW didn't move. Rocky said something else to him and got an answer. Then he grinned at Julian. "At twenty-one hundred, what's left of this guy's battalion is supposed to gather in that village and hit this CP around midnight. He says twenty-one hundred, but I'm not so sure. I'd blow hell out of that village, say about five to seven until five after; repeat five to eight, nine, and then ten. If this shit has lied either way, we'll catch his bunch. Would you believe how many gooks we've been killing? This jerk claims he's the battalion CO. Says he's the only officer left."

"The artillery," Julian said. "Give them and the 4.2s the coordinates to that village. Then bring at least two tanks of the 72nd up for supporting fire. As the sergeant says, before and after the hours. And Rocky—take this carrion out with you, but don't send him back to the cages until he sees what we do to his collecting point."

Charley Heath nodded, and Rocky Watanabe toed the Korean to make him get up. Then he said, "Damn, colonel —I believe you're going to make it just fine here with the 38th Infantry."

CHAPTER 12

The Pusan Perimeter, Republic of Korea, Sept. 4, 1950—The
hard-fought great offensive of the North Korean People's Army is
about out of steam, but attacks are still going on.

닭 쫓든 개 지붕
쳐다 보기.

"The dog that chased the chicken stares at it on the
roof." (Korean proverb: He has sought in vain
something now out of reach.)

She was very old, a toothless grandmother past *han-gap*,
her sixtieth birthday, when the full cycle of life had been
completed and the new one begun. She was twice lucky,
this *halmonie* who had been caught rolling hand grenades
down the slope into the command post of the 11th Regiment. If any man had noticed her first, if any of the grenades she rolled had exploded, she would lie dead on the
hillside.

Senior Lieutenant Lim said, "They gave her a sack of
grenades and told her what to do. No one told her to first
remove the pins."

Chong Nam Ki sighed. "Leave her with me. Grandmother—why do you try to kill us?"

She exposed discolored gums; a dirty white string of hair hung down one wrinkled cheek. "Kill you, officer? I do not understand. The other officer commanded me to roll the iron eggs. I obeyed."

Of course she obeyed; her long years had been spent in obedience, first to her father and older brothers, then to her husband and his family, most notably submitting to the complete dominance of his mother. If she had also been fortunate back then, perhaps that woman did not make her life miserable. Lost now, a wanderer farther from home than she had ever been, of course she had obeyed authority.

Father Chong had spoken of this, of how difficult it would be to alter such submission, for only women were true victims, and men did not care.

Nam Ki squatted beneath the joined shelter halves that roofed his CP. Soon it would be night; soon the darkness would bring desperate men across the shallowing Naktong. Desperate the *balgaengi* were now, starving, battered and frantic because the Pusan Perimeter was denied them. They were even more dangerous.

He lifted his voice: "Soldier—give this grandmother rations and escort her to the *Me-in* aid station to our rear. They will see to transport tomorrow." If everyone was still here when the sun next rose, including the old woman.

"Yes, captain. I will return quickly to my post."

Nam Ki's smile felt weary but still tasted proud. Every man of his unit was a good soldier, even the stragglers he had picked up on the retreat south. Sam Connover had helped by bringing supplies and food from American units that would never have cooperated otherwise. With the black sergeant, Sam Connover was tireless, and Nam Ki appreciated the few messages that came through about the Chong family safe in Pusan.

Rising, Nam Ki ducked from beneath his tent flap and lifted field glasses to peer through them at the mist gathering below his position. There was the narrow cut in the earth that his flat trajectory guns could not efficiently cover. At his foreign brother's suggestion—and with the drum of jellied gasoline Sam Connover brought from an airstrip far south—Nam Ki had readied a surprise for the night. The fuse was a small block of plastic explosive wired uphill to the plunger at his feet. A party of infiltrators would cook in that defile a moment after an unwary foot touched the wire with its pebble-filled rattle cans set to warn.

He cocked his head, mouth open to catch the flavoring of twilight and know its promise of coolness after the fried air of the day. He heard a sound that would have jerked his intestines only weeks ago—armor moving—but this evening the tanks bore the proper markings. Nam Ki could not see them, but he had learned to sort the differences in their voices. Not T-34s, these, but General Shermans of the 38th American regiment upon his right flank. No more than two tanks, he decided, moving up to protect against some anticipated thrust in that other line.

Fading, the sounds reminded him of his school days when the rail cars thrilled him so. . . .

> Hearing in memory
> The last car depart,
> I step over
> The membrane of sleep,
> And a fruit falls in my dream.
> I will ask the wind
> That departs in the morning
> To what depths the fruit has fallen.

Shin Dong Jip wrote fine poetry, but why was it that poets produced their finest work in solemn moments? Nam Ki would have liked to brush joyous songs upon silk, great ringing shouts of laughter so that the world would at least smile with him. Now he had forgotten how to smile, and the morning's harvest could only be death.

Swiftly then, flinging down like some knife slice of the earth's inner belly, night came upon the banks of the Naktong and the silent waiting began.

General Wright said "ho damn" several times and bit the end off a fresh cigar. Every houseboy in the rear area was talking about the coming invasion by sea, and most of the Eighth Army ignored the gossip for what it was; how the hell could a bunch of ragged-ass Koreans know about a landing at Inchon? Of all places, Inchon of the thirty-foot tides and mud flats. And why was a landing behind communist lines needed? Another couple of weeks and the *Inmun-gun* would dissolve on its own. Any T-34s left on the Naktong were piles of junk rocketed and napalmed, and every night the river floated with new bodies.

True, casualties were not on just one side, and attrition was a problem to the defenders as well. But Eighth Army was almost keeping up with replacements, and the Red Army couldn't bring them down from the north fast enough to stay ahead of the air strikes from fields in Japan and Pusan, and from carriers cruising at sea. Wright suspected that the enemy no longer had a pool of reserves.

But the ho damn landing at Inchon was a fact to be. It was a grandstand play that would sprout headlines across the free world and perhaps get MacArthur a shot at the presidency. The man had incredible luck and might get away with the landing, since it would generally be unopposed. If it shortened the war by a single day or saved the life of one U.N. soldier, fine. Another huge but—would the north collapse or struggle on? Would the U.N. command have to drive to Pyongyang and beyond? Already the Chinese were stirring, issuing thinly veiled warnings about the sanctity of their borders. And that was where The Omnipotent himself might step in shit because he was too high-nosed to look down.

"Sir?" Lieutenant Orr shifted restlessly on the phone. "There seems to be a probe at the far left of the 38th. Few reports so far, but they're worried about their aid station."

Danny Orr was a skinny kid who worried, a good sign in a staff officer, even if he fretted as the one-man staff of a general *non grata* in Tokyo. Wright realized that he had been sent to Korea as spare parts, and while generals were in short supply, he had been able to throw a little weight. Tokyo had even harkened to his suggestions a time or two, until he turned caustic in questioning screwups. Then his lack of awe and the importation of division generals who would always outrank him sent him out to pasture. Butt Wright was still in the combat zone, but how long until orders sent him home?

"Try to raise Connover's fire brigade," he said. "They should be close enough if they're needed."

"Yes, sir."

At least this kid didn't argue and didn't have something personal going with Sam Connover. Colonel Barron had stopped bitching long before going to the 38th Infantry, but the antipathy he carried for the sergeant never stopped smoldering. Wright thought he had puzzled it out. Since the men had never soldiered together and Barron had never wanted a field command before now, the problem had to be a woman, and Connover wasn't married.

Wright sat on a water can and looked off beyond the rice papering of the shack's door. He could almost see his wife and the tiny smile that flirted with the ends of her full mouth as she passed along one of her bits of officer knowledge. *Darling, the quickest way to ruin your career is womanizing.*

Shocked, he had stuttered and rightly claimed that he tried to avoid the general's cocktail party in the first place, and failing that, had only been coldly polite to the general's much-younger wife.

Frances had laughed at his discomfort. *Oh, my dear, I know that. The trick is to seem to be womanizing while not actually carrying through. The trick is to be more than coldly polite without promising intimacy.*

The woman he loved, had been lucky to love, never failed him. She steered him through the mazes of protocol and military bureaucracy, ever protecting him. *Because I love you, of course. But also because you are better suited to command than any of them, all of them.*

And now, Frances? Now that I am where I'm needed, where I can do my best, they will rid themselves of me at last. I've been so ho damn weak since you left.

Her smile reached through the rice paper door and warmed his cheek. *Weak, my darling? Never you.* He could almost touch her, she was so close, nearer than she had been in a long time. And then she was gone.

Lieutenant Orr said, "I have Connover, sir."

In two strides, Wright had the radio phone. "Sam? Looks like third bat's aid station will be hit. Can you cover?"

"On the way, sir."

No bullshit questions; given a job, Sam Connover would do it and do it well. Suppose the upstairs brass wanted to get rid of Sam? Already there had been orders to get him out of the Korean theater altogether, and already Sergeant Connover had ignored them and gone on to form his own little fighting force, his fire brigade able to rush to hot spots anywhere on a thin defense line that usually held few or no troops in reserve. Butt Wright's single star carried no such weight as Sam's Medal of Honor. But soon—after the flamboyant invasion to come—perhaps both the star and the medal would become weightless. Faded laurels and musty memories would not be enough for either of them, but they would be the only ones to give a damn.

CHAPTER 13

Pusan Perimeter, Republic of Korea, Sept. 5, 1950—Heavy casualties hit U.N. troops on the Naktong River when a last-gasp assault by communist soldiers overran an aid station.

개천에서 용 난다.

"A dragon rises from a ditch." (Korean proverb: The son of a humble family may rise to glory.)

Rich knew the difference now, and maybe he'd keep it in mind. It came to him here in Miryang because he had never screwed a Jap, and this little Korean girl had just turned him every way but loose. He was damned near sober, and when he stumbled into the cathouse he couldn't hit the floor with his hat. Hell—he couldn't find his hat.

Propped on one elbow, he looked down at her. Maybe all Korean women had only a dime's worth of hair between their legs, but this one didn't look or feel clipped. He'd have to check that out with other women. Her eyes were closed, and her body gleamed with sweat. If she didn't enjoy her job, she sure put on a terrific act. Rich reached across her for the bottle of *soju* and had a drink.

She opened her slant eyes and stared up at him. He said,

89

"Well—you're a cute little prostie, at that." How long had it been since he made love to anything but a bottle? Screwing wasn't necessarily making love, but it was a relief to know he could still make it. She didn't have word one of English, so it must have been his tone, because she smiled.

It hadn't taken businessmen of Miryang long to discover a good return for a small investment, and half a dozen whorehouses opened around the little town. Already the booze merchants were making runs to Pusan for resupply; Second Division Rear and various transient outfits had changed the area's economy.

One cigarette and two drinks later, the girl still looked good to him. Her slant eyes didn't really bother him. He knew she had them, but he didn't get that old twist in his belly when they glanced his way. Maybe that eased off when he learned how much the Koreans despised Japs. He didn't need more reasons, but in case he ever ran out of hate for the little bastards, Koreans could keep him in good supply.

At least, he felt that way at the moment. The next nightmare might turn it all around again, the next time he heard the goddamned *banzai!* echoing in his head and woke up screeching back at Japs behind their long bayonets. Every time that happened, his hands dripped sweat; every time, he had to see if it wasn't really blood. Away from the comforts of this girl, he might be normally abnormal again. Leaving her with a good tip, he recovered his bottle and cigarettes and went forth into the real world to see. Chained and booby-trapped with nonlethal alarms, his jeep was safe; he drove off to find Sam Connover and Stonewall Jackson and the Korean outfit. Tokyo was asking why a Medal of Honor winner hadn't been sent home. Rich knew it was because nobody sent Sam anywhere he didn't want to go, but he wouldn't tell *Stars & Stripes* that. Not right away.

Hadn't everybody at that exalted office thought he was

crazy for not hanging around Japan? He couldn't make himself leave the post, for one thing; for another, all those fucking Jap civilians at Hardy Barracks kept him in hiding. What the hell was he doing in the Far East, anyhow? Because he got pissed and pissy-assed drunk at the same time and demanded to be sent to Europe. Yeah, Europe.

S&S thought he was doing all right, though. Surprised, the civilian editor said, and the officer in charge added a pat on the back. But how about more features to go with the spot news? So many wire-service guys were working the daily stuff that Rich should be digging for deeper copy. Like Sam Connover; like refugee stories and anything heroic he could find, even if he had to stretch things a bit.

Fat fucking chance. If you knew somebody like Sam Connover—and yeah, Jackson and that tough ROK lieutenant—you wouldn't cheapen their valor by creating a phony hero. It was done, had been done in the last war; every time things got sticky, up popped somebody glorious for the country to focus upon.

The stench of humid paddies clogged Rich's throat, and he cleared it with rice whiskey. Just once after Seoul's fall, he had passed close to Sam and his group. He knew that the refugee truck had been sent down to Pusan, and Sam had yelled that an orphanage of sorts would be set up there.

So where are you heading? Rich had yelled back, and popped a couple of flashbulbs on the Speed Graphic. Just where you'd better go, Sam shouted—the other side of the Naktong, buddy.

Halting the jeep at a crossroads correctly, Rich now considered over a few gulps of booze. If he remembered correctly, this should be about the left flank of the 38th Infantry, and therefore the extreme left of the division. Somewhere west and south was the 6th ROK division—maybe.

Late afternoon sun lay along the deserted road, and a valley to Rich's right front purpled itself in shadow. Where was an outpost or even a listening position? The bird that sounded from a copse in the valley must be ragged ass, he thought; its cry was like worn rags, thin and tired.

"Well, laddie buck," he told himself, "you can't park out here in the open." He wasn't spooked. In fact, he felt good after having his ashes hauled. He just knew he'd better find some friendly cover before dark. Anybody would fire on movement close to the river, gooks and GIs alike.

Cruising slowly along the dirt road, holding motor noise to a minimum, and without lights in the gathering dusk, Rich drove with a carbine across his lap. He smelled dust of travel along this back stretch, smelled the utter silence, and tasted the quietness heavy upon his tongue. It wasn't the same as coming into an area after a bloody firefight; that silence was bone-chilling, for no bird dared sing, and even insects were still. This was a waiting thing, and Rich fed more gas to the jeep, then fed himself a swallow of *soju*.

Brush hung to a dropoff hillside, and Rich couldn't see the end of the next curve. Pulling the choke out a tad, he let the motor idle and got down to walk, to take a careful look.

The *snik-snak* of a rifle bolt froze him in his tracks. Drop! his mind screamed—drop and roll and fire at the sound.

Shaky and tense, the whisper reached him: "You sure you saw something out—"

"You son of a bitch!" Rich yelled. "You stupid recruit! Don't you know enough to keep a round in the chamber and the safety on? Goddamnit, I near wiped you out."

"That ain't a gook," the sentry said.

"I could have been," Rich said. "Now stay awake and point that muzzle straight up. I'm driving in, and I don't want my ass shot off by a dumb recruit."

* * *

Major Ho Chuk Gun crawled slowly out of his hole as the dark came down. He despised the entire day he had been forced to hide underground like a terrified animal while the foreign airplanes soared high overhead or screamed down low to search. More, he hated the small *pihaengi* that circled so arrogantly below the clouds and looked for the slightest movement so the pilot could call in artillery. It was disappointing that the People's Air Force had not been able to retain power, but Chuk Gun understood that his position was too far south for direct support and that the MIGs were needed to beat off cowardly air attacks on Pyongyang schools and hospitals.

Medicines and food were in short supply because of enemy planes, not because the spirit of the *inmun-gun* had been broken. That would never come to pass; the hired mercenaries of the capitalist might destroy their bodies, but the spirit of the people was everlasting. This very night, Chuk Gun would show the dogs across the Naktong that his teeth were yet sharp. He might capture enough supplies to break through and keep striking south. News of his success would then pass all along the line, and other *kongsin-juie-ja* units would wheel and hurry to pour through the gap he had created. The communist flag would wave high again.

He sniffed the night, and his stomach knotted. Two days or three, it did not matter how long ago he had eaten. Had not the Japanese taught his stomach that it could feed upon air? Before this, foreigners intent upon raping the country and beating the last vestige of dignity from peasants had also taught Ho Chuk Gun to wait. It would have been good to smash ahead and drive the *kho-jaengi* into the sea, to rid the land of invaders and traitors alike. That would come; the moment was only delayed, and a mighty strength concealed itself in patience.

They came silently out of the darkness, and Chuk Gun could smell the earth ground into their uniforms, into their very skins. He must carry the same odor, that honest smell of farm toil and sweat. He was the only officer, and there were but two sergeants. So few men of that proud, strong group that had been first to liberate Seoul, but all were men hardened in the flames.

He said to them: "We attack again this night, immediately upon the setting of the moon. I shall lead you." He heard a sigh pass through them and hardened his voice. "Are we *yongdu sami,* the head of a dragon and the tail of a snake? This night we shall spill much blood and supply ourselves, remembering *koji kamnae*—that sweet things come after hard times."

Of course they stood taller and did not complain as he described to them the action they would take. The decision was Chuk Gun's and his alone. There had come no word from regimental headquarters, much less higher up. The decision was his as a leader; therefore the victory would be his also.

He said, "Until the time, ten thousand years."

Softly they repeated the cheer: *"Mansei."*

And short hours later, in the dark of the moon, Chuk Gun waded quietly through the warm river ahead of his men, his submachine gun held chest high to keep the breech clear of water. His stomach ached, and his mouth filled with saliva at the thought of the food cans they would capture. Stopping often to listen, he heard no warning sound. The careless soldiers of the rich were sleeping on full bellies.

Reaching the bank, he climbed it stooped and quiet and hesitated when the *sangsa* eased to his side and touched his shoulder, then pointed out a cut in the bank, a short and narrow defile leading upward.

"Very well," he said. "Take three men that way. I will move to the left. Do not attack until you hear my gunfire."

Without a sound, bellied down to the earth like a snake, he moved inch by slow inch across open ground, stopping every moment to feel ahead with his bare hand for trip wires. Finding none, he knew a deep glee; the *Me-in* were asleep, certain of victory presented to them by the superior numbers of their cursed air force.

Dimly silhouetted against the lighter sky, a bulky vehicle loomed, and Chuk Gun heard low voices. He smelled coffee. The men behind him knew to spread as skirmishers when he began firing. Standing boldly erect because Americans would not expect to be set upon that way, he walked right up to the truck.

"Hey—" the enemy soldier said, and Chuk Gun opened fire, the vibration of his weapon reassuring, the crash of his shots music. He tasted powder smoke, and it was beautiful.

"No!" one man screamed, then another. "No, damn it— the wounded—this ambulance—"

Chuk Gun did not understand, but the message was also shouted in Korean. As if that made any difference, being wounded or whole. He screamed, "Kill them all!"

Sam clicked off the handset and looked at his friend's face in the light from the candle set atop his steel pot. He had seen that dark and steady face in all kinds of light— notably the hot floodlight that hung over a ring, but more so in the harsh and scary flare of bursting shells. Stonewall Jackson always stood as solid as his fight name.

As if keying in on his thoughts, Jackson said, "Trouble. Shee-it; I knew damned well I should have told that re-up officer to kiss off. Trouble is, then I'd have had to pay some cornerman; my freebie guy, his uniform got grown to him."

"Captain Chong's ROKs," Sam said. "They don't stretch as far as the aid station, and the 38th is worried." He blew out the candle and snapped it off his helmet to drop into his pocket. "If you kept fighting, somebody's glove would

95

have grown to *you*. I'll take down this stuff and check the weapon loads if you'll get our people on the stick."

In the heavy, humid darkness, Matt Jackson's voice was familiar as the mantle of calm settling over Sam. "You know how come I didn't let you up in the ring that day and beat hell out of you, white boy?"

To the left, down river, a white flare popped high over the hills. The echo of a single rifle shot rolled up to Sam, and in the night behind his jeep men shifted and stirred with a soft tapping of equipment. Two rebellious KMAG sergeants, ten National Policemen, technically deserters from their safer posts in Miryang, and seven mean little bastards from the annihilated 12th ROKs; a dozen civilians who had come first for food and stayed to ask for weapons and how to use them. A ragtag bunch indeed, but motivated and tough. Not even a full infantry platoon, but going in fast and hitting hard with plenty of firepower, the Fire Brigade was useful. Probably more so than a bigger line unit.

"You felt sorry for me?" Sam asked, forcing himself out of the combat tightness for just a moment and willing himself back into the Fort Lewis gym. There he smelled wintergreen and resin, the sharp sweat of fighters, and heard the shuffle-dance of feet, the whip of jump ropes and *ratawhap!* of the light bag. None were sounds to tighten muscles and speed the blood. Not Sam's way; not as he ever expected to happen again.

He had been pounding the heavy bag, and the black middleweight in the ring had to yell down at him twice: *Hey, badass! You want to get up here and see can you do that to me?*

No, Sam said.

The black drummed both gloved hands against the top rope. *Bag don't punch back, huh?*

And Sam walking over to look up. *I don't know what's with you, soldier. Maybe you have a beef with all whites. I don't care, and don't make me care enough to get in there and kill you.*

Shee-it, Matt Jackson said, but he said it softly and shadow boxed away. Later, in the dressing room, he saw Sam's blouse with its ribbons and walked over to put out his hand.

Now he said, "One look into them fay eyes and I saw you were crazy. Not a little bit crazy—I mean full clip, load and lock crazy. Us colored folks respect crazy people; figure they're touched by God."

The combat cocoon was binding him closer with silken cords, but Sam got out a laugh. "You signifying son of a bitch, that's certain Indian tribes."

Jackson chuckled. "You learning, Mister Charlie; you learning."

Sam was ready for his men when they appeared out of the night, different from GIs in that they were not bitching, even in whispers. Stoic, yes; emotionless, no. White men usually made that mistake. They had mastered the art of silence, and in the weeks since Seoul had been lost they had toughened physically and mentally. The 12th Regiment men hungered for vengeance; the police—Sam wasn't sure, but they might have loot uppermost in their minds. The civilians had debts to pay, sure, but Sam thought they were so eager to fight because they had discovered something new and precious to them—their own dignity. Stonewall was along because he wanted to be, not because Sam had any special influence over him. And Sam Connover?

Because this country's banner was good to fight under. This war was more tangible than the last one, considering it was being fought for survival, not for four freedoms or to end all wars, but simply to exist. At least it figured that way for Sam and the other professionals who happened to wear made-in-America fatigue uniforms.

"No jeep," Sam whispered. "Move quickly but silently. Extra grenades are atop the jeep hood to take as you need them. There is plenty of ammunition, so do not stint. Follow me, and I will rap my rifle butt twice for you to spread as skirmishers."

He didn't ask if there were any questions. This was not a democratic army, and he was certain these men understood. Head turned, he spoke even more softly to Matt Jackson. "Stay close."

Punctuating his words, another flare rose to his front, this one bright red, and gunfire cracked back at them. Loud now, he said, *"Kapshi-da!* Let's go!"

Sam's ranging hound instinct guided him unerringly along the path between rice paddies whose dikes had been broken to let out the water. The smells were strong in the damp soil, but he thought those would never leave; it had taken thousands of years to build them. Warm, clinging wind stirred his face as he trotted on, sweat oiling his joints and loosening his muscles. He breathed deep and rolled the excitement upon his tongue, a lifting of pulse and power that was almost sexual.

Up ahead someone screamed in English, ". . . the ambulances . . . oh, God, the wounded . . ." Carbines popped through the lengths of banana clips, and Sam heard the fast beat of burpguns. He ran faster and swerved to throw a shoulder into another running man.

The man spat his surprise in Korean, and Sam shot him up close. No call for signals or silence now, and the firing broke all around him, sometimes overwhelming the screams of pain and the harsh slaps of bullets through metal. A flare got loose on the ground, exploding with a blinding whiteness that illuminated the whole scene—the ambulances with doors gaped wide and bodies strewn about, their unfurled bandages whiter in the glare, but stained, stained.

Sam leaned toward a cluster of enemy soldiers, and to his left front another light hurtled skyward—the fingers of scattering flame that could only mean napalm. Yes, he

thought, the drum he had brought to the 11th ROK. He
fired twice and knew men running on both sides fired, too.
Shadows all, the enemy dissolved, and Sam chased after
them. Red-white, a muzzle blast in his face blinded him
and seared his flesh. He stumbled into the side of an ambulance and went to his knees.

"Fucking Jap—Jap!—fucking Jap!"

Unable to see, left hand brushing at his eyes, Sam
yelled, "Rich! Goddamnit—Rich?"

What the hell was Rich Shriver doing here? Firing an
entire clip through a grease gun, the .45 caliber slamming
close to Sam's head while Rich shrieked about Japs. Sam
struggled to one knee in the eye of the storm, the roar and
spinning all around him, the crash and shatter that had no
pattern, but he recognized the rhythm of its song.

Hands snatched at him and jerked away his rifle. "Sam,
Sam! Okay, man—be cool!"

"My eyes—oh, shit—" and suddenly he could see. The
flare was still burning, and so was one of the ambulances.
His men dragged the wounded and the bodies away from
it, more live wounded than Sam would have thought.
Where was Rich Shriver?

A medic shook himself away from the upright ambulance, blood streaking his face, his eyes wild in the shuddering light. Toward the river, directly in front and off to
the left also, a few bursts of fire still searched the ripped
fabric of the night. "The shits; the murdering shits," the
medic said. "My patients—I couldn't get out after dark,
and they came right at my ambulance—oh, God, nobody
was hit bad enough to die, but those murdering shits—"

Sam's eyes burned, and he tasted singed lips. "The guy
yelling about Japs—"

"If it wasn't for that crazy bastard—bedded down by his
jeep, went apeshit when the gooks hit—hey! Who's left
over there? Where the hell did you guys come from—all
those gooks with you—"

"Matt," Sam said, and Jackson led the medic over to the line of rescued wounded just as the flare burned itself out and the ambulance's gas tank blew up.

Sam sat down, rifle flat beside his leg. He poured a mouthful of water from his canteen and splashed some into his left hand. It was cool upon his eyes. Lucked out again, and the gook got away who had missed him by an inch. By the grace of God, father—or just a hurried shot? Either way, this time he wouldn't be joining Connover *Moksa* in that common grave outside Chunju Prison.

Two of his men hunkered beside him in the dwindling light of the smoldering vehicle, offering cigarettes, guarding him. The napalm trap in Chong Nam Ki's area had stopped burning, but a vagrant drift of wind carried the stench of crisped flesh. One file section of Sam's mind recognized that the attack probably hadn't been launched directly at the aid station but was a probe of the 11th ROKs. The wounded and the medics of the 38th, hidden in a flap of hill beside a clear road to the hospital in Miryang, just happened to get in the way. That didn't help the poor bastards, and some of the killers got away, including the one who almost blew Sam's head off. He drew upon his cigarette and took comfort in the fact that some of the attack force got an early sample of hell when the napalm cooked them. Chong Nam Ki had been alert.

Looking up, Sam saw Jackson come back with Rich Shriver by one arm. "Here's the one-man army. All you fucking fays are crazy. Had to stop this mother before he followed them across the river."

Shivering, although Sam could smell his steamy body, Rich sat down beside him. "You got a drink?"

Sam reached him the canteen. Rich took a pull, choked, and handed it back. The top rattled in his shaking hand. He said, "That'll have to do. Goddamn Japs pulled the same shit in the South Pacific. No ambulances to hit, but there was this long line of wounded guys down by the beach with a couple of medics looking after them. Bastards bayoneted every one of them; over and over, they stuck those long fucking bayonets in those kids."

One more machine gun raked the Naktong River with a long burst. Nothing answered. Sam ground out his cigarette, found and wet his handkerchief, and sopped his eyes.

Rich said, "We painted this big sign and hung it between two coconut trees for the replacements coming in. It gave the day and time and how many guys were butchered by the slant-eyed sons of bitches on that spot. It ended up by saying KILL THE BASTARDS. Only we never killed enough. Look over there—fucking Japs all over again."

Sam rubbed his cheeks and mouth with the damp handkerchief. "Not Japs, Rich—Koreans." Then he looked away, because Shriver was crying.

"This morning, I damned near believed that. They're Japs, and the replacements better know it. We have to kill the bastards—*kill the bastards!*"

Sam had no answer for that.

CHAPTER 14

Pusan Perimeter, Republic of Korea, Sept. 5, 1950—Americans reported today that Red troops are driving helpless refugees ahead of them in an effort to penetrate U.N. lines.

벙어리 냉가슴 앓듯

"A man without speech groans alone at the pain in his chest." (Korean proverb: Sorrow so deep it cannot be expressed.)

Julian liked the sun. It was hot and drew steam from the dirt road as they walked toward the forward observation post above the Naktong. It was where the river could be most easily forded, the most carefully watched part of his battalion's front. Snugged into camouflage that made them seem part of the rolling hilltop and one with the rain-splattered brush, two of the 72nd's tanks stood guard. On their flanks were light machine guns and a squad of riflemen, or what passed for a full squad these days, Koreans included. Julian had learned how uncooperative tankers could get if they had no infantry protection.

Just before dawn the rain had brushed over the area, laying dust that would thicken the air again in a few hours.

But now there was the smell of freshness, of beginnings that warmed Julian through his clothing and made him conscious of his thighs, his groin.

"We'd better duck to the side here," Charley Heath said. "Even in daylight, this road has to be under observation. Maybe it's nothing—especially since we broke up the strike from the village last night. I don't think Luke the Gook can mount another attack."

"It's a nice day for a walk," Julian said, "and if they've spotted movement . . ." He let the words trail off because he didn't know what he could do to stem another assault. Regiment offered nothing, not even replacements. Of course, the battalion CO wasn't required to personally eyeball a sore spot in his lines, but Julian was getting the hang of command. The troops were reporting to him now, looking to him instead of the exec.

There was strength to that, and when he ducked under the camouflage netting with Heath, he had to take off his helmet and use it to hide his erection. What the hell? He had so many things to think about, so much responsibility, that Maggi should not appear even on the fringes of his mind. But her presence was woman, not wife, warming as the Korean sun and damp as the steam being sucked off the pine needles by that sun.

She had betrayed him. He could not forget that even for a moment. From their wedding night onward—and for a wild second, he smelled the frangipani blossoms of Hawaii and not the muddy river—he had done all right, a proper bridegroom and regular husband. If Maggi was somewhat of a disappointment, he hadn't minded all that much. His bride was the daughter and granddaughter of generals, a good girl, a virgin, and any junior officer would be damned glad to have her. Advancement was slow in the Regular Army. A wife was one thing, a performing whore was another. Maggi Barron, army brat of big brass, should have kept the distinction holy.

"Sir." The tank commander was a kid with old, tired eyes, only a corporal.

"Where are your officers?" Julian wanted to know.

"Dead, sir; Sergeant Davis is across the road, if you'd rather talk to him—"

"No. I'm sorry, son." The right touch. "What have you seen?"

"I ain't sure, sir. I mean—there ain't supposed to be no refugees still coming for the river, but I swear I seen a bunch of them, women and kids, mostly. Then they kind of disappeared in a gully or something, but they sure as billy hell were heading this way."

Julian put on his helmet. He was in the shade now, his tension easing. "Maybe they just turned around. Even refugees know damned well they can't cross this river. How many would you say, corporal?"

"A bunch—forty, fifty; all them white clothes, and kids with them. I saw them kids plain in my glasses."

Considering this, trying to understand what it meant, Julian lit a cigarette and remembered to offer the kid one. Charley Heath climbed up on the tank and aimed field glasses through the netting. He said with a catch in his voice, "They're in sight again, colonel. Damn! They're coming right for the ford."

Julian wheeled around and pointed to the infantry squad leader. "You—take your people down there on the double. As skirmishers in case it's a gook trick." The sergeant looked perplexed and slowly rose from his foxhole.

"*Move!*" Julian ordered. Turning again, he shouted for the tanks to zero in on the water crossing, for the machine gunners to stay alert. Just before the sergeant slid over the slope behind his squad, he twisted his head around. "Sir— what do we do down there?"

"Stop refugees from crossing that ford."

"But if they just keep coming—"

"*Goddamnit, sergeant!*"

Charley Heath said, "They're coming; a few old papa-sans, but mostly women and children. The kids aren't scooting around; mama-sans have them by the hands. Good lord; it's as if they're on parade."

Below the position, Julian heard the sergeant yelling across the river. Julian said sharply: "Have one of the ROKs sound off. Tell that bunch to stop in Korean."

While the skinny kid in too-big fatigues shouted some-thing guttural over and over, Julian climbed atop the tank, too. Heath legged over the long gun to give him room. No glasses were needed; Julian saw them plainly—five and six abreast, they trooped slow and steady for the river, not turning to look at corpses rotting on the bank. Baggy white clothes; dark, drawn faces; old men who had trouble walk-ing down the slope, women pacing with their bundles, children whose swollen bellies hung over thin bamboo legs.

The women had small bundles. They carried no earthen jars, no piled-high bedding, not a precious little table. Jul-ian cupped his hands and roared: "Stop them, damn it! There's something wrong. At the river—fire warning shots over their heads!"

Heath's voice was edged. "In the middle of the pack—farther back: young guys hiding their faces. The bastards are using civilians as shields—gook soldiers!"

They must have rounded up every scared Korean trapped behind their lines, gathered all the people they could lay hands on, and forced them to trudge for the Naktong. Jul-ian clamped his hands together as an acid taste rose in his throat. Inside his head he screamed *stop! stop!* and knew they couldn't, knew they had gun muzzles at their backs.

The first ranks entered the river, the turgid brown water rising to their knees, then to their hips. Now the women swung their children to hip or shoulder, and late summer sun glistened in their black hair tied tightly back. Julian heard the high, fragile cry of a baby.

"Colonel," Heath said, and warning shots rang out below. "Colonel?"

"Not the whole damned bunch, major. Jesus Christ—didn't you hear that baby? Machine guns!"

"Yes, sir!"

"Take out those two old guys on the right flank."

The tank's armor plating turned hot in sun that speckled down through camouflage netting. Julian closed his eyes and braced his hand on the 75mm cannon. The LMGs fired, one short burst apiece, and the gunners were good. Both old men fell backward into the water kicked up by bullets.

The others waded around or over the dead men and kept coming. Now Julian saw their faces clearly, the glazed eyes, the tears streaming down cheeks. At the river, the squad leader yelled *colonel—colonel!* Oh, you sons of bitches; Julian's mind banged itself inside his skull, a crazed animal beating against its cage. Oh, you bastards. It's up to me, only me because rank has its responsibilities and they won't let me quit now.

"Fire on them!" The words ripped his throat, and he climbed down from the tank, trying to close out the quick thunder of machine gun and rifle. That lasted only a few seconds, but the single scream of agony that rose into the silence that followed would remain with Julian for the rest of his life.

A full-auto carbine drummed the obscene air, and a GI yelled, "I got that son of a bitch running. You see him drop that burpgun?"

Fighting the bile that clogged his throat, Julian got a cigarette going. It helped some. He leaned against the back of the tank and shook. When he looked up, Heath said, "You couldn't avoid it. I figure a dozen soldiers were driving that poor damned herd. If they got here, we'd have lost the tanks as well."

Slowly controlling his shakes, Julian wanted to say

things like us or them—somebody had to do it—or even the fortunes of war. He could only shake his head and push away from the tank. In shared silence, Heath walked beside him back up the road to the CP. The dirt was dry now, and the sun too hot to linger in it.

But it wasn't over. He couldn't even crawl into the muggy shade of his command post and lay his cheek against the cool earth there. Sgt. Rocky Watanabe hunkered at the entrance with two small boys kneeling before him. Their heads were shaved, and hunger had lifted their sharp cheekbones; they were perhaps eight years old, ragged. They kneeled on the ground and stared at Julian.

"What the hell, sergeant?"

"Caught them cutting our phone lines to Division Artillery, sir."

They were only babies, not much younger than Winfield when he was sent off to military school. Fishhooks caught at Julian's stomach; he'd be damned if he would take all the blame for that. Not after the goddamned Naktong ford. Nobody could have foreseen the hazing accident, and it would have happened to an older kid, even one much older.

"Better trained than the little old grenade lady," Rocky said. "If we can't reach Divarty when we need their guns—"

"I know," Julian gritted. *"I know."*

Winfield Barron had deserved a chance to get the jump on his someday class at the Academy. The kid tested at genius level and would have two years of college behind him when accepted at West Point. Would have had; everything past tense and all his fault, according to Maggi.

"Young and sharp," Rocky said. "The gooks had to pay these two; five hundred *whan* apiece. Less than two greenback dollars."

"The river looks like a butcher's counter," Julian said. His nostrils flared, but surely the dead hadn't begun to stink this soon. "What am I supposed to do with two more kids?"

Rocky shrugged, and Julian recognized the gesture as the enlisted man's disclaimer of responsibility, that smart-ass response that said an enlisted man wasn't paid to think.

"Let's see." Digging into the C-ration cigarette packet, Julian ripped open his last Camel. "I suppose Genghis Khan would have one of these little bastards shot and free the other, so all of South Korea would understand that cutting phone wires is a no-no."

Dropping the ruined cigarette and its box, Julian said, "Well, fuck that. Tell them we'll cut off their balls if we ever see them again. Then kick their asses and send them home."

"You got it," Rocky said, and he stood up to drag the boys away.

Weak-kneed, Julian ducked into his CP hole in the hillside. It was no cooler inside, and the water in his canteen still had the flavor of a urinal. He took off his helmet and sat on it, staring at the situation map but not seeing it.

Surprised, he took the lighted cigarette Heath handed him. Then Heath said, "I've discovered that combat is a hell of a leveler. It's also a purveyor of truth, whether we're shopping for truth or not. We have to out-tough these gooks or let them cut our throats. But if we have to *be* gooks, I'd just as soon pack it in."

Julian dragged on his cigarette. After a while he said, "Thanks, Charley."

CHAPTER 15

Chunju, Republic of Korea, Sept. 20, 1950—The bodies of more than two thousand men, women, and children were discovered at a prison in this city. A U.N. spokesman said they had been beaten to death.

백번 죽어도 싸다.

"It is cheap though you die a hundred deaths."
(Korean proverb: One death is not enough for an unpardonable sin.)

He had never known such bitterness, even when the island dwarfs were beating him. Ho Chuk Gun trudged through the deserted marketplace of Chunju, a few tattered soldiers straggling somewhere behind him. They were many *li* from the Naktong River, every one edged in blood of the *inmungun*. Some might say they were fortunate, that only the blessing of the dragon started these paltry survivors north before the foreign armies broke out of their defensive positions and before the armada landed more *kho-jaengi* at Inchon.

May they all rot unmourned by sons. No matter how many mercenaries the People's Army executed upon the

Naktong, they were inexhaustible, more and more coming across the oceans every day. It was not their war, and yet they came with their air fleets and sea fleets, just to make richer the arms merchants who controlled their country.

Chuk Gun stumbled and caught himself. He would not show any sort of weakness to gaping fools who would be watching from inside their miserable hovels, not realizing that they were about to be turned over to the long-nose rapists again, that once more the peasants would be robbed of their food and dignity. If they were not all fools, then they should be packing to follow the retreat of the *inmungun* north.

Instead, they hid themselves. It was the safety of rats in stacked barley straw, where they would lie quiet and then slowly come out to be eaten by the cat. He wished that somehow he could drive them all before him, herd them to Pyongyang like the low animals they were. There they could be educated and trained, even if they were willing slaves now.

Sergeant Pek dragged up beside him. "Sir—at the prison there is food and help. If—"

"We pause there," Chuk Gun snapped. "See to yourself, *sangsa*, and bring the men together; remind them they are soldiers."

Chunju Prison; Chuk Gun turned toward the great walls. The Japanese had built this huge, ugly pile, and he had heard that the occupying Americans used it for holding orgies with innocent Korean girls. Of course they imprisoned peasants there, so the peasant women could be made into whores.

And of course, dedicated political officers followed the combat troops who struck down into this province from Seoul, and the traitors who refused to be cleansed would have been separated from the population so others would not be infected. What, Chuk Gun wondered, would be done with such prisoners now? He walked a little faster, forcing himself and ignoring the pain, the belly he had filled Japanese style, with air.

Was it possible for *Me-in* to be kept in this prison? Perhaps all had not been killed on the Naktong; possibly a few prisoners had been chosen for interrogation and to show the world what aggressors were doing in Korea. Chuk Gun could taste fresh saliva, for even more than the food he needed to keep going, he wanted to crush more of the foreign dogs who had humbled him and the People's Democratic Republic.

Once a man knew dignity, it became more precious than his life. The paid troops of the warmongers had caused Major Ho Chuk Gun to lose much face. He would regain it if he could, and right here in Cholla-do Province. This was the birthplace of hagglers, the province known throughout Korea for its sharp dealings and love of money. No wonder the people were in hiding from the *inmun-gun*; the merchants intended to stay rich, to reappear and lick American boots.

Looking cold even in air so hot that it wavered, the prison walls loomed before him. Chuk Gun's knees were weak, and the shoulder wound ached. He had taken that on the night raid across the river, when the madman leaped screaming and firing into their midst. It was the same night four good soldiers died in the cruel, cowardly trap set for them in the earth itself. Chuk Gun remembered the screams as they burned, screams of agony cut mercifully short.

Sergeant Pek and three others came to attention before him. Four men! Four, the number of bad fortune because it was so near the Chinese character, the *han-mun* symbol for death. Chuk Gun pulled back his own shoulders and hung his submachine gun properly. Then he led his entire battalion of four through the prison gates and into the courtyard.

Dead men filled the open space, Korean civilians who had been beaten to death by the small picks and shovels used by *Me-in* to dig holes to hide in. The signs were obvious—blood where flies buzzed as they fed, blood scattered upon the ground, along the walls. Beyond these bodies, uniformed soldiers of Pyongyang were bringing women from a shadowed passageway.

A second lieutenant stepped up to Chuk Gun. "Sir." He saluted. "We have been ordered to dispose of all traitors to the state before evacuating the city, and the Americans are coming swiftly from the south. If you would care to assist—"

Chuk Gun shook his head. "My unit needs food, water, and ammunition. We cannot wait. But"—he peered up at cloudy windows—"If you have any American prisoners—"

"We are not so fortunate, major. As for supplies, I suggest you turn and march left. There you will find a Christian church, and beyond it a rectory. We did not catch the foreign minister when we came, and his poison infected many we were forced to kill. They would not inform upon him. The rectory is our headquarters, and supplies are there."

"The women," Chuk Gun said, "are they all yankee whores?"

"Not all." The lieutenant seemed disappointed but brightened as a small shovel glinted in the air and fell with a melon-bursting sound. "Some dedicated themselves to learning English, that language of barking dogs; some worked for the U.S. military occupation and are therefore spies."

"In some fashion," Chuk Gun said, the blistering sun making him light-headed, "they are all *yang-khalbo* and deserve to die."

Small, still able to wear a clean uniform, the lieutenant saluted again. "Of course, sir. Go in peace."

The sounds began—chopping noises and splitting noises that rose and fell steadily beneath the screams and the pleas for mercy. Behind Chuk Gun, he heard one of his men gasp.

Automatically he responded, "Stay in peace," and wheeled his men about before any of their weaknesses should cause him to lose yet more face. And he wondered why it was necessary to beat the prisoners to death. That made it slow work, and if many awaited their punishment in the bowels of Chunju Prison, some might escape justice. For as the lieutenant said, the Americans were coming in their fast trucks and fast tanks, while their speeding airplanes swept down from the sky.

Yes, the so-called United Nations men were carried swiftly, for their kind of war was only machinery. They did not understand that the *inmun-gun* was spirit, and spirit could not be crushed. Whatever had happened to allow their temporary victory for the *Mi-kuk ku-nin*, it was a hollow reed. The people's armies would return, stronger than ever.

But for now, they must save themselves for that day. Chuk Gun marched his unit of four toward the rectory. He wondered again why the wardens were not shooting the prisoners and hoped it was not because of a shortage of ammunition.

Rich Shriver put the camera back in his jeep. If he never took another picture, that would suit him just fine. Despite the cigar clenched in his teeth, the smell got to him, and he removed the cigar to brace both hands against the jeep hood. Then he turned his head and carefully vomited. In that other war and in this one, he had seen the dead torn and obscene, the dead shattered and degraded. Chunju Prison was too much.

The broiler of September sun had bloated the corpses quickly, and their gases made them swell even as the skin began to darken. They stank; the island smell, Jap smell was strong, thickening the air of this abattoir. Air trapped inside the prison walls had a peculiar texture, like almost visible fish scales; like the belly of an ancient feathered serpent, slithery and disgusting.

The fucking flies. Black and green and greasy, they carpeted the crushed heads, crawling and buzzing and eating. The animals, the fucking Japs who did this to their own kind. You killed the fathers, but the sons grew up to carry long bayonets and sharpened entrenching tools. Who would kill the grandsons?

He saw the women, although he tried not to look, and one face was clear, only the back of her head beaten. She looked like the little prostie he screwed in Mlryang. The whole courtyard was filled with bloating corpses, but there was movement among them—a G-2 team from the Second Division, pale shadows of Koreans who inched along the edges seeking identity. The flies rose in a dark and angry cloud when disturbed and quickly settled again.

Pulling at the cigar, Rich drifted smoke through his nose and turned for the bottle in his jeep. It was time to get out of here, past time to get blind drunk and let the war pass him by. His wife had been right; patient Saint Teresa had been right; he should have gone on through medical school and treated dandruff and hangnails. But of course he couldn't, because the only way to stop the bleeding was a tourniquet of flies. He drank deeply of the warm booze and his eyes watered. When they cleared, he saw the kid.

The boy sat between two bodies, fanning off the flies. He had already covered the faces, the broken heads, but still he fanned the flies away. He was small and sat erect, his soul leaking out of his eyes. Rich wet his kerchief from his canteen, tied it across his nose, and picked his way through the corpses.

"Can't do no good, kid. If you stay here, you'll come down with something."

Glancing up, the boy shook his head. Rich asked, "You speak English?"

"Mama-san, papa-san." He continued to wave over both bodies, but the flies settled quicker each time. Now Rich noticed the ugly welt along the kid's temple and the crust of blood so thick he didn't notice his own flies.

Bending, Rich took the thin arm and moved him out. The boy was too weak to struggle even when Rich sat him in the jeep and cleaned the wound with iodine. Remembering on their own, Rich's hands moved deftly and with some sort of caring: butterfly tape to close the skin, a dusting of sulfa powder, the bandage. When the boy sank back to cry quietly, Rich looked at his own hands, and they did not tremble. But the kid had stopped bleeding long before Rich saw him.

They used bastardized Japanese and GI English and sign language, and Rich understood that the gook butchers had thought they killed the boy first, a delicate touch of forcing his parents to watch. A blessing for him not to see them murdered. They were beside him on the stained earth when he came to, and the communists were gone.

His name was Kim Soo Man, he was eleven years old and now he was an orphan. He hadn't known what else to do but sit there and take care of his dead parents as best he could.

"What happen them?" he wanted to know.

Rich stared at the boy and took another drink. Well, laddie buck, he thought, you're making me walk back through all those goddamned dead this time, but nothing else. Finding the kid's folks was easy; their heads were the only ones covered. Convincing G-2 and Graves Registration to plant two gooks apart from the rest was the tough part and cost Rich two bottles of good *soju*.

"Okay," SFC Leonard P. Frusha said, "but just remember to send a story on me to Texas. That's Weirgate, Texas. We can have some live gooks put them down yonder by that old mass grave the Japs left."

When Rich got back to the jeep and explained, he noticed that Soo Man held a can of ham and lima beans between his knees but hadn't tried to open it.

"Okay?" Soo Man asked.

"Sure; what the hell." He showed the kid how to use the P-38 opener and drove slowly out into cleaner, fresher air, into some kind of sanity. Keeping sane was the main reason Rich Shriver, the GI's Ernie Pyle, wasn't about to burden himself with any slant-eyed orphan, now or ever. If Kim Soo Man couldn't make it on his own, tough luck.

CHAPTER 16

Seoul, Republic of Korea, Sept. 26, 1950—This city was recaptured today by hard-driving forces of the U.N. Refugees began flooding back into town immediately. Survivors of the rape of Seoul by the Reds are celebrating the end of the Korean war.

설마가 사람 죽인다 .

"'Surely not' kills a man." (Korean proverb: False security is a great foe.)

Major Chong Nam Ki quieted himself in the fairyland of the Secret Garden behind the Changdok-kung Palace. He tried to remain open to the centuries past so that he might hear the whispers of ancestors who had walked within these ancient walls. He breathed greenleaf shadows and saw golden coins of the sun fall softly upon his hands. It was difficult to refill his soul; so much of the lining had worn through, and many teachings had leaked out to lie behind him upon the long and twisted roads he had traveled.

Here in this sacred place, time was the texture of watered silk, soft layer upon gentle layer, the embroidery stitches of the years barely discernible to all but the most sensitive fingertips. Here his aristocratic forebears had strolled in court gowns encrusted with gold and jewels. This worn earth knew the tread of their slippers as they spoke with kings and paid respect to gods.

At least the animals of the north had not destroyed this shrine of Korea, or perhaps they had not had the time. The Japanese had not managed to strip the palace of all beauty, although they had used thirty-five years of colonization. All things, even spread far and wide, were drawn back to be funneled along the path chosen by time. Confucius had described such a path, preordained for each man. But since man was also given thought, it followed that he must guide at least part of his own destiny. Therefore, the seven gates. At each crisis in life, the path divided into seven, and man chose which one he would follow.

The killers from the north had chosen gates that led away from ruining this loveliness, these intertwining roads linking wooded slopes, lotus ponds, and pleasure pavilions. Perhaps all sensitivities of the *inmun-gun* were not burned away by the acids of communism, and high-ranking officers who entered the gardens yet felt the echoes of those here before them. Still, their armed and swaggering presence had profaned this place, as did the hidden stainings of Nam Ki's uniform. The Secret Garden was made for love and beauty, not the rattling of butchers' knives.

A dry leaf fell, slow drifting from side to side as it sought rest upon the ground. There was little reason for the leaf to make Nam Ki think of Wha Ja, but he did, and there against the wall he saw her memory, graceful and fragile. Wha Ja was not of earth and resting places, but born to incense, moonlight, and fireflies toe-dancing the air.

> My mind is a candle light.
> Please close that door.
> I'll quietly burn to the last drop,
> Flickering by your silken dress.

Nam Ki did not dare linger upon the midnight deeps of her eyes, nor the flowered lips that could melt away all cares. Songs of the willow and sweet bloomings of the night, wondrous though they were, could not lift the burden of duty from the shoulders of a youthful Chong Nam Ki. Even if war had not come, she must mourn with the fog that sometimes came to teardrop the gray loneliness of Myongdong street. And he must forever remain the eldest son of the family Chong.

He bent to capture the fallen leaf. It rested lightly upon the palm of his hand.

> My mind is a dead leaf.
> Please let me stay briefly in your garden.
> When the wind rises again,
> I'll leave you, lonely as a wanderer.

Lifting his head, he listened to sounds beyond the wall, to the movements of Seoul resurrected. The population was returning day by day, packing the trains running upon repaired rails, clinging to ROK vehicles and begging lifts from the *Me-in* trucks. Mostly, they walked back from all the terrible places they had gone—those who could still walk. Many homes in Seoul had been burned in the first orgies of communist liberation, but many families would never come back, either. The city would balance itself; the old and new, the live and the dead; Yin and Yang.

But newly promoted *So-ryawng* Chong Nam Ki would not balance. Standing up, he made his way back past the lotus pond, noticing a communist cap in the water, its red star like some dead mud worm. All had not gone well here, then. Perhaps a *balgaengi* soldier was weighted with stones at the bottom of the pond, and perhaps the cap had been discarded by some minor priest now pretending to be a good Korean.

Adjusting his own cap, he strode for his jeep and driver

parked just beyond the palace gates. Had all the holes in his soul been filled? No, but the few moments he had used to walk with yesterday reminded him of who he was, and that was as important as what he was. It had assured him of beauty yet remaining in a world gone ugly with bleeding. He wished that Father Chong could have sat beside him for a little while. Then, nodding at his driver, Nam Ki realized that his father might have been.

The 11th Regiment command post was in a middle school building beside the highway to Uijongbu. By this end of September and well into the season for *Chusok*, he had hoped to see the students coming back and life beginning anew. It would not be the same, but nothing was. Father Chong could not return from the dead; Nam Ki was forever a soldier, never to be a poet. But the saved children could be poets or artists or whatever they wanted, given the chance.

"Many Americans are here now," his driver said. "Will they ever leave again?"

Nam Ki looked sharply at this corporal, this *hasa* but recently arrived in the regiment, along with this precious jeep and its radio. "After they left, the communists came. The Americans fought; did you, corporal?"

Expertly, the driver twisted the wheel and turned the jeep smoothly around a shell hole in the road. "My father is *Chun-jang* Kang Jo Su, general staff." Evidently as an afterthought, the man added: "Sir."

A younger son—one who had displeased his father, to be of such lowly rank—but a soldier who had not battled the enemy and probably never would. "We are fortunate that the American general from Tokyo remains with our regiment."

Nam Ki appreciated the expertise of General Wright and was grateful that the man did not order, but suggested. There had been moments, though, when Nam Ki wished the responsibility was all the general's. He had been surprised to learn that Sam Connover and General Wright were old friends. They were shaped from the same strong clay, but the idea of closeness between enlisted man and high officer was still strange.

It won't work in the ROK army, Sam said, *not yet. It's rare in my own and usually a mistake. Butt Wright and I fought together in another war.*

His American brother and the general were at the CP map when Nam Ki entered the old schoolhouse. Now two telephones sat at the ready, and a large radio. Supply had grown steadily since the early days. There was even a folding table and chairs, and an American lieutenant heating coffee.

"Ah—the major," Wright said, his face lined and perhaps pale beneath the sun's darkening. But the eyes were those of the hawk.

"My brother," said Sam Connover. "Just in time." This one lived within the stripes of the tiger.

Rapidly, Nam Ki moved to the map. "Is there trouble above Uijongbu?"

"Not yet. When trouble comes, it will be much farther north."

Frowning, Nam Ki stared at the overlay, prim now with stability and no heavy red markings of the disintegrated communist army. "North? I do not—" He turned and went to sit with them at the table. The young lieutenant said hello and set out another canteen cup. "Not the Chinese," Nam Ki said.

"Not yet," Sam Connover said, "but soon after we move for the Yalu River."

Nam Ki's hands closed tightly around the metal cup. He did not feel the heat when coffee was poured into it. Steam rose past his eyes like fog. "MacArthur sends us over the Parallel?"

General Wright lit a cigar; the fog around him was blue.

"In spite of clear warnings. When we reach certain points, Lin Pao's armies will swarm all over us."

Nam Ki sipped coffee. "He will not change his mind?"

"MacArthur?" Wright grunted.

Sam Connover said, "We have a few days for supplies and all the transport we can hang onto. General Wright has been ordered back to Tokyo and then home."

Wright blew smoke and leaned back, both hands holding the canteen cup against his belly, as if needing its warmth. "We never received such orders, did we, lieutenant?"

"Garbled in transmission, sir."

Nam Ki said, "I must see to my family."

Sam nodded. "We think three or four days. There is time. The black sergeant and I will travel with you and the general. Please convey my respect to the Chong family."

Back at his jeep, Nam Ki ordered the driver onto the road to Seoul. Fisting his hands upon his knees, he rocked with the motion of the jeep until he thought it was like the swaying of women in mourning. "I must stop at my home," he said. "The road ahead on the right. Turn at the crossing."

The driver nodded. "I know of the Chong estates."

Rushing wind fanned Nam Ki's face, and the sun's warmth had not yet thinned. In the north, if they reached beyond Pyongyang, winter winds would have the edge of an executioner's ax. There, mountains steep and black reached high and icy. The Chinese would wear fur hats.

He said to this driver who had not heard gunfire: "Know this also. Speak only when you are told to. From this day forward, you are part of a fighting regiment, where I am the only man who knows your father's name. And I do not care."

Sullen lips clamped together, the young Kang drove in silence. Perhaps he could be formed into a soldier, for soldiers were still few. The Red Army had been driven back north, and a happy population of South Korea busied itself finding its scattered parts in rebuilding. What need of soldiers now? They had not heard of the waiting Chinese.

The Chong house wore a different face. Sedate and calm it had been; now it boiled with laughing children. Nam Ki left his jeep and walked past the truck and trailer parked outside the main gates. When he sat upon the entrance porch, a pair of small girls rushed to take off his boots.

In the highest form of politeness, he said, "Thank you, ladies."

Giggling behind their hands, they ran. No adult ever used such language to children, so this was a huge joke. Nam Ki wished he had something funny to tell his mother, his sister; he hated to think of his younger brother's face.

Mother Chong had been ecstatic to find her home virtually untouched. Now she must abandon it again, for the war was not over. Some children here might find their own families some day, but the task would be more difficult after they moved south again. There would be more lost children to gather along the way, more food and medicines to be found.

All had to become refugees again, and this time there would be no home to take them in.

CHAPTER 17

Seoul, Republic of Korea, Oct. 6, 1950—Morale is high here. Men who fought the war go on pass to Seoul, and fresh troops arrive daily, as do mountains of equipment and supplies. MacArthur calls upon North Korea to surrender.

속히 더운 방이
쉬 식는다.

"A quickly heated room cools quickly." (Korean proverb: Quick success will not last.)

She was silken, a triangle of downy smoothness beneath his hands. Sam had always been gentle with women, and he took special care with this one. It was strange, but she would be his first Korean. Seventeen years growing up in Chunju, and before now he had only kissed a Korean girl. And that had been in boyish wonderment, before he realized that Christianity and acceptance for the church stopped at the rectory door.

Was it also strange that Sam Connover should be in a whorehouse? Hardly; this was standard operating procedure for a combat man, this buildup of tension that demanded relief in the oldest of methods. A long time ago, he might have looked over his shoulder for an avenging

124

angel to strike him down. But now Sam stroked the woman's body, finger walking the curvings, tracing the delicate valleys and breathing the perfume of her hair. A woman made special on a special afternoon; black hair perfumed and flowing loose; that shuddering moment of readiness when she arched her pelvis to him.

If this was not a blessing, Sam didn't know another. Ever gentle within her, deep and lingering within her, he allowed her to set the pace and concentrated upon feeding her desires. But she wasn't Maggi Barron. Damn it—she was giving and exceptional, but she wasn't Maggi, and that meant no other woman could be.

"*I-go!*" she hissed, coiling beneath him. "Ah—you are a strong one. If they were all like you—"

And moments later, holding her close, holding her tenderly, he whispered back in her own language that she was beautiful. The woman flinched against him, and the fine intimacy was gone. She rolled over on the *chimtae* and reached for the rag in the water pan, but he took it from her and rinsed himself.

"You speak our language so well, but how does a foreigner—"

Drawing on his pants, he went barefooted out upon the entrance porch. Stonewall Jackson leaned back against a support post, sharing a D-ration bar with his girl of the day. The rice paper door to Rich Shriver's little room was open to the afternoon sun that angled softly into the tiny courtyard. Rich himself stuck his head out of the kitchen lean-to, grinning as he stirred one of the pots built into the stove.

"Make yourself to home, sergeant. Chow'll be ready in two shakes of a prostie's tail. Hey, Jackson—eating dessert first don't mean you get to pass on this stew. Papa knows best."

Jackson grunted. "My daddy was some darker than you, boy. What you got in that mess, anyhow?"

125

Sam sat cross-legged on the porch that had been polished smooth by a thousand feet. He lighted a cigarette, and the woman sat not too close to stare at him, at the Korean way he sat.

Shriver said, "Five cans of Cs."

"Say *what?* Spaghetti, ham and limas, what?"

"Yeah. My little prostie chopped up garlic and onions and all the peppers in the house. *Kimchi* on the side."

"No wine," Jackson said.

Shaking his canteen, Shriver said, "Medical alcohol, a hundred and ninety proof. Unpretentious little label, but a good year."

Jackson turned his head. His girl snuggled to him as he said, "Shee-it, Sam; this fay is crazy as you."

"Chow time," Shriver called, and from the porch across the courtyard the boy appeared, mess kit in hand.

Watching him go quickly to the lean-to, Sam saw more than one kid wearing a cutdown fatigue outfit and always hungry. He saw orphans and mascots and houseboys, or whatever else you wanted to call them—the children GIs picked up and took along. They adopted dogs and kids, too, looking for tenderness, for small lives they could guard instead of taking. Sam had been surprised by Shriver, though. Rich didn't believe in complications. More than simply feeding and clothing this kid, Shriver was halfway protecting him. All afternoon, the boy had been stashed with the landlady, all happy whoring out of his sight.

Jackson untangled from the girl. "You know how else you ain't got good sense, man?" he asked Shriver.

Sam field-stripped his cigarette butt and tried for the lotus position. It didn't work. His woman—was her name Kil Ja?—lifted her eyebrows and whispered that he was a great mystery to her.

Jackson strolled to the lean-to and pulled a spoon from his shirt pocket. "Anybody with good sense be in Tokyo drinking that dollar-thirty-a-quart Canadian Club, man. Halfass smart man be laying up in Shimbashi, talking trash to them cute little whores. But you over here—and where you get that kid?"

"Chunju Prison," Shriver answered, and no more.

"Hell of an atrocity story you did," Sam said, and he lighted the cigarette the woman—her name *was* Kil Ja— took from his pack.

"Easy; it was a hell of an atrocity."

Jackson persisted. "The kid?"

Shriver dipped stew into his canteen cup. "He was there. Get your own damned chow. Fatten up for Joe Chink. Temperature drops to twenty below up there, and those fucking shoe paks will freeze your toes."

"The man really going across the line?"

Shriver poured more stew into the kid's mess kit. "We are; *he* ain't. He's back in Tokyo."

The stew was savory, if you didn't mind the mixture, and the seasonings sort of blended the ingredients so that it was really only one hot taste. Sam ate.

Kil Ja said, "Are you a great scholar, a teacher? I have never known a scholar."

Turning, Sam looked more closely at the woman. She was pretty and young enough so that the wear didn't show. In Japan, her profession was semi-legitimate, especially if she was supporting her parents. In Korea, there was no such absolution. Kil Ja was forever branded *yang-khalbo,* a Yankee whore. Was it worse to make love for food, or to kill for it?

"Only a soldier," he said, but in Korean. If he wanted to keep to himself, Sam would have to watch that. But ever since he arrived, it was only natural to go with the language. Everything seemed too damned natural, a homecoming, and it should not be. To Shriver he said, "Chunju Prison—was a mass grave just outside the walls? Old, maybe not marked."

Frowning, Shriver thought for a moment, then put down his stew cup and took a long pull at his canteen. The raw alcohol choked him, made his eyes run, but soon he said, "Yeah. That's where Soo Man's—" Breaking off, he glanced at the boy and lowered his voice. "That's where his folks got planted, next to that old grave. How'd you know? You didn't come out through Chunju?"

"I came out in 1938," Sam said, "all the way out."

"Son of a bitch," Jackson murmured. "That's where your old man got murdered—that same prison?"

"They gave him a break," Sam said quietly. When Shriver handed him the medical alcohol, he took a swallow. It tasted awful, like a mouthful of rancid grave dirt must taste. "The Japs had him stand on the edge while they filled the pit with his parishioners, all those people who believed in justice and eternity, in everlasting life. Mostly, they believed in him, for was he not the great Connover *Moksa* come to save their immortal souls?"

Sam took another drink from the canteen. This one burned all the way down to his crotch. They waited, all of them—even the Korean girls who knew only a few English words—for what Sam had to tell them, what was forcing its way up from a strapped-down place where it had festered for many years. Sam said, "They kneeled him down and cut off his head with a samurai sword. Then they kicked his body into the grave, and when Koreans covered it, the Jap officer stuck my father's head on a stick. That night, this old bell ringer buried it, too. The samurai had missed the bell ringer, never caught up with him."

"Samurai, my ass. Fucking Japs," Shriver said. "If you weren't here, how'd you—"

Drawing hard upon a new cigarette, Sam got off the porch and slipped his feet into combat boots to walk across the courtyard. The buckles rang *ting-a-ting-ting*. He stared up at the warm sky, glad that he had not gone west with troops that raced for Chunju, but due north. Someday he would return to Chunju, but not now; not now.

The woman Kil Ja came to put her hand upon his arm, her *komu-shin* whispering rubber across the yard's hard-packed clay. For a time she stood like that beside him. He said thank you and looked north toward the line he could not see, the Parallel they had to cross. Maybe someday he'd be able to deny this eagerness, this straining against the leash, but not now.

Of course Ho Chuk Gun was proud. Not every newly promoted officer was given a tour of the capital building and allowed to look into Premier Kim Il Sung's private office. The great leader was in China, the guide explained. The man's face was lumpy and the color of old rice; he was nervous and eager to move along. Faintly, he stank of fear.

"Do you not believe our great leader will return with Chinese troops?" Chuk Gun asked. He had almost used the derogatory *dwae-nom.* Chuk Gun did not think much of the Manchus.

"Oh, no, regimental commander," the man answered, making small, jerky bows and rubbing his hands together. "It is only that we have been ordered to evacuate the capital. If you will excuse me, senior colonel—"

"The foreigners have attacked the Democratic People's Republic?"

Riceface padded down the hall for the stairway. "By dawn they were in Kumchon with many trucks and tanks."

Following the man downstairs, Chuk Gun said, "The general named my regiment. Where is the 204th?"

"Where indeed? Please, senior colonel, I have many important—"

Chuk Gun caught the thin arm. His own strength had partially returned since he had come back to Pyongyang, and he used it now, squeezing hard. "Civilian fool! There is nothing more important than the regiments. Get me transportation to mine, or the enemy will find you here without your head."

"But the general needs every truck to—"

Chuk Gun shook him hard, and the man said, "Very well! But you cannot kill everyone as you did the deserter in the road. The 204th—what is left of it—should be near Sunchon. You—*Crae, crae!* There is a jeep at the statues. The driver awaits orders and is anxious to be gone, as am I; as you should be. The Americans can be standing right here by nightfall. If they should find us—"

Sunchon; many hours, many *li* north of Pyongyang, and a rail center, if the American airplanes had left any trains. Too far for walking, especially since he had worn off his feet hiking all the way from the Naktong. Somehow, the deserter from his old company, the proud company that had led the way into Seoul, had beaten him to Pyongyang. How fortunate he had been to find the cowardly dog right at the capitol building yard. In sight of the general, Chuk Gun executed the man on the spot.

"The jeep," Chuk Gun insisted. "You will take me to it." He dragged Riceface down the corridor. As if he would release this bureaucrat, this vestigial *yangban* to report him to the general, or deny him the chance to reach his troops. The lower nobility, the arrogant junior lords who bought or inherited their way into government positions, the *yangban* had self-destructed soon after the Russians came to liberate them. A few remained to crawl into the structure and slow the wheels.

When he had ejected the frightened driver and spun Riceface away from the jeep, Chuk Gun settled behind the wheel. He had but small practice in driving, but he would manage. In the back was a box of canned food with Russian markings and a new PPSH with much ammunition.

As the driver scuttled off to tell his superiors how he was robbed the bureaucrat stepped back just beyond reach and hissed at Chuk Gun, "You are a fool. Everyone has fled into China; there is no 204th Regiment, no regiments of any number. The war is lost, was lost when the *inmun-gun* failed so miserably, when Pusan was allowed to remain in United Nations hands."

"Not the army! The army did not fail. It was the *pi-haengi*—the damned airplanes—and so many big guns—and we had no food, no water; the food and medicine stopped. *We* did not lose!"

Riceface stepped farther back, his left hand resting now upon the base of the great statue of a farmer and his wife striding proudly into the future. "Twice fool! It does not matter the cause. The war is lost and the Americans are coming, and our leader is in China. So are the cowards from the Naktong."

Chuk Gun brought his pistol around and fired, but the dog expected it and ducked behind the statue. A whistle shrilled in the compound, and men shouted. Chuk Gun jerked the floor stick around and got the jeep in gear; then he rolled it out of the capitol grounds—the near-empty buildings and grounds soon to be abandoned to the advancing enemy.

The war lost? He gritted his teeth. Never, so long as a true soldier breathed. The trouble with *yangban* was that they had never been peasants. They had not lived by the old proverbs like *Chiljon Palgi*. Any struggling farmer knew that if misfortune continued to befall him, that even if he fell down seven times, he must get up eight times.

Let the cursed Americans come deeper into the north; with all his mind and body, Chuk Gun hoped they would. The *inmun-gun*, with the Chinese at its side, would strike again and again until final victory.

CHAPTER 18

New York, NY, Oct. 7, 1950—The U.N. sanctions defeat of North Korea and reunification of the country. U.N. forces cross the 38th Parallel. General MacArthur says his troops will be home by Christmas.

법은 멀고 주먹은 가깝다 .

"The law is far, the fist is near." (Korean proverb.)

Julian Barron felt great. He was conscious of his skin and the sun upon his cheek, conscious of the sliding of his thighs within his pants as he walked. The woman was a marvel, pliant until she sensed his need for aggression, then turning tigress. He could do anything he wanted to her, with her, and the taste of her was still in his mouth, the golden sweat of her still in his pores. Her memory excited him.

She had long black hair like Maggi, but he didn't want to think of that, of his wife and a whore at the same moment. Was an adulteress as reprehensible as a whore? Maggi had only bedded one other man—or had she? There might have been others; she had plenty of opportunities right there on post. She didn't have to slink off to town and go to bed with that goddamned sergeant. Still, it was better that way, going in to Tacoma. Less chance of gossip spreading on Fort Lewis.

Bullshit; he could not think rationally about Maggi's grimy little affair. Turning off the lobby and into the bar so quickly stocked with black-market liquor from officer and NCO club stores in Japan, Julian ordered a double bourbon, water chaser. There was no ice. The Bando was the only western-style hotel in Korea, but it had a long way to go. It was much like the Korean people themselves, a veneer of civilization laid thinly upon centuries of savagery. Finding no cigarettes in his pockets, he signaled the barkeep, and the man brought C-ration smokes dumped from their small boxes onto a tray. They sold for 25 *whan* apiece, 500 *whan* to the Military Pay Certificate dollar.

Turning to prop his elbows on the bar, Julian wondered if the woman still slept upstairs in his room. Probably not; whores didn't waste time lining up other customers, and he hadn't been certain how long he might stay away from the battalion. If she hung around and no alert was called, he could use another day and another long, sweaty night with her. God knew when he would have another opportunity; if he'd have another chance.

He drank off half his whiskey, cleared his throat, and sipped chaser. Then he pulled hard upon his Phillip Morris and wondered if Maggi had lined up another lover since her husband shipped out to the Far East, because her first lover had shipped, too. Was an original lover like original sin?

That bastard wasn't Maggi's *first* lover; Julian Barron took her cherry on their wedding night. No, Connover was Maggi's first betrayal, and no more than that. The last betrayal for Connover, at least, if it could possibly be arranged. The bar filled with junior officers, only two field grades among them, and since Julian was high-ranking, they all let him alone. He wanted it that way. Charley

Heath was the only man around who understood Julian, who had fought beside him. Charley knew he was a good battalion CO. He might have to sort of outflank Charley to get information from Division G-2 on Sergeant Connover. The man wasn't immortal; maybe he was already dead or hit and on his way back to the Zone of Interior. Not the ZI, damn it; there he would again be in close contact with the woman he had seduced. The son of a bitch ought to be dead. But a Medal of Honor man—wouldn't his death be headline news for the herd of civilian newsmen here? Maybe the division PIO would hide the news, especially since Connover had been ordered out of Korea months ago.

What made Medal of Honor winners so special? Julian had seen brave men every day in his battalion. Everybody said that the Big Bong came to men who had gone crazy for a few minutes, so blindly insane that they didn't give a damn about living. Either that, or they were driven into a defensive frenzy by overwhelming terror, so that they attacked, like a field mouse cornered by a cat. Whatever, Connover shrugged off orders as if he were immune to discipline.

"Good morning, colonel." Charley Heath stood before him. "Buy you a drink?"

"I'll buy you one. Anything new? Do I have to come home?"

Heath drank his double and blew through his nose. "We're saddling up, but the last to ride out. We drew backup this time while the 9th is point and the 23rd follows."

"How far?"

"Pyongyang is the best guess. If there's no opposition."

Julian finished his drink and ordered another round. A few wild bullets had chipped the walls and knocked out window glass. The glass had been replaced by rice paper panels. Light came in, but you couldn't see out. Clever people, these gooks. "The war's over, then?"

"Home for Christmas, MacArthur says."

"What do you say?"

Heath drank and stared into his glass. Ordinarily a smiling man, his expression seemed fixed as he said, "I hope the Chinks celebrate the holiday at home. I hope they never leave home."

It was the booze, because Julian had no intention of saying it: "My wife hasn't written one damned letter since I've been over here."

"It happens, and no mail beats a Dear John, I figure."

Julian considered. Divorce was no longer impossible in the army, but in the church— He didn't like the idea of Maggi marrying anyone else, much less Connover. But would Connover even ask her? Any EM who broke up an officer's home would be fair game for all officers. He wouldn't last.

He said, "Maybe some of the mail hasn't caught up."

"Probably. My round, and then we should go. Leave anything in your room?"

"Only a woman I'd like to take along in my musette bag."

Heath's smile broke through again. "Aren't they something else? A lot of wives will have to turn over a new leaf when these guys go home."

Julian's lips became numb. Carefully, he formed the word: "Connover."

Blinking, Heath said, "What? The guy who saved our aid station?"

"Never mind. Let's go saddle up. Home for Christmas and all that crap." He couldn't say anything about Connover without bringing Maggi into it, without cheapening himself. There was no sympathy for a man whose wife played around; there was only contempt. Julian would see to Connover himself—if the Chinese didn't beat him to it.

* * *

135

It was brutally cold. Butt Wright pulled his head deep into his field jacket collar, glad it had been lined with dog fur in Pyongyang. Beside him in the parked jeep, Lieutenant Orr stamped shoe paks against the floorboards. Issue side curtains were long lost, and they had rigged blankets to cut some of the wind.

"That wind comes right out of Manchuria," Wright said. "Blows across the Yalu River, which is solid ice about now, and comes romping over those black ho damn mountains. The farther north we go, the steeper and higher the mountains get."

Orr stamped his feet again and tucked gloved hands into his armpits. Wright nodded approval at how his skinny young aide adapted to the weather change. He simply wore all the clothing he owned. It made him look like an olive-drab pumpkin, but he stayed warm. The boy didn't have to be on this windswept road, below frowning mountains rimmed with snow. By rights, he ought to be back in Seoul, or even Tokyo. Being loyal to Butt Wright might cost him his career.

Lifting field glasses to his eyes, Wright flinched at their icy touch. He slowly scanned, swept the road as far as the curve a long way ahead, then the precipitous slopes on both sides. They'd gotten caught in a traffic tangle just past daylight, when the division moved even farther north. A lowboy with a disabled tank aboard had slid crossways off the road and blocked movement for hours. Now they could find no other vehicles, and it was as cold as an MP's heart.

"Let's go back," Wright said. "Not all the way back to pasture as Eighth Army wants; just to that warm little schoolhouse."

"If the general really means that," Orr said, his breath hanging crystal in the air over the steering wheel. "But if you're thinking of protecting me—"

Lowering the glasses, Wright said, "I'm cold to the

marrow of these ancient bones." That much was true; he couldn't remember weather affecting him this much. "The thing is, we don't know where in the hell we are, and there's no damn whiskey to be found in these boondocks. If you plan staying in the army, you should send a relay back that I'm Section Eight material and disobeying lawful orders. That'll cover your ass. Remember that I'm only a spare-parts general fired by God himself, God in profile, who wears scrambled eggs on his visor—" His teeth chattered, and a shiver rocked through him. Ho damn, he was cold.

"We can get a routing from the ordnance outfit back at that schoolhouse," Danny Orr said, and he put the jeep into gear. "This road is mighty narrow, and all that ice—"

He was a good boy, Wright thought; Frances would have liked him. She always had a soft spot for young officers who might be helped up the ladder. Wright thought that was because Frances never forgot the miscarriage. And right now, as he always did when that memory came up, he damned the thoughtless medic who had told her the fetus was male.

Children are not so important, she had said, tremulous smile denying the dampness of her eyes. *I have my little boy in you—child and lover and husband in you, and I shall always love them deeply.*

"Hang on!" Orr shouted. "The damned thing is skidding!"

Wright felt the lurch and took a grip on the sides of the seat as the jeep spun across the road and went backwards over the side to crunch into the ditch. A great weight slammed down across Wright's hips. Dirty snow got in his mouth, and he spat.

Darling, you must take better care of yourself. You're not so young anymore.

But not so old that I must retire. There's so much I can

do, Frances. You know that; so many of the high brass can't reach the troops, and worse—they don't care. I don't know what I'd do out of uniform. I've been a good soldier—better than these fancy playactors. I deserve something, Frances; a little dignity, something.

Yes, my darling; at least dignity.

"General! Oh, my God—are you trying to tell me something? I'm so sorry—the damned ice—"

It wasn't bad. He twisted his head and got the dog-fur collar under his cheek to cut the penetrating cold from the ground. Then he tried to move his legs.

"Wait—I'll try again—oh, God! I can't lift it! I—ahh! Oh, God."

"Take it easy, son. This ditch has us. On the flat you might pry me loose, but not in this ditch. How's the radio?"

"Smashed, sir. What am I going to do? No traffic, lost way the hell out here—"

Wright's arms were free. Pinned down on his left side, he searched in his jacket to find a cigar. Sniffing the air, he smelled no gas and let Danny Orr furnish a light. It would be nice if he had a quart of Old Bushmill's Irish whiskey. Of course, you weren't supposed to drink in such cold, but Wright didn't think that would matter much now.

"Son," he said, "you can hike back to that ordnance outfit and get help. Pile blankets over me and give me the carbine, some grenades."

"But—but you could freeze. And the jeep is hard to see in this ditch, if something does come by."

Wright drew upon his cigar and told the boy to make an oil fire on the road; dirt in a helmet would burn a long time like that. He'd be all right, he insisted. Besides, there was nothing else to do.

"I don't want to leave you, general. These mountains

might be full of Chinese. You wouldn't have a chance. Oh, God—if I'd only been more careful—"

Beneath his blankets, Wright held the carbine snugged to his chest. There was some pain now, but he could handle it. "Every battle could be refought a little better," he said, "but we can't give time an order to rear march. The thing is to do something; right or wrong, *do* something."

While the boy made a fire and fussed around with blankets, and after Orr slid the three grenades they owned into Wright's nest, he straightened and said, "I'll hurry, general."

"Do you know," Wright said, "how I got my nickname, why they call me Butt Wright?"

Poised to climb out of the frozen ditch, Danny Orr turned, frowning. "Sort of, sir."

"We carried the old Springfields on parade, the '03. I had this bad habit of pulling the butt in too close, and that made my bayonet swing out of line, made the whole outfit look amateurish. Somebody in the file behind was always hissing it at me, butt right, Wright. It got to be a joke."

"Yes, sir," Orr said.

"Go on, son."

"General—"

"Go on."

As he lay there listening to the lieutenant trot down the road he hoped the boy wouldn't kill himself hurrying. It was a long way back to the ordnance unit's warm schoolhouse. Wright's cigar went out. Chewing it lightly, he released the carbine and felt his grenades, two frags and a white phosphorous; thirty rounds in the carbine's banana clip. Hell, he was an arsenal.

After he couldn't feel his legs anymore, he got warm and nodded off. So he wasn't sure if he heard it—a sound, not a truck on the road above, something lighter but not too close in. Turning his head slowly, he tried to see up the mountain slope, but the lip of the ditch cut off too much, that and the corner of the jeep's crushed top. He could see a curl of smoke from his signal fire.

The bullet *spranged* off the jeep frame and whined away. Wright snugged his cheek into the fur collar. That enemy rifleman couldn't see too well, either; his angle of fire was bad. Bending all he could, he tried to fold completely from sight. It was possible that the enemy hadn't really seen him, that the shot was a probe.

Sprang!

And that one, too. Curled under his blankets, Wright waited. That was something old soldiers knew how to do
wait. It was surprising how many of the enemy got sucked in if you waited. When the rifleman didn't fire again, he waited some more, then pulled the pin on a frag grenade and held it to his chest, the handle clamped down tightly. He watched the edge of the ditch, and he listened.

Jerking awake, he called himself seven kinds of ho damn fool for falling asleep. Old; he was so old that the army wanted to be rid of him, and he was proving the high brass right. His reports hadn't helped, reports critical of almost everything the Far East commander did in Korea, critical of the ambassador who came close to losing some two thousand people when he didn't evacuate in time, especially critical of KMAG and the poor performance of Korean troops.

If Frances had been with him, he would have toned down those reports. Maybe; Frances kept him calm, but she also kept him honest.

He heard them; his ears were good as ever, so he heard them shuffling across the frozen road and whispering. Pulling down the blankets, he flexed his right arm and backhanded the grenade up and over. It went off with a blast that rained icy dirt in upon him.

Later, he couldn't tell about the other grenades, whether

they did any damage. They didn't throw any back at him, so he figured they wanted the jeep. He wished he'd saved the Willy Peter grenade. Then they did just what he would have in their position: they came at him from both sides, down in the ditch with him and firing as they came.

"Ho damn, you sons of bitches!" he yelled, holding back the carbine trigger. "Thank you!"

The bullets raked him, and he only had breath left for Frances. She said, *Yes, darling—with dignity.*

CHAPTER 19

North Korea, Nov. 26, 1950—The U.S. Second and 25th Divisions are locked in a tremendous battle with superior Chinese forces along the Chongchon River in the west. General MacArthur claims entrance of Red China makes this an entirely new war.

불난 끝은 있어도 물난
끝은 없다.

"There are relics from a fire, but the flood leaves none." (Korean proverb: A torrent sweeps all away.)

Ahead, to the right a bit, bulked the mountain so like a burial mound for kings, smoothed and appearing pillared. There was a hint of eternity come too soon; blackness and shivering moon.

This also Nam Ki would have painted, his brush dripped heavy with night; then the white trails left by the moon dragging pale skirts.

> Sadness shades your lips, beloved!
> Do you too love that snow?
>
> Snow falls;
> It is time to pray together.

Blanket wrapped tightly around himself, he stood beside a twisted tree next to the road. He heard icicles move where no wind blew, and the chill that lay over this brutal land fingered into his heart. Somewhere in the frozen night many men stirred against the harsh earth. Not even the moon could see them, but Nam Ki felt them, the in and out of breaths like fog drifting to blanket the valleys. And echoing mutely from the stones came the gathered beating of the great common heart.

Sadness would stain many tender lips back in Seoul when that mighty host moved, and if any man here was familiar with his gods, he would do well to pray.

Did the Chinese still light joss sticks and waft paper gifts to their ancestors by way of heaven-bound smoke? So many, so many Chinese herded across the Amnok *gang,* that river foreigners called the Yalu, padding quickly and silently in their new British Keds from Hong Kong, their stocky peasant bodies rounded in quilted uniforms and ear-flap hats. So many of them, an endless brown flood, all carrying long rolls of rice over one shoulder like a bandolier. That was four days' rations. In four days the *chung-guk* could be down at the Parallel.

Seoul would be emptying, for the people would believe reports from the north, even if General MacArthur did not. Koreans still remembered stories of the Khans come raiding, the burned cities never rebuilt, the rape and pillage. Seoul abandoned once again to invaders, the old men, the children—and women? The *kisaeng* with her melon-slice mouth; Wha Ja, who would make of him a poet.

Father Chong had often warned of China, of the Russians and the Japanese. Because of our borders, he said, it is the destiny of Korea to live surrounded by enemies. Remember—live. There must be no promises with the Bear, the Shogun, or the Dragon. The proverb says that when whales fight, the shrimp is crushed.

Now the Chinese were in Korea, their massive army replacing the destroyed *inmun-gun;* the dragon had been invited into the house, and who would chase him out?

Nam Ki heard the crunch of boots on crusted snow: Captain Lim making his rounds of advance positions. It seemed the length of dynasties since Lim stood beside him at the Seoul railway station and helped pass judgment upon a pair of deserters. Sam Connover had been right; Lim was fine officer material. Where was Nam Ki's foreign brother now, and was Sam Connover as uncertain about this night? Probably not, for he was one of his country's great heroes. Men such as he were not afraid.

"Sir," Lim said softly, an outline darker than the night.

Nam Ki shrugged deeper into his blanket. "They will come. They are thick out there, the *dwae-nom;* I sense them. How are the outposts, our lines?"

Slowly, sedately as if she had not been dragging her skirt like a careless girl, the moon slid down the sky. Lim said, "We have done what we can, major. I would like more mortar shells, more three-point-twos, more of everything, including soldiers."

"I fear this will always be so," Nam Ki said. "Is there any contact on the right flank?"

Directly ahead, where a humpback mountain stretched across the 11th Regiment's front, a red flare popped high in the air. The color of arterial blood, it drifted by small parachute, shedding droplets as it came toward them.

When Lim swallowed, Nam Ki heard it clearly. But the captain's voice was steady when he answered. "No contact at all. On the left, the American division we have been beside for so long, but the other—"

Nam Ki tilted his head. Far off, the high, mournful notes of a bugle rode the frozen air. Flares, bugles and whistles: the Chinese method of communication in the field, primitive but effective. Now the horde was rising from forty thousand holes, fifty thousand holes that hid them from American planes throughout the day.

"The village we passed through," he said. "What is the name?"

Lim cleared his throat. The air became thinner, impossibly colder. "Not even a village, major; poor rocky farms beside a river full of rocks. It is called Kunu-ri."

Marking that on the map in his head, Nam Ki followed the ridges and broken valleys to the east. From what contacts his radio man had been able to make, and those sparsely, Nam Ki knew that somehow a ninety-mile gap had been left in the lines; ninety open miles that invited the Chinese to smash through and roll up entire divisions, if not the U.S. "Eye" Corps. During his last radio contact with Sam Connover, he had asked about that gap. Sam Connover replied only, "MacArthur." Nam Ki still did not understand.

He said, "A cigarette before the next bugle, while there is yet time." And Lim did not have to be told how to smoke beneath a blanket, ducking his head for each inhalation, making certain the red glow would not become a target for a sniper. To exhale, your head came out of cover, and since you did not see the smoke, the taste was different, flat. Still, a soldier smoked every chance he got; it helped with the drawn-out waiting.

Lim said, please move back to the company command post when the attack begins, and Nam Ki agreed. Sergeant Small Kim clicked the hand switch of his backpack radio and cursed the cold, but under his breath.

"Chagun Kim," Nam Ki said, "follow the captain now. After we reach the hole, try again to contact Ivanhoe—*anybody* at Second Division. Tell them the Chinese are attacking here, and they will be next."

But the mortar shell, running ahead of its warning hiss, exploded upon the listening post and killed Small Kim. It tore the SCR 300 radio in half and drove screams from the two riflemen on duty. Chong Nam Ki stared into a darkness blacker than the night, than any night ever known. He could not feel his skin, and the blackest of blacks ate the edges of his mind.

. . . and then he saw his father coming. Father Chong did not wear the uniform soaked in his blood, and not the western suit he had come to like, but the traditional *hanbok* of an impoverished farmer. . . .

My son, look upon my clothing and see all Korea. On my stained collar is the breath of exhaustion. See the broken string of hemp sandals and ragged socks. A ribbon on my blouse moves in the wind as a prayer of common people who have lived waiting for a thousand years.

"Yes, father," Chong Nam Ki said into the darkness. Gathering strength, he shouted it into the black mouth that was eating his brain: *"Yes, father!"*

. . . and then he could see. Slowly, leaving claw tracks of pain, the darkness withdrew, and Nam Ki did not die . . .

Around him, the night was not so black. He put his hand to his head and found much blood, so he used the bandage from his first aid pouch and bound his head tightly. His hands found a great hole in Small Kim's body, a hole no man could repair. Then he crawled to the riflemen and cared for their wounds. Mortar shells came one after another to rock the gully and the open place behind with gouts of yellow-red light. The air turned thick with flying dirt, with smoke that breathed acrid upon the tongue.

A tiny piece of silence grew until a bugle blared and whistles shrilled. Nam Ki said, "Stand up; we will help each other." His voice made roaring sounds inside his hurt head.

One soldier sagged hard against him. "Surrender—let us surrender—"

"There is no surrender," Nam Ki said.

Oh, shit, Rich Shriver said to his jeep's smeared windshield, and when the next burst of fire stitched along the road and chewed up the six-by ahead, he said to Kim Soo Man: "We leave it here, kid. You understand, damn it? Jump out and follow me. No—oh, hell, no! No food and that carbine of yours? You'll be lucky if the Japs don't shove it up your ass and run the clip."

The road was a mess. Vehicles burned and exploded, and from the ridges on both sides of the narrow valley the enemy poured heavy fire down into the Second Division. Soo Man snatched blankets and the bottle of native booze. "Just the goddamned ammo, you little bastard! Come *on!*"

"No *soju* for you?"

Rich stuffed his field jacket pockets, cursing the icy cold, the stupidity that had sucked this outfit onto a butcher's block, and the kid he should have left away the hell back at Chunju Prison. "No booze. Ain't you got sense enough to know that a soldier can't walk on whiskey? Shit —you ain't smart enough to be scared of them fucking Japs. Hit the ditch!"

"No Japs—fucking Chinese."

Rich grabbed the kid's arm and jumped into the ditch with him. A deuce-and-a-half on the road above them opened fire with the 50 caliber ringed upon the cab. Other bullets chopped the frozen dirt along the lip of the ditch. A heavy explosion shook the earth, and Rich wished for a drink.

Putting his mouth by the kid's ear, he said, "Don't be a smartass. And don't curse. That's the trouble with you slant-eyes; you're smartasses with bad mouths. Don't let me hear you talk bad anymore. You understand, you little shit?"

Jesus; the 50 caliber stopped firing, and all along the road men yelled and other men screamed in agony. A carbine popped slow and uncertain. Rich didn't lift his head above the ditch. He knew the layout: five miles or better of narrow defile, now packed end to end with trucks and tanks, with jeeps and ambulances. Burning vehicles, men dead and wounded and a lot more soon to be; some replacements new to Korea just sitting huddled in the stalled trucks, weapons in their laps, and waiting to be killed, not firing back. They just sat hunched and helpless. Jesus Christ; this had to be the deadliest ambush in the history of the army, worse than Custer and the Seventh Cavalry; more casualties than Bastogne and Corregidor.

Chinese; so damned many Chinks hit the division front before the pullout that you couldn't count them and didn't want to. The black field artillery outfit, the 503rd; Rich had been with them when the first wave came in behind the goddamned bugles. Pinned down with the operator of the dug-in switchboard, Rich scrawled notes in quick and hidden flares of his lighter, hoping he'd be able to decipher them come daylight. Twice, he left the hole and helped Preacher Lindley beat Chinks away from the nearest 155. Then Sergeant Lindley would come back to his switchboard and try to keep communications working. Big-eyed but not panicked, Kim Soo Man had sat quietly in the hole with them. Then and now, Rich wished he had left the kid at division rear, or even back in Seoul.

The firing slacked, and Rich peeped from the ditch. Moving south, long-legged and erect in their old-fashioned uniforms, mustaches proud, men of the Turkish brigade marched past and began to climb the slopes. The Chinks cut them down, but they continued to climb. Rich was sorry for them, so damned sorry that these manhood-proud volunteers were dying because of American high brass stupidity.

"Get out! Take your asses in both hands and get off those damned trucks!" The company commander of Head & Head, 9th Infantry, stalked the road where the bullets wasped by him and *clanged* into the trucks. "You bastards, you heard me! Get down and we'll take to the hills. These trucks aren't going anywhere but to hell!"

Some men listened and clambered over tailgates; some

just pushed farther back into the tarpaulin shadows, not realizing there was no place to hide. Rich nudged the kid. "Come on; we're falling in with this bunch."

Luckily, the planes came then, roaring in just over the ridge tops, firing as they came, loosing rockets as they swerved, wheeling high only to shriek down and lay napalm behind the mountaintops. Good thing, that, Rich thought as they trudged for the skyline and what might wait there. If the 5th Air Force fighters hammered the forward slopes, they'd kill too many GIs; there was no room for near misses.

Rich felt a tug on his sleeve. He was breathing hard already, and his legs were in no kind of shape to hike mountains. If he kept going to wars, he'd have to get into condition. Combat correspondents weren't supposed to fight, but the Chinks didn't know that. No more than the fucking Japs paid attention to the red crosses the medics first wore.

Soo Man tugged again, and Rich's eyes followed his pointing finger. "Horse," the kid said, loud enough to make GIs close by look up. "Chinese horse."

Left hand pressed against the small of his back, Rich stared at the skyline to the south, where a long column of horsemen moved in the open. Peering hard, he could make out fur hats and shaggy ponies. Cavalry in quilted uniforms, horses moving faster than the stunned gaggles of U.N. troops trying to make it out to safety.

"They're tearing our asses, laddie buck," he said. "Now save your strength."

So damned cold, with steel-edge winds sawing at your skin and swirling into any gap in your clothes. The shoe paks issued for cold weather could not breathe through the outer rubber, and inside, Rich's sweating feet ground their toes together, the socks building blisters. The planes came again, this time gull-winged Corsairs off a carrier, and low enough to make Soo Man duck. But the Chinks had been dug in for a while; they'd had time to burrow deep and to cover some gun positions. How long had they been here, waiting? Long enough to set up the perfect roadblock; probably ever since the division moved through this same valley of death going north, despite China's warnings.

Valley of death, appropriate as hell and a good slug line for his story, if he ever got to write one. Sorry, boss, no pictures. That Speed Graphic was just too damned heavy for anybody in a hurry. Sorry, Turks; you were too damned brave. Thinking bravery brought Sam Connover to mind, and Rich wondered if Sam and Stonewall were still running their own little army, still attached, in a loose fashion, to the 38th Infantry. He hadn't seen them since their short vacation in the Seoul cathouse.

Led by the 9th Infantry captain, the column reached the ridge top without being fired on. Rich pulled the kid close and kneeled with him beside a leaning boulder. "Ain't you got no sense, laddie buck? Stay off the fucking skyline. If the GIs don't pop you one, the Chinks will."

Automatic weapons opened up to the column's rear, and everybody hit the dirt, but Rich realized no fire was coming their way. He got to one knee, his carbine propped. How many men followed the captain—less than a hundred? Some lay flat in exhaustion, and some drank from precious bottles of hoarded whiskey. Rich saw one man loading extra banana clips for his carbine. Wind howled out of Manchuria and razored at the ridge, and a scrub pine, twisted and tired, shed its last needles.

The captain waved his M-1 rifle and called out, "Saddle up and move out! More Chinks are coming—look back along the ridge."

There they were, tall bastards in fuzzy hats and purple padded uniforms. They didn't fire into the valley or across at the column; they just kept coming. Gunfire raked the road, and burning trucks sent thick spirals of black smoke into the air. Rich could smell burned oil. Not blood, damn it, just oil and powder smoke. Maybe there was an odor to panic and defeat, but high on the ridge with the cold wind blowing, Rich couldn't smell that.

Nobody stopped until they dipped into a valley and then struggled up the next slope. Then some men fell out, especially those who carried bottles. The column was drawn out now, snaking over the ridge and out of sight below, leaving pieces of itself behind. Rich plodded on, reaching out from time to time so he might help Kim Soo Man up a steep place.

Once everyone rested, gasping the icy air that left their lungs to drift like tiny shrouds. The wind blew, and Rich could hear a man crying. It didn't sound out of place. Hunkered down, he saw half a hoofprint in snowy clay, and horse apples where they had rolled downhill. He moved his feet and listened to the squish. Jesus, if only he hadn't been so quick to leave his combat boots for these damned blister makers. This time, some stragglers didn't rejoin the column when it moved on.

Soo Man said, "What matter them, Rich?"

Shifting his carbine strap, Rich said, "Easier to quit than to keep on. Same kind of soldiers that couldn't make it back from a field problem; too tired, cramps, blisters, anything to keep from walking. The ambulances used to pick them up. Here there ain't ambulances and nobody to beg them to please come on."

Soo Man walked beside him. "They die. Fucking Chinks kill."

"You better Hong Kong believe it, and I told you about that bad mouth. When we get out of this shitstorm, I mean to flog your ass."

Time was wind and ice and climbing up, sliding down, so it might have been three hours or six when a Chinese patrol caught up and fired on them. Throwing the kid down, Rich sprawled between him and a blue puff of smoke rising from behind a rock. Putting the carbine sights atop that big rock, Rich waited, his ungloved hand freezing. A Chink fired to his left flank, another to his right front. Farther up on the ridge, an M-1 threw back its two-beat answer—*ka-chung! ka-chung!* The captain, Rich figured; the man was a field commander. He must have screwed up somewhere, to be given a headquarters company, but Rich was thankful for him. If they made it out, he'd write a big story on the guy—duty, honor, and country. Where the hell was Sam Connover? That crazy bastard ought to know his luck couldn't hold forever.

Ah; the fucking Jap lifted his head over the rock, and Rich put a bullet through his face. Two more came around the rock very fast, running low to the earth like jackals. Rich triggered a short burst at the bastard on the left, and the other fired as he came, his bullet throwing icy dirt into Rich's eyes. At his right ear, a carbine went *whack! whack!* and the Chink slammed into the ground, so close that Rich smelled him.

Wiping dirt from his face, Rich leapt up and caught Soo Man's arm. "Haul ass!"

Jesus Christ; eleven years old and just killed his first man. Worse, the little bastard was smiling about it. Then Rich remembered Chunju Prison, and the kid with blood all over one side of his head, sitting there in the midst of hundreds of swelling corpses, fanning flies off the beaten faces of his murdered mother and father. And Rich thought that the homegrown communists had made a major mistake. Kim Soo Man would make no distinction; imported or homegrown, he meant to make them pay.

Time blurred with pain and fatigue; time's destroyer was the cold, now chopping down, now jeering wind, and twice more the column survivors had to turn and fight off their pursuers. Rich staggered and didn't try to shake off Soo Man's support.

Then the captain labored up the last hill and turned to yell through cupped hands. "Come on, you bastards! We made it! There's our tanks—oh, those beautiful sons of bitches—our tanks!"

Half an hour later, wobbled into a CP of the 72nd Tank Battalion, sucking on a cup of coffee as if it were the best whiskey, he found there was no radio traffic open and no phone lines reaching back to I Corps. The story could wait; MacArthur would sit on it, anyhow. Rich would make book that Tokyo headquarters would try to make the bloody debacle into some kind of Dunkirk retreat victory. That was bullshit, because the casualties—uncounted as yet—couldn't be hidden.

A few minutes later, he found a master sergeant who knew about Sam Connover. "Him and that big black guy? Got them some tough gooks? Yeah—I seen them all away back in the valley. Lost my tank there and bugged out on foot; damned near froze. This shitty cold ain't for me, son. I'm from Mississippi, a little town called Shubuta. You *Stars & Stripes* guys send stories anywhere?"

Rich's eyes were gritty, and he was out of coffee. When the sergeant offered a smoke, Rich took it. His hand was slow, but he slapped a cigarette out of Soo Man's fingers. "Connover," he said to the sergeant, and had to wait for an answer until his ears stopped ringing from the rapid slamming of tank guns as some observer found a way to clobber Chinese troops and keep an escape route open for the Second Division.

"Connover, damn it! Where the hell is he now?"

"Can't be certain sure," the sergeant said, digging at his ear with a dirty finger, "but last time I seen that bunch, they was digging in as rear guard so part of the 38th could come out. I'd say Connover's fire brigade has had it. Just too damned many Chinks."

"Oh, Christ," Rich whispered, and squeezed the small hand that Kim Soo Man slipped into his.

CHAPTER 20

Kunu-ri, North Korea, Dec. 1, 1950—The U.S. Second Division is badly mauled by Chinese hordes that poured over the frozen Yalu River into Korea and down through a ninety-mile gap left in U.N. lines. On the east coast, U.S. Marines are being ground up at Changjin Reservoir. The Second Division can no longer be considered a fighting unit.

화약을 지고 불로 들어간다.

"Carry gunpowder and walk into a fire." (Korean proverb: A suicidal adventure.)

Sam winced as the empty shell casing slapped his shoulder and watched other 50 caliber brass skip and bounce over the slope. On its last strafing run the navy Corsair arched up and over the ridge, and he envied its flight. Maybe he envied its armament more. If his outfit had all that firepower here on the ground, some of them might get out of this valley. He doubted that, though. Half the Chinese in the world swarmed along the road below, and no organized resistance was left—if there had ever been any.

What a mess; an overwhelming, inexcusable defeat for the Eighth Army and the U.N. But what the hell, sergeants didn't make high-level command decisions. But this foul-

up offended his military sense, the rightness that was basic
to his soldiering.

Smoke rose from truck after truck, and oily black from
burning tanks, but most vehicles had been abandoned intact. Chinese troops were pillaging those now, shouting in
triumph and waving blankets, ripping the guts from sleeping bags, emptying ration boxes and spinning them into the
fires.

In the hole with Sam, Stonewall Jackson muttered,
"Ain't that a bitch? Maybe Joe Chink will eat himself to
death."

"I wish they'd find a hundred cases of whiskey. Then we
could walk down and knock them in the head. As it is, we
hold fire until they start around the curve."

Jackson set carbine clips in a row along the rim of their
hole. "I ain't anxious to call attention up here. But you
better check the ROKs; they're real edgy."

Sam nodded and gave the order in Korean to be passed
along the line: Do not fire until I do.

Through the sights of his M-1 he followed an officer
along the road. Chinese officers didn't sport red shoulder
tabs, and the big brass dressed in plain, peasant blue, with
no insignia of rank. This one gave orders, pointing here
and there with authority. Sam was glad for the looters; they
gave a little more time to the 38th Infantry stragglers scuff-
ing along beyond the bend, beaten and dispirited.

Somebody in that outfit had screwed up; if they'd taken
the east branch of the road, they'd have made it home.
They took the west fork and headed right into the inferno
of Kunu-ri because some officer misread a map or couldn't
find one.

The fire brigade had gotten one break. When Sam
steered his jeep into the ditch and led them in a charge up
the slope, the convoy was still trying to ride out of the
ambush, the troops reluctant to leave their transport. The
Chinese were concentrating fire upon the trucks, and Sam's

bunch reached the ridge to flank and chop down a squad in their prepared holes. The bodies lay outside on the icy ground, and Sam's people occupied the position.

He had taken one long and sweeping look at the tactical situation and knew they were lost. They'd started the retreat too far back in the column, and the Chinese were too efficient; pouring out of the hills, they had moved too fast. Cut off, Sam's little outfit had the choice of dying on the road or hanging tough up here and covering for the stragglers. Either way, they had bought it, but no man tried to run and hide. Lighting a cigarette, Sam glanced along his line and approved. He was damned proud of these guys and only sorry that he had drawn them into this moment.

From the time he had taken the oath on his first enlistment, his destiny had pointed him to this place and led him to this time. Of course it had to happen in Korea; ashes to ashes, from birth to death and the mystic circle completing itself; the dragon eating its tail, Yin and Yang. It made as much sense as the proprietary religion his father expounded from the white man's pulpit at Chunju.

Hey, *Moksa*—hey, reverend: Your errant son won't even rate a mass grave. They'll loot us and leave us where we fall to make the magpies fat. Maybe you left a prayer behind for us, but it won't take, Reverend Connover. Too many unregenerate heathens are here, Koreans who hold to their own gods. And nobody will be able to tell us apart, anyhow.

It was so damned cold. The air was sharp and clear, but for the smoke and the stench. Down there, more than the trucks were burning; so was human flesh. A truckload of wounded GIs crisped in a gasoline bath. The blue-uniformed officer had applied the match.

Jackson said, "Preachers been wrong. Hell ain't hot; it's all ice and freezing wind."

"Some sulfur and brimstone on the road," Sam said. "I'm holding one of the bosses in my sights. Sorry, Matt; you could have been in Tokyo."

"Sorry for me being here? Shee-it, man; I knew you were crazy and could have cut out any time. Tokyo—man, I'd be fucked out and fucked up. Never could stand spit-shining my boots. Made it like I worked at the Chattanooga Choo Choo. Hey, boy—give me a shine! But, Sam, we gave the bastards some badass rounds, didn't we?"

"From bell to bell," Sam said, and braced his elbows in the cold dirt. He thought of Maggi Barron, not of bugles and drums, but of Maggi. Before her, no woman had ever intruded upon combat. He'd never be able to soldier and be all he should to Maggi. Even if he had the chance to live with Maggi, he could not become a civilian. Smiling into the cold, cold wind, Sam thought that wasn't a problem now.

Forcing her from mind, he thought of Kelly Connover. Kelly was always a soldier, the roaring boy-o who told wonderful stories, tales of gunsmoke and hookers and exotic ports. Kelly Connover, who had at the end come to die with the only family he had.

The Irish, me boy; so sentimental we are. Don't ask me what happened to your father's humanity. He left it at the Orangeman's altar. Don't let it happen to you, lad. There's a wondrous world beyond this arsehole of creation, and love beyond words in a book.

The wages of sin, said the reverend; strong drink and harlots have brought you to an early grave. Now you attempt to poison my son's mind. Samuel is to take up the burden and become a man of God.

"There goes their point," Jackson said, "scarfing C-rations. Die with full bellies, anyhow. Do we wait on the main body?"

Sam zeroed in on the officer waving his troops away from the trucks and on down the road. "As beat up as those

GIs are, a handful of Chinks could finish them. Might as well let them know we're here." Then he shot the Chink—low in the belly—for striking the match.

Disciplined soldiers that they were, the fire brigade opened up with careful, spaced shots, and the mountain ridge didn't seem as cold. This side of the road curve, men twisted and fell. Some milled uncertainly until other bullets cut them down. Sam breathed the familiar tang of gunsmoke and settled to the slow thump of the M-1's butt plate against his shoulder. He was into his second clip before return fire reached up the hill. Then it came heavy from the road and accurate from ambush positions across the valley. Mortars set up behind the trucks and finned shells hissed down upon the ridge.

Slam! Pebbled dirt slashed across Sam's hole; Jackson said *shee-it!* after each explosion, and Sam's ears hurt. A hot needle stung his cheek. "Here they come," he said, knowing that nobody could hear him or needed to.

Spreading up the slope, they climbed as skirmishers under covering fire from mortars and machine guns. Sam picked off one man standing erect and another crawling up a steep place. A bullet kicked dirt in his face, and the skirmish line folded upon itself, leaving huddled brown lumps.

Slam! Slam! The mortars came *shushing* down again, and the ridge bucked, the foxholes vanishing in geysers of flame and dirt. Another line of Chinese climbed the slope. Sam worked inward from the advancing right flank until two more empty clips leapt from his M-1. This line also crumbled, but one man crawled close enough to heave a grenade.

"You making it okay?" Jackson asked. "If you got both hands left, you might plug me up."

Working swiftly, Sam dusted and bandaged, stopping the leak in Jackson's left shoulder and wiping the gash in his cheek. He had a moment then to yell for a head count, and his stomach knotted when so few men answered. The mortars were doing their work well, and peering through smoke, Sam thought he saw the shadows of men approaching along the ridge. The position was being flanked, and a third line of infantry plodded up the slope, burpgunners firing as they climbed, riflemen aiming, firing, and working the bolts on their long guns and carbines. Their leaders didn't give a damn how many men they lost; they'd never run out of peasants.

A grenade thumped on the edge of Sam's hole, and he reached out to throw it back. It exploded downhill, but something hacked him viciously across his right forearm, and something steely axed his forehead. He fell back in the hole, and the light dimmed.

Sam . . . the voice was far away, garbling from a well of darkness . . . Sam . . . and Hill 409 in Tunisia was dark, too—the Krauts laying in those bastardly 88s—who died there?—Jo-Jo and the kid from Tennessee . . . Sam! . . .

Blinking fast, he got his eyes open, and Jackson helped him from the hole. Chinese were all around them, bulky in winter uniforms, slant eyes peeping from beneath ear-flap hats, Chinese behind ready burpguns and rifles with long bayonets. Flat-faced they were, with brown lemon skin and dirty hands. None of them glanced at their dead comrades scattered down the slope and all the way up to the foxholes. They stared at Sam and Jackson and the two wounded ROKs who were left of the fire brigade.

In a floppy blue uniform of cheap, dyed cotton, the officer pushed through his men. His hand chopped the air toward the sitting ROKs, and he said something abrupt in Chinese. Sam flinched and hung onto Jackson when the burpgunner stepped out and killed both Koreans.

Into the echoes, Sam said as loud as he could: "You son of a bitch."

The officer looked hard-eyed at Sam and Jackson, pointed, and rapped out another order.

Julian couldn't control his hands. If he tried to light a smoke, everyone would see him shake. A 9th Infantry CO had been shipped back to the ZI when he began flinching at every sudden noise, and Julian wasn't about to go home; not yet, and maybe not ever. What the hell did he have to go back to? Maggi hadn't written in months, and for all he knew she could be filing divorce papers in Honolulu. As if she were the injured party; as if she could deny their life together by hiding in her old home.

Charley Heath passed him a lighted cigarette, and Julian said thanks. He tried to return to Maggi, but when the regimental commander walked into the old Jap schoolhouse south of the Han River, Maggi wasn't that special. Important, yes—but not mind-numbing. Julian had enough going on in his head. And when everybody sat down again, Colonel Peploe stood straight and neat at a makeshift dais.

"Holy mother," Julian whispered, not meaning to say anything, but since Kunu-ri, words popped out of him at odd moments. He took the cigarette out of his mouth and his hand shook, spilling ash on his OD pants, dropping a spark. Heath slapped it away and laid a hand on Julian's shoulder.

"Easy," Heath said.

The colonel spoke in a strong, even voice. He wasn't a tall man, but he made you think so. He had a reputation for scaring hell out of regimental headquarters people by setting up his CP on ground that hadn't been taken yet. Julian dropped his cigarette and tucked his hands into his field jacket. He tried to concentrate upon every word, but only the figures stuck. Holy mother of Christ—he wasn't certain he had heard correctly. So many lost, each individual the toll of a death bell: six thousand, eight hundred and forty casualties from the division at Kunu-ri.

And Julian was to blame for some of them. Sharp, by-the-book Julian Barron, hotshot on field problems at the Academy, had blown it at the ambush. He didn't know how it happened. Two roads on the map, and he led his battalion down the wrong one. He fed his men into the holocaust because for that one confused moment, he let it all get away from him.

". . . three quarters of our rolling stock," the colonel went on, "all our field pieces and most of the division doctors. Eighth Army has classified the Second Division as unfit for combat. But we *will* be fit, gentlemen, and damned soon. This regiment will stand ready sooner than anyone believes possible, including you commanders. Get . . . it . . . done. Dismissed."

Charley Heath sighed. "I think I'd rather face Joe Chink. That man means business."

Standing up as the room emptied of officers, Julian said, "I'll go see the colonel and try to explain."

"Explain what? Everybody screwed up, everybody. We're liable to do it again."

"Six thousand men—oh, my God."

Heath nudged him toward the door. "Come on; we have to hustle our own replacements, if that means bribing the first soldier at the repple depple or kidnapping. Liberate a few vehicles from rear echelon outfits, raid ordnance companies for weapons—get the jump on everybody. Peploe damned well means what he said. He'll whip the Chinks next time out if we have to throw rocks. I'd rather it be mortar shells."

Julian allowed himself to be led to the three-quarter that

was the only wheels for his headquarters. He couldn't shake his depression. But as he locked his fingers tightly together, his hands didn't shake. He wanted to cry, to hide his head, to go to confession. Do not bless me, father, for my sins are too heavy. You cannot absolve me, for I cannot forgive myself.

CHAPTER 21

Tokyo, Japan, Dec. 10, 1950—General Douglas MacArthur asks permission to bomb Red China and to unleash half a million of Chiang Kai-shek's troops from Formosa. President Truman denies permission.

정들었다고 정주지 마라.

"Do not tell even a close friend your true feelings."
(Korean proverb: Today's friend may be tomorrow's enemy.)

He accepted the Chinese because he must; Ho Chuk Gun did not show his displeasure because he must not. Their officers acted as if he were not here, as if he and his men were not worthy of notice. *Chang-mal,* they were so few, compared to the Chinese many, but also, in truth, the Koreans were better soldiers. The *chung-guk* depended upon greater numbers to overwhelm the enemy, and upon capturing enemy food and ammunition if the battle lasted more than three days.

They were such animals, the lower ranks, uneducated and dull-eyed. Caring only for their warmth and bellies, they knew nothing of communism or the reason they had been sent to Korea. Yet a political officer told Chuk Gun that these peasants were better off in the army than if left to scratch their poor fields and slowly starve.

Since this army of Mao Tse-dung did not speak Korean or Japanese, they had brought Koreans with them as interpreters, Koreans who lived in Manchuria for generations and acted like foreigners themselves, speaking with a heavy singsong accent. Chuk Gun liked them even less than the arrogant Chinese.

When the *inmun-gun* was rebuilt and refitted, there would be a problem getting the Chinese out of Korea. Drawing a deep breath, Chuk Gun strode from the headquarters hut, happy to be returning to his own unit, his own kind. His rank entitled him to command a regiment, but there was less than a battalion to lead.

Still, they were Koreans, and mostly men who had only remained in China long enough to be regrouped, men who kept their uniforms and their honor. Some among them had been caught by the military police and returned to duty, and some were young boys rounded up and brought to the army for the first opportunity to prove their dedication.

In time this unit would regain the face lost when the People's Army almost dissolved under constant bombing and strafing by U.N. planes. When all Korea was secured, the flat-faced peasants from the Middle Country would have to get out. Too many times, they had come raiding into Korea for treasure, but more often for women. Korean women were long known for their beauty and obedience, and the Khans, the Manchus, and Mongols rode in to take them by force.

Moving into his own small hut on the back slope of an unnamed farm community, Chuk Gun inclined his head to return the deep bow of his aide. On the folding camp table, part of much equipment abandoned by the cowardly Americans in the north, sat a carton of foreign cigarettes and cans of rich food. He took a cigarette and allowed the lieutenant to light it.

"Tonight we return to Seoul," he announced. "I would have attacked much sooner, but these uneducated soldiers—"

"I understand, sir," Lt. Che Sun Ap said. "Shall I prepare the evening meal?"

Nodding, Chuk Gun returned to the hut door and stared out at the low, rolling hills between him and Seoul. He would attack from a different route this time, and Intelligence said the city was almost empty and would not be defended. Chuk Gun hoped enemy troops would try to keep him out. He needed to show these superior Chinese how well Koreans fought. His aide pumped and lighted a gasoline stove, another gift of the fleeing *Me-in,* and Chuk Gun heard cans being opened. Too much foreign food could make you ill, and he thought to find rice and *kimchi* in Seoul.

Thinking of beautiful Korean women made him moody, and twilight coming to soften the hills made the feeling worse. A-jah had been beautiful. He listened to his battalion come alive, waiting only for the full cloak of night to come from hiding into the open. Soon they would ready themselves for the drive into the city, eating hurriedly and seeing to their weapons. The foreign airplanes could not stop them at night.

A-jah, he thought, as beautiful and graceful as a flower. He was young then, denying his dignity so that he might not be noticed by the cruel Japanese, being less than human day by day, so that he might feast upon A-jah in the gentle nights. Ah, yes, she was beautiful, and only slowly did Chuk Gun come to understand the curse of such loveliness. No squat and heavily muscled farm girl, his A-jah, but a young woman of high family who had even attended middle school. How fortunate he was that such a woman accepted him.

And how quickly fortune changed. He had thought that none of the old ways could be good, for had they not brought the island dwarfs to stalk the conquered land? But there was also the ancient custom that said a woman should deny her beauty, that she should not keep a mirror in the house, lest she be tempted by willful pride to stand preening before her looking glass instead of caring for her husband and home. A-jah should have disguised her beauty and not attracted the Japanese captain.

"It is ready, sir," Chuk Gun's aide said.

Sugared coffee and beans with shreds of meat, hot and foreign. Chuk Gun used a brass spoon he had carried for months; the Americans put so much water into their food that the spoon was better to use than chopsticks. He had stopped being hungry when he first thought of his wife, and she intruded upon him now.

The filthy Japanese, forcing himself into A-jah's slim, warm body in Chuk Gun's small house; unwise woman for not telling her husband. Chuk Gun could not help knowing, for the Japanese captain bragged, and Ho Chuk Gun became an object of ridicule. Of course he left the city and slaved in the rice paddies owned by other men, but the shame did not go away, and slowly the righteous anger grew stronger, its edge sharp and clean.

The gods were good, for when the war ended and the Japanese waited, defeated, for orders from their conquerors, Chuk Gun came home. He came silently in from the back-breaking fields to take his revenge.

The island dwarfs were always so intent upon samurai steel, shining honor, and *seppuku* that they could hardly be shocked when Chuk Gun killed the captain with a farm knife. Especially since he had used the proper gutting strokes: in, up, and across, but with no swordsman standing by to relieve the agony with a single slash. The officer had taken a long time to die.

Not so with A-jah, for although he had the right, Chuk

Gun had not the heart to draw out her deserved death. Her eyes, deep and afraid, widened at him when he stalked toward her, the dripping knife in his hand.

It was not my fault, she breathed. He took me with his strength and kept me prisoner because he is Japanese and therefore our master. I did not want him, my husband. I did not tell you because he would have you killed. It was not my fault.

As in the Chosun dynasty days, he said, you should have made yourself ugly so you would not be desired. Failing that, you should have killed yourself to protect my honor and your own. It is the custom; it was your duty.

Closing her eyes then, kneeling demurely upon the *ondol* in the proper position for a woman, she waited for her death. Chuk Gun did not shut his eyes when he stabbed his wife in the heart but looked into the pale oval of her face.

Rich Shriver said, fuck it, and left Korea. He left his jeep and the kid with the Second Division Public Information Office. Captain Duke Davis could be trusted to care for both. More so than Rich, anyhow. PIO gave him a lift to a muddy landing strip where an L-6 spotter plane took him to Taegu and a Crashmaster flight for Tokyo's Haneda airport. He was short of pictures, but he carried a thick sheaf of stories that were fact and fiction. He knew to clean up facts that were too gory or defeatist, knew when to embroider. He was sick of both truths and lies, and at times since the bloody mess at Kunu-ri, he'd been unable to tell the difference.

The flight sergeant on the C-47 had two bottles of Canadian Club to swap for the Russian carbine Rich had brought along for just such an emergency. So the trip wasn't bad, considering that flying scared the shit out of him, and considering that no amount of good stateside booze could drown Kim Soo Man's face. What more could the little bastard want of him? Rich Shriver wasn't daddy material, or husband either; Saint Teresa could attest to that.

Damn it; the kid would be okay with division PIO, better than all right because he wouldn't get dragged into danger or feel he was forced to hold onto a drunk in order to survive. As best he could, Rich explained all that before he left, tried to tell Soo Man that *Stars & Stripes* insisted that he come back to Japan. Yes, the kid said, yes, I understand—but he didn't. He stood big-eyed and fighting tears as Rich moved off alone.

Not Rich's fault, unless he should have left the kid in that stinking prison yard, fanning blowflies from his dead parents. It was nobody's damn fault, just the way of the world and especially the style of a war, when any decency got blown all to hell.

He drank, seated upon rolled canvas and parachutes in the long, dark body of the flying freight car. And he thought that Teresa might not have remarried, that at least she owed him a long talk. The plane dropped into an air pocket, and Rich took another drink. She didn't owe him the time of day; nobody owed anyone.

Look at Sam Connover; the whole nation was supposed to be indebted to Sam: above and beyond the call of duty; one of the gloried few. The nation paid off Sam with a medal and a pretty ribbon, and now because great leaders just couldn't stay out of other wars, he was MIA—missing in action. Fighting a rear-guard action with his faithful ROKs and Stonewall Jackson, he was left in Massacre Valley, that miserable fucking Kunu-ri. Twenty below zero and a high wind-chill factor; MIA meant dead and bodies never to be recovered. Even if Sam had somehow been taken prisoner, which Rich doubted, it might be worse on him as soon as the Chinks found out he was a hero. They'd make propaganda hay out of his medal, show him off like a zoo animal, and maybe, after squeezing him dry of PR value, put him on trial as a war criminal.

Mumbling to himself, then crawling beneath the canvas for warmth, Rich dozed, holding fast to his bottles. And when he left the plane, clean-shaven kids in starched, pressed uniforms stared at him. He was a peasant in aristocrat country, grimy and wild-looking with his taped-clips carbine, his booze and cruddy OD bag. But hell, two bottles of booze made him rich.

"Rich as I'll ever get," he muttered, which caused the staff car driver to hurry their trip even more. The slant-eyed *banzai* bastard could take the edge off a man's drunk that way, weaving in and out of Tokyo traffic with his foot on the floor and one hand on the horn. His mellow buzz ruined, Rich took his bag from the car and leaned over the driver.

"Did they ever tell you that Tojo was queer?"

Then he wandered across the small parking lot and into the building that housed *Stars & Stripes, Pacific*. Half an hour later he discovered how much chickenshit it housed, as well. He was to get a haircut ASAP; what the hell did he mean, bringing a loaded weapon here? And why didn't he bring the up-to-date trip ticket for the S&S jeep?

It was some better in Editorial, where they sort of appreciated his stories, although most of them were dated, they said. No matter now; they were sending his replacement to Korea tomorrow.

". . . and you'll want to get a haircut," the major said.

"As soon as possible," Rich said, "yes, sir."

Then he went outside to the parking lot and stole the staff car that had brought him here. Maybe the driver would commit hara-kiri, he thought, and sucked one-handed at a bottle while he figured how to get back to Haneda airport. Now he knew why he'd stayed away so long; it wasn't the fucking Japs so much as the rear echelon troopers.

Give me two armies, von Clausewitz had said—one all spit and polish to look great on the parade ground, and the other grimy and grisly to do the fighting. Never the twain should meet.

Rich tried to give the staff car to a blue-uniformed Jap guard at the airport, and while the bowlegged little shit was trying to figure out his "presento," Rich flashed his press card at a disinterested Air Force pilot and climbed aboard another C-47 aimed for the Land of the Morning Calm. Fuck them all; any replacement would play hell finding the *S&S* jeep. Rich would recover it and have the numbers switched before any journalism major in a clean uniform discovered the difference between his ass and his elbow.

"Going back to work for Second Division PIO," he announced to cases piled the length of the plane. "Let Duke Davis confuse the brass at *Stars & Stripes;* them and their goddamn barbers."

He was out of booze and crawled atop a section of the strapped-down cases and crates to nap awhile. Lying on his back, he stared at the cabin ceiling close over him and told himself that Kim Soo Man had nothing to do with Rich Shriver heading back to Korea. He couldn't fuck around with shoeshines and yessirs while Sam Connover and Stonewall Jackson were carried as MIA. If the bodies were found, or eyewitnesses who saw them fall, then Rich might find another plane—one to take him all the way stateside and to hell with the fucking army and every slant-eyed son of a bitch in the world.

Anyhow, the kid would be glad to see him and needed somebody to make him keep his head down when the shooting started. That didn't mean Rich was taking him to raise, the little bastard.

Sighing, he turned onto his side and stared down at lettering inches from his nose, white letters across brown cardboard: LORD CALVERT. Holy shit! He was riding a planeload of fine whiskey, the army's Class Six being delivered to Korea's deserving troops.

He sat up and used his carbine barrel to pop a binding and liberate a bottle. "Damn," he said, "who claimed I ain't ever going to be rich?"

CHAPTER 22

Seoul, Republic of Korea, Jan. 4, 1951—This battered city was captured by Chinese communist forces today. U.N. and ROK troops are strung out along the south side of the Han River.

번개가 자지면 천둥을
한다 .

"If lightning flashes, thunder follows." (Korean proverb: Signs show coming events.)

He knew he was somewhere in Yongdung-po, south of the Han River and beyond reach of the Chinese in Seoul—for the moment. But Chong Nam Ki also knew the folding over of images, as a rice paper screen folds to be put away. Sometimes the window in the converted schoolhouse allowed the thin sun to crawl inside; at other times people and scenes smeared across the painting like a rag and cleaned it of the window, the hospital, and Nam Ki himself.

This Nam Ki dissolved into other Nam Kis gone before and the stooped graybeard to come. The young ones were solid; he could feel the rush of their excitement and know the leaping eagerness of muscle and expanding mind. The old figure was shadowy, and when Nam Ki extended a trembling hand, he felt only the chill of winter.

His head throbbed, but he sat up on the folded quilt, bracing his hands in order to remain erect. The mortars; always the mortars. Nam Ki flinched at the evil hiss of an incoming shell and lost his balance. On his back again, he awaited the explosion that never came. Of course there was no explosion; he was in a field hospital, and the Chinese had not attempted a river crossing.

"Ah, colonel; you are awake. Is there much pain?"

He did not recognize the man; not of the 11th Regiment, for certain. "How long—*wee-sa?*"

The man signaled to a woman who came to kneel beside him. "Not a doctor, Colonel Chong, only a medical student. We have so few qualified men left—the *han-yak* first, then prepare the needles."

Nam Ki closed his eyes as they lifted him, and the brass bowl pressed his lips. Black steam surged into his head through his nostrils, and his stomach rumbled. There was no bitterness like that of the boiled-herbs potion used by doctors and shaman for a thousand years. Nam Ki choked on the hot, stinging liquid and barely won the battle with his stomach.

Easing him back, the man said, "Yes; I would prefer penicillin, but the Americans guard their supplies well. Nurse, careful with the colonel's head as we place him upon his side."

The turpentine rag drew across stretched paper, and the lines of painting blurred. By closing his right eye, Nam Ki could see movement in fog that drifted mournful willow trees.

> With her basket hung on a bare branch,
> Where has my maiden gone?

The silky haze
Glimmers about the branch.

The blind fortune teller told them long ago, squatted in his tiny house in the Miari district as candles flickered; his voice like dried leaves blowing along Myongdong street. He whispered to them of sadness and impossible love. But in their hearts they already knew, and had only been hoping for intervention by some compassionate god.

". . . Nam Ki! My brother . . . Nam Ki?"

He recognized the voice, but it was silly to think that his younger brother would be at the fortune teller's; Wei Ki was only a child. Besides, he might tell Father Chong of the *kisaeng* girl.

Nam Ki opened his left eye and peered upward past the acupuncture needles in his head. "How did you find us, Wei Ki? Foolish child, to be upon the streets so late. Ah— did you bring my *saju*, so that the blind man may know more through the four pillars of my life? Perhaps the hour, day, month, and year of my birth will change fate."

Never, said the fortune teller; the fate of both is written in the woman's destiny; never.

Written? Nam Ki snarled; written? Blind man, how can you read?

I read the wind, aristocrat; I listen to the stars, *yangban*.

". . . older brother, do you know me? I am here."

"Yes," Nam Ki said. "Our mother, our sister—are they well? Why have you left them alone in Pusan?"

The boy sat beside the folded quilts, his young face tight with worry. "The orphans are safe in Taegu with our mother and sister. Taegu is the American Eighth Army headquarters, where food and medicines are easier had."

Having difficulty with his eyes, Nam Ki got them focused and frowned at his younger brother. "*Tong-saeng*, you wear a uniform."

"Yes, it is my duty, especially since you have been wounded. I can take your place when you go to our mother."

The canvas wavered, shimmered, drab colors sliding one into another. Nam Ki concentrated upon holding them steady, upon making all around him solid. "My place, boy? Even as I slept, I was promoted to colonel. You—you are a lowly lieutenant. My place, you would take? I command the regiment. I remain in command. Return to Taegu."

Wei Ki shook his head. "I am the lowest of officers, but I *am* an officer. To honor our father's memory, I must fight."

Nam Ki wanted to hold his brother close, wanted to explain what the 11th Regiment meant to the country and to its leader. Instead, he said—as acupuncture needles ached in his neck—"You are assigned to my regiment?"

"As I requested, older brother."

There should be no intrusions now, but Nam Ki saw the palace garden and eyes softer than a summer midnight; he smelled the lotus.

"The war has moved to the west," his brother said. "The Chinese do not risk crossing the Han, but Wonju is attacked, and the enemy is moving down upon Chipyong-ni."

The nurse came back and stooped over Nam Ki. He heard her say something to his brother, but the words crumbled upon themselves. When next he opened his eyes, the needles had been removed and he was rolled upon his back. The sun was gone, but a candle flickered close.

"Wei Ki?"

"I am here."

"Our foreign brother—what of Sam Connover?"

Wei Ki shifted upon the floor where he sat cross-legged. "Gone. His name has not come out of the north. I have asked at the *Me-in* headquarters. I have said prayers for his spirit."

Pain slashed through Nam Ki's head. "No."

Wei Ki sat quietly, and Nam Ki said it again: "No. If he was taken prisoner, it would not be known yet. This is a great soldier."

"A small dagger may bring down a dragon."

Against his eyelids, Nam Ki watched the slow dance of the candle beside his bed. Wha Ja danced like that, with slow grace, moving the long sleeves of her dress like the wings of circling butterflies. Wha Ja was light and warmth. Sam Connover was a brother, and a brother was closer than a woman, however beautiful.

He said, "I will rise from this *chimtae*. I am not killed and will not believe It of Sam Connover. I will rise and lead my men again."

"Yes," Wei Ki murmured.

And this time, when Nam Ki stared into the palace garden, its earth moved beneath him, and he had to hold tightly to a tree to keep from falling off the world.

A pair of flat-faced guards held Matt Jackson in the doorway. One kicked him behind the knees, and the other slammed a rifle butt between his shoulders. He pitched forward onto the floor, and they backed out, jerking the papered door shut.

Sam had been waiting, legs stretched out and his back against the wall, hoping that Stonewall Jackson would make it back to the hut before the Chinks threw him in the Hole. In midwinter a man had to be prepared before his first trip, or he wouldn't come back. Finally they were getting around to all the colored guys, understanding at last that they didn't buy that Progressive crap.

Drawing in his feet, Sam had only to lean out and touch Matt. The room wasn't that big, but nobody else moved; nobody came from the other rooms to see how Jackson made it through interrogation. The lethargy was getting worse. Although two other men lay along the walls, their faces were turned away, and only old Smitty sat up to watch.

Body jerking and shoulders shaking, Jackson rolled onto his back. Sam said, "You crazy bastard—you're laughing!"

Coming to his knees on the hard clay floor, Matt showed gray at the corners of his mouth and blood seeping from over his right eye where old scar tissue had built up. "Man, it was funny. Joe Chink trying to jive. Shee-it, you fays fuck it up good, but you got to *hear* a Chink."

Smitty's floppy hands slid from his blue quilted jacket, making uncertain motions like dark and crippled birds. "Slide your laughing ass over here and get warm. Be the last chance you get for a spell."

Jackson hesitated. "Hell, I'm good for ten more rounds or ten days in their fucking Hole."

Sam watched Smitty's hands, watched the man inch along the papered wall and give up the hut's hot spot—only warm this time of day—on the *ondol*. At night, when the pale sun slid behind frozen Manchurian mountains, and after a twig fire was built for the cracked corn soup or boiled millet for Hut 6, the men began their rotation. The clay floor would be too hot right over the kitchen flue, and the room flues would cool before reaching all the way through the shack. So at intervals during the night, men shifted themselves and their thin blankets from cold to warm, from sweat to shivering. It worked for the betterment of all; Sam and Matt had seen to it. Smitty's hands wobbled below his bent wrists as he said, "Be more than ten days, and you be dreaming of this fine hut. Just try and remember you be dreaming."

The black guy from the 503rd Artillery Battalion, Smitty had been taken at Kunu-ri, too. He was the man with the floppy wrists, older than anyone else in the hut, his hair ragged and gray. Pushing the backs of his useless hands together, he always tried to steady his spoon and feed himself and got pissed when anybody tried to help. The Chinks let him live as an example of what happened to reactionaries who held out too long. At least he didn't have to make those office hooch interrogation treks anymore, but it was probably too late for Smitty. Every day showed on him.

"—just had to laugh," Matt said.

Sam stared at him. "You laughed at One Hung Low?"

"Uh-uh; some new cat sent in to shuck this poor o-pressed colored boy. You know those Chinks that talk like they from different places in the States? How they buddy up to you? Well, that shucks you componee, but this slant-eyed motherfucker says, what's happen-ing, baby? Man, I dig his clean threads and dog-fur hat, him all cozy in his warm hooch. Then he says, ain't nothing shaking? I couldn't help it; I laughed in his signifying face. Shee-it; you got to *be* black to talk it."

"Come here, stupid," Sam said. He pressed his ragged handkerchief hard against Matt's cut eyebrow. Pressure, ice, and collodion—before the boxing commission barred that coagulant because it had to be dug out later. Remembering, Sam saw Matt on his stool in the corner, and the blood. He saw himself turn to block the doctor's clear view while he bore down hard on the smooth, iced iron.

He's okay, doc. No need to stop the fight.

Because Jackson had a family and needed the money; because his heart was bigger than his head, and he'd rather get punched out than have a fight stopped.

Sam eased off on the pressure. Where the hell were the referee and ring doctor now that they were really needed?

Smitty's loose right hand nudged a canteen cup toward Jackson. "Weed root tea with a dab of sugar. You need vitamins because it be ten below and cold as Commander Ding's heart."

Tucking his handkerchief away, Sam thought how rough it was on the others, swallowing their spit while holding back a few grains of rice or millet seeds. This was gummed together for emergency rations while the men saving it were on the edge of starvation themselves. But it might keep the next poor bastard alive in the Hole, and any of them might be next.

Lately there had been less food to save, and Commander Ding blamed the shortage on American planes that routinely bombed and strafed peasants working in the fields. When they were not attacking schools and hospitals, of course.

His back propped against the wall, Sam crossed his legs and tucked them under himself. Day by day, he was reverting to his childhood in Chunju, for reacting as a Korean now helped. He half listened to Smitty warn Matt Jackson about the rigors of the Hole. It was five by five feet, and seven feet deep, a grave for too many men in the frozen earth along the Yalu River.

The Chinks had screwed up, leaving Smitty alive. His horrible example might work with the weak men, impressing the Pros all too ready to sign confessions. But to everybody else, old Smitty was an object of pride. The interrogators had pulled his hands behind his back and wired them tight. Then they looped the wire over a beam and dragged him off his feet. Time and again his arms had been pulled out of their sockets in terrible pain, but the wrist tendons were ruined first. Smitty hadn't given them a damned thing.

". . . both your feet in one pants leg tied with boot laces. Fold the other pants leg and your jacket under you to cut that ground chill. Roll up in your blanket and keep your hands in your armpits." Smitty's hands swung back and forth.

"You probably won't shit much on what little they give you to eat, but scrape a hole and cover it. Them motherfuckers want a man to lose his dignity, so don't live with your own shit."

"Hey, man," Jackson said, "I heard all this before."

"You ain't been in the Hole before. One more thing—" Smitty nodded, and Sam reached over to fish in Smitty's pocket. He brought out the American dime.

"United States money them bastards missed when they took my watch and pictures of my family," Smitty said. He tucked his loose hands under his arms, a difficult move for him.

Matt grinned. "You want me to call a cop?"

The grin showed Jackson's white teeth, the teeth he'd be lucky to keep. Scurvy made them fall out, and indoctrination officers took them out with pistol butts.

"This ain't funny, youngblood," Smitty said. "Down in that Hole, you run out of things to keep your head busy. That's when you use this dime, at night when you freezing and ready to holler *yessir, Mister Chink, I confess anything you say.* But you flip this dime away and search for it with just one finger. Play games with it, anything to keep your head on, man. And you hear me, Stonewall Jackson— bring me back my dime."

Thin and shaky with the whine that was always laced through it, a voice reached from the next room. "If you damn guys keep making the Chinese mad, everybody will be dog meat."

"Buckbee," Sam said, "shut the hell up."

Stooped and pasty-faced, Buckbee had been transferred into Hut 6 only a week before. Now he stuck his head into Sam's room and said, "You can't pull rank in here. You heard the political officer. Everybody's equal here. They shipped the chickenshit officers to another camp so they wouldn't push us around."

Sam whispered it: "All I hear is a Pro talking."

Buckbee faded from the doorway, his whine trailing after. "I didn't mean—"

Smitty flopped his hands. "I be setting a watch on that one. He don't belong in this badass hut."

"Hut 6 badasses," Jackson said, but he wasn't smiling now. Guards were coming back, their feet crunching snow.

Smitty said it fast: "Wiggle your toes and fingers all you can so they don't fall off. If they drop hairballs and fish bones down to you, don't make no never mind—eat it. Now they don't give a goddamn you black and supposed to split off from the fays. Don't get smartass, or they throw a bucket of water on you and you be wasted, man."

"I'll make it," Matt said.

Sam caught Matt's right hand. It would never lift in another ring. A bullet had wrecked it. Matt wore his entire Chink issue—thin summer uniform underneath the winter one. Every rag that the men of Hut 6 could spare was stuffed into his clothes, and that might not be enough.

The door slammed back, and a whip of arctic air lashed into the hut. A man groaned, and another cursed. Two guards glared at Matt, and one pointed: "You come."

Stooping under the low ceiling, Matt made a deep bow. Holding his face straight, he said, "Right in your ear, slopehead."

When they marched him away, they left the door open. Sam crawled there to watch his friend walking off, walking proud. Wind sawed at him, and he closed the door. Smitty crawled back to his warm place, and the other guys rolled over then—Marotta with dark hair cropped to his scalp; Joe Lavoie's thin face showing every bone.

Lavoie said, "Jackson will make it."

Marotta whispered, "Jackson will come out of that goddamn Hole, if he wants to."

"That be the trick"—Smitty squeezed his arms across his chest—"wanting to bad enough. Fucking Pros, they want to go home and sell out for the chance."

Leaning on one elbow, Marotta tugged his ear-flap hat. "Everybody wants to go home."

"Not more than anything," Smitty said, "not if you count yourself a natural man."

"And a soldier," Sam added.

Smitty nodded, deep lines around his eyes and the set of his mouth. "Can't be no man, you sure as hell ain't no soldier."

Sam couldn't improve on that, so he pulled his knees up and crossed his arms around them, then put his head down. This was Hut 6, the toughest in camp, but even these Reactionaries were crumbling—the young ones, anyway. It was hard to blame them, for at least they had resisted. Other kids gave up without a fight because they hadn't enlisted to be tortured. They only wanted the GI education bill, and they were those that mom protected so fiercely with assists from her Congressman. The kid never developed the legs he needed to climb Korean mountains because he rode everywhere, even to the rifle range.

After the Reds took him, mom and the Congressman weren't there to promise him dessert if he ate all his cracked corn. So he hid his head in his blanket and died, and only the wild dogs waited to tuck him in. The dogs— bony, slinking beasts that gathered in the edge of the woods beyond the wire to snarl over the day's corpses. Somehow that made dying worse, knowing how you would end up.

"You thinking on Kunu-ri again," Smitty said. "If you got to lay that on somebody, lay it on MacArthur sitting away off in Tokyo and telling there ain't no Chinks in Korea. We caught this one, and the interpreter say: This motherfucker don't understand Korean or Japanese for shit. If Joe Chink ain't in Korea, who all these night-runnin' bastards blowing bugles?"

Kunu-ri, all his ROKs dead; he and Jackson wounded. Sam only had a moment to bury his dog tags, and only Jackson now knew he wasn't *Kelly* Connover, RA 5989593. He had remembered his uncle's serial number as well as his own. Sam didn't know what that had done at Second Division headquarters, or even if the name had gone out to the International Red Cross.

The Chinks used that ploy as the first step in turning a POW into a Progressive. Just sign here, and your loved ones will know you are alive and well. If Maggi Barron thought he had bought it, that might be better all around. Away from her husband, she may have cried a little.

". . . bugles," Smitty said, "whistles like traffic cops and them flares hanging high up in the night. My whole outfit got run through a meat grinder."

More cold crept into the hut, and now Marotta and Lavoie snuggled together for warmth. Sam said, "Hell of an outfit, Smitty." He knew the story, but it helped the old guy to talk. Sam thought of Matt Jackson in the Hole.

Smitty went on: "We stayed while all them other outfits hauled ass by our position. I heard this white colonel tell the battery commander that we better get the hell out. The old man say, shit, we ain't running. Black outfit like us, we had to show we badass as any fays. So the Nickel-Oh-Trey laid them guns in three directions, and the fuses cut one-point-five. Shell blows at a second and a half from the muzzle, and that be too close, man. Jerk that lanyard and holler: Kim, count your men!"

His head sagged, and Sam murmured that the whole division was proud of the 503rd. Smitty's chin lolled on his chest, and Marotta grunted. "He keeps going in and out, and someday he won't come back. What good is pride, sergeant? The dogs get you just the same."

Icy wind moaned around the hut, and Sam pulled his blanket close. Days dragged into months and on into forever, and in winter you saved strength by doing as little as possible. It was hours until chow time, so Sam closed his eyes. Another blast of wind shook the hut, and a thin, agonized voice rode it; some poor bastard being indoctrinated.

CHAPTER 23

Somewhere south of Seoul, Republic of Korea, Jan. 4, 1951—
This capital city was lost for the second time today. Chinese communist forces poured through the devastated town from the north
and east. Last summer at the start of the war, North Korean
troops overran a stunned populace for an orgy of bloodletting.
Observers see little hope of anything else from the peasant soldiers of Manchuria.

사람새끼는 서울로 보내고
말새끼는 제주도로 보내라.

"Send young men to Seoul and young horses to
Cheju." (Korean proverb: In the city there are
chances to rise or fall. Lush grass grows on the
mountains of Cheju island. To each his own.)

Julian was conscious of the letter folded into his shirt
pocket. Beneath his field jacket, it lay warm there, penetrating to his skin despite the sawtooth wind so cold upon
him. Even the dark and snowy mountains looked not so
menacing. At last Maggi had written, and the mail clerk
brought her letter to Julian just before the line troops buttoned up for the defense of Wonju. He had been afraid to
open it, expecting bad news, expecting to learn that she

had filed for divorce and wondering what he would do without her. He had never considered that.

Priorities changed when life was reduced to survival; duty had a different meaning, and responsibility—Christ's cross could have been no more difficult to bear. Julian wanted help to carry the load, the sharing that only Maggi could give. He couldn't run crying to the general that his rank was too heavy for his shoulders; not and face the specters of infantrymen who depended upon him to lead, to know the right answers at the right time.

He had never run crying to Maggi, either, but she had always been there. Again touching her letter in his pocket, Julian wondered how she would react if he let her see actual tears. She'd probably ask for his AGO card, so she could check his identity. Julian Barron in tears? God, if she only knew. Because he didn't show emotion at their son's funeral, Maggi thought he didn't care. But now—every casualty became personal, magnifying that earlier grief. When a soldier died, Winfield Barron died over again and made Julian another degree older.

He walked beside Charley Heath, their combat boots crunching dirty snow across a stubbled and frozen rice paddy. Three paces in front of them walked Rocky Watanabe, his M-1 at port arms, his breath drifting back in small, frozen clouds. He was point and connecting file for this mobile CP of Julian's that also carried a radio operator and a runner, just in case. Rocky hadn't liked it a damned bit when Julian pulled him in from his line company. He was more important at Battalion as an interpreter, but that wouldn't have held him. He was another of the don't-give-a-damn breed, defiant of chickenshit and more than worthy of his stripes. Giving him a free hand with the security platoon kept Rocky on his toes and interested. It also made sense to Julian, since command posts were prime targets for the Chinese. Rocky had put together a guard platoon from spare parts—off-duty cooks, drivers who had lost their vehicles, a few clerks, and the rest Koreans.

Twice now, Rock Security had picked up infiltrators before they could reach the regiment's nerve center. Rock of the Marne—the 38th Infantry's other war motto. If there was confusion about Rock and ROK, it was compounded by the sign on his six-by truck: ROCK ROKS; commanding officer, Rocky Watanabe.

Unorthodox and non-regulation, and it worked; beyond the classroom, that's what counted for tactics and for people. It had taken combat to teach that to Julian. Now he breathed icy air and grunted as they started up the ridge he'd chosen for an observation post. Somewhere north of Wonju, so many meters up, other units an inexact distance from his battalion's flanks. War was an inexact science, he thought, and wondered who had said that first.

Maggi's letter was that way, too—nothing definite, nothing pinpointed as to their future. But she had written, and although she refused to accept guilt, she had admitted to some blame for her affair. *Not really an affair, Julian; one night and two meetings over coffee in the PX. I was lost and very angry at you. I am still angry, only not as much and not as blindly. I realize that you must have loved little Win, too. If only you had not sent him off to military school so soon . . .*

Holy mother; if he had taken the other road past Kunu-ri; if he had followed the path his mother laid out for him, he wouldn't be responsible for men's mortality, only for immortal souls. Father Julian Barron; colonel; the military title lay easier upon the tongue and easier upon the mind. But a priest never married.

And if he had not married Maggi Scott, great-great lineal descendent of General Winfield Scott? At first it was for her connections, for contacts desperately needed by a young officer determined to make a high career of the army. Later it was for her comfort and stability. When had it become for Maggi herself? Maybe not ever; not yet.

"Good hole here," Charley Heath said. "Good as any, that is. Foxholes decided me upon cremation, if I live long enough to be choosy. Every time I climb down into a hole in the ground I feel as if I'm getting into my grave."

"Hell, major," Rocky said, hunkering down. "Just think of it as a step toward being with your honorable ancestors, like us Japs. Room there for the radio guy and you two; me and the runner'll be next door at the Waikiki Hilton."

Julian got down and belly-leaned against the cold, stony earth. Slowly, he swept the front with his field glasses— rough, miserable ground, ice in the shadows and slabbed with rocks, marked here by a twisted sapling and there by scrawny brush. All mountains, one damned Korean mountain after another, divided by stinking paddies or faintly trailed by roads. Not as tall and brutal as the peaks up north, but tough to fight over. Julian never wanted to see another mountain.

Behind him, Heath said, "Our old buddies are back; G-2 claims four North Korean regiments are out there, plus unidentified units of CCF."

Nodding, Julian shivered at the cold air drawn into his lungs. Happy New Year, he thought; auld lang syne was zero on the thermometer tonight when the blackness came down and brought the communists along. New Year's Eve and a celebration due; the fireworks had been saved for this afternoon. This time, they were as ready as could be expected, and Julian could only wish that the trainload of ammunition had come in days earlier, so a thorough distribution would have been made. A hell of a note, when the U.S. Army had to depend upon a Korean steam engine for firepower. So many trucks lost at Kunu-ri, so many men, and neither casualty list had been caught up yet.

He said, "That ammo train worries me; if we lose Wonju, it's just sitting there for grabs." He peered through the glasses. "And that bridge. I know the river's frozen, but how thick is the ice? Can the gooks cross there?"

"The engineer platoon has the bridge under control. You didn't talk to that lieutenant, did you? Funny thing—he's another technical AWOL. Danny Orr was old Butt Wright's aide, and the driver when Wright bought it. The general's attitude must have rubbed off, because he said, damned if he'd go back to Tokyo when he was ordered. My God—Shimbashi, all those beautiful whores hanging out of windows, hot food, hot *sake* and hot women. I could bug out to Tokyo and forget this frozen-ass country in a split second."

The radio corporal clicked his handset and muttered into it, hunched over the SCR 300. "Impel Three, I read you five by five."

"You'd crawl out of an ambulance to stay with this regiment," Julian said. "General Wright, this Lieutenant Orr"—damned if he'd mention Sam Connover—"disobeying orders to stay in combat rather than avoiding it, the army doesn't punish people for that. But I didn't really understand it before. It's what we do for a living. Damn; I must be getting battle rattle. I never talk this much."

"Does you good," Heath said. "Incoming mail—duck!"

Ka-rump! The first mortal shell exploded on the ridge.

"They're not waiting for night," Julian said. His ears rang. "Those NKPA units must be back at full strength."

Something made a *thock* sound into the earth close by. Julian said, "Radio—have the companies reach our CP here. Do you have contact all around?"

"Pretty good, sir," Corporal Giblin said.

Again the *thock!* From the next hole Rocky Watanabe said, "Fucking buffalo gun. I hate them; always too far off to reach. It ain't that they're all that accurate; it just bothers me to get shot at and not shoot back. Hell of a thing to use on a man."

Julian nodded and continued to peer through the binoculars. The far-off sniper was using the Degtyarev 14.5mm antitank rifle, a bolt-action, ungainly weapon designed to punch holes in the light armor of early WWII vehicles. In Korea it might knock out a truck or shatter an individual.

Thock!

"I'll shove that up the bastard's ass," Rocky said, "all five feet of barrel. Then I'll kick the stock off it."

Wind probed Julian's field jacket and made a light, weird sound under the brim of his helmet. Down the ridge, mustard-colored lumps detached themselves from the snow and moved forward. Enemy mortars increased their fire, shells whistling in to throw frozen dirt and rock splinters.

"They're coming," Julian said. "Corporal—call in the companies one by one; tell them we're being hit and to report any action on their fronts." The right command, the right time, easy now before the real confusion, before casualties mounted and important cogs in the defense mechanism went missing or got broken.

Maggi had not mentioned Sam Connover; the missing Sergeant Connover. Julian wouldn't make a point of telling her, for she would think he was gloating, and he was. But maybe it was something more, a different feeling since her letter. Suppose she really loved the guy? He didn't want to believe that, but if she did, then telling her would only hurt. That was something else; until their son was killed, Julian didn't think that Maggi could be hurt, or even reached beneath her cool exterior.

Not actually an affair, she said; just one night of being screwed by another man; not actually an affair. How many orgasms made an affair? An anonymous hotel room, Maggi's slim body presented to a strange man. Maggi Barron in a one-night stand to punish her husband for the death of their son. All right, damn it; he'd buy that, but why the meetings in the PX coffee shop? Had she meant it to go further, her not-really-an-affair? Christ on a crutch, she may have divorced him in her pain and rage. But surely she wouldn't have married Connover; not because of one night's screwing. What else had the man done to her, with her?

Closing his mind against any fantasy pictures, Julian still couldn't shake Connover. Division G-2 had come to question him after Kunu-ri, because Connover's makeshift fire brigade was unofficially attached to the 38th Infantry. Julian was the last man they should have asked, and when he wanted to ask a few questions in return, G-2 cut him off with a warning to keep quiet.

"Divarty," he said to the radio man, "get me Division Artillery." Speaking into the handset, Julian checked map coordinates and asked for registering fire. Within seconds, the first shells came howling down into the corridor. Julian corrected and called fire for effect.

The day cracked wide open as batteries to the rear hurled shells onto areas of approach, the 105s screaming in with accuracy. The ground shook, and the air curdled with smoke and pulverized earth. For a time, Julian couldn't hear the small-arms fire, but he smelled burned powder and gutted earth. With the near misses he could feel the texture of the air around him, splintered and slapping against his face, the lash of miniature ice shards and tiny barbs of fire.

It always turned into forever, Julian thought, filled with slash lightning and impossible thunders, forever stretching itself only to snap back into a cocoon where there was no hope of growing wings. Julian took messages from his line companies and sent orders back; he argued with Division Artillery about how many HE rounds he needed and talked them into a short barrage of Willy Peter. Flaming the scrub on the mountain's downslope, the white phosphorus burned hot and bright, and the attack broke up. At the foot of the slope, a North Korean's body burned slowly.

Into the lull, Charley Heath said, "The bridge, damn it!"

With his glasses, Julian picked up engineers fleeing the mined structure and thought only seconds would pass before the bridge went up in fire and smoke. But long minutes went by and no explosion; across the field, the communists trotted on, laying a curtain of burpgun fire.

"There!" Julian said. "A man running back to the bridge —an officer, I think. Good Christ—he'll never make it."

Heath used his own binoculars. "It's Orr! What the hell is he—"

His hands shook on the glasses, blurring his vision. Julian forced himself to be steady and said a short, long-unused prayer under his breath. Advancing gooks fired on Orr as he reached the bridge and checked fuses or wiring. Nothing happened, and again the man took off, only to come circling back like an ungainly bird, running lopsided because he swung a five-gallon gas can.

"The crazy bastard—he'll destroy the damned thing somehow!"

Then the flames leapt skyward, and Julian lost sight of the guy; the explosives caught and blew up with a hell of a roar. The beautiful, crazy bastard, Julian thought, and pulled in his neck because a handful of dirt slammed his helmet. Wiping his face, he looked down the slope where no gook stirred. Beyond the smashed bridge they backed away shooting, and concentrated fire from the engineer platoon chopped them down.

It got so quiet that Julian's ears ached, and he was grateful for Charley Heath talking: "They won't leave this party so soon. Luke the Gook will be back for the cake and ice cream."

Corporal Giblin spoke up. "Some birthday party. I used to figure I was lucky because everybody celebrated my birthday on New Year's Eve. But now I'm wishing me a wish—not for the whole fucking year coming up; nobody has to promise me all of 1951—just give me a tomorrow."

More, Ho Chuk Gun thought; somehow they had to do more and drive the foreigners into the sea. Only when

Korea was cleansed of all invaders and alien thinking would the People's Republic reach its promised place in the world. That included the Chinese, of course, but they must be left to the future. Now the major obstacle was the cursed Americans. Why did they fight so well now? Had every lowly soldier among them been promised loot and women? Surely they had stripped the country already and could see that victory over the *inmun-gun* was impossible. Chuk Gun wanted every one of the detestable long-noses out of Korea. It was better to kill them, because then they could never come back to rape and burn. That was ever their fashion, the so-powerful, so-rich *white* men; the tall, arrogant, and well-fed, the *white* men. Only the Russians helped, and even so, at times Chuk Gun thought he saw a certain look in their eyes also. But you could not challenge men who educated you, trained you, and finally presented you with arms.

The road south and the crossroads west lay beyond Hoengsong Valley and the town of Wonju. When the *inmun-gun* captured this road hub, Seoul and provinces to the south would again lie open and helpless. This time no mistakes would be made, and with the great power of China to assist them, Ho Chuk Gun's men would conquer.

He cranked a field phone and spoke into the handset. "Battalion commanders report to me immediately after dark. Wonju is to be taken this night, or I will walk into the town upon your dead bodies."

CHAPTER 24

Below the 37th Parallel, east central front, Republic of Korea, Jan. 14, 1951—United Nations forces savagely mauled by Chinese human-wave attacks are regrouping here along a line calculated for a strong defense. A highly placed source said, "We're lucky the Chink doesn't have wheels. If he had, we'd be learning to kowtow. He has to chase us on foot, and that just gave us the edge."

대문 밖이 저승이다.

"Hell waits outside the door." (Korean proverb: A caution to travelers in a strange land to watch for danger.)

Rich Shriver thought about kicking the stool out from under the clerk at Division Rear. He thought again and decided against it, but only barely. He said, "What the hell you mean, I can't adopt the kid? Some kind of law against it, laddie buck?"

"Actually, yes." The clerk had five stripes and was so clean he looked pretty. "It would take an act of Congress, literally, to allow one Korean, or any other Oriental, into the United States."

"Literally, huh?" Rich drawled the word.

The guy sniffed. "It doesn't help to get snotty, you know. Because for another thing, we have no records on you, nothing at all. Yes, you claim to be Division PIO, but we don't have your 201 file."

"It's on the way from Tokyo," Rich said, not at all sure of that. "Okay, if you ain't worth doodly shit to me, where's the Judge Advocate General tent?"

Sliding back his stool, the clerk kept the table between himself and Rich. "Find it yourself, wise guy. When I do get your file in here—"

"Protect it with your ass, because if it gets fucked up, that's what it's worth to you—your ruby-red ass."

Outside the tent, a furry taste in his mouth, Rich slung his carbine and tilted his helmet back. He glanced along the line of olive-drab tents dusted with brown streaks, no different here than they would be set up on maneuvers in the States. Everyone carried a weapon, even moving between tents, but there were no sentries out in the daytime. People back here thought that fifty miles from the nearest reported fighting made them safe. Maybe they'd learn a bloody lesson from infiltrators. Korea had no front lines and no true rear areas.

There it was, the JAG office; why couldn't the army just name it lawyer? Several tents down, where vehicles had to park—shit, they had even painted some big rocks white to mark the area—Kim Soo Man sat guard in the jeep that once belonged to *Stars & Stripes Far East*. Its bumper markings now read 23rd Infantry, and the hood numbers were changed. The 23rd's boss didn't know that, but Rich figured Colonel Freeman to be understanding. A jeep on the line was worth six anywhere else.

Rich went into the tent and found the JAG captain to be equally understanding, and a pretty nice guy. For the hell of it, Rich took his name and address for a hometown release and left the man beaming. Rich smiled himself down to the motor park and unlocked the chains on his jeep. To anybody else, Soo Man was only a gook, and a little one at that. Some yoyo might have tried to steal the jeep, but he'd have stepped in shit. The kid was tougher than he looked.

"Hi, *sonsaeng*. You finish business?"

"Come off that *teacher* shit, boy-san. Anything you learn from me will probably cost you your gook hide. Come on, we'll slide on into the village and you find me some paddy piss; *soju*—right?"

"Yes, *sonsaeng;* this not always teacher, Rich. Meaning polite mister, I think."

"Don't let it go to your head. Watch for *soju*."

A story worked in Rich's head, not the stock release that the commanding general had been relieved in December because somebody had to be blamed for the more than six thousand casualties at Kunu-ri and MacArthur was untouchable. About the only thing the next general did was to order everyone in the division to grow beards. An old China hand, he claimed the Chinks respected beards as a sign of age. Rich thought it boosted the morale of a beaten outfit, gave the GIs something to bitch about. Then Nick Ruffner took the division in mid-January after Wonju had been lost. Shoulder stars were popping like popcorn: Lose a town, lose a command. Rich hoped the last guy would stick around awhile. The troops needed someone to believe in, someone permanent.

Rich's feature story would be Father Carrol of the 38th. A boozy Irish priest, the regimental chaplain was special. Captain Carrol begged whiskey from everybody returning from Rest & Recreation in Japan. Most men brought back AWOL bags filled with miniatures, and these suited Carrol just fine. It got so the lucky guys on R&R would buy one batch for him and another to hide for themselves, and they gossiped about their drunken churchman.

But as much as Father Carrol liked his liquor, he carefully hoarded the little bottles until wounded came into the aid station. Then every GI without a belly wound got to drink a toast with this angel in ODs. The story's best quote came from an ornery first soldier peppered by mortar fragments: "Beats hell out of holy water."

And the good priest answered, "My boy, my boy—this *is* holy water."

Carrol made up for eightballs and chickenshits and arrogant bastards of all ranks.

"Soju," Soo Man said, and Rich pulled the jeep to the roadside. Shabby lean-tos played at being stores, offering small wares that might be of value to someone—a few eggs in twisted straw, chopsticks wooden and metal, brass bowls, three boxes of GI-issue cornflakes. Rich saw tall green bottles of rice whiskey and the wizened old man in baggy white clothes, a smile above straggly chin whiskers.

"We'll take every bottle he's got," Rich said. "Six, ain't they? And how about chopsticks? You ain't too handy with a fork, you know. A set for you and a set for me."

He lighted a cigarette while Soo Man had the order filled. It was cold, and the old man probably wore all the clothing he owned, but it wasn't enough; his gnarled hands were blue. Those thin rubber shoes couldn't hold much warmth, either.

"How much?" Rich asked Soo Man, and added the rest of his Korean money to the total. It wasn't much, only a thousand *whan* extra. The old guy handed back the tip.

"Take it," Rich said. "Goddamnit, kid—tell him it's okay."

Soo Man offered the blue one-hundred-*whan* notes. The old man smiled his stumps of teeth and shook his head. *"Animnida."*

"He say, no, thanks."

"What the hell's wrong with the old bastard? He can use the money to buy shoes."

Soo Man bowed to the man and passed *soju* into the jeep, then gave Rich a pair of metal chopsticks. "I no can

196

say. He is papa-san; many old. Take nothing no work for. Understand?"

"Proud, damn it," Rich muttered. "A proud old man."

He climbed from behind the wheel of the jeep and walked around. There he bowed to papa-san and wished he could speak Korean. The old guy bowed back, and Rich figured they understood each other anyhow. A big difference from the fucking Japs. The longer this war went on, the more Rich learned that Koreans were a long way from being Japs.

Tapping the rice whiskey, he rolled the jeep along a reasonably graveled road away from Ivanhoe Rear and away from too-clean clerks. Back there was some sort of imitation civilization, hot showers and a daily routine, even a few hookers hidden out in the nearest village. Most nights, there were movies. The rear echelon didn't know they were living a lie, that it wasn't maneuvers and business as usual. They kept clean and didn't bleed and went on R&R as if they were deserving combat troopers.

The jeep's top was up, but there were no side curtains. Cold wind sliced across Rich, and he checked to see if Soo Man was well wrapped in blankets. The kid was looking good these days, filling out on C-rations and sharp in fatigues and overcoat tailored to fit his small body. Even his boots were handmade, because whenever Rich drove into a town not completely torn up and fought over he'd find a tailor, a shoemaker. What the hell.

Late in the chill gray day, he picked up the small blue flags that pointed the way to the 23rd Regiment. The twilight came down like a shroud dipped in ice, but Rich was feeling no pain. Slowed to a crawl, using only the tiny blackout lights on the jeep, he inched along. Out of the dark, a sharp challenge stopped him.

"Hey, man," Rich called out, "ain't nobody but us chickens—just me and a kid and the PIO jeep and a big drink of gook booze."

They trotted up to him, riflemen on each side of the jeep. The big shadow said, "How'd you get through?"

"Is there a roadblock? We didn't see any. You want that drink or not? The kid and me got frozen asses and empty bellies."

The little shadow said from behind his rifle, "You got one hell of a lot of luck, man. The regiment's surrounded and cut off by a million Chinks, and here you come, right through them."

Rich treated himself to a big drink. "No shit? I'd better get off this perimeter, then. But are you guys sure? We didn't see a damned thing, and nobody took a pop at us."

It was the big shadow's turn. "Colonel Freeman passed word that we can't expect help. We have to hang tough with the French battalion. He said we can expect the fight of our lives, and you know the Old Man don't bullshit."

And the other soldier: "Get that jeep out of here before you draw fire."

Rich heard it coming and slammed the gas pedal to the floorboard. The jeep leaped ahead, and Soo Man grabbed for support.

"Mortar!" Rich yelled. "Hold on, you little bastard!"

Sam had never seen two of the interrogators before. Both were wolfish and hard-eyed, dressed in the dark blue quilteds of the Chinese, but they were not Chinese. They spoke to each other openly before him in Korean because they had no idea that he understood the language. He had kept that secret, although if he spoke with the Korean guards in their own language, life might have gone easier for him. But Sam continued the deception in case it might give him an edge someday.

The other man was One Hung Low, his beady eyes set deep into heavily folded eye sockets, his catfish mouth never completely closed. Hung was a Manchurian, a peasant lumpish and brutal who enjoyed his work. His methods turned fewer GIs into cooperating Pros than the smooth, insidious system of the camp boss, Commander Ding. Both had worked on Sam before this and gotten nothing. Therefore this trip to the office hooch had to do with the two Koreans.

One man's eyes were so slanted they almost met at the bridge of his nose; the other had a nose that flattened across half his face. Sam made the required bow and sat in the straight chair facing them. The bow didn't cost Sam anything, and he could save his resistance for the important things.

Nose said quickly, "We will show this ignorant Chinese that Koreans are more capable." Slant put a sheaf of paper upon the rickety table and nodded. "This prisoner hides something. We must prove that we can expose his lies." Then Slant walked over and tried to tower above Sam in the chair.

He was too short, and that angered him. He slapped Sam across the face. "Your army number is wrong. Why do you give a wrong number?"

Letting his head hang, Sam said, "Serial number RA 5989593."

He was slapped again. "Too low. You are not an officer."

The North Koreans wanted a hand in running the PW camp, if for no other reason than to maintain a jealous presence. Being temporary allies had not altered the basic time-honored distrust that Chinese and Koreans had for each other. Checking serial numbers was a shrewd move.

"It's the only number I have," Sam answered. "Connover, Kelly, Sergeant, RA 598—"

This time a fist almost knocked him off the chair. No more open hands. Sam blinked at the floor. Of course the serial number was too low for any soldier in today's army. The real Kelly Connover had worn it when Black Jack Pershing pursued Pancho Villa into Mexico. Only a few men carried seven numbers, and those were pre–WWII be-

ginning with 6 or 7. Now all were eight numbers, with no
Regular Army identification up front. Still, it was slick of
the gooks to sort this out.

"Why do you, of all American aggressors in this camp,
have such a number?"

It was time to go into the stupid routine. "Aggressor? I
don't understand. That's a big word—aggressor."

Slopping tea, One Hung Low laughed. Sam knew that
Reactionaries, especially the guys from Badass Hut 6, had
been feeding him this kind of return for months. He hadn't
said anything to the Koreans and was obviously enjoying
their irritation. Sam hoped he would choke on the dumpling
he took.

"Unschooled," Nose said to his partner, "an ignorant
man."

Slant pawed through papers. "He has been disciplined
repeatedly for sleeping during indoctrination classes. He
criticizes himself, but only by repeating what he has been
told. And in the beginning, he caused his entire group to
stand for hours because he insisted that the North attacked
the South. You are correct, comrade—ignorant and unschooled. This Chinese dog has chosen his most difficult
prisoner to make us lose face."

Nose changed the tactics and offered Sam a cigarette.
Sam took it. Nose said, "How did you become a sergeant?"

Blowing smoke from the harsh Korean tobacco, Sam
said, "Sergeant? Oh, yeah—my uncle is a captain." Any
Oriental understood and approved nepotism; their worlds
were based upon it. "Hey, this is a good cigarette."

They kept trying, using the good cop–bad cop routine.
They threatened to have him shot and tried to bribe him.
Now he took food and tea, but when they wanted him to
inform on his hut mates he became puzzled, then came up
with Buckbee's name. The guy acted funny, he said, and
always talked about going home.

Delighted, the Koreans took notes until One Hung Low

laughed and told them that Buckbee was a Progressive who reported to Commander Ding. Sam kept his eyes blank and his face straight. Hut 6 had suspected Buckbee for a long time; now they had him by the short hairs. Whenever they needed to twist him, they would. If Buckbee didn't bend, he would snap. "Watch how you speak," Slant said. "This Reactionary is listening."

Hung finished the dumplings. "You have said yourself that he is ignorant. Do you expect such a man to understand Japanese? He stumbles over his own language."

In Chunju middle school the Japanese professor led the students in criticizing Sam, in mocking his clumsy height and peculiar eyes. The *sensei* pointed out that America-*jin* thought only of safety and riches. Even their god was weak and cowardly, unfit to stand with the proud gods of *bushido*. And this foreigner was the son of the Christian priest who refused to go back to America.

He did learn Japanese, Sam thought; like all the other Korean students, hating every syllable of every detested word, the son of the Christian priest learned Japanese. Now he was glad.

He just hoped the PWs wouldn't be kept here long enough to speak Mandarin. It could be a long and stalemated war.

CHAPTER 25

New York, NY, Jan. 25, 1951—Today the United Nations voted overwhelmingly to end the Korean conflict by peaceful means. These means were not discussed.

공한 쥐는 고양이를
문다 .

"Birds listen to day talk, and rats to night talk."
(Korean proverb: Communists do not speak the
language of others.)

It was the Second Ice Age, and they were the dinosaurs, and the world would never be warm again. Julian Barron crouched in blanketed misery in the canvas lean-to CP. Around him the dug earth was cold, gummy in spots where small fingers of heat and busy feet had thawed it. He missed Charley Heath, sent to Regiment for a meeting with Colonel Peploe. The S-3 sergeant kept up the Operations map and had a neat hand on the overlay, but the threatening red symbols were all over it.

"Below the 37th Parallel," Julian said. "All the fighting, and all this endless winter, and we come up a parallel short."

"Yes, sir," Corporal Giblin said.

Julian fumbled for a cigarette and lighted it. The Coleman lantern fizzed and pretended to throw out warmth. The stove was a five-gallon coffee can punched with holes, heat tablets stinking. Julian said, "I guess it beats being jammed back on the Naktong, though at least it was warm there."

"Yes, sir," Porky Giblin said, a round, bundled-up man not much for talking. He wore a shoulder holster strapped over layers of clothing and had a short civilian pistol tucked into it. Noticing Julian's look, he said, "Thirty-eight Bulldog my old man sent. I mean, a two-inch barrel is plenty for a desk soldier to haul around. I mean, with any handgun, I'd probably shoot myself in the foot."

That was the most he'd said for the night, and as if it tired him, Giblin scrunched down beside his map and between the radio and field phone. Lantern light shone dull blue from the butt of his little pistol.

It was quiet, and Julian appreciated that; it was cold, and he didn't like that at all. Inched closer to the heat, he brought out Maggi's second letter. One for each shirt pocket, talismans both, to protect him from harm. The superstitious carried Bibles there, a sheaf of family pictures or a deck of cards; bulletproofing.

What did she expect of him? Mother of God, more than he could give. A Dear John letter would be kinder; and so would divorce papers. The whole damned move was wild, a backhand in the face, and yet—a thing gut-honest and jolting. He hadn't asked for a report on her affair with Connover; he hated the very idea, but the way she presented it—goddamn! Was he some kind of pervert to feel it was also sensuous?

Julian pulled hard on his cigarette, and smoke mixed with the fog of his breath. She might have written this letter with a view to turning a knife in his guts, but at the end, that wasn't what she said, not what she meant. Thousands of miles away, an unfaithful wife, Maggi was more vivid, more real than she had ever been, even in his arms.

"Sir." It was Porky Giblin, and Julian blinked at him. "Sir—Dog Six reports probing movement on his front."

"Alert the tanks and the four-point-twos. They have their fire missions. Then touch base with the other companies."

"Yes, sir."

They had been massing for days, perhaps weeks. G-2 reports said Chinese Communist Forces and North Korean units were mixed along the division front. Every signal reminded Julian of the debacle up north, and he hoped the troops were ready this time. As ready as could be, because the enemy they waited for was less than human and more than deadly. When the enemy did not care about losses, when they had the men to burn, any position could be overrun.

The thick letter rattled in Julian's hand, and he unclenched his fingers to smooth it out. It was almost as thick as the storied Bibles whose bullets penetrated only to inspirational passages and saved the fine, Christian soldier who carried the Good Book in his breast pocket; right over his heart, of course.

Maggi's missive would never be read in Sunday school, but a porn king might bind and distribute it. Julian crushed out his cigarette butt and unfolded his wife's letter. Be honest, he told himself; a shrink might be more interested than anyone else. And where would that doctor lay the blame, where assign the guilt? Eleven years of marriage, and this letter was either a new beginning or the dismal end.

Tararataa!

"The bugles," Giblin said. "Those lousy goddamn bugles."

"They're not mystic," Julian said. "Joe Chink doesn't have radio, so he signals with bugles and whistles. It works okay in the dark."

"And flares," the sergeant said. "I wish I could run those red flares up a Chinaman's ass."

Julian's hands held to Maggi's letter. "We'll do it this time."

The bugle notes rang high and clear over black, icy mountains, the echoes reverberating in every line trooper's heart, Julian thought. There was nothing he could do now except wait. Rocky Watanabe's backup platoon also marked time in a damned thin reserve, and Divarty had the valleys registered, waiting a call from Forward Observation Posts. Come daylight, direct air support was on tap, with the Ground to Air Control flyboy at Regiment praying for clear skies. The problem might be in lasting until daylight.

Bending over Maggi's letter, holding it close to the low sputter of the Coleman lantern, Julian separated himself— part of him drawn tight and conscious of every minute sound, running each contingency through his mind like a wire recorder, he was yet able to put the rest of himself into the letter. Maybe it was a protective move, like the fixed grin some combat troops wore, or the tough guys saying, yea, though I walk through the valley of shadow, I shall fear no evil . . . because I'm the meanest son of a bitch in the valley; and the lips mutely sincere with Hail Marys.

. . . I remember the smell of that day, Julian. It was piney scent and the caress of springtime that was a lie. For me it was cold and dark, and I rolled up the car window to shut out the lying wind. The MP at the front gate saluted our license tag, and I wondered if enlisted men think of officers' wives as women and not just trouble, if they see us as women sometimes reachable and vulnerable—oh, hell, yes, vulnerable. I thought that the War Department put out the same commandment for all ranks: know ye that the line between officer and enlisted is forever drawn, and woe unto him who crosses it. Or unto *her*, Julian? . . .

"Sir—Baker Six."

Julian took the handset with his left hand. "John? Okay —hang tough; the four-twos are coming. Watch your right flank. If the ROKs start to fade there, Divarty zeroes in. Don't wait to let me know."

Over the darkling ridge, he heard small-arms fire and the thump of Chinese mortar shells. Within seconds the deeper slam of his 4.2s drowned them out. The sound power phone rattled.

"Rocky," Giblin said.

"Tell him to sit tight."

"Sir."

Where the hell was Charley Heath? If Colonel Peploe got rolling, Julian might not get his exec back for a while. Julian waited, his body picking up the rhythm of battle noises. He couldn't hear the bugles now, and his phone didn't ring, his radio didn't insist upon help—yet.

. . . driving into Tacoma, I wanted to scream, Julian. I wanted to throw up, but I did neither because I knew what you would say: *Get hold of yourself, Maggi.* Every goddamn cadet must memorize that line before all the rest of the recitable bullshit at the Academy. My father said it— *Get hold of yourself, Maggi.* Yes, Daddy; sorry, sir.

And you: *Maggi, damn it! Get hold of yourself!* Yes, husband; sorry, sir.

But not that day, Julian. I was sick and angry and thought, fuck you all . . .

Wincing at the crudity he had never heard his wife say, Julian nodded at Porky Giblin's question and said, "Tell Able Company that Divarty's fire mission is on the way."

. . . I stopped at a bar in the daytime. I meant to get drunk and do anything to embarrass you and the goddamned army. Not the fancy hotel bar Fort Lewis officers habituate, Julian—this was a dark place smelling of beer and sawdust, and I heard Glenn Miller and that vocalist I can never remember doing "Perfidia." Captain Glenn Miller lost with his band in the English Channel when the war was winding down. The army can louse up music, too . . .

WHAPP!

"Incoming," Giblin said. "Close. You want Rocky to sweep the CP area?"

"Hold him in position. Not much here the gooks can damage; just us." Julian didn't doubt that the enemy was up to his usual tricks, slipping through the forward outfits to strike at command posts. Julian's CP perimeter was well dug in, and even set about with a few trip flares.

WHAABOOMM!!

Spitting dirt, Julian lay his carbine across his knees and thought that the Chinks might mortar a position their own troops were about to hit, but if so, they'd back off soon.

"Sir—goddamnit, sir."

"Get hold of—" Julian swallowed the rest. "Hang loose, corporal. We also serve who sit and wait."

"Shit and wait, sir."

"That, too."

The lantern flickered; Julian looked back at his letter as the smell of smoke eased into his shelter. . . . I ordered anything but Scotch on the rocks, because that's what you always drink. It was dark in there, and when I paid the barman I couldn't make out the picture in my wallet. You know the one—little Win in his fatigue uniform, the colonel's kid, so cute. Holy mother of Jesus, you kept our child military beyond the end of his short life by burying him in Arlington. Dress right and cover down where ranks of heroes lie awaiting the call to Valhalla. Such bullshit, Julian. Little Win was no hero, and how many goddamned soldiers are only eight years old? . . .

Sharp and quick, explosions running over each other, an automatic weapon cut loose within the battalion CP area.

"Gooks!" Giblin said.

"Get Rocky. He's to use that bullhorn and make everybody else keep their heads down."

Sudden quiet dropped like a net, the weird, listening kind of silence that sometimes happens in the midst of battle. It was worse than violent noise because you kept expecting it to blow apart.

. . . nobody asked me, Julian, if I wanted my son in that hallowed ground beneath a stern marker; name, rank, serial number; the dates. Nobody asked me a damned thing because I was outranked by you and mother. You two made funeral arrangements while I was still reeling from the notification. Good Christ; no official telegram—the War Department sincerely regrets to inform you? . . .

Julian felt then as Maggi must have, felt it more deeply now because death had walked with him for many months, because as someone wise once said, each soldier's death diminished Julian Barron. His own son dying in a stupid hazing accident. The prestigious military school would never lose another cadet that way, especially after Maggi's mother had her attorney plaster half of Virginia with legal papers.

. . . what good was that then? Winfield Scott Barron was dead, and I knew the coffin would be West Point gray and refused to look. I stared down at the folded triangle of flag and squeezed it so hard that my knuckles ached . . .

(Small sound, scratching sound as if a night animal clawed gently at the earth. If the silent net was not about them, Julian could not have heard it.)

"Watch it, Giblin!"

A fraction late, Julian slapped the lantern off its ration box. Light still flooded the little tent when the Chinese burst in, one slamming through the opening at each end, bayonets extended.

Just like that, Julian thought, bringing up his carbine. To his right, over the quilted shoulder of the Chink plunging directly at him, he saw Giblin firing the snubbed .38 pistol, and firing again.

The muzzle flash of the carbine was light enough then, and its flame drove the Chink rifleman back and down hard. Julian went down, too—but to roll out of the tent and into the open night.

"Everybody down!" Harsh, metallic, the bullhorn's warning rang loud: "Anybody not in a hole loses his ass!"

Rocky didn't warn twice. Winking red and yellow, muzzle flashes from the Security Platoon raked the CP. Close and hot, bullets snapped the air close over Julian's head. That close, they didn't whine; they popped like firecrackers.

"Colonel?"

Lifting his head, Julian said, "Rocky—the tent! Giblin's in there with two Chinks!"

"Shit! They got by us anyhow. Wait—"

Porky Giblin lay on his back cursing, a dead Chink pinning him down, the Chink's bayonet high in his chest. Julian rolled the corpse off his corporal and shielded the lantern to get it going again. Suddenly the medic was with them, kneeling over Giblin and trying to keep him still.

"Scratch two," Rocky said. "You guys did okay."

"Okay, hell," Giblin grunted. "I hit that son of a bitch three times, and he stuck me anyhow."

"Cute little handgun," Rocky said.

Giblin grunted again. "Hey, medic—you want this fucking .38?"

The kid looked up. "Medics ain't armed, son. I tote a GI .45 in case the gooks don't know that."

Julian got a man on the radio and took the phone himself. It wasn't a snap, but everywhere the battalion was holding. He treated himself to a cigarette.

Outside, where they'd hauled the Chinese bodies, he heard Porky Giblin: "*Balls?* You know what the old man was doing when all that shit hit the fan? He sat there reading a letter from home. Old Balls Barron!"

CHAPTER 26

Chipyong-ni, Republic of Korea, Feb. 14, 1951—Ringed by mountains, this crossroads village was a salient reaching deep into enemy territory. It has become a gigantic trap for the 23rd Infantry Regiment. Cut off and surrounded by communist troops, the regiment cannot expect help; it must stand or die.

누더기 속에서 영웅 난다 .

"Out of rags comes a hero." (Korean proverb: Fire is the test for gold and adversity the test of a strong man.)

Because he had been educated and trained at length, and because he had struggled to absorb all that opportunity had to offer, Ho Chuk Gun could read in its entirety the pamphlet authored by Supreme Commander Lin Piao. Some of the *hanmun* characters were applied differently than Koreans used them, but with a bit of thought, the meanings became clear. *The Primary Conclusions of Battle Experience at Unsan* was a small book whose wisdom was mightier than the *Thoughts of Chairman Mao*.

It was why Chuk Gun had his junior officers gathered in this cave of limestone, to go through the instructions and information Commander Lin Piao thought important. He stood up and faced them now, three short rows of young officers whose units waited below the ridge. Already motivated, these men only needed guidance and control so that they might gain better dominance over the enemy. Dominance and, in the end, annihilation.

There was no need to call for attention; the audience was rapt and hungry, for the Americans were again within the reach of honor. First he read them much of what they already knew—that the *Me-in* coordination of mortars and tanks was excellent, their artillery very active. Although the words threatened to choke him, he continued: "Planes' strafing and bombing of our transportation and troop concentrations has become a great hazard, while in turn, their convoys move swiftly and unhindered."

No man nodded; hunkered upon the stony floor with chill evening wind sliding among them, Chuk Gun's men listened intently. Praising the enemy was up to him, his responsibility as commanding officer; they did not have to agree, only to learn and obey.

Departing from the pamphlet, he said, "They are men of machines—depending upon their machines because they realize that only the tanks and airplanes and trucks are strong. As men, they have no strength of their own. Cut off from the rear, they abandon all equipment and their heavy weapons," he told them in a strong, lashing voice. "American infantrymen are weak and afraid to die; they lack the courage either to attack or to defend. They may fight fairly well by day and at long range."

The junior officers stirred, a felt rather than seen movement that Chuk Gun interpreted as eagerness. He continued: "They cringe at night fighting and hand-to-hand combat; when defeated, they have no orderly formation of retreat and become lost, dazed, and panicked. The infantry loses its will to fight."

The brush-stroke characters blurred upon the page, and

Chuk Gun reminded himself to have the book written in pure Korean. The Chinese had deliberately ignored passing this vital information to their Korean allies. But it was not that slap which caused the pictographs to shimmer before Chuk Gun's eyes. It was the woman in the small house he had found for a command post. She, too, had lost her will to fight.

Clearing his throat, he said, "We will use the *Hachi-shiki*, the battle formation shaped as a wedge of flying geese. We move the open end against the foreigners, then close about their flanks while a special force pushes through to the rear and blocks reinforcements."

The woman—she had not told him her name, and he had not asked—at first fought him like a wild thing, but as his superior strength overcame her she melted to him. He had been too long without a woman and would have killed her, because it was obvious that her own man was away in enemy uniform. Also obvious from the first moment she stopped clawing and spitting was her own body hunger. The woman's house was perfectly situated; a small land-slide had toppled trees to form a natural roof. American airplanes would not find it or waste a bomb if they did.

There was something—not A-jah's grace but a kinship; not the glow of A-jah's lips, but a shimmer, and perhaps the woman required punishment for her husband standing against liberation, and for her fearlessness. She had re-mained in her house while all others fled the mountains.

"As a main objective," he continued, "one of our units —your battalion, Major Yun—must fight quickly around the enemy and cut off his rear. All units avoid highways and flat terrain and thus avoid tanks and artillery."

The woman—there between the snug, padded *chimtae* she flamed to him, taking him into her arching body as if he were her lover. For those dizzying moments, perhaps he was.

"Keep your men at the level of the Chinese," Chuk Gun

said. "They must be warm and well-fed as possible. The foreigners do not believe we can carry upon our backs all that we need to fight well. We have courage and obey orders and will fight to the death. We can and we will!"

Softly and sincerely, they applauded him then, an approving buzz passing among them. Striding through them with his aide trotting at his heels, Chuk Gun rolled Lin Piao's *Conclusions* in his hands. When this war came to its conclusion, the woman would return to Pyongyang with him. She would be proud to do so, and grateful to be concubine to a hero of the People's Democratic Republic.

At the cave entrance he turned and planted his boots apart, facing the lower ranks of his regiment. "Tonight," he announced, "at the first notes of the bugle, we attack. Chipyong-ni must fall to us."

Rich Shriver frowned at the kid. He couldn't get out now; nobody could cut through the murderous ring locked around this crossroads. Rich still didn't understand how or why they had gotten through roadblocks last night to join up with the 23rd. But Joe Chink did a lot of goofy things. Like that night across some river when they blew bugles and lighted torches, when they chanted and circled with those torches as if it were some homecoming parade.

For several minutes, all the GIs could do was stare and phone around to check their own vision. Some spoilsport called the map coordinates to Divarty, and the 105s, the 155s, put an end to the rites. If the Chinks pulled many stunts like that, the war would be short.

Several times, the Chinese—never the goddamned gooks—sent captured GIs back to their own lines; goofy and good propaganda. And sometimes, in attacks, they would come in standing straight up and laughing their lemonade asses off; goofy and a stash of heroin like the stuff found at Kunu-ri. Maybe the Chinks would pull back and let the regiment alone. And maybe there was no front seat in hell reserved for Rich Shriver.

He drove the jeep behind a Sherman from the 72nd Tank Battalion, and that worried him, how the tankers had dug in the monster until only its turret and guns were clear. When armor GIs worked that hard, everybody could expect a hairy fight.

Pulling a shovel from the jeep, he handed it to Kim Soo Man. "Dig deep, you little bastard, wide enough for both of us. I have to check in with the colonel and see what's going on. Then I'll come back and help dig."

"Guns, ammo?"

"Hell, yes, but get the hole dug first."

"Shit hit fan tonight?" The boy's smooth face hinted at a smile.

Rich slung his carbine. "I told you about that bad mouth. Keep your head down. Some fucking sniper may not wait until tonight."

He knew a few guys in the CP defense perimeter, but they were all too busy digging to do more than nod hello. Rich paused to look around. This wasn't the best defense position he'd ever seen, down in a little valley with a half-destroyed village around the nerve center. To the left front, he saw a line across frozen paddies, and on the right flank, the main line of defense must wind across a set of low hills.

Sighing, Rich ducked into a hut that still owned half a thatch roof; a folded squad tent covered the other half. Silver-haired, tall, and with the hawkish look of old-line aristocrats, Colonel Freeman was a busy man, flinging an indoctrination lecture over one shoulder to three second lieutenants. They were replacements, new to the army, not to mention to a combat zone, and were trying to look casual.

Freeman said, "The enemy is well-fed, well-clothed, and sturdy. They are rough, gentlemen; they're not afraid to leave their own lines; they carry their food and ammunition on their backs. They don't need trucks."

A captain handed Freeman a radio handset. The colonel spoke into it: "No, damn it! I know we're out on a limb, but nobody pulls out for any reason." Turning on the replacements, he said, "The Chinese soldier is an illiterate, simple peasant; he has nothing a modern army needs—no radio and very little artillery. He's not much good with artillery and has no tanks, no mechanized food supply or stockpiles of equipment."

Rich eased into a corner and took notes. Phones rattled, and the radio was busy; S-3 at the map was represented by a warrant officer. Rich looked over the new lieutenants, lucky to have gotten in before the ring shut, unlucky to draw the upcoming fight as their first combat duty. First blood was one thing; trauma was another.

Freeman folded himself onto a gas can padded by a rolled field jacket. "The Chinese can move no faster than they can trot, which means they can't shift rapidly to meet a changing situation or exploit a breakthrough."

He hesitated, and one of the new officers said, "Well, sir."

"Well," the colonel said, "this tough little son of a bitch, short of everything but guts and a willingness to die, has already inflicted upon American troops the worst defeat we have suffered in this century. He will be coming at us tonight, and you gentlemen will help stop him. Get to your platoons."

Writing fast, Rich thought that this professional was one of those who made the army worth a damn, that held it together despite changing tides, vote-conscious senators, and mom's my-poor-boy letters. Easing over to the warrant officer at the map, Rich introduced himself as PIO and got a rundown on troop strength.

Boxed into the Chink trap was the regiment itself, the attached U.N. French battalion, and in support the 37th

Field Artillery, a battery of 155s from the proud, black Nickel-Oh-Trey, a Ranger company, and a small detachment of engineers. This was stronger than it might have been, Rich noted. "What's against us?"

The S-3 man shook his head. "Nobody wants to count."

Putting his story notes away, Rich hurried back to the hole Soo Man had started. As the day lengthened, he felt the tension build, the rise of adrenaline brightening rays of the weak winter sun, making the smell of fresh-turned earth stronger. The CP tightened upon itself, voices dropping as the sun lowered, and before sunset Rich and Soo Man had a good hole. Shelter halves floored it, and they sat upon mountain-type sleeping bags. Shelves dug into the sides held ammunition and their few grenades, C-rations, and a canteen of water.

Blanket drawn around his shoulder, Rich spooned cold ham and limas. In his head, he fiddled with the story and sidebars. Any time an outfit was surrounded, it echoed WWI's Lost Battalion. But this might not work into a big deal; the Chinks could probe and get beaten off; tomorrow the air force would clobber them with napalm and rockets; a tank column could break through from the rear. But there was the goddamn *feel* of everything, the brassy taste of the air. It was coming, and when it got here, it would be a son of a bitch any way you looked at it, a true, revolving son of a bitch.

The ham and limas turned greasier to the taste. He shoved the half-eaten can into a shelf and stood up. His field of fire was narrow, but there was clearance; he could line up on the slope that led to the CP hut, but he'd sure better know his target. Rich decided he'd drop by again and help figure a signal or password, something. Maybe the CP would not be hit because the line outfits would all hold and no infiltrators would slip through.

Yeah, and maybe no kid would bleed to death tonight.

"Eat," he told the kid, "and don't lift your slope head

out of this hole unless I tell you it's bugout time. If you get into your sleeping bag, don't zip up. You might have to leave it in a hurry."

He remembered that it was this regiment that lost the first men trapped in their sleeping bags, unable to get loose and fight back when a sudden attack caught them. It was so damned cold in these mountains that staying warm might mean staying alive, so the men had to get back into their bags. But now they cut footholes in the bottom and stitched the rims with the soldier's next-to-favored companion, his "housewife" sewing kit. It happened, of course; the unexpected firefight, and three guys galloping away in sleeping bags, much like frenzied caterpillars.

What the hell; Rich climbed out and brought his Royal portable from the jeep. Before the light faded, he had typed a pretty good piece on the French battalion, culled from memory and earlier conversations.

Chipyong-ni, ROK—Already drained by their war in Vietnam, the French sent only one battalion of infantry to Korea. But they're good; they're all professionals, and many are Algerians who think war should be fun.

Putting the machine aside, Rich made certain that the kid was bundled up, then sank into a light sleep himself. He didn't dream but remembered being glad that he wasn't out on the perimeter where he'd have to stay awake and alert.

The Chinese waited until 0200. Rich checked his watch when the first brassy bugles echoed the frozen air. Shrill whistles picked up the noise, and flares went up to pop the black sky; white flares hissing and dripping, American. Jumping, Rich wondered what the hell. A siren—an old fire-engine siren—split the night, hand-cranked, by the rising squall of it. Down there on the south rim the flares drifted and hand grenades went off—four, five. Small arms popped in that area, then farther up along the line. At least two outfits were being hit, and that damned siren slowed.

217

The first attacks were quickly over, and three more exploded before dawn. Each time Rich jerked awake, had a drink of *soju,* and shoved Soo Man's head down. The CP force didn't have to fight, but when the day oozed gray tentacles over the hills and across the stripped paddies Rich hadn't been able to catnap for hours.

"Make a cook hole," he said. "I'll go see what happened last night. You make coffee and heat some Cs; don't go after the little stove. Use heat tablets and stay in that hole."

"Okay; you think I'm some dumb gook?"

"Laddie buck, I know damned well you are."

Last night's light attacks couldn't be all. The Chinks had the whole regiment surrounded, boxed in tight. Rich looked skyward as the C129 transports lumbered over and spewed equipment parachutes. The 23rd Infantry was still cut off, or it wouldn't be getting airborne goodies.

That meant the fight at Chipyong-ni wasn't over; it was just getting started.

CHAPTER 27

Central front, Republic of Korea, Feb. 14, 1951—Although the world's attention remains focused upon the village of Chipyong-ni, where an American regiment is fighting for its life, the war continues elsewhere. Twice today, the Chinese tried to drive south and reinforce troops blocking U.N. relief columns. A tired ROK unit broke both attempts.

집과 계집은 가꾸기 탓

"A house and a woman depend on how you care for them." (Korean proverb: To keep a house and woman safe, each must be well guarded.)

Chong Nam Ki tilted his head forward so his brother's gentle hands could loosen the ache in his neck. It would take Buddha himself to halt the pain in his head, and he was grateful that it did not remain but came and went like slow waves on a shore.

> My mind is a lake
> Please come in your boat.
> Clasping your white shadow
> I'll shatter like jade
> Against the bow.

Nam Ki did feel brittle, more like porcelain than jade, a hollow vase of celadon kept too long in the kiln. But his shaping was still his own, and although chipped, he was not yet crumbled. He was still his father's son, still a senior colonel.

"*Komahp-da,*" he said. "Thank you." He used the lowest form of politeness, because as his younger brother, Wei Ki was not entitled to more. Was this in part what Father Chong had meant about the new Korea adapting? To retain the good and discard that which had outlived its usefulness; must they begin with the language, which established not only stature, but caste?

"There is tea," Wei Ki said. "One tires of coffee, and our mother knows this. She entrusted tea to a wounded sergeant returning to duty in our regiment."

"I would like tea," Nam Ki said. He put on his helmet and took it off again because it was too heavy. "Our mother would be an excellent intelligence officer. There is little she does not discover."

She had not known of his love for Wha Ja, but suspected something. He had refused even to meet with the marriage broker and turned away from her subtle maneuverings to interest him in *yangban* women from suitable families. The bloodline must be kept fine and pure. An entertainer, a woman whom only training and tradition raised higher than a prostitute? A *kisaeng,* my son? He could not have mentioned such a thing.

Blinking, Nam Ki stared about the hut, stared at his muddy boots worn inside the house. Mother would be furious; see how the papered floor was ruined. But this was not the Chong home; it was a battered hut in the central mountains. Of course; how could he have thought otherwise? He said, "Younger brother, do you think the marriage laws should be changed?"

Wei Ki frowned. "We await an attack that may destroy

us, and you speak of marriage laws? My brother, my colonel—"

Nam Ki took the hot tea. Somehow, it had always tasted better from a brass bowl rather than a canteen cup. "As for the attack, we have prepared as best we could. So now I think of what father wished—a new Korea built solidly upon the old strengths, stronger because the old weaknesses are gone."

"Lee cannot marry Lee, Kim cannot marry Kim. It has always been so."

Sipping tea, Nam Ki shook his head. "Even though ten generations have passed? This should no longer matter."

While jealously protecting the family lines, the emperors, the scholars, and the people themselves refused to accept any outside blood; the *chingol* true bone was the standard. Chinese, Japanese, and any other foreign taint was scorned.

Perhaps this began with Korea's great mistake, that of thinking it had the best of all possible worlds and denying any intrusion by barbarians, denying progress while the world passed it by.

Even if that were so, the result was Korea's ethnic individuality. If there had been no genetic prejudice, there would be no Korea—only a nameless appendage of China, or a colony absorbed by Japan. Changing tradition for reality was one thing; racial suicide another. Who would be wise enough to draw the line?

"The tea is good," he said, closing his eyes against a ripple of pain in his head. No written law said he could not marry Wha Ja, but duty was stronger. He wished it was not so. "Are the replacements cared for?"

"Yes, brother. But every day there are fewer veterans to guide them."

"Ah; then you no longer consider war an adventure?"

Wei Ki shook his head. "Only an atrocity. But there are tigers in the world."

Rubbing his temple where the thick scar pulsed, Nam Ki said, "As our father knew. We do not become tiger hunters by choice." He finished his tea and allowed his body to sag back upon the floor. "I will rest now."

Major Lim came quietly from his corner and murmured, "We will wake you at the first bugles, colonel."

Nam Ki's eyelids fluttered. "You and I have gone many *li* since the railway station in Seoul. Friend Lim, I thank you for watching over my brother; I thank you for your loyalty to our country and to me."

"Sir—"

He was tired, and the pain waves lapped inside his head, but he felt the uneasiness of his officers. There was no cause for fear, he wanted to tell them.

"We will travel many more *li* together, Colonel Chong."

And Wei Ki said, "Yes, older brother."

Against his eyelids Nam Ki saw the fortune teller in the Miari district of Seoul and heard the whisper from *The Book of Probabilities*. Old man, what do you know of love, what can you see with your blind eyes? . . . I hear the stars, *yangban;* I taste wind upon the moon, and your future sings of sorrow. . . .

Fortune tellers, shaman priestesses, superstitions older than carved stone gods that guard village gates—must these relics of honored centuries be discarded in order to compete with newer countries? So much should be retained for the children to know the full measure of Korea.

Crash!

Sitting up quickly, Nam Ki knew an echoed crash of pain. Mortar? Recoilless rifle? His ears were not as clear as they should be. He shivered and pulled on his coat, locked the end-to-end banana clip into his carbine. Swaying, he stood up; before Korea could be guided into the modern world, first it must be saved from the Chinese and the *inmun-gun.*

A dim voice calls
From a distant field
But I can see no one
In the fine haze.
Another call comes
Dimly from far away.

Sam Connover worked the bit of broken straw into his left earlobe. The irritation gave him something to concentrate upon and stopped him from wondering if it was day or night. The Chinks hadn't noticed yet, and if the right GIs kept their mouths shut, they wouldn't realize that only the Reactionaries wore the symbol of defiance. The indoctrinators would think it only another aberration of Yankee capitalists. Stonewall Jackson started the fashion, coming out of his last trip to the Hole wearing a wood-splinter earring. It gave some of the men, the hard-core resisters, something to keep secret among themselves, gave them a badge of pride. Matt Jackson deserved a medal for lifting spirits and toughening resolve. If they made it out of Camp #5, Sam would see to that medal.

He sat cross-legged upon the bare floor and stared at the bare wall. He had never learned the art of meditation, but at times he could take himself almost out of his body. Now the bare electric bulb dangled lighted from the ceiling, but that didn't mean anything. A basic trick of the communists was to confuse the PW's sense of time. The light might burn endlessly; the room might remain black for eternity. Either way, they didn't want you sleeping much. A guard would come in and shake you awake at odd hours. Anything to make it easier for the bastards to feed their line of bullshit.

The Chinese had stopped the beatings, the physical torture, and bore down upon psychological abuse. It worked better; the list of active collaborators among the prisoners grew almost daily. Then there were those who merely cooperated. The real spies were difficult to count. It was easier to just go along, to write criticisms of yourself and memorize "socialist" dogma. Going hardnose put you in this private room.

His uncle's serial number still confused Commander Ding-dong and his slick indoctrinators, but Sam held fast to his stupid act and usually got by. Lately, however, he was drawing more attention because somebody, some goddamned Progressive, had fingered him as a resistance leader. His "huh—beats me—huh" routine didn't get him trotted back to Hut 6, but to solitary confinement. At least no idiot in Second Division G-2 or KMAG—if Korean Military Advisory Group still existed—had blown Sam's cover with queries to the International Red Cross. If anybody had noticed. How long to the evening—or morning —bowl of boiled millet or corn and tepid cabbage soup that might have a film of grease on it, if he got lucky? Who could tell?

Look at the wall, Sam. See something on the wall, and the next step is to see something *in* the wall and people it with light and shadow, with faces . . . Maggi Barron's eyes, sea-deep and sea-green, surging tidal eyes that were so soft in the next dawnlight. She might even have been silently crying as he watched her when she didn't know, as she thought she was sneaking out of the room without waking him.

It was a maneuver usually his own, leaving without commitment, without lies. He didn't want this woman to go, ever. But that was stupid. He hadn't even known who she was, if Maggi was her right name, and a one-night stand, no matter how wondrous, could not mean a set of discharge papers from the army. Until this moment, no woman had even made him think of it, and Maggi didn't make him dwell on something he couldn't handle—civilian life—longer than it took her to slip out of the door. For

224

a long time afterward he lay on the bed and stared at the ceiling.

Sam rocked forward, and his forehead bumped the wall. Cold, the special, damp Manchurian cold, probed into his clothing. He struggled to again divorce mind from body. It worked in part; he still felt the numbness of his face and feet, and he had lost Maggi.

. . . Samuel, you must not demean yourself. You must not associate with the Koreans beyond the church. You are white, *white*, and never forget that, and never demean yourself to the Asiatic.

Is bowing to the Japanese demeaning, father?

. . . Samuel, Samuel—I have spared the rod and spoiled the child. Render therefore, unto all their dues; tribute to whom tribute is due; custom to whom custom; fear to whom fear—you do know the quotation, Samuel?

Romans 13-7, but doesn't it end with honor to whom honor? Koreans are honorable, father.

. . . I do not recall that you have as yet learned Zechariah and Malachi; excellent discipline, Samuel, and knowledge that will help you in divinity school.

Sam jerked back, came hurrying mentally back from the rectory at Chunju. His legs were stiff, and he had trouble standing on them. Genesis, Exodus, Leviticus and Numbers, he had memorized them all, kneeled on a cold stone floor, and because he felt he had no choice might actually have gone to divinity school, if for no other reason than to get away from vicious little Japs, or get the hell away from hell.

Still, it might have taken more guts than he had back then to defy God and his father, because it also meant breaking his promise to his mother. But there was Kelly Connover, glorious black sheep of an otherwise staid family; Kelly and his vivid stories of far and exciting places. Why had the roaring boy-o come all the way to Korea at a time when the Japs showed openly they hated all white men? Kelly Connover had retired from the army, just barely. He returned to all he had left of family, to those of his blood. At the end, the miserable end of his life and the ancestral fear of banshees brought him to his holy brother's side.

Where he shortly died, not at last by enemy steel, but gutted by cancer. When it was time for the church to send Sam "home" to the land he had never seen, past time by the Japanese timetable, Sam first realized he had a choice. He didn't go to school. He went to the first recruiting office he could find in San Francisco.

Four years later the Japs beheaded his father at Chunju Prison.

Rubbing his arms and then stooping to rub feeling back into his feet, Sam lowered himself into the cross-legged position. It was Korean, and perhaps the many ghosts of Connover *Moksa*'s butchered parishioners would help his son survive.

CHAPTER 28

Chipyong-ni, Republic of Korea, Feb. 14, 1951—This tiny outpost
of the free world hangs on tonight, despite repeated heavy attacks by fanatic communist troops.

궁한 쥐는 고양이를
문다.

**"A cornered rat bites the cat." (Korean proverb: The
desperate fight to live.)**

Ho Chuk Gun trembled within himself and showed nothing. It would not do to allow a woman to believe she had
any sort of control over him. But he still could not understand how a woman so sleek and beautiful would live in
the mountains on poor land, with some brutish farmer.

Eyes properly downcast, moving with the innate grace
of a temple dancer, she served the American coffee he had
brought. Kneeling before him, pale hands at rest upon her
simple dress, the woman sat upon feet tucked beneath her
buttocks. Her back was straight, and light from the single
small candle gleamed softly in her hair.

He had less than an hour before the night's attack, and
he had earned this privilege of his rank. The woman was as
much his right as lesser spoils belonged to his men. For

them the food, cigarettes, and watches, the warm clothing of the foreigners, as well as their weapons. For the commanding officer, his choice. The regiment understood that. Under the great leader Kim Il Sung, an intelligent and ambitious man could rise high. Only the oxlike remained peasants, held to the muck of rice paddies by their own lack of ability, not because some rich and powerful landowner chained them there.

When he put down the brass bowl of coffee and drew out a long American cigarette the woman made a small bow and lifted the candle plate, leaning toward him to offer the flame, using both hands as inferior to superior. She had been well trained by someone, and surely not by her husband. Chuk Gun would not ask, of course. He smoked and listened to the activity outside the hut, the muted movement of a thousand men flowing through the narrow draw. This night they would go up and over the ridges, then down into that valley where the stupid foreigners waited to be killed. The Chinese would be impressed by the skill and valor of Ho Chuk Gun's soldiers.

So it was only right that he celebrate in advance, for tomorrow he would see to executions and interrogations in Chipyong-ni, too busy for the ministrations of this woman.

He said, "After the battle I will send my aide for you. You will ride north in a captured vehicle. Captain Sunoo will take you to my quarters in Pyongyang, and as soon as the *khojaengi* are driven from Korea, I will return to you." He had not asked her; he commanded and did not doubt that she would obey. Beauteous or not, she was only a woman.

Drowning his cigarette in the coffee bowl, Chuk Gun leaned above the candle flame and put both hands upon her breasts. She quivered and thrust the full globes hard against his palms. He did not have to order her to remove her clothing; breathing heavily, she already fumbled at her dress. Warmth lingered within the floor from charcoal that had cooked the evening rice, and the quilted bedding, although not richly embroidered, was clean.

Chuk Gun stretched upon it and waited for her to finish presenting her nude body and then take down his pants. There was no time for his complete and more satisfying nakedness; that would come later. Only her breasts were bare when she turned toward him upon her knees, the dark cherries of her nipples aimed downward at him. Her hands worked at the puddle of her spread skirts.

He did not see the knife until it flashed in her raised hand.

It drove at his throat, and he barely jerked aside in time. He heard the violent hiss of her breath as she struck again, quick and deadly as a serpent. She did not miss him this time.

Searing pain burst in his head and exploded through his body. He struck out blindly and rolled to his knees. His pistol—where was his pistol? The she-dog! He would shoot holes in her belly. Right hand clapped against the agony of his eye, he lunged at her, but she knocked out the candle, and he missed her in the dark. Her blade raked his arm, and he cursed. Scuttling backward, he pawed for his coat and pistol belt.

A gust of chill wind touched him as he turned, gun in hand. Oh, the cunning bitch—she snatched open the door and was gone into the night. Chuk Gun pushed hard against his cheekbone, against the eye that poured blood down his cheek. On his knees, rocking with unbelievable pain, he choked back the shout that rose in his throat. Outside the hut, his men gathered for the attack. He could not scream at them to find the woman, the cursed she-devil who had waited until just before this important battle to try to kill him. Insane; she must be a crazy woman, to do this and refuse the great opportunity he had offered her. After the battle he would have the mountains searched for her, run her down like the low, sly animal she was. It would give him intense pleasure to open her belly and slowly pull out her intestines.

It took a mighty effort for him not to cry out. In the dark, he ripped cloth from the bedding and felt gingerly about his face. Soft and grapelike, his eyeball fell into his hand. Shuddering, he flung the thing against the black wall and wiped his hand upon his jacket. Steeling himself, knotting his stomach against the sickness that threatened to spew forth, he forced the cloth into the empty socket and bound it there.

Head spinning and gone weak in the knees, Ho Chuk Gun fought his weakened body with the strength of his mind. The pain—the stabbing, excruciating pain—he used it as a focal point, as a throbbing center of hate to strengthen his resolve. Crawling, he reached the open door and eased out upon the entrance porch. Sitting erect then, he belted on his pistol and tightened the bandage around his forehead. He would not let his men see his wound. If every drop of blood ran out of his body, he would lead them until he fell.

The planes thundered in low over the ridge tops, guns hammering and rockets smoking out ahead of the jets. Rich Shriver leaned against the lip of the hole he shared with Kim Soo Man and watched the explosions flower against the mountain slopes, saw the tracers ricochet and arc skyward. Close air support kept the Chinese army under cover this day, and when the jets went home the Corsairs would come winging in with their loads of napalm. Rich watched the terrible beauty of the Sabre jets scream down and claw high in a graceful ballet.

And he remembered the Zeros in his other war, whipping over at treetop height and shooting the shit out of the jungle and everything in it. Washing Machine Charlie making his nightly run with a couple of bombs; if he didn't kill anybody, he ruined sleep. Having air control was a hell of a lot better than being on the receiving end.

He slid down and sat on his rolled sleeping bag. He was the only correspondent at Chipyong-ni, and if he were a civilian, the copy he sent out with the medevac choppers would make him famous. As a GI, he'd be lucky if it bought him another stripe. A rocket explosion shook the earth and sprinkled dirt upon his portable typewriter.

"Fucking flyboys," he said, and he shook the dirt off, balanced the machine on his knees, and continued to write. *Ten crazy men of the French battalion last night faced a fierce Chinese attack. They cranked off a fire siren liberated from somewhere in Pyongyung, gathered hand grenades, and boiled out of their foxholes with fixed bayonets. About 40 shocked Chinese broke and fled down the hill.*

Cute story, great color, and it might divert attention from the fact that an entire regiment and some support troops were still cut off, and the next time the Chinks came their sheer numbers could roll them right over the 23rd's desperate positions. The real story, the straight news story, was how this outfit was toughing it out, clinging to every yard of contested ground despite everything the Chinks threw. No choice because the outfit was surrounded? Like hell; they could always quit, throw up their hands and yell *"Tow Shong!"* like it said in the Red propaganda leaflets.

There's where old Mousey Dung could use help, rewriting those leaflets. Rich had one in his pocket: "Don't be the sacrifices of moneybags and warmongers. . . . You never dream that this winter you would come to a foreign land 5,000 miles away from your home and creep in the cold trenches with your lives in danger every minutes." Another raggedy bit of paper was addressed to officers and enlisted men of the U.S. aggressive army. Not exactly an auspicious opening, but no doubt better than Rich could do in Chinese.

A deeper, slower sound floated down upon them, transport planes; Rich looked up to see parachutes spill out and mushroom accurately down upon the crossroads. A supply drop, the first of many, replacing ammunition burned during the night, bringing in medicines, food, and water. There would be no bugging out from this position; even if the Chinks allowed it, Eighth Army wouldn't. Now, if about a battalion of paratroopers would drop in— He felt warmth and smelled gas. Turning, he eyed the steel pot that the kid had upended and filled with dirt. When the firing stopped after daybreak, Soo Man had scooted around and come back with a rectangular can, the kind issued to kitchens. It was half full of gas, and the kid used it to fuel his makeshift field stove.

"You little bastard," Rich said, "you'll make out okay. If you don't get hanged, you'll probably end up running this two-bit country."

Looking up from a cup of issue chicken noodle soup he'd mixed, Soo Man said, "What this two bit?"

Rich smoothed a crumpled cigarette and lighted it before explaining about small change. Another flight of supply planes thrummed overhead, and an M-1 rifle cracked twice on the far edge of the perimeter.

Soo Man said, *"Hankuk* no small change one day. We fix."

He held up the warmed canteen cup, and Rich took a long swallow before passing it back. "Give you the chance and you might do that."

"Fucking-A right."

"Watch your mouth. You want to grow up ignorant?"

Or just grow up, Rich thought. All the Korean kids whose lives were cut short already; the thousands more who'd get blown apart or just be starved; the skinny kids made orphans by bloody-handed liberators from north of the Parallel. Trying to reach maturity in Korea was a full-time job with no overtime, holidays, or bonuses. Hell, he had just described the Regular Army soldier, the difference being that the RA clown had a choice and got paid for it, more or less.

"Stay in the hole and eat something," he said. "I better not look out of the CP and catch your lemonade ass running around outside."

Soo Man grinned. "No sweat, Rich."

Command post people were busy deepening the regimental nerve center for the coming night. Rich said hi to a couple of them and got close to the S-1 sergeant. "Casualties getting out?"

"The bad ones; those choppers only haul two at a time. Not many KIA, considering." The man was an old-timer, another of those who thought they'd made their war and could sit it out until retirement. How did the old quote go . . . Give him a break, St. Peter; he's served his hitch in hell.

The old guy said, "It'll hit the fan tonight, though. The sons of bitches will keep coming. G Company got a prisoner who says last night was just a probe." He grunted and rubbed an unshaven smile. "They can't get the guy out, so they wired him to an 81 base plate. If I know George Company, they'll have him loading. Son of a bitch is lucky they didn't pop him in the first place. This way he earns his rations."

Rich hunkered down. If he thought any paper would print it, he'd get a shot of a Chink soldier loading an 81mm mortar tube. The Geneva Convention high brass would scream, and liberal papers stateside would jump at the chance to show how GIs flaunt the Rules of War. Whatever the hell those were. The Geneva Convention was okay, but North Korea and Red China hadn't signed in. Who saw or cared what happened in the field? Only the poor bastards who died there.

As for rules, Rich knew only two: stay alive and don't bleed. For Christ's sake, don't bleed.

He scribbled some notes, passed his typed copy to the

sergeant to get out with the next medevac chopper, and picked up some C-rations. He avoided the aid station and went back to his hole. Soo Man was asleep, but a new shelf had been dug for his helmet-stove and gas can.

"Just like home," Rich whispered, and climbed down to key open a can of cold hamburgers with gravy. The P-38 worked perfectly, and he wondered why the army couldn't put out something else as good as the little folding can opener, the best equipment ever issued.

Seated on the sleeping bag, Rich took off his tin pot and leaned back. Any rest would have to be this afternoon; anybody the Chinks caught asleep this night would wake up in hell. He looked over at the kid, at the smooth young face softened in repose. Again he wished there was some way to get him out of danger. A tough little bastard, Soo Man welcomed an opportunity to draw blood on behalf of his parents. But damn it, he was still only a kid and ought to be doing kid things.

Rich nodded off and awoke to twilight, to a sense of oh-shit all through the CP perimeter. Around the low ridges, and across along the rice paddy defense, the line outfits had long ago buttoned up, and all they had to do now was wait and pray. No planes could help them now; no armor would break through in the nick of time. When the gritty turned shitty, it was always the ragged-ass infantryman who had to stand and take it.

The kid was gone.

"You little bastard! Soo Man—" Rich stood up, put one foot onto the firestep, and shouted the name.

Behind him, noise. He whirled, and Soo Man dropped into the hole. "Watch your mouth. Many fucking Chinks."

"Where the hell you been?"

"Look jeep, dig more."

Rich found a cigarette and crouched low to light it. "Damn that jeep. You stay here and cover your own ass. Understand?"

Now he could just make out the expression on the kid's face when Soo Man said, "Okay, papa-san; no sweat."

Papa-san, the GI-bastardized-Japanese term for old man, but the kid wasn't using it that way. He meant daddy, and Rich turned away quickly. Terry would have loved this kid. If she got the chance to know Soo Man, maybe she'd think things over. That was part of their trouble, Rich thought— no kids, nothing that stayed alive and bound them together.

What did he want, for Christ's sake? He could hear St. Teresa's comeback: a child, and you in the army? A child, and you off playing war? Terry did the right thing, walking out on him. The army was no place for kids and wives. Like Chipyong-ni was no place for anybody with good sense. Real estate wasn't worth one drop of blood, but killing Chinese was important now. Rich could see the reasoning behind this stubborn defense. Eighth Army and especially this Second Division needed to know that the Chinese weren't supermen, that firepower and heart could stop their human sea attacks.

Maybe. This was the time and place to find out.

Rich pulled a deep breath at the first Chinese flare popping high over Chipyong-ni: singly and in groups, a dozen others spread evil red blooms into the black and breathless sky. And there rang the bugles ahead and to the rear, on both flanks, keying upon the drifting flares. Surrounded; cut off—spook words to the GI, evoking memories of Custer's last stand and the glory poster in every small-town barbershop in the country. Give the American soldier a back door, and he'd fight well. Not for him the fight-to-the-last-man bullshit. Leave him a way out, and he would return to fight another day; he turned claustrophobic when boxed in. But there were enough survivors of Kunu-ri here, enough men who saw North Korean atrocities along the Naktong, to keep the replacements from pulling the plug.

"Hell," he muttered, "I can't sit here and know what's

going on. Soo Man—you stay in this hole, understand? Promise, you little bastard. You understand promise?"

"Damn right. You promise come back."

"You got it, son."

With that he climbed out and covered the few yards downhill to the CP, which was turning into a creditable bunker that could do with a thick roof, but roofs were short around Chipyong-ni. As Rich slid inside firefights broke out on all sides of the perimeter; not quick bursts and wait, but the long, rolling fire that said big trouble. Everybody in the bunker listened, heads cocked and eyes serious below frowns.

Thump . . . THUMP! . . . deep, somewhat muffled explosions that weren't mortars, and not grenades.

"Satchel charges," the old sergeant said. "Probably pole charges, too; like they ran at our tanks with."

Colonel Freeman said, "Isn't that George Company's area? Get them on the phone."

"Coming in now, sir." The commo man had a long, pale face. "They're getting hit hard and want help."

Freeman took the phone and said there was no help, except possibly drawing some men from the artillery battery. The old sergeant squatted beside Rich and told him how Chinks ran at the foxholes and blew them apart with big charges. Outside, a star shell was so bright that Rich caught a flash of it through the canvas bunker cover.

"Outgoing," the sergeant said. "Gives George Company a look at the Chinks. They'll follow with HE and Willy Peter. Maybe that will stop them."

"Reports from first battalion," the commo man said. "Everybody's under fire. Not much mortar, though."

Outside, a shell fragment hit a rock and whined off. Then the noise grew, ballooning with explosion after shell burst until the whole area rocked.

Head down as he wrote on his pad, Rich pictured the unadulterated hell at the foxholes below. The action might as well be on some lousy South Pacific island. No jungle here, and cold instead of heat, but otherwise the scenario was the same—slant-eyed bastards charging and screaming, dropping grenades into foxholes. They would die by the hundreds, but what the hell did goddamn Japs care about life, even their own? Jap, Chink, gook—

"I'm gone," he told the sergeant. "If they break through George Company and get in here, I can cover a ten-yard stretch to your right front."

"Do me a favor," the old guy said. "If you don't have a good eye, hang onto your grenades. Last time the CP got hit, some asshole threw grenades all over the place; damned near killed everybody but Chinks. If you're going, make it now. In a few minutes anybody moving around outside is suicidal."

Bellying down before he reached the hole, Rich felt the tightness of muscle tension across his neck and shoulders. Nature, the survival instinct; flex the muscle, and the club won't do as much damage; ready the body with terror and hate, and it drew quick, saving strength when most needed. Only nobody told Mother Nature that she was running a few thousand years behind, that today's club had an average muzzle velocity of 2,800 feet per second. That was enough to knock a dinosaur ass over tea kettle, and those damned things wore armor plate and stood yea tall. So much for tensed muscle.

"Soo Man—hey kid! Don't get itchy. I'm coming in."

The voice eased to him from the darkness, thin and whispery as his own, toneless. "Yes—come."

Rich turned cold all over. Head up, propped upon one elbow, he zeroed in. This was the right direction, and just ahead was the hole they had dug. But that was not Soo Man's voice. Good God; some fucking infiltrator had reached the kid, killed him. Oh, Jesus, oh, goddamn. His throat aching dry, Rich had to be sure and hissed, "The little bastard there with you?"

Snick. Burpgun bolt or grenade pin? The voice: "Yes—come."

Oh, goddamn, laddie buck. I'm so goddamn sorry I left you alone. See what I did, Terry? See what that deaf god of yours let happen? You couldn't intercede, St. Teresa?

A heavy shell rocked the ground, and Rich dug fingers of his left hand into frozen dirt. Forgive me, kid. Forgive me, Terry.

"Hey, gook!"

Little Sir Echo, slimy echoing son of a bitch whispering his only English into the night: "Yes, yes—come in."

"Hey!"

"Yes—"

Rich aimed for the voice, a sound shot. Bam-bam-bam-bam!

The son of a bitch never finished his sentence. Barely able to breathe, Rich crawled to the hole, to the darker shadow sprawled over its lip. Inching close until he could put out a hand and feel that this wasn't a little dead kid. It was a heavy-bodied Chink. Rich put the muzzle of his carbine to the guy's head and kicked off more shots—bam-bam-bam! Then he dragged the corpse the rest of the way out of their hole. his and Soo Man's. At least the kid deserved privacy.

CHAPTER 29

Bern, Switzerland, Feb. 15, 1951—Officials of the International Red Cross returned from an inspection tour of North Korean and Chinese prisoner of war camps today. The diet is adequate and the treatment humane, they said.

익은 밥 먹고 선 소리 한다.

"Eat ripe rice and speak green words." (Korean proverb: Talk nonsense with a well-fed mouth.)

He stopped being cold. He lost track of time and couldn't find his feet or hands. Sam knew only that he was still tied beneath the downspout, and icy water was beating him to death. He wanted to curl up in some dry corner of his mind and have it done, just wait to be dead.

Lifting his head, he sucked water and coughed. It was crazy to drown standing up. St. Michael, you're supposed to watch over soldiers, so where the hell are you?

Graven images, Samuel? You have strayed far.

His father had never been to Manchuria, but Connover *Moksa* had long echoed from that mass grave at Chunju Prison. Sam tried to close him out.

This wasn't war, he thought; it wasn't even a decent place to die.

A thousand years ago, Kelly Connover said if a soldier was real lucky he could pick a way to die, a day to die. But even Kelly was forced to shrivel in pain and lose his dignity.

Oh, Christ; oh, St. Michael. Hell would be nice and warm. Ah—there's the rub, Horatio. The sons of bitches have turned hell into a frozen punishment of ice and snow and razored wind. Heaven must shine with long rows of red glowing heaters and open fireplaces that pop with sparks. Heaven wasn't angels and pink clouds; it was never being cold.

Heaven is the kingdom of God, Samuel.

Water; water beating his brain to mush. If he cried, the Chinks couldn't tell it now. His head was sore, his face ached. They wanted him to beg, to sign a confession . . . forgive me, Father, for I have sinned. But he wasn't Catholic; he wasn't even a man, only a huge, throbbing boil.

Maybe uncle Kelly Connover hurt this way, the cancer beating him from inside, whipsawing his guts and boring through his ribs. And Kelly toughed it out . . . remember, kid—fuck them all but six, and save them for pallbearers, and two for road guards. If you go first class, save two more—one to count cadence and one to piss on the grave.

Let's have a drink on it, kid.

Anything but water.

Blessed be the meek, Samuel.

Dead be the fucking meek, kid. Old soldiers never die, but the lovers of soldiers pass like the seasons. The army is like Texas, kid—hell on women and horses, and all the horses have been used up. If you give a damn about a woman, fuck her and forget her. She'll never understand that you've already crawled into a big olive-drab cunt that won't let go.

Women pass like the seasons, but Maggi had not passed.

Army wives were soldiers, too. Daughter and granddaughter and great-granddaughter of soldiers, she was one with military posts and wars and separations. Duty; Maggi Barron knew about duty. What more could Sam want from her, what more she of him? Soldier to soldier.

Onward, Christian soldiers.

Sam hung against his ropes. Old soldiers never die. They brace under a downspout, and water beats down on them until their head explodes. He was winning now because even if they wired his wrists and jerked the tendons apart like Smitty's, he wouldn't feel it . . . how the hell was he supposed to confess anything? Forgive me, father —for not going back to Chunju to die with you; forgive me, for I have killed and been killed.

Water will never be holy again.

"You got to help!" Sam's head rocked with the slap. "Damn it—come on, pull out of it."

More goddamned water, but this time it was hot, and he choked on it. Opening his eyes, he saw Stonewall Jackson's intent face. "Sergeant Connover present and accounted for, sir."

"Shee-it," Matt said. "I told you they couldn't kill this crazy fay. Help me peel him out of these wet clothes. Marotta—Joe Lavoie, give me your blankets."

Smitty said, "Rub him with my shirt."

It was warm in the hut, the floor soft as feathers. Sam sank into it, eyes closed against the drumbeat in his head. He still felt the water pounding down, pounding down. Commander Ding had refined torture; the downspout was worse than the Hole.

Shaking his head, Sam hunched in blankets to see Jackson leaning from the hut to wring out the sopping uniform. He said to Smitty, "Who turned me in?"

Hands flopping, Smitty said, "Be that mean motherfucker in Hut 5 or Buckbee here. Both be running scared of you."

Sam pressed his head between his hands; it seemed to help. The sergeant in Hut 5; over there they lived in fear of the man. There were stories that he snatched rations from the sick, that he had thrown men from the hut to freeze in the night. A Progressive of sorts, Kallager used the Chinks as much as they used him, mouthing their propaganda and signing anything put before him because they kept him in power in his hut. Sam and Matt Jackson had paid a call on Kallager and told him to ease up.

Buckbee was a typical Pro, giving in at the first pressure, criticizing himself and others, bowing and scraping to the Chinese in hopes of staying alive. He reported everything to his masters and dutifully read Marxist literature. Buckbee had been told to find another hut, to ask for a transfer.

One or both of these men had gotten Sam the waterspout treatment. "I heard the Koreans talking," he said. "Nose and Slant. They were bitching about the Chinks losing a big fight and sacrificing Korean troops. It's the first time the bastards have been stopped, and they must have gotten a real ass-kicking."

"Good," Jackson said, "but what's that got to do with them fucking Pros?"

Rubbing his head, Sam said, "The Chinks will be busy saving face and making excuses."

"Now you got it," Smitty said, waving his hands. "Waste them motherfuckers while Joe Chink busy."

Jackson grunted and massaged Sam's hands, his own right hand thinner and more clawlike now. "Who's close in Hut 5?"

Smitty's head bobbed, and he took a while to answer. "White boy—Richards, Richardson, something like that; dying fast. Man gets down in that hut, fucking Kallager holds back rations, says they dying anyway."

"Switch names," Sam said. "Put Kallager out for the

dogs, and if the other guy buys it, hide him until the next day. We all look alike to Chinks."

"Shee-it," Jackson said, "I thought that was just us niggers." He nodded at the other room. "How about our homegrown Pro?"

Sam pulled the blankets tight about his body. His hands were shriveled, and he felt that way all over, inside and out. He could still hear the roar of water. Maybe they had waited too long already; the Chinks controlled the camp like no other jailers in other wars, through indoctrination classes that were a sort of mind control and a network of informers. Worse, they reached kids who never had a clear idea of values and confused them even more.

He didn't know about the other PW camps, but no escape had been made from this one. That was the soldier's first duty after capture, to escape; nobody in Camp 5 had even tried. Everything was against getting away—the open terrain; the population, where any GI would stand out; and the language. Sam might have made it himself, but only by faking a Russian uniform and with a lot of luck. Keeping a project like that secret was almost impossible under the present camp setup. Sam realized that he was also at fault, that personal resistance wasn't enough.

"Hold off on Buckbee," he said. "We can use him if he's more scared of us than the Chinks." His teeth rattled a bit from the cold still inside him, but he looked at the others in the room. "Anybody thinks they can't handle this, you don't want to hear any more."

Marotta looked at Joe Lavoie, but neither moved.

"Good," Sam said. "Matt, you and I—"

"Don't want to hear no shucking about let's draw straws. I got dibbs on Kallager my ownself. Motherfucker thinks he's badass, and I want to see how bad. Besides, Joe Chink be watching anybody, it be you fresh out of your shower bath."

Softly, Marotta said, "I got a piece of sharp tin that would easy cut his throat."

Sam stared. "That guy who committed suicide—Coyner; the Chinks never found the weapon. You did."

"Thought it might come in handy, one way or another."

Jackson said, "Hang to it. Kallager is set for a couple of rounds with me and no referee."

Julian heard the nickname and liked it. Balls Barron put him in a category with Blood and Guts Patton and Vinegar Joe Stilwell. He was accepted. All through childhood he had never had a nickname, and his wife had never called him anything but Julian.

Maggi; he couldn't get her out of his command post. She hung just over his shoulder, so that if he concentrated, he could catch a remembered wisp of her perfume. He didn't have to bring out her letter again; he practically knew it by rote.

. . . I never could drink and got kind of numb. I wouldn't have been there at all if you hadn't cleaned out Win's room when I was gone . . .

She had made a scene about that, but it was unhealthy for her to hang onto the toys and clothing, the small tailored uniforms.

. . . Was two months past regulation mourning? Was that listed in your goddamned army regulations—so many sobs issued, no more than X amount of tears? . . .

Your ARs too, he'd told her; his mourning also. Didn't she think he had loved Winfield as well?

. . . So you shipped him away the hell off where he could be killed . . .

Not fair, Maggi.

. . . I didn't give a damn about fair. After my son was killed, there's no such thing as fair . . .

"Colonel?" Corporal Mason, replacing the guy who had taken a bayonet. "Sir—Division says just sit tight, that the

23rd kicked hell out of the Chinks and they may slide off our way."

"Thanks." Division, Corps, and everybody else had been worried about the other regiment, surrounded and hammered by too many CCF. But the bugout syndrome, the haul-ass response was finished. The division was getting in its licks now, and Julian felt good about it, about his battalion's part.

Charley Heath stretched out on a sleeping bag, hands behind his head. "Missed something, did I?"

"Not much. It's just—hell; everybody holds. Joe Chink won't push us any farther back."

"Colonel Peploe thinks they'll try again, harder next time; more men."

Julian nodded. "Then we'll kill more of them."

"Yeah," Heath said, and fell asleep.

In time, Julian thought, he might also. Right now, he was pulled tighter than ever before. In the early years of marriage, Maggi would see his tension—caused by things that didn't mean a good goddamn when placed in perspective—and she would rub his neck, his back. Sometimes he pulled her down upon him and made love; sometimes she drew away. He never thought of Maggi as highly sensual. He didn't try things with her because she was always so calm, so standoffish cool. She was meant to be a wife, not a mistress.

. . . I said something aloud about Tommy Atkins, and he said not many women read Kipling. I was ready to go back to the post. Army wives never go home, Julian; have you noticed that? They return to quarters, wherever the hell that is—Fort Lewis, Germany, Japan. No roots and nothing to hang onto, not even the residue of a dead child . . .

Ah, Maggi, Maggi—I shouldn't have given his things to the Thrift Shop. That seemed to hurt you more, that other boys would wear his things.

. . . It wasn't a pickup the way I imagined one. I don't

remember what we talked about, but I remember the easy silences. So it seemed natural when we went to the room —not a motel room, a neat little place belonging to a friend of his. This man knows women; he knows things you have never bothered to learn. I never believed it could be like that . . .

Julian frowned. Was that it? He couldn't remember the next lines, the pornography. With a glance at the situation map and the corporal standing by, he brought out Maggi's letter, much creased and handled. Page by page, he went through it and found nothing else about spending the night with her lover. Had he imagined it, dressed it up in his mind with added frills? Evidently, and what did that do to his self-image?

. . . You always rush to take a shower after, Julian, as if sex stains you, as if I make you dirty. I refuse to feel grimy for anything I've done; I will not feel guilty. If you can't handle that, I'm sorry; I will wait until you come home to start proceedings . . .

Divorce. He didn't want a divorce, he wanted Maggi and a chance to tell her all the things held back, some of them even from himself. Mama and her constant harping, her self-pitying prayers grating like steel wool; the rape that produced him. Oh, blessed Jesus; oh, holy mother Mary, oh, that her own child, conceived in sin, should also be a burden—oh, oh, oh.

"Oh, shit!" Julian said.

Corporal Mason looked around. "Sir?"

Combat was the great leveler, and death had no respect for rank. Julian said, "I was thinking what a different perspective I get, looking back from here, thinking what I'd do differently."

"You mean at home, sir? I know what you mean. I hope I get the chance to correct things."

"Yes," Julian said, and the mortar shell exploded almost

on top of the CP hole, ripping the canvas cover and splattering the map board.

Spitting, coughing smoke and dust, Julian got to his knees to shake off debris. Charley Heath sat up, too, saying, what the hell? Corporal Mason didn't get up. He couldn't; the top of his head was missing.

Mason didn't get his chance. Julian might not either.

CHAPTER 30

Mokke-dong, Republic of Korea, Feb. 15, 1951—The 11th ROK Regiment fought a desperate delaying action here today. Pounded by three times its number of enemy, it blunted a major Chinese drive and held fast despite breakthroughs and heavy casualties.

날개 부러진 매

"A hawk with broken wings." (Korean proverb)

Chong Nam Ki moved forward into the night, guided by muzzle flashes and ground bursts. The map he normally carried inside his head shifted and blurred, so that he feared to trust it. Chinese flares soared, reaching up from the valley floor in a tumult of whistles and bugle calls. The regiment's positions were good, deeply dug in and with good fields of fire. More than that, his regiment had heart. They hated the Chinese, and all had suffered losses by the *inmun-gun*. They would fight.

"Older brother—"

"Wei Ki; what are the reports?"

His brother touched his arm and drew him to earth beside a boulder. "Many *chung-guk*. They climb the mountains like insects, like ants with a single purpose—to feed upon us."

"They will need sharp teeth," Nam Ki said.

"Come with me, brother; you should remain back in the hut, but since you will not, join Major Lim and me in this pit."

The night smelled crisp, and the air was clean despite gunfire. A land of embroidery upon silks, he thought. Century after century of pain and pillage, and still the land breathed in beauty. We will defend; we will progress, because if we are to remain Korean, we must.

"Please, colonel." Major Lim tugged at his sleeve. "The fire is heavy."

"Yes." He heard the music of the bullets, and the drum song of mortars. Inclining his head, he listened for the strumming of the *kayagum*, the stringed instrument of court entertainers, and it came softly from the valley, but not as sweet, never as soft as Wha Ja's voice of silver.

He had known little but the name when first he went to the *kisaeng* house. Young and arrogant and ignorant, he was determined to act the part of an experienced man with this whore. Actually, he was a boy and much afraid.

The phone buzzed, and a star shell flashed, lighting the slope. To right and left of the command dugout, machine guns opened fire. Nam Ki looked down and saw Chinese falling like millet before the harvest sickles of farmers.

"*Jotah!*" Wei Ki shouted. "Good! Good!"

Major Lim said something into the phone, then turned and spoke to Nam Ki. "Our left flank, colonel. The *daenom* strike hard there. Shall I commit the reserve company?"

Nam Ki said, "I learned that *kisaeng* and whore are not the same." He pressed one hand hard against the thick scar along his head.

Wei Ki said, "His wound, major. Please take command."

That was not quite true, Nam Ki thought. There were three ranks of *kisaeng,* and only the lowest were outright prostitutes. Wha Ja was of first rank and did beautiful calligraphy; she sang in that voice of polished silver, and she danced—ah, how Wha Ja danced. Eyes closed, Nam Ki smiled as he watched the styled movements, the magical grace of sleeve and slipper.

"Artillery," Major Lim said to the radio man. "Reach the American artillery if you can. Third Battalion is in danger of being overrun."

Wei Ki said into the sound power phone: "Mortar section. Give me light shells on the same coordinates. What? That is all? Then fire one of them now." He looked at Nam Ki, then at Major Lim. "Only one left. Shall I have the defense company fire flares directly along the ground?"

"Excellent," Nam Ki said. "That will confuse them and give enough light for our gunners, but only in small circles. Where darkness remains, order constant grazing fire."

Wei Ki looked at Major Lim, who nodded.

First-rank *kisaeng* were taught proper ways to walk, talk, sit, and dress beautifully. No school could have instructed Wha Ja in the great tenderness she showed a young fool, nor the deep understanding. She did not have to be taught to love. That was a golden treasure she showed him how to spend.

The machine guns opened fire again. Down the slope men screamed and screamed again, closer each time. When the down-drifting white sun winked out, flares slid and bounced along the tortured earth. They made puddles of light like small lakes.

> Each night I cover the lake
> with my dreams

lest this shore be untidy
the day the white swan returns.

"Older brother! Come now—come with us."

Nam Ki was being shaken. "What?"

"We cannot hold the Chinese here. We must fall back to the next defensive line. Come—hurry!" Wei Ki rose to full height and fired a burst from his carbine, then pitched a grenade over the lip of the dugout.

"I will stay," Nam Ki said.

"What? You are ill—your wound—come with me. Major—help me lift him."

"One grenade," Nam Ki said. "Leave me with one grenade."

"Brother—no, no! You cannot—"

Nam Ki did not feel the winter wind, but a gentle breeze off a reflecting pool in the Secret Garden of the emperor. The guns chimed joyfully, and the temple bells were no clearer than Wha Ja's song.

"I can do no more," he said. "You must, Wei Ki. I charge you with the duty of our father, with the promises made. Korea must find its rightful place in the sun. To discard the bad and hold to the good. This is what Father Chong said."

Major Lim fired twice and pushed the radioman from the dugout. He ripped the phone from its wires and threw it out. Then he handed Nam Ki a grenade. "May we meet in another life, Chong Nam Ki."

"My brother—no, I say—"

"Major," Nam Ki said, and Lim dragged Wei Ki into the night.

Rising, Nam Ki lighted a cigarette. He allowed the candles to continue flickering, for did not light draw insects? Facing front, he pulled the pin on the grenade and placed it behind his head, the spoon held down. Its serrated metal was cold against his neck, but he did not mind. Cautiously, hissing among themselves and, as he thought, curious about the lights and knowing full well where the command post was located, the *chung-guk* came.

Although the taste of the words was dung upon his lips, Nam Ki called out to them in their dog language: *"Tow shong! Tow shong!*—I surrender."

> With a heart that sings of the stars
> I will love all dying things.
> And I must fare the path
> allotted to me.

> Tonight also
> The winds sweep over the stars.

Jabbering, they climbed into the hole close around him, and one of them wore the blue padded uniform of an officer. Nam Ki said, *"Tow shong,"* and released the grenade spoon. Then he said, "Wha Ja—"

And in the red, flowering explosion, she answered.

Eased down into the hole, Rich Shriver went weak in the knees. Goddamn it, he should have left the kid back at Division, or at Chunju Prison. What did laddie buck Shriver know about taking care of anyone, even himself? His foot touched something in the bottom of the hole. Sleeping bags—no, Soo Man's body. The goddamn Chink had been standing on him.

Steeling himself, Rich crouched lower and put out a hand. Above the hole, bullets snapped and hissed; incoming. The Chinks were throwing all they had, and fireworks answered them in a blazing ring around Chipyong-ni. He fumbled over the kid's body, so small, too thin. The side of Soo Man's head was sticky, and Rich flinched.

But he also felt breath stir the back of his hand. The kid was alive!

Feet thudded on the hard earth, and the yells were high-pitched. Hell—the kid needed help, and here came these slope-headed sons of bitches. Whirling, he stood up and emptied the first banana clip at crouched shadows. Thumbing the release, he switched ends and fed the full clip into the carbine. One slant-eye yipped like a dog when hit, and Rich fired until the hill around him was wiped clean. Then he dropped to his knees and found two more magazines taped together.

He listened hard to the night above them, listened harder for the beat of Kim Soo Man's heart and heard both things —death above and life below. A white flare broke low over the CP, and machine guns worked the hillside. Chink burpguns answered, quick and flat-sounding. He slid fingers over the kid's head and found a bullet crease along the temple, messy but not as deep as he feared. Unless the skull was fractured—

Something heavy dropped on Rich's back and damned near flattened him. What the—satchel charge! Jesus Christ—he wasn't a fucking tank! Whipping around, he grabbed the thing with both hands and heaved it up and away as hard as he could. The blast rocked him back on his heels, and the light showed him a pair of Chinks hunkered with their candy asses a foot off the ground. He ducked for the carbine, brought it up, and raked both of them. There was so much noise he couldn't make out his individual shots.

"Goddamn it—let us alone!" Back under cover, he sought and found the kid's carotid artery. Beneath his fingers it pulsed steady and strong. Cursing the night, he got hold of a first aid packet and ripped it open.

Moving on their own memories, his hands powdered the wound and bandaged it tight. Not much blood; thank God there wasn't much blood. He could never stop heavy bleeding; nobody could.

Soo Man moved and made a small sound, barely audible. Rich whispered, "It'll take more than a lick in the head to kill you, you little bastard."

Rising again, he braced his feet on each side of the kid and told himself that the prognosis was good. He had felt no shifting bone in the skull. Of course, a blow like that, a bullet gouging a path along the head, could scramble things inside. But the kid was tough. He'd better be, goddamn it. Rich Shriver hadn't packed him over half of Korea for him to crap out now.

The command post fell silent, so quickly that the quiet itself was shocking. Out on the perimeter—there were no flanks, just a great bloody circle—firing continued heavy for long minutes before dropping off. A star shell from the 37th Field Artillery battery spilled white light over the CP, and one downed Chinese soldier moaned close beside Rich's hole. Before the light burned away, Rich zeroed in on the bulky uniform and silenced the bastard. Then, to make certain, he popped a round through every prone body he could reach. The light blacked out, leaving a greenish stain against his eyelids.

One side of the defense line went quiet, but on the other, firing intensified. If they held through this desperate night and continued to punish the Chinks, even that mindless carpet of raw manpower would have to curl back upon itself and lick its wounds. If nothing else, the 23rd Infantry's valiant stand here had shown the rest of the world, and, more importantly, an edgy U.S. Army, that GI guts and firepower could kick Chinese ass.

CHAPTER 31

Koje-do Island, U.N. Prisoner-of-War Camp, March 12, 1951—A neutral-nations inspection team, aided by the International Red Cross, toured compounds here today. Behind wire are some 86,000 prisoners. Inspectors reported the POWs short of athletic equipment and flush toilets.

가랑잎이 솔잎머러 바스락
거린다고 하다.

"A dead leaf tells a pine needle, 'Do not rustle.'"
(Korean proverb: Find fault with others and ignore your own.)

This much of Sam Connover was Korean, the stolid patience, his knowing how to wait. Kallager had been sent on a tour of other camps as a showpiece for Commander Ding's successful indoctrination program. Kallager could spout Marxist dogma upon cue. He would return, and in the meantime the sick man in Hut 5 had died. There would be another; there always was.

Taking lessons from the Turkish PWs in the compound, Sam and Matt Jackson scrounged the earth for sprigs of green, grass or weeds that showed through melting snow. Every man needed vitamins, including the Pro Buckbee;

255

they took him along on foraging expeditions to lull his suspicions and give him nothing to report.

When they came back to the hut with a handful of bitter weeds, Smitty was gone. The man with the floppy wrists had been taken to the hospital.

"We tried to keep him here," Marotta said. "Guards looked in and couldn't wake him up. He'll die in that fucking hospital."

Sam closed his eyes. The camp hospital was an old school building with a high roof; it was heated by two iron stoves without stovepipes. Green wood was the fuel, so smoke lay thick in the building like a nauseating blanket. The two medics assigned there had to crawl on hands and knees to keep from choking. The medicine issue was four sulfa tablets—per day, not per man—for the entire hospital. The sick and wounded died first, and then the young men. They refused to eat the boiled millet and maize delivered in a bucket like the hog slop it was. But as Jackson said, it was root hog or die. The kids chose to die.

"The protected kids," Sam whispered, settling into his Korean squat inside the hut. "Mommy can blame herself for their deaths. All the mommies who gave their kids everything but a belief in themselves and their country. They drove them to school and picked them up, so they have no legs. They cooked special dishes if the kid didn't like what was on the menu. Here's five bucks—go to a movie. Work? Are you kidding? Mom sent her little boy out into a world where tigers walk, and not only did she not tell him about tigers, she sent him out naked."

Matt Jackson folded the weeds into his canteen cup. "You sounding like a country preacher."

"Not like my old man. He preached turning the other cheek, but he had only one neck to give the Japs." He didn't want to dwell on that, so Sam focused on present problems. "Smitty won't come back, damn it. If he was conscious in that hospital, he'd tell the kids to fight and show them how."

Jackson glanced at the other room and lowered his voice. "Hold onto Smitty's stuff before that fucking Pro grabs it."

Sam motioned with his head; Marotta and Joe Lavoie collected Smitty's pitiful possessions, his blanket and mess gear, a ragged but prized pair of socks. Marotta said, "Look—he left his dime. Jesus, I always feel like a grave robber. How come a guy like Smitty has to die, while the fucking Pros go on? That goddamn Kallager—"

"Easy," Sam warned. "Kallager won't make it home, but you guys have to—so you can testify against the Pros. Good sharp hate can keep you alive better than a full meal."

Samuel, Samuel—love thine enemy.

Did you kiss the Jap, Father? The one with the samurai sword?

Tucking his knees into the wrap of his arms, Sam rested his head and fought against guilt. Honor thy father did not mean die with him, die needlessly, stupidly, because it was wonderful to be a martyr. He could have gone home when the Japs first showed their teeth; but no, if Jehovah delivered Daniel from the lion's den, He would surely deliver His faithful servant. But Connover *Moksa*'s god must have been looking the other way—or didn't know the difference between lions and tigers. The *Moksa* of Chunju was a Christian soldier who did not believe in other soldiers, who grudgingly allowed his brother Kelly to die upon hallowed ground. Some fought heavenly battles by choice; the GI fought for his pay and to save his own holy ass.

. . . Oh, it's Tommy this and Tommy that, and Tommy how's your soul, but it's thank you Mister Atkins when the drums begin to roll . . .

She had breathed lines from "Tommy Atkins," not realizing she was saying them aloud. Maggi Barron uncom-

fortable upon a bar stool, unused to bars and pickups but
understanding Kipling because she was army, too. Sam
guessed that, although she said nothing about the post. He
didn't know she was an officer's wife. It wouldn't have
made any difference that special night, no more than her
wedding ring. But in the PX coffee shop, seeing her across
the table from Colonel Barron was different. Sam hadn't
expected more than the great gift of that night, and he
didn't think she did, either. She had left him in the bed as
he had left so many others, in silence and without promises. But accidental encounters and the jolt he got when
their eyes met made it seem all right to talk about it over
coffee, surrounded by the undreaming military post.

Maggi was army and always had been, but now she
wanted no part of it. He discovered that was why she had
been in town that day. They talked at more than arm's
length, separated by a table, with the rattle and laughter of
the morning break around them in the coffee shop. Once
the colonel walked in, and Sam left without comment, as if
he'd just been filling a chair. It was dangerous for her, and,
in the long run, for Sam also.

Neither said, let's meet somewhere else, the bar, that
little room, but the tension was always between them. And
he realized that she wanted, needed, something more, a
thing he was not ready to give.

"Is it stupid to say I love you?" she asked.

"It's beautiful," he said.

Her eyes were big. "I mean it."

"I know."

"You could say something. Like you love me, too. Isn't
that traditional?"

"Maggi, Maggi—as crazy as this is, I do love you."

Her eyes probed him. "But?"

He looked down at his coffee. "I put in for transfer to the
Korean Military Advisory Group. If I stay here—if we see
each other—"

258

"Jesus," she said, "I should have known. You and the damned army. You *are* the damned army."

"I couldn't stay in uniform if we were together; you know that."

Twisting a spoon in her long fingers, she said, "Your medal; there are plenty of firms that would give you a job—public relations, advertising, something."

"You know better than that, too."

"Oh, good Christ! What is it with you people? What do you want, a cluster to the Big Bong? The damned army will use you up, wring you out, and throw you away. *You* know that."

He couldn't talk to her about tigers; Maggi saw only a dead child and the bastard she had married. She saw only the dusty specters of army posts and the general who fathered and ignored her.

"I'm sorry, Maggi."

"Sure."

Sam lifted his head and stared at the shadow creeping across the hut wall, at the guy sleeping out the day or pretending to. Had he been as stubborn, as stupid, as his father? One throwing away his life in hopes of eternity, and the other worshipping at a bloodier altar? Maggi could have been Sam's blessing, his comfort, with that deep quietness in her.

Joe Lavoie slid back the hut door and crawled inside. "Smitty died and Kallager's back, fat and sassy in a new uniform."

"Ain't this Christmas?" Jackson sat up and rolled his shoulders. "I got a present for that motherfucker."

"Matt," Sam said, "let's just strangle the bastard."

"And miss letting him know how it feels to beat on sick guys? Shee-it, I been planning on this."

Sam sighed. "Nail him good before he can yell. Remember, he's been eating well."

"Oh, I ain't forgetting that, man. Ain't no way I can forget that."

They waited until night, until word came back of a dying man in the next hut. They needed a legitimate body, and it would have been great if Smitty could have been used, but even Joe Chink would have noticed the difference.

Marotta said, "How about the other guys in his hut?"

"He'll wish he had a friend," Sam answered, "but he doesn't."

Kallager had taken possession of an entire room, crowding the others into smaller spaces. It wasn't big, and the ceiling was low, but it would have to do as an arena. Big and pink-cheeked, Kallager looked up as Matt Jackson came in and Sam stood in the door.

"What the fuck you want, nigger?"

Jackson smiled. "I'm glad you said that, motherfucker. What do I want? Your fay ass out on the hill for the dogs to gnaw on."

Kallager moved, and Sam said, "Watch it, Matt."

"I see the knife," Matt said, and as Kallager rose stabbed him twice over the eye with a long left hand.

Kallager staggered and sliced at air. Matt feinted with his crippled right and hooked off the left. Kallager's knife flew away, and he sat down hard, blood leaping out over his right eye.

Moving inside, Sam closed the door and was poised to boot Kallager in the head if he opened his mouth to scream. The man saw it and spread his hands. "Ding will hang you bastards for this." Blood dripped down his face.

"Badass, ain't he?" Matt said. "Shee-it, you know what old Ding-dong wants, right?"

"Look," Kallager said, "I can fix it for you guys—more rice and even some meat, cigarettes from the Red Cross packages."

"What you know, Sam?" Matt said. "Red Cross packages came in, and only this motherfucker knows it."

Kallager tried to throw himself backward and yell. He didn't make it. Sam kicked him in the face, and he fell over onto his side. At the other room door, a pair of wan faces peered out. Sam said, "You got a dead man in there?"

"Ed Johnson," one man said. "Don't let that bastard wake up."

"No sweat," Matt Jackson said, and kneeled over Kallager. "Never worked him over like he deserved, but this'll do."

Sam said, "Drag your dead guy in here. In the morning, tell Joe Chink it's Kallager. We'll have him over at Hut 5."

Jackson got his hands around Kallager's throat and bore down. Kallager kicked twice before his legs stiffened out. Jackson leaned back and looked at his hands, at the mangled right he could never use in the ring. "Shee-it, thought I'd feel something. I don't; it's like stomping a snake. Got to be done, but ain't no fun to it."

Outside the hut, somebody scratched on the door. "Hush," Jackson said, and Sam heard the quick whisper as well: "Chinks coming."

Sam said, "You guys—back in the other room. You don't know anything, didn't see anything." He looked at Matt Jackson. "Maybe we can fake it, if they aren't coming especially for him."

"Yeah," Matt said, and stood up. "Get back against the wall, Sam."

Something in Jackson's voice made Sam hesitate, and the singsong of approaching Chinese guards grew louder. Sam said, "Damn it, Matt—"

And that was as far as he got. He never saw the punch coming. The lights went out.

CHAPTER 32

No-Name Line, Republic of Korea, May 16, 1951—GIs dug into these narrow, rugged ridges braced for an all-out communist attack today. Enemy troops massed along the Soyang River are reported as 137,000 CCF and 38,000 NK. Facing them and anticipating wave after wave of human sea assaults are the U.S. Second Infantry Division and an understrength ROK Corps.

가랑잎이 솔잎더러 바스럭
거린다고 한다.

"No spider catches insects without a web." (Korean proverb: Preparation is half the battle.)

Julian had been expecting the first blow on May Day, as a communist demonstration for the world that saw the Chinese bloodied at Chipyong-ni. He hoped it wouldn't, because his troops were not ready then. They were now, as prepared as sweat and equipment could make them. Long ago, the 38th Infantry had learned that airpower was nice to have, but the planes could not stop the continued reinforcement of CCF. Joe Chink relied on darkness and muscle to move men and supplies down the peninsula, but the logistics had a flaw that could be fatal. When troops had to carry everything they used—ammunition, food, and medicines—they planned on capturing what they needed after initial supply ran out. G-2 had calculated that to be four days of sustained fighting.

"Four days or forty," Julian said. "This outfit will stay as long as it takes."

Julian turned to the man who had become more than just his right arm. Charley Heath was the first man Julian could call friend, and that beat hell out of jockeying for rank and playing office games. It had taken him a long time to discover his own capabilities and learn what the job meant. Julian Barron would never kiss ass again, and what he gained, he would earn.

"We have the rest of the day, Charley; I could wish for more, but Division thinks it's tonight. When I hiked over and saw Colonel Hanes's layout, I realized we have to kick ass here and make the men dig deeper. Hanes has sandbagged dugouts and concertina wire."

"We have more *fougasse*," Heath said. "Every chunk of dead space to our front is covered. When Joe Chink starts up those gulleys—egg foo yong."

Fougasse—a WWI leftover term for a fifty-five-gallon drum filled with napalm and triggered by a quarter-pound block of Compo C or a white phosphorus grenade. Liquid flame soared thirty yards long and ten yards wide, its 3000 degrees Fahrenheit destroying all it touched. This was one of the surprises the regiment had waiting; there were others—not much wire, but strung in nasty, unexpected places; artillery test-fired and accurately zeroed in on all approaches; and Hail Mary shells with proximity fuses for air bursts called down upon the outfit's own bunkers if the defenders were driven inside. The Chinese had made another major mistake, Julian thought, worse than the miscalculation at Chipyong-ni. They had given the Second Division two full weeks to prepare. The war had been fluid before, chasing up and down the country. Now the Chinks would run head-on into real defensive positions, manned by hard-nosed GIs eager for revenge. This coming battle could change the whole aspect of the war.

Heath said, "The men have learned to hang tough, but they still hate to work. We're a mile piggyback from the nearest supply road. Damned good thing we have Korean bearers. If I hadn't seen what loads those guys can carry on A-frames, I'd never believe it."

"Chinese pack the same loads," Julian said. "But goddamn it, we'll see that they won't climb back down Hill 800. Now let's get out and make those positions safer."

They separated beyond the CP dugout, and Julian made for the right flank of his battalion. If the CCF stuck to their standard battle plan, they would first strike the ROK troops to the east, and strike hard. Those ROKs were tough and battle-hardened and would fight, especially the 11th Regiment, which was fast building a reputation. But Julian didn't think the ROKs could hold, and when they retreated, the Chinks would swing west and hit his flank.

There was a flavor to mountain air, the kiss of springtime that he breathed deeply. Pausing beside a jagged slab of granite, he stared down at a clump of the biggest, brightest violets he'd ever seen. Maggi liked violets, he remembered, but he had never surprised her with a bunch. He had missed doing a lot of things.

"Not quite the chrysanthemum and the sword," Rocky Watanabe said at his elbow, "like the Shinto bullshit, but close enough. Flowers and *fougasse* and kick ass. Whatever works, man."

Julian shifted his slung carbine and sighed. "Who the hell told you to leave the CP? I don't need a baby-sitter."

"Just taking a stroll, colonel. If that pisses you off— shanghai me; ship my beach-boy ass clear back to Hawaii."

"You wish." Julian grinned. "Watch for trip wires. This company's got mines all over the slope."

An earth-stained lieutenant climbed out of a hole and came to them. "Colonel?"

Julian keyed his memory. This tired young man was the company commander by virtue of survival, and the only officer left. "Lieutenant Kirkland. It looks pretty good, but I want every position as deep as you can get them by dark. Do what you can about top cover, and then button up. They'll hit the ROKs over there, then peel off and come at you. There will be no bugging out. Is that understood?"

A frown crossed Kirkland's grimy face. Beyond him a lanky sergeant rose from his air-cooled machine gun. "Sir, goddamn it! This outfit don't bug out. Not as long as the lieutenant has the company and I run this fucking platoon."

The whisper drifted up from an unseen position. "That son of a bitch ain't got the only set of balls on this hill."

Stifling a grin, Julian said, "Carry on, gentlemen—but do me a favor and use your shovels. I need every mean son of a bitch on this hill to stay alive and kill Chinks."

Kirkland nodded and smiled. "You got it, sir."

That wasn't in the manual, Julian thought as he strode away. They didn't teach it at West Point; pride was an intangible, and so was truly reaching your men. He had damned near blown it, but he was still learning. He might need a lifetime to learn. Would Maggi also grant him some learning time?

With Rocky sometimes walking ahead, behind, or beside him as self-appointed bodyguard, Julian toured the next company. Overhead, a magpie sailed in startling colors against a low and threatening sky. The clouds meant little or no direct air support today, and maybe not tomorrow. They could use every plane when the Chinese came down from their darkly brooding mountains in force. In open daylight attack, they were vulnerable. In panicked retreat, they were helpless targets—and Joe Chink had proved he could panic, at Chipyong-ni.

The next unit had sent men to the rear for trip flares and antipersonnel mines, for all the wire that could be "liberated." The infantrymen had left some bruised air force and rear-echelon people behind, but their forward slopes were well covered. Here Korean oxen had been used to haul the 4.2 mortars up a thousand feet of steep mountain. The battalion hadn't had it easy, for water, ammunition, and food had to be backpacked up the hill, and it took about three hours for a round trip. Again, ornery GIs and uncomplaining Korean bearers made it all work.

Winded, but back at his own CP, Julian told Rocky to check out the security platoon positions and reminded him of the bullhorn technique they had used before. Stay down or get wasted was the order, then small-arms fire would rake the command area. Chinese caught above ground would be chop suey.

Charley Heath had coffee heated, and Sgt. Porky Giblin was back on duty, his bayonet wound not enough to keep him hospitalized for long. Now the S-3 sergeant wore an issue .45 and had an M-2 carbine propped close by. Sergeant Majefsky sat at the switchboard and EE-8 phones.

Heath said, "They're bitching, but they're working. There was a call from Ivanhoe 2. He named off the units we face—12th, 15th, 20th, 27th, and 60th CCF armies plus 38,000 rejuvenated North Koreans. Spotter planes report a muddy river of Chinks flowing south. Only the L-5s are flying today, ceiling too low."

"Gee," Julian said, unslinging his carbine and sitting upon a ration box, "didn't we have any bad news?"

Passing a canteen cup, Heath said, "Bad news for the Chinks. Task Force Zebra made it into position between us and White Battalion; every vehicle of the 72nd Tank Battalion is waiting—tanks, the quad 50s and twin 40s of the AA outfit, all emplaced."

Julian sipped coffee. "Good. It's time the Chinks learn who's boss."

Outside, twilight came soft and gray upon the hilltop, and Julian heard his security platoon, Rocky Watanabe's fire brigade, getting into position. He got out a can of meat and beans, wiped the can, and placed it in the coffee cooking on the little stove. Nobody blinked. Julian opened a can of dog biscuits and munched one while his supper heated. He used to bitch at Maggi if the meat was overcooked or undercooked. It was difficult for him to remember what a practicing asshole he had been.

Rescuing and opening his meat and beans, he ate mechanically, too tired to sort flavors. Korea had done something to him, split him down the middle. No—it was more like combat had peeled a layer from him, shed a phony outer hide that he had never needed. Like a growing snake discarded his skin? Jesus—he had so much to say to Maggi. Once he said it, if she still wanted a divorce, if she still clung to her image of Sam Connover or would find someone else, Julian would simply have to let her go. Not simply, damn it.

Connover was MIA since Kunu-ri, which meant the poor bastard's bones were back in that five miles of hell. Julian still wouldn't tell Maggi; sooner or later she would use her mother's Pentagon contacts and find out for herself. Maybe she had already done so and still meant to leave.

Poor bastard, Connover? Yes, because he had known Maggi for so short a time. Who was worse off, Connover or Julian Barron, the dumb bastard who had lived with her so long and never really known her?

The first bugle call jerked Julian's head up. Rubbing his eyes, he swallowed the last of his cold coffee and lit a smoke. "Charley?"

Heath turned with a phone in his hand. "By the book; they're beating up the ROKs on our right."

Sergeant Giblin made a mark on the overlay and said, "The ROKs are doing pretty good." He went back to the radio. "But there are feelers all along our flank already. It won't be long."

The hilltop rocked, and Julian coughed on a deep drag of

smoke. "Joe Chink must have run into Task Force Zebra—Jesus! The armor is cutting loose with all they have."

From behind his position, he heard outgoing mail as the 38th Field fired on predetermined targets, immediately firing for effect—laying a barrage without adjusting fire. Julian kept his mouth open and covered his ears. Dirt sprinkled down from the bunker covering—what small tree trunks the ridge had offered, and three feet of dirt and rocks. Wave after wave of violent sound vibrated the earth and shattered the air. Julian had never heard anything like this, and for certain, the Chinese hadn't either. He could almost feel sorry for any poor sons of bitches on the receiving end of so much firepower—the 105s and 4.2s, the tank cannon and machine guns, the 81 and 60mm mortars clearing their throats steadily—almost sorry, but not quite. The more goddamned Chinks that died now, the more GI casualties would be reduced later. The human sea could be dried up, and now was the time. If only the defenses held—

"Charlie Company is hard hit, sir," Porky Giblin said. "Wait—they're overrun. Goddamnit, Jonesie—get the hell out! Get—oh, shit." His eyes were anguished as he looked back at Julian. "Radio contact gone. Shit, I went through basic with Jones. Crazy bastard stayed with his radio."

Major Heath rang off an EE-8 phone. "Charlie Company's hanging together; no panic, and the Chinks lost so many men they can't follow right away. Item Company's being forced back, too. Second Batt is moving back to a prepared line."

CRASH! CRASH! CRASH!

It was several seconds before Julian could speak and be heard. He said, "Charley—what the hell else can we do? If all we're throwing doesn't stop them, we've shot our wad. Send the French battalion to plug the gap. There goes our reserve."

He waited then, fielding calls from his line companies, adjusting artillery fire when called for, and two companies called the Variable Time blasts down upon their dugouts. Gleefully, they reported wiping Chinks off the bunkers and off the ridges. Julian silently thanked Wally Hanes, whose idea it had been to use the proximity fire.

Rattle! Crash—crash—CRASH!

Heath said into the echoes, "It's easing off some. The French failed to retake Charlie's lost position. Colonel Peploe says the 72nd Tank and the 23rd Infantry are side-slipping over to block." Heath grinned big and wide. "We're holding, Julian, damned if we aren't. Even Joe Chink can't afford to keep losing men like this."

Sergeant Majefsky spoke into his own phone and said something to Porky Giblin, then looked up at Julian. "Chinks breaking off, sir."

"For now," Julian said. "Soon as it's light, let's get the litter bearers and ammo bearers back to work. Charley— ask for air at dawn. If our spotter pilots have the guts to fly in pea soup, the fucking air force can."

Reports filtered in during the night, and by checking the situation map, Julian began to see the big picture. It was like opening the door a crack, but nailing down the hinges. Division had the same thought—that the Chinese armies would not accept a bloody nose but would try again and again, until that flawed logistics plan collapsed on them.

Time blurred for everyone in Julian's command post, and he saw his crew sleep when they could and eat when they had to. He did his job, and so did they. All along the Soyang River the CCF took a beating, and although the door opened more for them, they never sprang the hinges, and they poured down into the valleys only to find themselves running short of ammunition and food. The skies cleared on the third day of the attack, and the Chinese died in heaps, in rows as they were strafed and bombed, as deadly accurate U.N. artillery followed them back out of the gigantic cemetery they had created for themselves.

Stubble-faced and drawn, red-eyed and shaky, the CP crew stared at one another on the fourth day. Charley Heath said, "Ivanhoe 2 claims 65,000 Chinese casualties—65,000! They no longer have a chance of cracking the line, and General Almond is bringing in the 187th Paratroopers to attack. Damn, Julian—we're attacking once more! The Chinks will sure remember the Second Division after this."

Wearily, Julian smiled. "Payoff for Kunu-ri. Send word to all companies—goddamn it, we're proud of all you sons of bitches. Sign it, Balls Barron."

Heath's grin was lopsided. "That reads better than well done."

CHAPTER 33

Eighth Army Headquarters, Korea, June 30, 1951—U.N. Commander-in-Chief Gen. Matthew B. Ridgway, responding to a Russian speech made in the United Nations General Assembly, today radioed the commander of communist forces in Korea as follows: "I am informed that you may wish a meeting to discuss an armistice providing for the cessation of hostilities and all acts of armed forces in Korea, with adequate guarantees for the maintenance of such armistice."

원수는 외나무다리에서
만난다.

"Meet an enemy on a single-log bridge." (Korean proverb: Face bad luck you cannot escape.)

Captain Chong Wei Ki kneeled upon the warm earth and said his daily prayers for his father's peace and for his brother Nam Ki. This week he had returned from a rest in Seoul, where he felt a stranger to his own family, in what was left of his own home. It had seemed that only the orphaned children were real, and yet at certain moments their laughter rang oddly in his ears. His mother wore deep new lines about her mouth, and his sister was a taller stranger.

Rising to his feet, Wei Ki brushed his knees and looked

out at the hill mass to the regiment's front. Behind him in the headquarters bunker Colonel Lim and staff officers discussed the coming truce. Wei Ki spat. The family Chong had given its blood and treasure to fight the communists, and now, after the Chinese and *inmun-gun* had been beaten at the Soyang, the Americans were willing to talk peace.

Of course, the Chinese sent sly word that they might think about a cease-fire. When communists could not win by force of arms, they tried to win by talk. Any peace that grew out of such a meeting would be a lie and a betrayal of *Taehan Minkuk*, the Republic of Korea itself. Turning, he stamped along the path to another observation post cut into the dry hillside. The corporal behind the range finder started to come to attention, but Wei Ki waved him off. "Movement?" he asked.

"Like all dogs, they go to ground in the heat of the day, *taewi*, but they have not departed."

"I hope not," Wei Ki said. "Then we would lose the opportunity to send them to their ancestors."

The corporal smiled and bowed. "Yes, sir."

A man learns quickly to be a soldier, Wei Ki thought; he is a good student of warfare or he dies early. And even excellent soldiers expect death and face it. This 11th Regiment had been hardened in the flames, from the time of his father's command until now. They respected each other, the regiment and its leaders, and the 11th had forced the communists to respect them.

Other regiments, other ROK corps were strong and willing troops now, the equal of American units after a year of warfare. Properly armed and commanded, they were worthy allies. Why then would *Mi-kuk* accept less than victory now? Had not the U.N. proclaimed its intention to attack and destroy the communist army of the north?

Wei Ki knew he was not alone in his feelings of confusion and anger. President Syngman Rhee had also issued a statement this day, and his conditions for peace were stringent—CCF out of Korea, North Korea disarmed, an end to Russian and Chinese arms shipments; no settlement by the U.N. that would conflict with the sovereignty of the republic.

"A strong, clear statement," Colonel Lim had commented, "but for all practical purposes we must remain a puppet of America."

One of the new officers had leapt to his feet, outraged. "But, sir! What will we have gained? Our nation lies in ruins; we have sacrificed a million men; a million children beg for food in the streets. Korea cannot accept a continued division of itself. The *inmun-gun* will continue to make war, and Korea may never again be one land."

The junior officers applauded, and Colonel Lim had waited before asking the lieutenant if he was a college student.

"Dan Kuk university," the man said with pride.

"You are fortunate," the colonel said. "I am the youngest son of a poor farmer, and my only education has been in warfare. When the communists attacked, I was a corporal. Now I am a graduate of war, and my lessons have taught me much about the communists. What you say is true, and what I say is also true. Korea has no choice but to walk beside America. If we do not, where will we get our arms, ammunition, fuel, and even our food? Remember also that many American soldiers have died for a country that is not their own."

And at the last, Wei Ki had spoken: "Perhaps the U.N. will learn what Koreans already know—that much time will pass and much blood yet be spilled before this truce is settled. What we can do, officers of the 11th Regiment, is to continue killing *balgaengi*. We are experts at this."

Because there was much bitterness in his throat, Wei Ki rushed from the meeting before being thought a fool. Now he walked along his company's positions and considered the responsibilities fallen upon him as head of the family

Chong. His father had been a scholar of renown and proved to be a wise prophet. His brother had been a poet turned soldier. What, indeed, was Chong Wei Ki?

A soldier, yes, but if the war did not go on forever? And if it did, all soldiers would die without knowing another life. Wei Ki drew a deep breath of mountain air and tasted dust, tasted the bitterness of his soul. Keep the good, father Chong commanded; discard the bad and help our country gain its proper place in the sun.

Again, Wei Ki turned to stare at the range of dark hills that towered ominously before his regiment. Deep within them, the enemies of the Republic of Korea burrowed. Always, enemies poised to overrun Korea—the Mongols of Genghis Khan, generations of Manchu warlords, and lastly, the vicious dogs of Japan. But now, forged as steel in this bloodiest of all wars, the Korean people had found an identity for themselves, a national character—not of old men muttering of past glories, not of humble peasants bowing to their conquerors, but an identity of strength. Koreans always had pride, he thought, but pride without power is only ridiculous.

Whatever happened now, however this false and misleading truce might come to pass, the new Korea would stand and endure. More; somehow it would move forward.

CHAPTER 34

The Kansas Line, Republic of Korea, August 14, 1951—While representatives of the United Nations, Red China, and North Korea met again at Kaesong without settling any questions, the U.S. Eighth Army and FECOM (Far East Command) found a serious threat to U.S. Second Infantry positions on the central front. A triangle of enemy-held hills serve as observation posts for increasing artillery fire. For some time now, Chinese Communist Forces have succeeded in bringing heavy artillery into Korea. The division was ordered to attack.

찔러 피를 낸다.

"Prick and bleed." (Korean proverb: It is foolish to bleed on purpose.)

Rubbing his unshaven cheeks and blinking through bloodshot eyes, Rich Shriver sucked on a cigarette to steady his hands. "So I didn't need all five days' R&R. I got my I&I—intercourse and intoxication—done, and what the hell. Hanging around fucking Japs bothers me."

Captain Davis reached under his canvas cot and brought out a bottle. "Hair of the dog. You set some kind of record, sergeant; since the Rest & Recreation program began, you're the only man in this division, and probably the entire Korean theater, to return two days early."

Rich nodded his thanks, drank deeply, and shuddered. "Everybody is celebrating in Tokyo; the war's over. Goddamn, you never saw so many paper assholes. I guess I felt guilty screwing around over there."

Duke Davis nodded. "And you missed the boy."

Rich started to deny that, then he shrugged. "Couldn't figure a way to haul him with me. The little bastard came so close to buying the farm that if I got him to Tokyo, both of us would wind up stateside and fuck this war and the next one, too. But since that ain't possible—"

He collected gear and notes in the Public Information Office tent at Ivanhoe Forward CP. Looking out back, he watched the kid pack their stuff into the faithful jeep. Both Kim Soo Man and the jeep had been hurt, and although both looked some worse for wear, they'd made it.

Captain Davis repeated the hill numbers, and Rich shook his head. "Duke—numbers read off to me don't mean doodly. Me and numbers ain't got along since we hit short division in school. I'll just go up to the line and tag along with whichever regiment gets the shitty end of the stick."

Duke Davis lifted an eyebrow at the kid. "The boy's going with you? After he was hit at Chipyong-ni—"

Rich shrugged. "The little bastard won't stay where I leave him. Once out of the aid station, he hitched rides and found me. He'll do it again."

"You ought to ship him down to Taegu, put him in school. He's still a kid."

"Man enough to save my ruby-red ass when he dropped that Chink. But, yeah, you're right. We lucked out, getting him to an aid station and hiding him until he healed. Shit —I did stories and pictures on every goddamn medic in that outfit. After this Kansas Line bullshit, I'll try to talk him into school. I don't know; he owes the gooks for his parents. Over here, kids grow up quick or don't grow up at all." Slinging his carbine, Rich stood up and tucked away his notebook.

The captain said, "You're pushing your luck. You don't have to get into firefights to do your job. Remember that you're not a line soldier, and that dead correspondents don't turn in copy."

"Hey," Rich said, "I ain't no hero. Sometimes I just get caught where I can't haul ass. Let me know when the next booze ration comes in."

The captain squirreled his bottle back under the cot. A three-quarter truck passed on the way to the motor pool, raising a billow of powdery dust. Duke Davis said, "The CCF out there don't know a damned thing about truce. They've tunneled into those mountains from the rear, dug connecting caves like the Japs did in the Pacific."

Turning, Rich said, "Yeah, I know about Jap caves, captain. But, hell, this is the only war we got."

He backed the jeep from behind the tent and pointed northeast. Beside him, Kim Soo Man rode easily, M-2 carbine across his lap. The kid was an old soldier now, a seasoned trooper with a battle scar that showed hairless and angry from eye to ear across the left temple. His face was still pale, but the black almond eyes were harder. Hell of a note, Rich thought; the kid had a ways to go before reaching his teens, and he was rough as a cob. Kim Soo Man had left his childhood back in Chunju Prison with his murdered parents.

Rich said, "This time, keep your head out of your ass and don't let any fucking Chink slip up on you. In the first place, if I put you in a battalion CP, stay there. If I catch you following me up to the line, I'll kick your popcorn ass up between your shoulders. You got that?"

Soo Man grinned and hung onto the dash as the jeep skidded around a curve. "You better believe it, GI."

"You better *Hong Kong* believe it, you little bastard."

They were approaching the Punchbowl, Rich knew, a

miserable open space between ridges that nobody owned or much wanted to. Low ground was damned near indefensible, but both sides had to patrol it. The way he'd heard the battle plans down from Corps, the first assault was to come from the 36th ROKs, with priority air and artillery support. Whatever, taking any one of those well-defended hills would be no picnic.

All three GI regiments—9th, 23rd, and 38th—had targets, too. Laddie buck, Rich told himself, you're starting to think Pentagonese, and that ain't for line troopers or writers, only inmates of the Puzzle Palace.

Tooling the jeep along a beaten road that would lead him to the 38th Infantry, Rich digested more of the battle plan. Back at X Corps, MacArthur's fair-haired boy Gen. Ned Almond was running the show long-distance. The guy was lucky, though; he'd outlasted his former boss when President Truman pulled the plug on the general who could do no wrong. When Matt Ridgway took over, the word passed swiftly: no more bugging out. GIs first called him old Wrongway Ridgway because he pointed them north. Later they knew him for a hell of a commander.

He found a battalion CP in a ragged clump of trees. Commo wires snaked out of a tent and up a slope where riflemen gathered. "Sit," Rich told the kid, and tucked the jeep out of sight. He ducked inside and paused to accustom his eyes to dimness.

Somebody said, "The flyboys worked over all three hills pretty good, and that B-26 with the fat bombs—"

". . . 500-pounders," somebody else added. "Too bad they weren't atomic. That's the only way those goddamned ridges will fall without a lot of blood."

Buzzword, Rich thought, and jotted it in his notebook: Bloody Ridge. The name would make a catchy headline. Taking a step toward the S-3 situation map, he said, "Sir— Sergeant Shriver, PIO. If the colonel doesn't mind—"

Two officers turned to look at him, a major and the light colonel. Rich knew one of them. "Shit," he said.

The bastard had learned how to smile. "My sentiments exactly, sergeant. It's been a while since we got some eyeball G-2 in Seoul for General Wright."

Colonel Chickenshit Barron looked different. Rich said, testing any change, "Butt Wright was one hell of a man—sir." The sir was delayed just enough.

Barron nodded. "That he was. What can we do for PIO, Sergeant—Shriver, isn't it?"

Jesus; he was even remembering the peasants' names now, like an honest-to-God officer. Something or somebody had run this guy through the wringer and brought him out pretty straight. "Yes, sir," he said, without any delay. "I'd like to get some copy and pictures when your outfit jumps off. From what I got at Ivanhoe Forward, the operation looks hairy."

"A bitch," Barron said. "Grab a cup of coffee—do you know Major Heath? Any scoop on the new commanding general? Big boots to fill, Nick Ruffner's."

Whatever turned the guy around had made a tight circle. For sure, he was no goddamn desk soldier now, and by the looks of him, Barron would be more apt to bite ass than kiss it. Sam Connover would never believe this turnabout; too bad Sam bought it at Kunu-ri.

He said, "Bull Boatner, buck general and old China hand, soldiered with Vinegar Joe Stilwell, even speaks the goddamn language. Nobody fucks with the Bull."

"Hey, now," Major Heath said. "We have another winner."

Barron turned back to the map, to the phones and radio. "Charley, this time I'll go with Dog Company for a look. Air and artillery softening aside, I have a hunch this is no milk run." He turned back to Rich. "Coming, sergeant?"

Rich grinned and checked his Rollieflex. "Wouldn't miss it, colonel."

CHAPTER 35

Heartbreak Ridge, Republic of Korea, Sept. 14, 1951—Blasting
bunkers, prying fanatic North Koreans out of their rat holes on
this brutal, ugly knob, one company of the 23rd Infantry reached
the top last night. Low on ammunition, they fought to the bitter
end. When a relief company reached them this morning, every
man had been killed, and not a single round of ammunition was
left to them.

달고 치는 데 아니
맞는 장고 있나.

"All drums sound when struck." (Korean proverb:
No matter how strong, a man falls to many attacks.)

The warmth of summer hadn't done a damned thing for the
chill in Sam Connover's guts. It was a black ice thing he
would carry forever. On his heels against the wall of Hut 6
and feeling a hint of returning winter in a lift of wind off
the Yalu River, he finished working a new and stronger bit
of wood into his left ear. Now it was more than a secret
symbol worn by the stubbornest of Reactionaries; the earring was a tribute to the brave man who invented it—Matt
Stonewall Jackson.

Closing his eyes, Sam sorted through the biblical files in

his head, the rote learning made indelible by force and repetition. He could find no comfort in any line beyond "greater love hath no man than he lay down his life for a friend."

Damn you, Matt. Both of us killed Kallager. You had no right to take all the blame. No goddamn right.

Matt had been dead since mid-May. He lasted sixty days through all the Chinks could throw at him. A man like that, dying at last in the Hole, tortured and starved, and not one Chinese or North Korean worth the sweat off his balls. If Commander Ding thought that Matt's death would spook the other Reactionaries, he was wrong. Those who resisted indoctrination and criticism and signing any kind of trumped-up confession only got tougher because they hated more. If nobody else in the compound had survival in mind, Sam did. He was determined to live long enough to kill as many communists as he could reach.

Thou shalt not kill, father? It was all right for Joshua and Samson, but not for Kelly and Sam Connover? Explain? No, simply believe, never question, but believe.

Sam had only been able to do one thing for his friend. Punches and bribes and the fear of death paid off for the corpse detail. The dogs didn't feed on Matt Jackson. His grave was shallow, but well protected by a cairn of rocks in the little grove of trees on the hill. His monument would last forever in the minds of all men who defied their captors, men who discovered it was tougher to fight back with only their minds.

"Sergeant?" It was Marotta, drawn even thinner and a little stooped now, but even tougher in spirit. His earring was a plaited bit of straw.

"Yes?" Sam pushed back his depression. That was becoming more difficult to do as the months crawled by, chipping away at men's determination and eroding their souls with the starving of their bodies.

Ah, Connover *Moksa*—you did not believe that soldiers

had souls. That wasn't your only mistake, father. Even the faithful are not always right, nor always blessed.

"Ding-dong announced a clean-up campaign. A pack of smokes for two hundred flies; three cigarettes for a rat."

Joe Lavoie leaned over. His earring was a polished rat bone. "If I can liberate some gauze bandage from the hospital, I'll hang a fly trap over that stinking latrine and flip out Joe Chink. It ought to hold a couple of thousand, and to fuck him up worse, I'll drown them in the river and let him go nuts trying to figure why they ain't squashed."

Marotta showed missing teeth in a grin. "Man, I'm from New York and I know about rats. Come on, Joe, we'll find some pregnant ones and collect for a shitpot of baby rats. Bastards didn't say how big they have to be."

Sam settled back on his heels and drew upon the sun. Always suspended between two countries and widely different cultures, he found it difficult to accept the fact that he was in China now, that he was ten thousand miles from the country he'd sworn allegiance to, that across the river lay the land of his birth, and even that had been altered by the stupidity of geopoliticians.

Land of the Morning Calm, of mists and soft mountains, a serene world where peace was a byword: not hello, good morning, but are you in peace? Go in peace, stay in peace, sleep in peace. Men of other lands made peace a lie and set brother against brother. Sam's mind drifted to a childhood of azaleas and a quiet stream, of respected grandmothers who always had rice cakes or *chopje,* fiery *kimchi,* and at special times like the sixtieth birthday—the *han-gap*—the long, involved meal of the Fairy Furnance, *shinsol-lo.*

Sam's stomach rumbled. It was hard not to think of food, any kind of food, but he fought his mind away from it. Maybe he was getting better at meditation, because once in a while he found a quiet place in his mind and crawled inside. Often Maggi Barron was there with him, because she was that special stillness of herself. When she wasn't there, he missed her. Sam only wished he could reach the astral plane mystics spoke of, leave his body behind and fly.

Too much soldier and not enough mystic for that, he thought. When he pictured himself flying, it always ended with his peeling off in a steep dive and rocketing the shit out of Camp #5. Jesus, Icarus and the Wright brothers; he'd genuflect to them or any guru who would furnish a strafing run and the holy purifying flame of napalm.

Father, you did not know how to hate, unless you hated me for betraying you and bypassing divinity school to join the army. I would never have made a preacher, *Moksa*. I have never felt the white man's burden, but my own is heavy. I am bent with the soldiers I did not save, could not save, and their weight bears me down. But hate is what keeps me alive, and I will stay alive, if I must reenlist to serve a hitch with the devil.

A flash crossed his closed eyelids, and for an awful moment it was the sun gleaming from the swift blade of a samurai sword. Shrinking, he peeped through slitted lids and saw only a wink off the Yalu River.

"All right," he whispered. "If—no, when—I make it out of here, I will go to Chunju Prison and bow my head beside your grave. I will not promise to pray."

Rich Shriver accepted Charley Heath's bottle and took a big gulp. It wasn't often he got to drink officer whiskey, and he made the most of the opportunity. It wasn't often he changed his mind about some of them, either. Barron was one of the rare exceptions. Even the kid liked the people in this command post, especially Rocky Watanabe. Soo Man's Japanese wasn't that extensive, but he'd been forced to study it through early years of school. Rich remembered Sam Connover explaining that part, that Imperial Japan did its buck-toothed best to colonize Korea, to wipe out thousands of years of a culture older than its own. If the truth were admitted, Sam explained, the Japs originally emigrated from Korea. Island cultures don't travel to the mainland, but the other way around. Too, Japanese grammar was identical to Korean, and many of the pronunciations were close. Sam had said that Japanese was easier to mouth, but both languages sounded weird to Rich. Besides, even if he was a brain, he wouldn't soil his tongue with anything Jap.

A lie, he told himself; you had a mouthful of that Jap moose in Tokyo on R&R. Moose wasn't Japanese; it was a GI improvement on the word for girl—*musame*. But shit, when did a stiff dick ever have a conscience?

Major Heath said, "This show is supposed to be the 23rd's, but I have a hunch it'll be like the last time, when Corps sent those poor damned ROKs up Bloody Ridge alone. The colonel has this battalion ready to jump in, although jump isn't exactly the word. Look up at that big, steep bastard and your legs start to ache. It's about seven miles long and yea damned high. It will take hours to climb that ridge, even if you're not under fire."

Rich nodded and glanced at Soo Man curled in a corner of the tent. The kid was turning into a soldier, sleeping at any chance, eating when he could, and only bitching when he was left behind, out of the action. The whiskey warming his gut, Rich lit a smoke and sat down beside the kid to wait for word on the attack. For hours Divarty had been pouring thousands of softening-up rounds upon connecting Hills 931, 894, and 851, but nobody would long remember official army designations. Guys like Rich or civilian newsmen would tag the mountain mass or the fight itself with a name. GI names were colorful enough—Bullshit Hill, Clap Valley, and the like—but newspapers were reluctant to print them.

He wondered if Teresa read about Korea, wondered if his byline ever appeared in stateside papers she might see.

Had she married again and maybe had a kid of her own? Saint Teresa was a woman first; he admitted that now. If he ever pulled the Big R and rotated back to the land of the big PX, he'd give her a call and tell her that. If he was sober enough, he'd even say thanks for the good years she had given him.

What the hell would he do on rotation with Kim Soo Man left here in what would soon again be Frozen Chosen? He could entrust him to Duke Davis, but it was possible that Duke would also end his tour and go home. Some clown might take over PIO, some idiot who would wear a tie and shine his boots and call all Koreans fucking gooks. Rich ground out his cigarette and thought that bigod, nobody could force him to take the Big R. If this goddamned war ever wrapped up, either upon the ground or negotiated at the communists' phony peace table, maybe then he could get something done to bring the kid to the States. Hell, if he had to, he would even get married again. There were a number of dumb broads out there who'd think hooking up with a GI was okay. He looked up and somehow he'd slept for hours. Colonel Barron was in the tent, and out on the ridge small-arms fire echoed in the night.

Barron stabbed a finger at the map. "The general said we'll go up here, the steepest damned part, at 0600. Air and artillery will keep working until we reach this spot." The finger stabbed again. "If we reach it. The 23rd had its heart broken trying. Every time one outfit grinds up to its objective, the gooks come back and knock it off. We're going to help."

Another turn of phrase that Rich wrote down: Heartbreak Ridge. Hell, he was getting poetic. The kid still slept when Rich stretched himself up and made a can of coffee, dumping in C-rat powders until the water boiled properly black. "We going to eyeball it again, colonel?"

Barron accepted a tin cup of coffee and nodded. The

phone made its goofy buzz-ring noise, and the S-3 sergeant answered. Barron said, "I'll take a radioman, too. Porky —see to an SCR 300."

"Two messages, colonel. The first is for you personally, and the next is PIO trying to reach Sergeant Shriver." Porky Giblin reached the handset up to Barron.

Rich wondered what the hell and waited his turn. The colonel passed him the phone, his face alternating between a smile and a frown. Rich said into it: "Class Six, come in? Hide my booze until after this action."

Voice thinned and distorted by miles of commo wire, Captain Davis replied: "Rich, this is strictly need to know, but since you were close to the guy—it's Sergeant Connover. Counter Intelligence says he's a POW and using a retired soldier's name and serial number so the Chinks won't dirty up his Medal of Honor. He's masquerading as his own uncle, Kelly Connover."

"Son of a bitch," Rich said, his face stretching until it felt as if it might crack around his grin. "Thanks, Duke."

"Oh," Captain Davis added, "tell Colonel Barron congratulations on his promotion."

Turning, Rich said, "It ain't always bad news that comes in bunches like bananas. Good on you, colonel. If anybody deserves a full bird, you sure as hell do."

"Believe it," Charley Heath added, "but we'll hate to lose you, sir."

"You won't," Barron said, "until this battalion is off the line and I'm damned good and ready to leave. Then Colonel Heath better take over."

"Another fucking troublemaker," Rich said. "The army can't get by without us, sir. My boss said, need to know only, but shit—if CIC could have found its ass with both hands, we'd have had this news long ago. I don't know if you know Sergeant Sam Connover, the Medal of Honor guy who went MIA with a KMAG outfit at Kunu-ri—but he's alive. Goddamn, old Sam is a POW away the hell up north, but he's alive! I was never real sure anybody could kill that hard-nosed son of a bitch."

Remembering then, reaching back to the first fall of Seoul and the mess at the U.S. embassy compound, Rich glanced at Barron. Sure, the colonel knew Sam Connover. They had some kind of hard on for each other. Damn, had he made a dumb mistake by spilling the news? Back then, to the chickenshit desk soldier who kissed ass around the embassy, yes. This wasn't the same guy.

Colonel Barron proved that by saying, "Good, the army needs every one of its brave men. I'm glad Sergeant Connover is alive."

When he left with the colonel and Corporal Jacobson— for once a big bastard capable of hauling the heavy back-pack radio up the Empire State Building, if necessary—the kid was still asleep in a corner of the tent. The poor guy was worn out, Rich thought, and popped a new roll of film in his camera. When they got back from the shit-fit on Heartbreak Ridge, maybe he'd drive the boy down to Seoul for a couple of days' rest. Rich was due for a wrestle with some cute little prostie, anyhow, some eager girl who might be so ugly she was cute, and carried about a dime's worth of hair between her short bow legs.

See, Saint Teresa—once I got back in uniform, no trouble getting my ashes hauled, and it makes no never mind about slant eyes.

Looking up as he legged it after the colonel and the radioman, Rich saw the sky gone gray in mourning. Not a good omen, he thought, though the ceiling wasn't low enough to hold back the jets. As he watched three Sabre jets whipped in low over the frowning ridges and laid silver eggs that hatched flaming napalm. Their next run slammed rockets into the rocky shale, and the third pass gave the pilots a chance to cut loose their guns.

"Goody," Rich muttered, panting as the slope grew steeper. "Trouble is, most of the bastards up there are away down in their rat holes. They'll bob up and show their teeth when we get in range."

As they climbed behind line companies of the first battalion, Divarty raked the ridges with a damned good pattern, 105s backing off to let the heavier 155s come in. "We could wish for Corps Artillery," Rich grunted, "those big-ass 240s, but what the hell."

The clouds dropped lower, and now Rich could see muzzle flashes far up the mountain as the rats showed their teeth. *Spranngg!* A ricochet skipped off a rock, and a handful of bullets chopped the air too high. Riflemen went to earth anyhow, but not to stay; by the book, they leap-frogged upward, firing as they climbed.

"Shit!" Rich ducked as a 62mm mortar *whumped* close by. Then something bigger, a scream of ripped air and a hell of a slam as it tore out a great chunk of earth. "Gook artillery," he said. "How come the goddamn flyboys didn't find those guns?"

Colonel Barron turned to say something to his radioman, his words lost to Rich in the hellish noise of enemy shells plastering the slope. Rich was looking at Barron's face when the radioman vanished in a burst of fire. The colonel disappeared, too, and a giant invisible fist slapped Rich in the head and knocked him down.

On hands and knees, shaking his head in an effort to see and hear, he struggled in a strange numbness that forced him to move inch by inch. Then the grip broke, and he jerked up to a crouch, his ears still ringing but his eyes clear. Too damned clear; he saw the top half of Corporal Jacobson and the bottom half of the radio horribly blended.

"Uhhh!" That was Colonel Barron, on his back and already white-faced, staring up at the dark sky. His hands clamped his belly, and the blood seeped through his fingers.

Rich said, shit-shit-shit, and crawled around the mess of the corporal to reach Barron. The shelling didn't stop, but it moved beyond this patch of torn ground. He watched his hands move on their own, the combat medic hands doing everything right—dust the wound, rip open the aid bandage—oh, shit; pressure point, hell; Barron was gut shot, and there was too much blood, too fucking much blood.

"Don't," Rich snarled, reaching in and finding the greasy tube to clamp as tight as he could hold it. "You son of a bitch, don't ask me what you can do to help. Just hang on, *hang on,* goddamn you. Don't bleed! Hear me, you pimple-faced bastard—don't bleed!"

The bullet punched him in the side, but he hung on to the artery. No slant-eyed turd could make him let go if he didn't want to. He pinched the slippery tube harder, harder. If he let go, they'd both drown in a fucking fountain of blood. Good Christ, how Rich hated blood.

Blazing hot, a metal fragment sliced Rich's forehead, knocking off his soft hat. Helmets were too damned heavy, always had been, and you couldn't wear a helmet on your belly.

Something was wrong with one eye now. "Hold on, colonel; don't wiggle around, because a real medic will be by sometime, and until the bastard shows up, don't move; don't fuck me up—you hear? Do you *hear?*"

Where were the Japs? The slant-eyed sons of bitches would be snaking out of the jungle any second now.

. . . What can I do to help, sarge? . . .

Don't bleed, you little shit.

"Sarge—sarge! We've got him. Let go, sarge. . . . Jesus, he's shot up bad as the colonel."

Rich didn't hear so well, and the dark clouds must have dropped all the way to the ground, because the medics that were trying to take away his patient were hunkered down in shadows.

"It's okay, sarge—you did it. The colonel's alive; he's going to make it. Sarge—"

He was so damned tired, but Rich managed to smile. "I did it. Goddamnit, at last I did it. I stopped the . . . I stopped . . . blood . . ."

But not his own. Not in time.

CHAPTER 36

Second Infantry Division, Republic of Korea, September–October, 1951—This American unit has destroyed the V North Korean Corps and has decimated the II NK Corps, causing replacement by the 67th Chinese Communist Field Army. Pressure along this front and heavy casualties inflicted upon the enemy have caused a reopening of stalled truce talks.

구시월 제 단풍잎

"Maple leaves of September–October." (Korean proverb: All things fade before a frosty wind.)

Major Chong Wei Ki looked up from the American ration box that served as his *pahp-saeng*, his rice table. His sergeant, looking confused, ducked beneath the tent fly and saluted.

"Sir—a boy wishes to speak with you."

Wei Ki frowned. "A child in this zone of battle? Why would such want to speak with me? Sergeant, are you—"

"I regret interrupting, major, but this is no child. Small and young, yes—but only one who has become a man in his heart could drive a jeep up here. He is called Kim Soo Man and is well armed."

Curious, Wei Ki nodded. "Very well, send in this boy

who is not a boy, but watch him closely. The communists will use any trick to reach us, since they cannot defeat this regiment in battle. They do not realize that this is the new ROK army and not dependent upon warlords these days. They think they can start panic by killing Colonel Lim or me, but they are wrong. Cut off one head, another grows to replace it, and that holds true down to the lowliest private of the 11th Regiment."

Sergeant Chae lifted his chin and stood a bit taller. "Yes, sir." Wheeling, he marched out and returned with the boy.

Wei Ki looked at him. He wore American fatigues, but so did the ROK army. The boy carried an M-2 carbine with casual case, canteen, first aid packet, and extra clips. He stood erect and looked Wei Ki in the eye. "I am Kim Soo Man of Cholla-namdo," he said. "I wish to join your regiment, major."

"Chang mahri-o? Really? Where have you lived, who have you served? You may be too young to be a soldier."

Soo Man answered, "I have lived with the American Second Division. I served only the sergeant who saw to the burial of my father and mother at Chunju Prison, and who took me with him. My"—and for the first time, Wei Ki noticed a falter in the boy's voice—"my *Me-in* father was killed two days past. I drove away in his jeep and brought our weapons with me. I have killed but one Chinese dog, but surely the 11th ROK Regiment can use another jeep and additional weapons."

Covering a smile with his hand, Wei Ki said, "And yourself as a soldier, of course. Why have you chosen this regiment to honor with your presence, small one?"

Soo Man frowned, his hand clenched pale upon the carbine sling. "I came because it is said this regiment does not flee from the *dae-nom* or the *inmun-gun.* It is said that two commanders of this regiment were men of great hearts, men not fearful of death. *Sahn-ae kah-yah pah-mul jahm-nun-dah.* 'Unless you go to the mountain, you cannot catch a tiger.' If I wish to kill communists, I go to the hunters of the communists."

At the tent flap, Sergeant Chae clapped his hands, then remembered himself and drew the sharp intake of breath that signifies surprise or embarrassment. He said, "I am sorry, sir."

Solemnly, Wei Ki nodded. "Yes, you have come to the hunters, and I think now that we are fortunate to recruit such a young hunter. Sergeant Chae—you will see to this soldier's needs now. After the identity numbers are changed upon the jeep, you will return to me for duty, Private Kim Soo Man."

"Yes, sir," the boy said, and, walking beside the sergeant who towered over him, said in English, "Come on, you little bastard."

Wei Ki caught himself somewhere between tears and outrageous laughter. This then was the new youth of Korea, the strongly forged metal that would stand against the communists. This young man who had stopped being a boy back at the prison where the *inmun-gun* had committed such a bloody atrocity, who had already killed one of the invaders of his country, strong as he might be, as sad as he might be, this was what Korea badly needed.

Head down and eyes closed, Wei Ki murmured, "Father Chong, elder brother Nam Ki—I think this is what you meant. Hold to the good and discard the bad. When this one becomes an adult, who will force him to bow in submission? Who will dare to snatch away his birthright?"

Turning back to his makeshift table, Wei Ki glanced at the battle map and wondered if the boy realized what was happening all along the front. The truce talks—he spat on the ground. The Americans had a good word for it: stalemate. No wins, no losses, except face, prestige, whatever they might name disgrace. The entire Orient watched and listened, and even if many countries hated the Chinese, they also knew a thrill of pride that the Oriental had not only fought the white man to a standstill but now had him asking for peace. It was the first time in history this had happened. Even Chong Wei Ki, if he did not know what this war meant to his country and to his family, might have felt a momentary gratification.

"The gooks, the Chinks, the yellow men, the coolies. They have fought with only their bodies against machines and science, and testing you, they have found the white man wanting in determination. Not your soldiers, who are brave as any men, but your fat and timid men of political power. When you have allowed the *balgaengi* to shame you here in Korea, they will find other countries to fight you in, and each time it will become more difficult for your hearts to remain firm."

He found American cigarettes, three Camels in the packet from C-rations. Peering into the rising blue smoke, he decided to keep this youth of the new Korea with him as—not as a servant, for this one was no houseboy; as personal bodyguard, then. If the communists were held at a line across the country, and if they did not again try to unify Korea by force and into their cold image, perhaps Kim Soo Man and Chong Wei Ki would have something to say about the path their country would take in the future. Korea had to move forward, always forward. If the country even stopped to rest from its labors, evil would catch up and destroy all that had been built since the Japanese were driven out. If that happened, there would be no next time for Korea.

CHAPTER 37

Letterman General Hospital, San Francisco, Jan. 18, 1952—Another shipment of soldiers seriously wounded in Korea arrived here today. The families of many of these Purple Heart veterans were waiting to greet men they had not seen in years.

집 태우고 못 줍기

"After the house is burned, search for nails." (Korean proverb: After a major loss, try to recover something.)

Julian had asked her not to fly to Japan after she received the official report of his wounding; asked, not ordered. He wasn't all that sure she would come, but he really didn't want to see Maggi until he was more or less a whole man again. It had taken long, tough months for him to get this far, with layovers and operations at Tokyo Army Hospital and Tripler General in Hawaii. The surgeons at the Presidio of San Francisco's Letterman were pretty sure they could finish rebuilding his hip. The torn intestine had been shortened and arteries stitched back long ago. He could eat most things now—so long as he didn't think too much about a dirty, exploding hillside; so long as he didn't remember a man holding Colonel Julian Barron's life in his body with what was literally a death grip. When that scene jumped up in full, agonizing color, Julian choked and couldn't swallow.

Maybe because he had asked, maybe because she didn't want to, Maggi had not flown into Haneda airport on a big bird with other anxious officer wives who could swing priority seats and dependent travel orders. Damned few enlisted ladies got to Japan without paying their own way. That was another reason he asked Maggi to wait until he made it back stateside. He didn't ride on Rank Hath Its Privileges these days; he'd learned the hard way that RHIR too—Rank Hath Its Responsibilities. He knew some things now, and Julian hoped to make changes, to pay Sgt. Richard H. Shriver with more than the posthumous Silver Star. He meant to equalize some things, although Shriver undoubtedly would be the first to insist that the goddamn brass stay on one side of the line and EM on the other.

Julian stood and caned his way to the wall mirror. The uniform hung loosely upon him, and his cheekbones seemed sharp. The major change, he thought, was in his eyes. Every so often they would revert to the thousand-yard stare of the combat infantryman, that glassy look of men who had lived through what they could not believe, who had seen too much.

Maggi would recognize him, of course, but she might also note a stranger peering back at her. He hoped his wife would see the change in him and not focus upon the double-barreled bastard she had always known.

He was nervous. His hands sweated, and the tender place in his gut tightened painfully. Maggi, he said to himself, and turned from the mirror to move a bit unsteadily down the long hallway; Maggi—and her name had a special flavor in his mind, a honey flavor along his tongue when he whispered it.

Oh, God—there she was in the waiting room. There

stood Maggi, lithe and sleek and beautiful. As each uncertain step with his cane brought him closer, he searched for changes in her also. Finding them, he was more uneasy. She looked more mature, but far from old, and her eyes— yes, set deeper and perhaps wary now. Did she still carry Sam Connover in them?

"Hello," he said, and she repeated it. At arm's length, he stared at her, and she did not flinch, did not look away.

Maggi said: "I didn't know you have to use a cane."

"Progress," he said. "Last month it was crutches." How could he do this properly? There was no easy way. He said, "Sergeant Connover is a prisoner of war."

"I know." It was as if she were discussing a recipe or something, and not the man she had gone to bed with.

"If the truce comes through, they'll probably repatriate the POWs. The Chinese still don't know who he really is."

She nodded, and light gleamed in the rich depths of her hair. "Because of his medal."

He took a step forward and wrapped her hand in his. She felt cool and didn't squeeze back. "I can't keep talking about him," he said. "Not here, anyhow. Are you staying close by?"

She didn't answer right away, and he said, his voice thickening, "I'm not trying to claim conjugal rights. You don't owe me anything, but I hope you'll let me talk about Connover and us."

"Come on," she said. "I have a rented car and a motel."

Releasing her hand, he said, "Thanks for coming. I wasn't sure you would."

"I wasn't either."

Her walk seemed different now, freer, more rolling. Did taking a lover do that to a woman? Careful, he warned himself; you're beginning to sound like Asshole Julian, not Balls Barron.

She extended her hand to help him into the car. He avoided it and lifted himself to the seat; the car smelled like new leather, and he became intensely conscious of Maggi's perfume. He couldn't recall that fragrance and wondered if she had changed the old one. But could he really name the other kind? He just had not paid attention.

The motel was close to the Presidio, and when she keyed the lock and he followed her into the shadowy room Julian felt like a kid sneaking into his first assignation, all nervous and trembly, wondering if he would do it right, if the girl would laugh. The sister of his West Point classmate had laughed.

Maggi switched on a light and sat upon the edge of the bed, her back straight and her chin lifted. She had a lovely line of throat, and her lifted breasts pushed against the fabric of her dark woolen dress, so that the single strand of pearls sought the hidden valley between them. "Please use the chair," she said.

Stiffly, he sat down. Some of the finish was rubbed from the chair arms; a print of the Pacific Ocean hung over the bed, and he couldn't help but wonder if she had laid Connover in just such a room.

With an effort, he put it together, the things he had practiced saying for months, the sincere thoughts of Maggi's happiness that meant more than his own. "Maggi—I was wrong not to listen to you about sending little Win away to school. I can't change that or bring him back, but I wish I could, for both our sakes. I learned a hell of a lot in combat, even before I was wounded. Mostly I guess I discovered how to be a man. Damn, I'm not doing this so well. I'm trying to say that Connover should make it home before too much longer. If you still think you love him—I won't stand in your way. A quiet divorce—"

Deep and dark, her eyes held his. It was so quiet that he could hear the low hiss of the gas wall heater and the slow thumping of his own heart.

Maggi said, "Why would you do that, Julian? I've never been more to you than a stepping stone for higher rank, and after that, a possession, sometimes a decoration, no more."

"But now I would let you go because—because I love you and want you to be happy. That's the most important thing in the world to me right now—your happiness. Don't feel duty-bound because of my leg. It will be fixed here. I won't be a cripple."

"Jesus," she murmured, her hands coming around to rest upon her rounded thighs. "I can't believe this is Julian Barron speaking, especially Barron as a full bird, and standing next to God."

"It's not Julian," he said. "The troops call me Balls Barron now. It takes guts to tell you to go to another man when all logic cries out for me to beg you to forgive me, to beg you to stay."

Her voice was so soft he could scarcely hear: "Not because you're using your wounds or another promotion as excuses, but only because you're thinking of me? Damned if I don't believe you."

"Believe me, Maggi. I'll even try to fix it for a post where nobody knows you used to be married to an officer, so you and Connover won't be hassled."

She lifted both hands to her elbows and rubbed them gently, never taking her eyes from his. "Then I must be honest, too. It wouldn't work with Sam because—in the first place, he wouldn't choose me over the damned army, and I have to be more important. I *am* more important. Whether you believe it or not, it didn't take an act of Congress to make Sam a gentleman, and he would marry me if I asked him. But I'd feel guilty the rest of my life, guilty for all of us. Somehow, some way, word would get out and ruin Sam. You'd be made a laughingstock, too." She hesitated and drew her knees together. Had he been staring?

She went on: "I already made up my mind to at least welcome you home. If it was still bad, if you were still a bastard, I could just walk away, but not hand in hand with

Sam Connover. I will always be grateful to him, Julian—
understand that. I will always share a little part of me with
him and be damned glad for it. If you accept that, then we
can try to make this marriage what it should have been,
ought to be. Again, if you accept that I'm being so goddamned noble for the good of Sam Connover."

"I've come to understand men like him," he said. "It's
possible I might even understand nobility. Just such a man
gave me back my life. Now may I come over there and kiss
you?"

The sound she made was something between a laugh and
a sob, and she was still making it when he sat beside her
and covered her mouth gently with his own. Oh, God, she
tasted of all good things, of wonders to be discovered, of
spices and heat and—thank you, God—a slow-moving
tongue.

It was only awkward for a moment, getting his clothes
off, and she helped him position his bad leg upon the bed.
She was smooth and silky warm, and when he reached for
the light switch she stopped him. Shuddering, she worked
the length of her body against him, more wanton than she
had ever been with him, daring to take the lead and to
gently dominate. This was not the supine Maggi of old, but
a sensuous, forceful woman.

Entering her, he thought of Connover; this was how she
had laid her lover that long-ago night. This was the way his
wife had ridden the other man, taking him deep into her
body, twisting and moaning, loving sex as she had never
loved it with Julian. Until now.

Damn, for a second there he had been jealous, angry
because Maggi had shared this magic with someone else,
because she had opened these marvelous secret places to
another man she loved as deeply for the moment. Of
course she had loved Connover—for that moment; Maggi
would have been unable to screw him otherwise.

Holding her tight but letting himself go, Julian allowed

his hidden fantasies to run free, to picture her vividly, then and now; and if this was perversion, it had never been better, and to hell with ordinary lovemaking. Maggi Barron—*Barron*, damn it—was no ordinary woman, and Julian Barron was glad for it.

"I love you," he breathed, "woman, woman—oh, how I love you."

CHAPTER 38

Panmunjom, Korea, July 27, 1953—The truce between China, North Korea, South Korea, and the United Nations has at last been signed by all parties. Communist delaying tactics ended suddenly when President Truman allowed a news leak that let the Reds know he plans to ship tactical atomic weapons here.

The U.S. Second Infantry Division licked its wounds and counted its blood cost. It has lost 50% more men than any other U.N. division in Korea. But to quote its successful commander, Maj. Gen. Haydon (Bull) Boatner: "We also inflicted more casualties on the communists than any other division. Which means we killed more of the sons of bitches, and we're proud of it!"

죄는 지은 데로 가고
물은 골로 흐른다.

"Punishment flows to the guilty as water flows to the valley." (Korean proverb)

Panmunjom, Freedom Village, Korea, Sept. 4, 1953—Screening and repatriation of prisoners of war began here today. The U.S. Army calls this Operation Big Switch, patterned after the previous exchange of seriously ill and wounded of both sides, Operation Little Switch. But knowledgeable observers here see much difficulty coming with both Chinese and North Korean POWs who are refusing to return home.

등잔 밑이 어둡다.

"It is darkest right under the lamp."
(Korean proverb)

The captain of engineers snarled at the freshly uniformed major with the staff insignia on his starched collars. "Yes, goddamnit, and if you people don't keep those fucking little weasels out of my way, I'll run over the next one. You want these compounds built, I'll see to it, but not with any fucking communist getting in my hair."

The major sucked in his belly and looked stern. "You're forgetting yourself—captain."

"Ho damn!" said Danny Orr. "I'm remembering what you rear-echelon types don't know, and I sure don't need this job or a cute uniform like yours. Keep fucking with me and I'll resign on the spot and go to work for the ROKs. So piss off, major."

Freedom Village, Korea, Sept. 16, 1953—They walked slowly over Freedom Bridge today, American prisoners of war who survived as much as three years in communist camps. They walked slowly, as if they could not believe they were really free. Some fell to their knees on this side of the bridge; some tried to hide their tears. One man wearing a scarred face turned and knocked down another man. Military Police rushed to both, but an American full colonel took charge of the scarred man and hurried him to doctors for examination. Reporters were barred from following.

정각각 흉각각

"Love is love; faults are faults." (Korean proverb: Love overlooks mistakes.)

Chewing his lower lip, he watched each thinned face as man after man limped or staggered or walked proudly over Freedom Bridge. Sam Connover would be one to stand tall—if the bastards let him go.

There he was! Scarred and stooped more than Julian remembered, but walking with that touch of swagger that marked the tough ones. But he didn't hurry, like most of the POWs who rushed to friendly hands before their jailers could change their minds. What made Sam turn and exchange words with that high-ranking North Korean who wore a black patch over one eye? Surely Sam Connover would not be one of those who collaborated with the enemy, not a sellout that Intelligence had begun hearing about.

The communist spat a hissing stream of Korean at Sam. Julian's eyebrows crawled up when Sam answered rapid-fire in the same language. The communist—a *general*, by God!—flinched and started for Sam.

"Come on, you son of a bitch!" Julian was halfway to the bridge, reaching for his pistol.

Sam Connover didn't run away. Cocking both hands, he invited the man to come get him. Shuddering, his hands shaking so hard that Julian could see the movement, the Red general backed up. Then he whirled and stamped away. Julian stopped himself and held out his hand to Sam.

But Sam had something else to do; closing on one hurrying prisoner, he spun him around and knocked him down. Only then did he report.

"Connover, Samuel, Master Sergeant," he said.

"I know who you are, sergeant," the colonel said. "Of everybody in the world, I should know who you are."

Sam peered at the man; there was something familiar, but after so long in Camp #5, it was difficult to be truly certain of anything, only the determination to give the bastards nothing.

"Barron," the colonel said, "Julian Barron."

"Shit," Sam said, and looked at the doctor who wanted to stick a thermometer in his mouth, at the medic who gingerly wrapped a rubber tube around his arm. "It's okay, chancre mechanic—I popped most of the lice this morning. You only have to watch for the ones that jump."

"Not shit," Barron said, and his tone forced Sam to glance back at him. "Chickenshit; I admit it and apologize."

"Apologize? Are you sure you're the right Barron?"

Barron sighed, and Sam focused more intently upon the man. He not only sounded different, he looked different. How, Sam wondered, and then it came to him: The bastard looked like a soldier; he had that inner something that said to the initiate, this is a bigod *man,* and best not fuck with him, because he's sure of who and what he is, sure he can handle any dirty job that comes down the road.

Barron said, "That's what Maggi said."

"Maggi," Sam repeated, pretending great interest in his blood pressure reading.

The doctor said, "Please, sergeant—I need all your vital signs."

Sam accepted the thermometer; it gave him a good reason for keeping his mouth shut. He saw Barron flick a warning glance at the doctors and medics swarming around.

The colonel—bird colonel, bull colonel who wore the Combat Infantry Badge, Purple Heart, and some other good ribbons on his OD blouse—said, "I'm sure you remember your—girl, sergeant. She's the main reason I volunteered to do another tour here, half-ass working for G-2. She wrote you a letter and asked me to bring it to you."

Sam spit out the thermometer. "Son of a bitch, and you did it."

"I did it."

The doctor snorted. "Damn it, sergeant—"

"Bug out," Barron ordered. "All of you bug out and let this soldier alone for a little while."

The doctor said, "I will not take any responsibility for—"

"I will," Julian said. "RHIR, doctor—if you short-arm inspectors know what that means. The responsibility is mine. Now get the hell out of here—all of you!"

"What did the gook say to you?" Julian asked. Sam just stood and held Maggi's letter.

Then Sam said, his words running together a little, "Oh —the bastard just had to run off at the mouth, figuring that somebody on this side would understand him and make a little more propaganda. He didn't know I speak Korean."

"Neither did I," Julian said, watching Sam slowly crush Maggi's letter. Maybe he wasn't crushing it; maybe he was trying to absorb it through his skin.

Sam said, "General Ho Chuk Gun wanted us to know who he is, and the son of a bitch is a true believer. He said that we begged for this truce, but that the war hasn't ended. When it starts again, he will wipe every foreigner from his sacred soil. I told him I'd be right here, too, and when was he going to rid Korea of the foreign Chinese, the foreign Russians? Then I called him dog shit, and a slime who begs and eats. Korean does have a turn of phrase."

"Go on, sergeant; read your letter. If you'd like me to leave—"

Sam collapsed slowly upon a canvas folding cot. For a long moment he sat there and held the letter without opening it. He said, "You called her my girl. What does that mean, colonel? Does it mean that you were only protecting your wife's name? Or your own?"

"If you'd like, I'll step out and let you be now," Barron answered. "I'm sure Maggi said it all."

Sam stared. "You read it."

"No."

"Damned if I don't believe you."

"She said that, too."

Sam fumbled with the envelope. He wanted to lift it to his face, to breathe the scent of her, the flower-musk fragrance that was solely Maggi Barron's. Not with her husband standing there, he wouldn't. He said, "Stick around, colonel. We'll both learn something." He opened the envelope and unfolded Maggi's letter.

Dear Sam, dearest Sam—You gave me your love when I needed it most, when I needed to reaffirm my reason for living. With you, I knew what it was to be a whole woman, unafraid to give, unafraid to take . . .

Forgetting that Barron was nearby, Sam rocked back and closed his eyes. He saw Maggi only briefly in bed with himself, saw her more in the quick, hurting talks they had in the PX coffee shop at Fort Lewis. He looked back at the letter, the strong, direct handwriting so like this woman.

. . . but I also learned—I guess I knew before I started —who you are, Sam Connover; Sergeant Connover. I wished you different, but then you would not be who you are. And later, when you were gone, even after I knew that you were alive, I learned something else. I discovered that a woman can love two men at the same time, that a woman, at least this woman, can share her heart. I love

*you, Sam, but I also love my husband, and that's different
—new and different, but then he's not the same man.*

*I'm not making excuses, Sam. When I had time to think
about us, when you were far away and carried as Missing
in Action, I had already decided not to leave Julian until I
tried. If he would try, I would try. I didn't think it would
work, but even if I divorced him, I would not have asked
you—again—to marry me.*

*I have been all my life in the army; you know that. And
when Julian came home from Korea a real soldier, even a
soldier like you, I realized that we are three of a kind, only
my uniform doesn't show. Thank you, Sam; thank you for
loving me and for letting me love you. I'll never stop.*

The gas lantern, Sam thought; the damned fumes got in
his eyes. She had known all along, this exceptional
woman, this woman above all others. Oh, God—if he
thought any woman could share his life, if he thought any
could mean more to him than the path he had so long ago
chosen to walk, Maggi Barron would be the one. But
Maggi was wise; she knew better; she was also a soldier.

Looking up, Sam said to the colonel, "You have one hell
of a woman, sir."

"I know," Barron said, "I know."

Slowly and carefully, Sam tore Maggi's letter into tiny
shreds. It was something like breaking a champagne glass
into a rock fireplace, so that no lesser toast could ever be
drunk from it. No other eyes, including her husband's,
would ever read what was written with her heart's blood.

"Thank you, colonel," he said. "If G-2 has any kind of
pull here, I'd like to ask another favor. Before all the de-
briefing starts, before the army starts trying the Progres-
sives—the Pros, like that bastard I dropped out there—I'd
like one day and transport to Chunju city. My old man is
buried there, and in the PW camp I promised to visit the
grave. I never have before."

Barron nodded. "Anything you want, sergeant. You have the right. If any laddie buck gets in our way, we'll just run over his popcorn ass."

"Rich," Sam said, remembering. "Sergeant Shriver; he couldn't cover this story?"

He listened as Colonel Barron told the story, and when it was done, Sam nodded. "His way; Rich did it his way."

And Barron added softly, "Because that's what really counts. So do we all, sergeant—so do we all."

All Sphere Books are available at your bookshop or
newsagent, or can be ordered from the following address:
Sphere Books, Cash Sales Department, P.O. Box 11,
Falmouth, Cornwall TR10 9EN.

Please send cheque or postal order (no currency), and
allow 60p for postage and packing for the first book plus
25p for the second book and 15p for each additional book
ordered up to a maximum charge of £1.90 in U.K.

B.F.P.O. customers please allow 60p for the first book, 25p
for the second book plus 15p per copy for the next 7 books,
thereafter 9p per book.

Overseas customers, including Eire, please allow £1.25 for
postage and packing for the first book, 75p for the second
book and 28p for each subsequent title ordered.